RAINBOW OVER THE BAYOU

Jim Crow Through the Eyes of a White Girl

By

LINDA LOWE ERLEY

hb
hope*books

ENDORSEMENTS

"*Rainbow Over the Bayou* is a courageous and tender work of remembrance that reaches across time, race, and culture to illuminate the path of reconciliation. Linda Lowe Erley's words honor both the beauty and the brokenness of the South, offering us a story that does not shy away from the wounds of Jim Crow but dares to imagine healing. Through the legacy of Lillie Mae, we are reminded that faith, love, and truth-telling can bridge divides and create spaces where racial healing can take root. This is a book of hope and light for our fractured world."

- Dr. Zoe Shaw
Psychotherapist
Author of *Stronger in the Difficult Places*

"Through the lens of one woman's journey from innocence to awareness, *Rainbow Over the Bayou* captures the sacred work of remembering, lamenting, and loving across the boundaries that divide us. Erley writes with grace and courage, showing how the gospel opens eyes, heals hearts, and redeems even the most painful histories. This is more than a story—it is a call to live as people who see one another through God's eyes."

> \- Dr. Lewis Brogdon
> Author, Executive Director of the
> Institute for Black Church Studies,
> Associate Professor of New Testament,
> and Black Church Studies—BSK Theological Seminary

"I've known Linda as a fellow church leader and dear friend for decades, and *Rainbow Over the Bayou* moves me in the same rich way she always has—enlightening with story not lecture; inspiring with compassion not condemnation; convicting with gentleness not force. She always leads by first admitting her own need to learn, to grow, to change. I know Linda, and this book is as authentic as she is."

> -Jeff Power
> Pastor and Global Humanitarian Aid Leader, retired

"Linda Erley frames her profound and engaging historical fiction by saying, 'I was born during Jim Crow. Lillie Mae was born into Jim Crow.' Linda invites us into a love story: a beloved story of two women, bound like family, but living in two different worlds. It's a narrative of awakening, awareness, and the horror of aspects of Southern life that were so typical they almost felt normal—until they slowly didn't. A beautiful telling of a difficult and hopeful story."

> \- Steve Cuss
> Author, Pastor, Speaker, and
> Podcaster of *Being Human with Steve Cuss*

READER ADVISORY

This book portrays the harsh realities of racial segregation and injustice in the American South during Jim Crow and the Civil Rights Movement. It includes depictions of discrimination, prejudice, violence, and the extreme dangers faced by Black Americans, including lynching and murder.

AUTHOR'S NOTE

This historical fiction draws from true events, the author's life experiences, and personal interviews. The town in which the story is set is fictional. Apart from select historical places, events, landmarks, and figures, all other characters, narratives, and locations are the author's creations. Any language used reflects the time period and is not intended to offend.

This book was not written to shame or impose guilt. Its purpose is to enlighten, spark meaningful conversations, and ensure we always remember.

DEDICATION

To Lillie Mae, my second mother
You loved so well, worked so hard, and held fast to
your faith through every trial and injustice, carrying
daily the yoke of Jim Crow on your shoulders.
Lil, we carry on your beautiful, extraordinary legacy.

And to all the women like her—
the unsung heroines who, across decades,
walked the long road of oppression with courage,
perseverance, and unwavering faith—
May your voices rise and resound
through the generations.
May we never stop listening.

TABLE OF CONTENTS

INTRODUCTION

I grew up in the deep South during the 1950s, '60s, and '70s in a small Louisiana town tucked deep in the bayous. It was a safe place, a quiet place—and to me, in those childhood years, a most magical place. It was all I knew, and it seemed perfect. But behind the fragrance of magnolias and the quiet hum of cicadas, another reality lived—woven into the fabric of our town and of Southern towns all around us—a harsh truth that would soon begin to unfold before me.

Before this truth found its voice—and before my innocence was ready to hear it—there were long afternoons and barefoot summers, when the world felt untouched and time moved slowly. We rode our bikes up and down oak-lined boulevards, where Spanish moss hung like icicles on a Christmas tree. I can still recall the sweet, heady scent of gardenias and jasmine in spring and summer, filling the air like an expensive Parisian perfume. Adding to the feasts of the senses were bright pink, lavender, and red azaleas, which lit up yards with bursts of color.

The alluring, slow-moving bayou waters curled around cypress knees that reached skyward—twisted and weathered like gnarled fingers. We often heard the whimsical music of a steamboat's calliope echoing up from the water as it made its way along the Mississippi. My sisters and I would run as fast as we could down the street to the top of the levee, eager to wave at the passengers before the boat disappeared around the bend of the broad and winding river.

In the hot, humid days of summer, it was common for us to walk to the corner store with sun-warmed pavement under our feet, picking out penny candy handed to us in small brown paper bags. We clutched it as if it were filled with treasures. If the day was especially hot, we bought a Sno-ball and walked home, sharing stories and giggling without a care in the world as watermelon-flavored syrup from the icy treat dripped down our arms. Later, I'd snuggle under the covers of my cozy bed in our comfortable home—safe and sound.

I often awoke to the smell of steaming hot biscuits waiting for me and my sisters on the breakfast table. My clothes were always in my drawers, cleaned and ironed, ready for me to pick out an outfit for the day. But one of my most comforting memories is the daily presence of Lillie Mae in our home—every day but Sunday.

Lillie Mae is my inspiration for this book. She was our maid—as it was called at that time. She was Black. And she was one of the most beautiful, brave, strong, loving, and Godly women I've ever known—an anchor in my childhood and growing-up years.

Lillie Mae worked for our family for three generations and helped to raise me and my sisters from birth. She became family. She taught me about faith, about love, and about cooking and baking the Southern way—measuring with your heart and tasting as you go.

As I grew older, I began to understand there was so much more to Lillie Mae's story. Beneath her joyful spirit and steady presence in our lives lay a quiet strength, shaped by perseverance through hardship. Even as a child, I sometimes caught glimpses of it—though I didn't yet have the words to name what I saw. A child's mind may be simple, but it begins to notice, to wonder, to piece things together without fully understanding.

For Lillie Mae, the weight of the South's Jim Crow laws—and their deep, daily impact on Black life—kept a constant grip on her world. Yet, as time went on, I also learned that nothing could truly hold her down or steal her joy. Lillie Mae was a child of the King, and she knew it.

Looking back, I now know that much of my younger life was shaped not so much by what I saw in the small world around me but by what I didn't see. I heard but didn't understand. I sensed yet couldn't fix. I was once told that if we choose to allow it and are brave enough to step into it, the hands of time will begin to reveal more depth and dimension into what our innocent eyes saw and our naive ears heard.

I share my words in this book as a witness to a dark time in our nation's history—a time I now understand—I was growing up right smack dab in the middle of it all. It was a time marked by a growing awareness of White and Black—but not yet the deeper, more complicated generational layers of what stood behind each color and what lay between them. As a child, I hadn't yet seen the darkness, but the stirring of it had begun. Those that, in time, I would no longer be able to ignore. "There is a time for everything, and a season for every activity under the heavens ... a time to be silent and a time to speak" (Ecclesiastes 3:1,7).

Today, I find it impossible to stay silent. I did not choose this book. This book chose me. Just as Dr. Martin Luther King Jr. wrote from his jail cell in Birmingham, Alabama, in 1963, "We will have to repent in this generation not merely for the hateful words and actions of the bad people but for the appalling silence of the good people."[1]

Dr. King's words are a call to awaken—not just in 1963 but today as well. The words and stories in this book are not to sit in judgment, to shame or accuse. My prayer is that they will first illuminate the past so we will always remember. Second, they will bring awareness and knowledge of the Jim Crow era and what led up to it, the truth of those times, and how echoes remain today.

This book is an invitation to you, the reader, to courageously use your voice—to step with intention into meaningful conversations with both Black and white brothers and sisters after reading this historical fiction.

Through these conversations and in these sacred spaces, may you feel the freedom to ask questions, share what's on your heart, and—most importantly—actively listen. May it all take place on the foundation of God's love, grace, forgiveness, redemption, and healing—across racial barriers. It's the only way. Dr. King boldly declared, "Darkness cannot drive out darkness; only light can do that. Hate cannot drive out hate; only love can do that."[2]

Growing up in the South, many stood in direct opposition to that truth, spreading hate, fear, racism, and violence. That part of my world in my younger years was hidden from me... but it wouldn't stay hidden for long. Darkness can never stamp out the light and the justice of God.

The origins of this darkness began aboard ships bound for the Americas from the 1500s to the 1800s. Enslaved people were packed in as human cargo, treated no better than livestock. They crossed those waters in fear, kidnapped from their families, torn from the rhythms of daily life in Africa, and stripped of everything familiar. These human beings, made in God's image, were legally labeled as chattel.

When reaching the shores of North America, these Africans were forced into slavery. Bought. Sold. Chained. Beaten. Raped. Whipped. Worked... literally to death. Hurled into a nightmare of bondage.

New hope and light came to them when slavery was abolished in 1865. Yet, was it really over? There were many challenges for Southern Blacks, especially during the Reconstruction period from 1863 to 1877. For fourteen years, "the U.S. government undertook the task of integrating nearly four million formerly enslaved people into society after the Civil War bitterly divided the country over the issue of slavery."[3] It was an attempt "to build an egalitarian society on the ashes of slavery."[4]

Soon, however, the dark shadows of slavery reappeared, this time under a different name. Something called the Black Codes continued to restrict the rights of formerly enslaved people and exploit their labor. As an extension of the Black Codes, yet another master emerged: Jim Crow (1877–1964). It was a convenient way to put Blacks back into captivity.

This time, it was not as much of a physical bondage, as it was one of intimidation and fear. It marginalized, dehumanized, and diminished the rights and lives of Blacks. Violence, lynchings, and hooded terror were always hiding in the darkness around the corner.

The great hope and light that had pierced the darkness with the abolishment of slavery began to flicker as the harsh winds of Jim Crow grew. Yet it was never completely snuffed out. Through the brutality, lynchings, fear, and marginalization of a people created in God's own likeness, the smoldering embers of a strong and passionate people were still there. Those embers were quickly fanned back into flame. The Civil Rights Movement caught wind, and it blew strong.

Being raised by Lillie Mae and drawn into her world, I saw things I didn't fully grasp then—but time and closeness helped me understand. I saw and felt something sacred, something placed deep in the soul of African Americans that I believe many of us will never fully experience or truly understand, including myself. It was something God had woven into their very being and carried through the generations. A unique and beautiful song, given just to them—one that could never be shackled or chained.

It had begun in their native land, then was infused with the groaning of survival once they arrived on this hostile soil hundreds of years ago. Over time, it became a melodic blend of the world they had left behind and the one they were forced to endure. Just as the Jews beseeched God to release them from Egypt, a deep cry for God's presence—pleading for their own deliverance from bondage—could be heard here on earth and high into the heavens.

Music was one thing that could not be taken from the enslaved. It could not be torn from the safety of their souls. Since they were not allowed to read or write, many of these spirituals carried biblical stories they had memorized and woven into song. These melodies helped them endure suffering, expressing their deepest emotions, their lived pain, their hope—and their lament. They were created extemporaneously, passed down from one generation to the next, etched into the memory of a people who refused to be silenced. These sacred expressions would come to be known as Negro spirituals, and they became anchors for their resilience.

Walk into any African American church today, and you'll feel something stir deep within your own soul. You won't walk out the same. When hands and voices rise in praise to God with such power, fear has a difficult time surviving. Across generations, these spirituals gave African Americans strength. I heard them often, sung by Lillie Mae as she worked in our home—sweet melodies that seemed to lift her to another place entirely. They are songs I long to know the sacred meaning, yet I understand I never fully will. Still, through Lillie Mae and her community, I was blessed to taste their sweetness.

Lillie Mae was an extraordinary woman. And like many others who walked similar journeys—a true survivor. These brave women and men carried a song that God placed deep in their souls, and it gave them a solid rock on which to stand. Lillie Mae's ancestors passed those songs down to her as well. They weren't just songs she sang daily; they were truths she lived by. Whether it was a good day or a hard one... still, she sang.

At this point, you might be asking: Who gives this white girl the authority to speak on such things? I would humbly answer, God allowed it to touch my world in a most unexpected and profound way. This historical fiction tells the story of two lives and two worlds, intertwined by God's hand, for that particular dot on the timeline of life—the era of Jim Crow, and the echoes that remain today.

Words and emotions often burn in a soul longing to be freed. At age 66, shortly after Lillie Mae passed away, I felt a calling from God—to be a voice joining in with the chorus of many that have risen over the decades. A chorus that has become a *Magnum Opus*, filled with strains of indignation and sorrow, yet broken by crescendos of resilience and sprinkled with notes of hope. It's a longing to be heard, respected, and set free. These emotions, at times, cannot be separated. They all belong.

Lillie Mae had a pamphlet of Jim Crow laws she kept in her home. She had them highlighted and underlined. I can't imagine carrying such a heavy yoke on her shoulders day after day. It is best understood through the lens of a historian's perspective on racial etiquette during Jim Crow.

Most Southern white Americans who grew up prior to 1954 expected black Americans to conduct themselves according to well-understood rituals of behavior. This racial etiquette governed the actions, manners, attitudes, and words of all black people when in the presence of whites. To violate this racial etiquette placed one's very life, and the lives of one's family, at risk... In general, blacks and whites could meet and talk on the street. Almost always, however, the rules of racial etiquette re-

quired blacks to be agreeable and non-challenging, even when the white person was mistaken about something. Usually it was expected that blacks would step off the sidewalk when meeting whites or else walk on the outer street side of the walk thereby 'giving whites the wall.' Under no circumstances could a black person assume an air of equality with whites ... Those whites, moreover, who associated with blacks in a too friendly or casual manner ran the risk of being called a 'n—lover'... The whole intent of Jim Crow etiquette boiled down to one simple rule: blacks must demonstrate their inferiority to whites by actions, words, and manners.[5]

By understanding and remembering this history of racial oppression, hate, and injustice, we are honoring and shining a light on those who bravely walked this incomprehensible journey—and on others who tragically lost their lives along the way. My hope is that this book will continue to give Lillie Mae, her ancestors, and so many others the voice they deserved—and still deserve—to have today.

We cannot choose the world in which we are born. We can, however, choose how we live our lives within that world. I was born *during* Jim Crow. Lillie Mae was born *into* Jim Crow. Yet, Lillie Mae did not let it be her master. She had another master and King, and His name was Jesus.

She never let the darkness of this world extinguish her light. It was something no one could steal from her. So many in our town saw it—the light that shone from within her. And of course, we saw it in our home, day after day, as we spent our growing-up years by her side.

She was on her knees daily, hands clasped in prayer, until the age of 96. Every day, with her Bible open, she bent over it—reading aloud the Word of God, which is living and active, a wellspring of hope passed down through every generation—offering truth, comfort, and strength.

This is how Lillie Mae lived her life—and I hope to carry the torch she lit in me, a legacy of hope and quiet strength. She and her strong community inspired this book. As I helped to clean out Lillie Mae's home with her daughter, after she passed away in 2019, I took a picture frame of Dr. Martin Luther King, Jr. off her wall. It had been in that same spot since I could remember as a little girl. It breaks my heart to think of her crushed hope when he was assassinated that dark day on April 4th, 1968. As a child, I was not sure who he was at the time. It was probably just another day for me. It makes me sad as I write about it. It makes me sad for Lillie Mae.

As her daughter and I continued cleaning out her home, we found a copy of an old Life magazine from April 19th, 1968, buried deep in a box. It had been published just 15 days after Dr. Martin Luther King Jr. had been assassinated in Memphis, Tennessee. The pages were tattered, browned, and crumbling—but the words inside were meant to live on. The author and photographer of the article, Gordon Parks, shared powerful words in *Life Magazine* from Dr. King's funeral.

The scratchy, taped (recorder) voice of the man we sorrowed for, echoed off the walls (of Ebenezer Baptist Church in Atlanta) and penetrated our hearts. '... and if you're around when I have to meet my day, I don't want a long funeral. And if you get somebody to deliver the eulogy, tell him not to talk too long.' The quiet was heavy as the magnificent revivalist voice of our murdered black leader rolled on. 'I'd like somebody to mention that day, that Martin Luther King, Jr., tried to love somebody.'"6

His audio-taped message still echoes today, along with these timeless words of his: "Hate is too great a burden to bear. I have decided to love."7

Lillie Mae decided to love. She had no room for hate in her life, even through those years of Jim Crow. As we were finishing up in her home, I found a passage in one of her many Bibles that her daughter wanted me to have. It was a verse Lillie Mae had starred and underlined. She exemplified this passage found in Philippians as she lived her life with an uncomplaining spirit. She would be so pleased to know that I am sharing it with my readers.

"Do everything without complaining or arguing, so that you may become blameless and pure, children of God without fault in a crooked and depraved generation, in which you shine like stars in the universe as you hold out the Word of life, in order that I may boast on the day of Christ that I did not run or labor for nothing."8

Lillie Mae knew we were living in a crooked and broken generation, yet she chose to shine like a bright star within it. In the middle of our two very different worlds, surrounded by the sting of discrimination, Lillie Mae and I discovered something deeper: love, hope, forgiveness, respect, and re-demption. Even in the darkest times—then and now—light can still be found, if we're willing to see it.

We have a choice of how we live our lives. We have a responsibility for what we have become stewards of over the generations. We can decide how we allow our past to shape us. What do we choose to carry in our backpacks through the decades of our lives, and what do we pass on as our legacy? Perhaps it's time to unpack some things—to look at them, be curious, share some, and maybe even lighten the load. When we set aside our biases, stereotypes, and assumptions, we open the door to truly listen. Speaking takes courage—but listening requires intention.

My hope is that you, the reader, might discover some-thing in these pages you didn't know—or have never consid-ered before—something that stirs a deeper curiosity within you. I've included a list of resources in the back of this book for those who want to explore further and engage in mean-ingful conversations about this part of our history.

Maybe, with that, a deeper truth can begin to unfold. What might it look like to see others not just through our own eyes, but through God's? And if we struggle to do this, maybe it's time to adjust our lens.

PART I

ECHOES REMAIN

Though the signs of Jim Crow have long been taken down, its echoes remain—woven into language, assumptions, and everyday moments. Sometimes they're loud and unmistakable; other times, they whisper through unexamined words or unnoticed glances. These echoes can often go unrecognized, especially by those who've never had to listen for them.

We've each been placed on this dot in the timeline of history to listen, to learn, and to build bridges of communication and understanding across racial divides. It's hard. It's messy.

Only by acknowledging the echoes can we begin to quiet them—and move forward together, in humility, in healing, and in our shared humanity.

CHAPTER ONE

"Not one of us was here when this house was built. Our immediate ancestors may have had nothing to do with it, but here we are, the current occupants of a property with stress cracks and bowed walls and fissures built into the foundation. We are the heirs to whatever is right or wrong with it. We did not erect the uneven pillars or joists, but they are ours to deal with now. And any further deterioration is, in fact, on our hands."[9]

-Isabel Wilkerson

August 6, 2019

Morning

"Come on, Mimi, sing with me," urges Willa Mae. Her words are strained and breathless yet carry the same gentle insistence they always have. The doctor says it will only be a matter of days now. Singing is the last thing Mimi feels like doing, but Willa Mae wants it... needs it. So, they must.

Music is the language of Willa Mae's soul—a source of comfort and connection no matter the circumstances. Even now, in the final days of her ninety-seven years on this earth, it remains her solace.

Mimi forces a smile, and her throat tightens with emotion. The familiar strains of a favorite hymn play softly on the Bose, and Mimi's voice joins in. They have sung together countless times over the years, their voices blending in joy, but today, every note seems to press against the ache in Mimi's chest.

"Let Jesus *fix it for you*," their voices rise together, "He *knows just what to...*"

Mimi's voice falters. A lump forms in her throat as she chokes back tears. Willa Mae stops singing, her frail hand reaching out, her dark fingers trembling as they find Mimi's. Her voice, raspy yet steady, carries the same quiet strength it always has.

"Baby, we just need to pray and trust in Jesus. He'll take care of the situation."

Those words... so simple... so familiar, are Willa Mae's pearls—her timeless wisdom offered freely to anyone she meets in her day. Whether it's at the back door of the Riverside Café, a friend on Magnolia Street, or one of her many church family members, Willa Mae shares her faith without hesitation, leaving each recipient grateful for the gift. Everyone in Bayou Grande, Louisiana, loves her for it, even if her feisty nature occasionally catches them off guard.

Mimi often says that Willa's faith, sprinkled with a little bit of peppery spirit, is how she survived all those years of being pushed to the back. It's her anchor, her shield, and her legacy. Now, as Mimi, sixty-five years old, stands by her deathbed, a flood of memories collide with the rawness of the moment. Childhood laughter mingles with the heaviness of impending loss. Succumbing to both, she realizes that each of those feelings has earned a place here.

As Willa Mae drifts into sleep, Mimi looks down at the beautiful dark hand resting over her own—the colors starkly different, but the bond between them seamless. That weathered hand has comforted Mimi through every trial, every loss, and every celebration. Now, as her eyes fill again, she wonders how life can go on without her.

Willa Mae has been part of Mimi's life from the very beginning. She came to work for the Benoit family in 1952, long before Mimi's birth—at a time when both Willa Mae and the Benoits needed each other in ways only God could orchestrate. For Willa Mae, in her late twenties, it was a chance to provide for herself, her daughter, and her mother in a world that had not made room for her worth, dignity, equality, and opportunity. For the Benoits, it was help for their growing family. Willa remained with them for three generations.

To Mimi, looking back, it had always been a divine appointment—a sacred thread woven into the fabric of their lives. Mimi's parents are long gone now, but Willa Mae remains a steadfast rock within the family. As Mimi stands there, the weight of the moment settles deep in her chest. How will she face the world without Willa Mae? She knows it will be hard, but she is sure of one thing: Willa Mae's strong faith, love, and the wisdom she instilled in Mimi will carry her through, just as it always has.

That morning, Willa was moved to St. Francis of Assisi Hospice Home, just outside Bayou Grande, Louisiana. As Mimi looks around the room, it is sparse and sterile, with little to distinguish it from the countless others in the facility. A hospital bed stands by the window, its clean white sheets tucked tightly with hospital corners. Along one wall sits a small wooden writing desk with a plain chair under it. Beside the bed sits an orange faux leather chair, sagging with age, a deep crease running through the middle of its worn seat. It looks precarious, as if it might split open at any moment, disgorging its foam stuffing across the floor.

Mimi eyes it warily before lowering herself into the chair with care. Settling in, she lets out a deep sigh, her body finally relaxing after a long, emotional morning, and it's still early. She finds herself imagining the countless people who must have occupied this very chair, keeping vigil over their loved ones. There has likely been laughter and tears, whispered confessions, heartfelt apologies, reconciliations, and... final goodbyes. *It all belongs here,* Mimi thinks. *If only this chair could talk, what stories it might tell.*

But restlessness soon overtakes her, Willa Mae having dozed off singing her comforting gospel songs. Mimi rises from the chair and walks to the window to take in the view. Outside, the bayou stands in vivid contrast to the starkness of the room. The sun peeks in and out of the fog as though playing hide and seek. It casts timid rays through the trees and across the water, sparkling like diamonds. Cypress trees stretch their branches over the bayou, their scratchy, beard-like Spanish moss draping gracefully and swaying slightly in the warm breeze. Mimi feels at home.

She cranks the window open to get a better view of the surroundings. A sudden blast of hot, humid air blows in, hitting her face and fogging up her glasses as though she has just opened an oven door. Summer in Louisiana is unrelenting, and Mimi knows better than to leave the window open too long. The reason isn't just to block out the oppressive heat but also to keep out the Louisiana state bird—as everyone jokes—the mosquito. With a resigned chuckle, she pushes the window shut again, sealing out the sticky heat and the threat of bites.

"Let's get her checked in."

A stern voice breaks the quiet, jolting Mimi from her thoughts. She turns away from the tightly shut window and sees a woman about her age standing near the doorway, her light skin faintly flushed from the afternoon heat. Mimi looks at her as though not clearly understanding what she has said—not to mention the tone in which she said it. She recognizes her as the supervising nurse they met earlier at the nurse's station upon arrival this morning. She carries only a clipboard. Nowhere in sight is the pain medication Mimi had requested for Willa Mae when they first arrived.

The nurse walks briskly to the side of the bed. Her eyes glance at Mimi, then back to the clipboard in her hand.

"Well ... let's get her checked in," she repeats, her tone cold and matter-of-fact, this time laced with a thin layer of annoyance. She says nothing more. No greeting. No acknowledgment of Willa Mae lying frail and vulnerable in the bed, nor even a kind word to Mimi.

How strange, Mimi thinks, her chest tightening. She can't believe the nurse has ignored them both so completely, as though Willa is merely an object to be managed and not a person nearing the end of her long, remarkable life.

Mimi moves around the bed, coming to stand on Willa Mae's other side, her presence instinctively protective. Before she can respond to the nurse's terse tone, the woman speaks again, her voice louder this time, cutting through the air like a blade.

"Have you chosen a funeral home yet?"

Mimi freezes, her breath catching in her throat. The words hang there, heavy and jarring. They're spoken mere inches from Willa Mae, as if she isn't there at all. Mimi's mind races. *Is she serious?* Her shock quickly gives way to anger. *How could anyone be so rude and thoughtless?* Her eyes dart to Willa Mae, who remains still, her frailty stark against the clinical backdrop of the room.

Mimi's gaze locks in on the nurse with a mixture of defiance and disbelief. Looking down at Willa, Mimi thinks, *No one is going to treat my Willa Mae this way.*

"Could we please talk about this in the hall?" Mimi whispers with a tone of practiced Southern politeness, though it carries a clear edge of reprimand.

"She can't hear what we're saying," the nurse replies with a dismissive scoff. "She's not with it."

Mimi's anger flares, simmering just beneath her composed exterior. From her own previous experiences, she has known hospice care to be a sacred, tender space, where nurses are angels on earth. God uses them as His agents of compassion toward the patient and the family as well. This brusqueness strikes a clashing contrast that catches her off guard. It's as though a dark cloud has entered the room, filling the space with its presence.

What an unexpected place to encounter such callousness, Mimi thinks, her frustration mingling with growing anxiety. *I am Willa's advocate,* she reminds herself, summoning her courage. *I must remember her words.*

Willa—a short name of endearment used by Mimi for Willa Mae—has often told her, "Mimi, God has given you a strong voice. Don't be afraid of that voice, baby. You speak it."

Mimi draws a breath and locks eyes with the nurse.

"She is actually quite with it," Mimi says quietly but firmly. "And I would prefer not to have this conversation right now—and certainly not in this room."

The nurse raises her eyebrows, her lips pursed in a show of exaggerated annoyance. With a sharp "humph," she turns and marches to the small table by the door, dropping a thick packet of papers onto its surface with an audible thud.

"I need you to fill these out," she says curtly, still avoiding Mimi's gaze.

"I'll be back to collect them," she adds, already heading for the door.

"What about the pain medication I requested earlier when we arrived?" Mimi calls after her, her voice rising slightly.

The nurse pauses in the doorway, turning with an impatient scowl. She pats her right pocket, then her left, before shrugging.

"What do you know?" she says, "I thought I had the syringe in my pocket, but it's not here." The nurse's eyes glance briefly to Willa. "She can hold on a little longer. She looks fine to me. You're not the only ones here. You'll need to wait your turn."

And with that, she leaves the room.

Mimi stiffens. A trace of cold indifference in the nurse pierces deeper than the moment itself. She looks down at Willa, her heart aching with a fierce determination to protect her, yet the feeling is all too familiar. It stirs something buried, something old and unfinished from decades ago.

In an instant, the sterile walls around her fade. She is seven years old again, sitting with Willa Mae on the levee bench high above the Mississippi River in her childhood town in Louisiana. The morning is full of joy, but Bubba Boudreaux's words cut through it like a cold wind off the river. Ugly. Demeaning. Directed at Willa Mae. Mimi didn't understand it all, not then. But she feels it—that sharp sting of cruelty, a sense of something that seemed unfair to her. She wants to speak, to shield Willa, to do something ... but in her innocence and fear, she doesn't know how. Now, nearly six decades later, that same helplessness wants to rise again— but this time, Mimi sees it for what it is and stands against its headwinds, hitting strong in the form of words.

Turning her gaze out to the bayou, she resolves, *these last days of Willa's life will be filled only with kindness, dignity, respect, and love—not marred by cruelty.* "I won't let that happen, not like then," she whispered softly to herself. Looking back towards the door, she takes a deep breath and pulls out her phone to call her sister, Anna Beth, who lives just a couple of miles away and is planning to join her later in the day. Anna Beth is Louisiana through and through—a true Cajun with a big heart. She loves a good time, shares a passion for all things LSU Tigers with her husband, Andrew, and has never wandered far from their hometown.

Mimi, by contrast, is always the quieter one, an introvert who mustered the courage to leave Louisiana after college to travel the world. It was during those adventures that she met her husband, eventually settling out West. Their older sister, Mary Grace, lives a world away in Germany with her husband, a retired military officer.

When she hears Anna Beth's voice, warm and familiar, Mimi feels a wave of relief wash over her.

"Anna Beth, I'm so glad you answered. I really need to talk to you."

The concern in her sister's voice is immediate.

"Is Willa okay?" she asks.

"Yes, she's doing okay. Sorry, I didn't mean to scare you. She's dozing on and off right now. I'm pretty sure she's in some pain, but I requested meds, although they seem to be taking a long time to come."

Stepping into the attached bathroom, Mimi quietly closes the door behind her.

"Okay, so what's going on?" Anna Beth asks, her tone softening but still alert.

Mimi's voice drops to a whisper, though her emotions are bubbling just beneath the surface.

"Maybe it's my imagination, but you know I'm a pretty good judge of character. The head nurse came in a little while ago to admit us, and ... well ... I just ..."

"Well, what? What is it, Mimi?" Anna Beth presses, a touch of urgency in her voice.

"Something feels off here," Mimi admits.

Her frustration begins to spill out.

"To be honest, Anna Beth, the nurse, was downright rude. She didn't even acknowledge Willa when she walked into the room! And then ..." Mimi's voice grows more animated as she recounts the moment, "... she had the nerve to ask about funeral home arrangements while standing right over Willa! Who would be so inconsiderate like that, as if ..."

"Take a deep breath, sis," says Anna Beth, you're getting yourself all worked up. Maybe it's something, maybe it's not. I admit it was very rude, but you've been through a lot this morning, and I bet you've been up for hours without eating."

Mimi opens her mouth to argue, but stops, realizing her sister is maybe right. "I'm ordering you Uber Eats," Anna Beth continues firmly. "I know what you like, so just trust me. Willa's resting comfortably, and you need to take care of yourself, too. Get some food in you, and when I get there, we'll talk about it."

Anna Beth's calm voice is like a balm to Mimi's frayed nerves. She nods to herself, allowing her sister's words to ground her. For now, she'll do as Anna Beth suggests and focus on regaining her composure. Mimi steps back into the room, trying to steady her thoughts. *Maybe I am just tired and jumping to conclusions*, she reasons. *The nurse could just be having a bad day.* Yet deep within, she still feels unsettled.

A faint mumbling breaks her thoughts. Mimi turns quickly toward Willa's bed, leaning in close.

"Willa," she whispers, her voice calm but filled with concern, "are you okay?"

The mumbling comes again, this time a little clearer.

"Daddy ... the stars ..." Willa mumbles.

Mimi reaches out instinctively, rubbing Willa's forehead with the same tenderness she has been shown throughout her life by Willa Mae. She pulls the worn chair closer to the bed and sinks into it, her mind turning over the meaning of Willa's words. She's heard stories about those nearing the end of life—stories of names called out and moments of recognition that seem to transcend the physical world.

One hospice nurse once described it as their "spiritual eyes" opening, a glimpse beyond the veil that separates the temporal from the eternal. Mimi has always believed in that veil and what lies beyond it. Of all the family members Willa has spoken of over the years, it is her daddy she mentions most often. She adored him, and the bond they shared left an indelible mark on her soul. But one day, that cherished relationship was stolen from her—her father's life was unjustifiably cut short.

By Willa's bedside, Mimi thinks back to the first time she heard that story—sitting with Willa beneath the old pecan tree on the Benoit property, where Mimi grew up.

Being a teenager then, her world was small and her understanding of life was still unfolding. On the swing, with late afternoon light filtering through the branches, Willa shared with Mimi her story of loss, resilience, and the unbreakable bond between a young girl and her father.

IT WAS 1933, and Willa Mae was twelve years old when her mother appeared at school, calling her out of the classroom with a solemn expression. She remembered little of that day, but the words her mother spoke still rang in her ears.

"Your daddy has died. You need to come home."

Once they arrived home, Willa overheard the hushed, anguished voices of adults talking in the next room.

"The hospital didn't treat him because he was colored," one said. "That's why he died."

At twelve, Willa didn't fully understand. Hospitals are supposed to help people—all people. How could this have happened?

The weight of that day pressed heavily on her small shoulders. Opening her daddy's clothes drawer, she grabbed his flashlight. Throwing open the porch door, she ran, her legs carrying her instinctively to the sugar cane fields across from their house in Bayou Grande, Louisiana. It was her and her daddy's special spot, a sanctuary they often shared under the stars. She needed to find him. Willa was in denial that her daddy had really died and was certain he would be there waiting for her in their special spot.

The path through the sugar cane was narrow, just wide enough for a horse to pass. As she ran in desperation, the familiar cane stood tall all around her as though trying to embrace her and bring her comfort. Willa knew this path by heart. She ran out of breath, getting closer and closer to the crossroads where they always stopped.

It was there, on so many nights, that her daddy brought her to watch what he called "the best picture show ever." The dark sky, free from town lights, was their private theater. "Front-row seats," he would say with a grin. "No sitting in the back for us." They lay on a blanket, swatting away the mosquitoes with the lavender oil her grandmother Sissy brewed each year. Willa loved those nights, especially the first glimpse of a shooting star streaking across the sky.

She asked him, "Daddy, why are stars so bright?"

"Each one is a twinkly little window into heaven," he replied.

Willa squinted, trying to peer through those heavenly windows, hoping for a glimpse of what lay beyond. Those nights under the stars weren't just about stargazing. They were lessons, moments when her daddy planted seeds of resilience deep within Willa Mae's soul.

"There are four things you must never forget," he always told her. She knew them by heart, but she loved hearing him say them.

"Number one," he started. "What are you, Willa Mae?"

"I am God's image bearer, Daddy," she answered, her voice proud.

"That's right, baby. You're made in God's beautiful image, just like everyone else. Don't ever let anyone take that from you."

"Number two," he continued. "What else do you have that no one can take away from you?"

"My voice, Daddy!" she shouted, her words were bold enough to reach the heavens.

"That's my girl," he said, beaming. "Some might try to dismiss you, but your voice is a gift from God. Use it, baby. Speak it."

"Number three," he said, his tone grew serious. Daddy always looked up to the stars, pausing, and then looked right at Willa.

"Forgive," he said, as though he meant it deep within his soul.

One night, Willa Mae confessed that she needed to forgive her friend Edmena for taking the bigger half of a moon pie. Her daddy laughed so hard she thought he might cry. But then his face turned solemn.

"If you don't forgive Willa Mae, you're the one who'll be bound in chains. Bitterness will take hold of you, spreadin' like poison ivy in the summertime."

Finally, he asked, "What do you do every night before bed?"

Willa teased him, always mentioning cookies from Grandmother Sissy's tin can. He playfully threatened her with a spanking. Then she answered truthfully.

"I recite the 23rd Psalm."

"That's right, baby. It's medicine for your soul. God's prescription for us. One day, you'll understand how much you'll need it."

On her twelfth birthday, he gave her a copy of that psalm, roughly written in his own handwriting and placed in a handmade wood frame. It hung above her bed from that day on.

But on that night in the cane fields, as she reached their spot under the twinkling stars, her daddy wasn't there. She collapsed, and her small frame shook with sobs.

"Why did you leave me, Daddy? I'm scared!" she cried out to the sky.

Hoping to hear his voice, there was only silence. But at that moment, a brilliant shooting star streaked across the heavens—brighter and longer than any she had ever seen. She knew it was him, sending her a sign, reminding her that he was still with her.

Through her tears, she feels him looking down from the other side of those heavenly windows, sending a kiss that floats down to her tear-streaked face.

From that day on, Willa carried her daddy's words deep within her, letting them guide her through a life of trials and triumphs.

MIMI LOOKS OVER to Willa lying in the hospital bed. She again thinks back. *It must have been there, that night in the sugar cane fields—where Willa's unshakable faith and resilience began. Willa has lived through so much—Jim Crow laws, the horrors of the KKK, and the injustice of losing her father. Willa Mae is a survivor.*

Yet, Mimi thinks, as she gazes at a tall cypress tree outside the window, its steadfast trunk rising from the water, *Willa Mae has done more than survive. She thrived.*

CHAPTER TWO

"The Lord is my Shepherd, I lack nothing.
He makes me lie down in green pastures,
He leads me besides quiet waters,
He refreshes my soul.
He guides me along the right paths for his name's
sake."[10]

-Psalm 23:1-3

August 6, 2019

Morning

A sharp whiff of disinfectant pulls Mimi from her deep thoughts. The pungent smell triggers a flashback to childhood, when her mother would break open ammonia capsules to revive her after fainting in Catholic Mass. Perhaps it had been the heavy incense swirling through the sanctuary like a dense cloud, or maybe it was just Mimi's fragile, anxious, and fearful demeanor.

She sits up in the chair, eyes wide from the potent smell, and looks up to see a custodian mopping the hall just outside the door. He glances up and catches her eye.

"Morning Miss…Can I help you with anything?" he asks.

The man appears to be in his late 60s, his Black skin creased by years of life and hard work. His kind eyes hold the wisdom of an old soul, an unspoken warmth that softens his presence.

"Thank you," Mimi replies. "We're just waiting on the nurse for some medication."

"Well, if you need anything, my name's Joseph," he says kindly. "I'm sure the nurse will be here soon. I'm gonna let her know that you need her, baby," using the old colloquial "baby" as so many Southerners do.

"Thank you," Mimi says with a sincere tone.

His gaze lingers past her. He's looking at Willa Mae, who lies in the bed, softly singing to herself. Something in his face shifts, as though a light has been dimmed. What was warmth turns to noticeable concern, a subtle sadness rising in his expression.

The silence breaks as he pulls the mop out of the sudsy bucket and splashes it onto the floor. Then, with a grace that feels both unplanned and deeply intentional, Joseph begins to sing. His voice, rich and familiar, joins Willa Mae's in perfect harmony. Their tones blend effortlessly, as though bound by an ancient rhythm that transcends time. Slowly, Joseph's voice fades as he pushes his mop further down the hall, his song trailing softly behind him.

Hearing a ping, Mimi glances at her phone. It's a message from Effie, Willa Mae's daughter and only child. She's sending her flight details. Relief washes over Mimi at the thought that Effie will soon arrive to be by her Momma's side. Anna Beth plans to pick her up at the New Orleans Airport after a long flight from Detroit.

It's been years since Effie last set foot on the Southern soil she once called home. She walked away from it decades ago, following the same well-worn road that so many others had taken—leaving behind the weight of a place steeped in its dark history, searching for kinder ground.

Willa has fallen back asleep. Mimi reaches for the portable Bose speaker and lowers the volume on the gospel music playlist—songs Willa Mae has loved her entire life. Close by are three cherished items that bring Willa comfort and a deep sense of security.

First and most important, her tattered Bible lies next to her pillow like an old friend she can't go anywhere without. It's barely held together by duct tape from years of reading, pondering, and praying over its pages. On the small table beside the bed sits an aged frame holding an intricate, colorful needlepoint. The fabric is yellowed and stained with time, yet its beauty remains untouched by the years.

Above Willa's bed hangs a framed copy of the 23rd Psalm that her daddy gave her when she was young. It had been placed carefully in a simple homemade frame, crafted from cedar. The faint, sweet, woody aroma drifting from it reminds Mimi of home.

Willa asked Mimi to hang the Psalm above her bed the moment they arrived. An old nail was already pressed into the wall, as though waiting patiently for what was to be hung there. For 85 years—ever since her daddy gave it to her on her 12th birthday—that Psalm has always hung above her as she slept.

Like a warm, familiar blanket, it's something she cannot rest without. She's committed every word to memory and prays its promises nightly. Most importantly, those words bring her comfort and strength, reminders of the faith that has always sustained her and carried her through life.

As "Amazing Grace" plays softly, a tender smile spreads across Willa's face. Her feeble hand lifts, moving gently from side to side in rhythm, as though directing a choir only she can see. It's a scene that feels both surreal and sacred.

Joy and singing are not what you often see and hear when someone is so close to making their final journey home, and yet, it makes sense. Willa Mae has lived for this moment all her life–the moment she will walk into glory and into the arms of Jesus. Whenever someone passes away, Willa always says the same thing with a sparkle in her eye. "They've gone on into glory." She says it as though they have just won the best prize ever.

Now, as Mimi watches her, a bittersweet truth settles in her heart. Willa Mae will be going home soon. It's her turn to go on into glory. And there waiting will be her indescribable prize and radiant crown–one that someone in the heavenlies has been polishing just for her, all her life.

Mimi walks to the window and notices for the first time how close Bayou Grande flows by their temporary home at hospice. The morning fog is beginning to burn off, yet patches of it still hang heavy over the bayou. *My heart is as heavy as this morning fog,* she thinks, as she looks back at Willa's frail body lying in bed. Willa has always been the strong one–a comforter, cheerleader, and advocate for Mimi.

As Mimi matured, she sensed a strength deeply embedded within Willa's heart that was almost palpable. Something higher and not of this world must have carried her through the unspeakable hardships and invisible chains imposed on her by Jim Crow. She lost her daddy early on because of those laws. She grew up being bound by them.

Unworthiness seems to have had a tight hold on Willa. Mimi knows, though, that this is not something that takes root overnight. It is relentlessly given in small, toxic doses over time, until it grows and grows, deeply rooted, becoming systemic. Mimi never forgot the day in her teenage years that she came to understand this earthly weight that Willa carried daily.

"WILLA MAE, LET me help you fold the rest of these towels so we can go shopping!" Mimi offered eagerly.

"Now, Mimi, you know I've got more work to do after this," Willa replied. "I still need to put away the dishes and take out the trash."

Then, squinting with a curious look, she added, "Your Mama said you could drive all the way to Baton Rouge over that bridge? You just got your driver's license."

"Yep!" Mimi grinned, smiling ear to ear. "Today's the day I've been waiting for, and only the brave will accept this invitation," she said, throwing her hands out with a mischievous smile.

"Now you know you are bad, baby." Then, with a smile, "Okay ... well, stop standing there and let's get this work done so we can go to town, just you and me."

Willa Mae's crisp white uniform stood out against Mimi's cherry red Camaro as she climbed in. They crossed the Mississippi River Bridge, the one that connected their small town to Baton Rouge.

Pulling into the parking lot at Goudchaux[11] department store, Mimi jumped out of the car, practically glowing with her newfound freedom. As they made their way toward the store, Willa—as always—lagged, walking about five feet behind Mimi with her head lowered. Even if Mimi slowed down, Willa slowed her steps down too, keeping the invisible space between them. It had always been that way, for as long as Mimi could remember.

But that day, something stirred inside of Mimi, something that refused to stay silent. Stopping abruptly in the middle of the parking lot, Mimi spun around, facing Willa with frustration written all over her face.

"Willa Mae!" she blurted out, her voice sharper than she intended.

Startled, Willa pauses mid-step and looks up, her expression a mix of surprise and confusion.

"What's wrong, baby?"

Taking a deep breath, her tone softened as she searched for the right words.

"If you keep walking behind me everywhere we go, you can't come with me anymore. And I'll miss you because we always have so much fun together."

Covering her mouth with her hand, Willa gave a nervous giggle, glancing back down. But Mimi was not backing down. She stood firm, her eyes locked on Willa's.

"Well?" Mimi pressed, lifting her eyebrows in expectation.

Hesitating, Willa dropped her hand from her mouth, looked up, and smiled. "Okay, baby. Don't get mad. I'm comin."

Mimi waited until Willa joined her, shoulder to shoulder. Only then did she move forward.

"Thank you," Mimi said quietly as Willa reluctantly fell into step next to her. Mimi's heart tightened. *What could make Willa feel so unworthy?* She wondered.

But it wasn't just unworthiness—it was something learned and lived. Willa had grown up knowing exactly where she was expected to stand. Social norms had placed her firmly in what the world saw as a lower caste.

After a moment, before they reached the door, Mimi stopped again, breaking the silence; her voice softened even more.

"Willa?"

"What is it now?" Willa asked, folding her arms.

Mimi turned with an uncertain smile as her eyes searched Willa's face.

"I'm sorry I got mad, but I just don't understand why you always have to ..."

Before Mimi could finish, the polite toot of a horn startled them both. A car idled a few feet away, waiting to turn into a parking space that Mimi and Willa were standing right in front of. Willa smiled faintly as though brushing it all away. "It's okay, baby. Let's just go shopping."

And so, for the first time, they walked into the store side by side. But then, Mimi began to question more. As a young child, so much of who Willa Mae was had been both seen and unseen.

Now, as a teenager, it didn't settle well in her heart. It never really had. She thought of Willa using a separate bathroom or drinking only from her designated plastic cup behind the kitchen sink. The sight of it all, now remembered through older eyes, gnawed at something deep within Mimi. She was beginning to shoulder some of the burden that weighed so heavily on someone she loved so deeply.

But Willa felt another weight—the weight of God's glory—wrapping her in a divine acceptance of who He created her to be. She knew there was a seat of honor waiting for her next to Jesus on His throne ... and she knew exactly who—and who alone—gave her true worthiness.

As the years pressed on, Mimi often reflected on the irony of it all. How strange, she thought, that so many Southern families, her own included, willingly and with much vigor placed their babies into the arms of these loving, hard-working Black women—expecting them to change diapers, bathe them, feed them, and soothe them through tears and tantrums. Even decades before, nursing them from their own breasts.

And yet, those same women and their families were deemed too "dirty" to drink from the same water fountains, too unworthy to use the same bathrooms, or swim in the same pools. What a strange dichotomy, Mimi thought ... a disturbing, yet often forgotten reality.[12]

MIMI WALKS OVER to Willa's bed, covering her with the light blanket. Willa's eyes open. Mimi gives a reassuring smile. She thinks about all they have been through together over the years. Mimi turns her gaze back to the bayou, trying to hide the tears welling up in her eyes. Even though she moved out west years ago, thousands of miles apart, they talk every day on the phone. Willa worries about Mimi. Mimi worries about Willa.

Looking back over, she notices that Willa has drifted back to sleep, as she has done so often in these final days. Mimi knows she must be strong for her. She takes a deep breath and wipes away the tears. *Where is the nurse with the morphine?* she thought. She can tell Willa is in pain, but of course, she never complains. Mimi presses the call button.

As she waits, she notices that the bayou is eerily quiet this morning. There are no boats or fishermen in sight. All she can see is one stately brown pelican, the true state bird, perched on a stumpy cypress knee jutting out of the water. It is as though he is standing vigil over Willa, who, along with her deep affection for rainbows, has always loved watching pelicans.

The pelican sits, with wings slightly spread, just as they often do. Willa used to tell Mimi that pelicans, like her, enjoy sunbathing. She'd teasingly call her the "Coppertone girl" from the 1960s ad, with the dog tugging on the bottom of the swimsuit to expose her tan against her white skin. Mimi had always liked that nickname as a little girl because with her sun-kissed skin, it brought her closer to the color of Willa's.

The pelican is beautiful, with dark brown feathers that resemble a natural tan. Perched on the cypress knee, he looks like the king of the bayou. Then, suddenly, he takes off. With just a few strong flaps of his wings, he soars across the water. With a swift dive, he plunges like a shooting arrow into the bayou, his long beak aiming straight for his target beneath the surface. His massive pouch quickly surfaces, full and heavy. Mimi imagines the pelican has just secured a satisfying breakfast–or perhaps just an appetizer. Two gulls, persistent and unapologetic, follow behind, hoping to find any leftovers in the churned-up waters.

Mimi leaves the window and eases herself into the worn orange chair next to Willa's bed, praying it won't split open beneath her. It is the only spot of color in the otherwise stark room. It is as though someone has decided that each space needs a "pop" of color for such a time as this, and, indeed, it does.

The intercom crackles, and the nurse's voice comes through, sharp and impatient.

"Can I help you?"

Mimi's voice, calm but firm, replies.

"We've been waiting for almost an hour for pain meds for Willa Mae in room 108. Will they be here soon?"

The nurse's clipped response comes back immediately.

"I need you to be patient. You'll have to wait your turn. We will be there soon."

With an audible click, the line goes dead.

Mimi stares at the intercom, her jaw tightening. *Well, that was once again rude,* she thought, shifting in her chair.

At this point, something is brewing inside Mimi, and it is not kindness. Before she can react, Willa's soft voice breaks through the tension.

"I'm okay, baby," Willa whispers faintly. "We just have to pray and trust in Jesus. He'll take care of the situation."

"I trust in Jesus," Mimi mutters under her breath, "I just don't know if I trust this nurse."

That's it. Enough of this Southern politeness, she thought— enough of waiting my turn. Mimi senses something is very off here, and every instinct inside her screams for action. *I am Willa's advocate, she thinks, and I will do everything I can to make sure she gets the kind of care she deserves.*

She bends down to Willa, her voice calm and reassuring.

"Willa, I'm just going down the hall for a minute," she says gently, brushing Willa's hand. "We'll get you feeling better real soon."

Walking into the hallway, Mimi immediately hears laughter coming from the nurses' station. Turning to the left, she spots the supervising nurse standing there, nonchalantly holding a cup of coffee. As soon as the nurse sees Mimi approaching, her eyes narrow slightly, and she purses her lips in irritation.

Intimidated, Mimi pauses in her steps for a moment. Then, familiar words fill her head: Courage does not mean the absence of fear. Drawing a deep breath, she straightens her shoulders and continues, her steps now steady and deliberate.

"Excuse me," she says, her voice firm but urgent. "Willa Mae, in room 108, really needs morphine, and she needs it now. I can tell she's starting to feel some pain."

The supervising nurse doesn't flinch. Her expression remains cold.

"Like I said earlier, you're not the only people here. We'll get there soon."

Mimi is momentarily taken aback by the nurse's continued icy tone.

Before she can respond, another nurse at the station speaks up kindly, her voice soft but confident as she looks toward the supervising nurse.

"I can get something to take to her now."

"No," the head nurse barks sharply. "You need to go to room 105."

The young nurse's countenance falls slightly as she glances at Mimi with sympathetic eyes. As she passes by, she leans in close and whispers,

"I'm so sorry. We'll be there soon, I promise."

"Thank you for your kindness," Mimi replies quietly, her gratitude sincere.

Mimi turns to leave, her emotions simmering beneath the surface. But then Willa Mae's words ring in her mind, "Speak it, baby."

Stopping mid-step, Mimi turns back to the supervising nurse, her tone unwavering.

"I'm sorry, but if someone doesn't get to Willa Mae with her medication in the next five minutes, I'm going to need to speak to the director of the facility. I know you think she looks fine when you see her. You don't know her, but I know her well, and she never complains, even when she is in pain." With Mimi's boldness building, "We need the meds now."

The words hang in the air for a moment, and as Mimi turns back around, she lets out a long breath. *That felt good,* she thinks, a small sense of triumph blooming inside her.

"I spoke it, Willa," she whispers under her breath, as if sharing the moment with her beloved second mother.

Walking back to the room, Mimi notices Joseph, the custodian, standing quietly in the shadows at the end of the hall. He meets her gaze, giving her a reaffirming nod, having heard every word. Mimi smiles, continuing to walk with renewed confidence.

As Mimi enters the room, she reminds herself to focus on Willa Mae and make her comfortable. Noting the time and expecting the meds to be on their way, she walks to the sink, letting cold water run over a washcloth before wringing it dry and folding it neatly. Placing it gently on Willa's forehead, she watches as Willa's eyes open slightly, her face softening into a faint, grateful smile.

"They're coming soon with medicine, Willa, to help your pain," Mimi assures her softly.

Willa's eyes shut again, and Mimi sits back down in the orange chair. The cool compress seems to ease Willa's discomfort, and Mimi allows herself a small breath of relief. The supervising nurse appears at the door, her voice curt.

"I'm going to get it now."

Without another word, she turns and disappears down the hall.

"I'm counting the minutes," Mimi muttered under her breath.

Her thoughts drift to childhood. She can still picture Willa leaning over her bed in her childhood home, placing a cool washcloth on her fevered forehead with the same tenderness Mimi had just shown her. And then, without fail, Willa would return with a tray—a perfectly folded napkin, steam rising from a bowl of Campbell's chicken noodle soup, and a few buttered saltine crackers beside it.

Mimi remembers how beautiful it all looked, as though the simple act of presenting the tray made her feel better. Willa had always done things with such care, making Mimi and her sisters feel special and loved. Yet, as a child, she had never thought about who cared for Willa's daughter Effie when she got sick.

Snapping Mimi from her thoughts, the supervising nurse reenters the room, a syringe in her hand. Without a greeting or acknowledgment, she walks to Willa's IV and administers the morphine with brisk efficiency.

"There. She has her morphine." Her voice is clinical. "That should keep her quiet for a while."

She then walks out.

Quiet? Mimi thinks, her stomach twisting at the words. *What an odd thing to say.*

Sitting back down, Mimi pulls out her phone to call Anna Beth. As her sister answers, Mimi steps into the bathroom and closes the door partway, just enough so Willa can't hear.

"Anna Beth," she says quietly, "something is not right here. This is not the environment we want for Willa Mae, and it's certainly not what Effie would want either. I think the supervising nurse is showing blatant racism toward Willa."

"At hospice?" Anna Beth says in disbelief. "Is the staff not treating her well?"

"The staff is wonderful. It's just this one person," Mimi clarifies.

"What?" says Anna Beth. "How could that be? The facility had such great reviews and recommendations, but maybe you are right in what you sensed with that nurse."

"I know," Mimi sighs. "But the rest of the staff have been so caring and kind when I talk to them. I don't know how this one nurse ended up here, but I don't think we want Willa anywhere near her. I guess I had hoped the South would've come further by 2019. But moments like this ..." She trails off. "They pull me right back to the 1960s—as if no time has passed at all. Do you think you and Andrew could look for a new facility?"

Mimi sees an incoming call.

"I'll call you back, Anna Beth. It's Effie."

Effie's voice comes through the phone, strained and anxious. She's at her layover in Atlanta, where thunderstorms have delayed her flight. *Typical*, Mimi thinks.

Southern airspace often comes with unpredictable summer storms rolling in off the Gulf. Effie has a fear of flying, so Mimi does her best to encourage her.

"I'm praying for your travels, Effie," she reassures. "All is well here. Your Momma is resting comfortably now that she's had her morphine."

After saying goodbye, Mimi walks back to the window, drawn to the view of the bayou that has always brought her comfort. The fog has lifted some, but now a drizzle falls over the water. A blue heron flies low, skimming the surface before diving down and emerging with a small fish in its beak.

The bayou is truly magical, Mimi thinks, feeling a pang of longing. She misses parts of this world sometimes. Her husband, a Northerner, often jokes that you need a passport to get into Louisiana. He's not all that wrong. It's a place unlike any other, filled with rich culture, unforgettable food, and music that seeps into your soul.

Yet today, as sacred as hospice always is, there's a palpable breach, a dark and toxic presence that taints the peace and hospitality of this space. Mimi sits back down on the edge of the chair, pressing her hand against her forehead. A gentle touch brushes her hand. She looks up to find Willa Mae's frail hand reaching out to hers.

"You okay, baby?" Willa asks softly.

"I'm just a little tired," Mimi admits.

"Rest yourself, baby," Willa says, her eyes drifting closed again.

That woman still watches me like a hawk, Mimi thinks with a faint smile tugging at her lips. She's going to watch over me until she takes her last breath. Mimi sits further back in her chair and tries to fake relaxing, so as not to be fussed at yet again. Once she's sure that Willa has dozed off, she stands quietly and walks back to the window. The bayou not only comforts Mimi but also helps her to think.

Mimi knows they have a decision to make: either move Willa and risk the strain it might cause her, or stay and shield her from this vile racist. Suddenly, her eyes catch movement as the pelican returns, making a graceful landing on the same cypress knee. He pauses, lifting his head toward the gray sky before turning, facing the window where Mimi stands. His gaze seems to meet hers, filled with a quiet empathy.

For a moment, it feels as though he understands the weight of the decision they need to make. His deep, penetrating gaze settles on Mimi, his pale-yellow eyes standing out against the earthy brown tones of his feathers. He stares at her mysteriously, as though trying to convey something unspoken. Mimi looks intently at him.

"Are you back to say goodbye," she asks, "or calling us to stay?"

CHAPTER THREE

"When the whole world is silent, even one voice becomes powerful."[13]

-Attributed to Malala Yousafzai, 2014
Nobel Peace Prize Laureate

August 6, 2019

Morning

A gentle knock comes to the door. Mimi turns from the window, walking toward it as it cracks open, followed by a cheerful, "Hellooo! May I come in?"

"Of course," says Mimi, "come on in."

Willa Mae's eyes flutter open as a young man, appearing to be a nurse's assistant, walks in. His smile and presence light up the room the moment he sees Willa. Moving to the foot of the bed, he meets her gaze with an expression of genuine warmth.

"Why, hi Miss Willa Mae," he says softly, his voice full of life.

"My name's Angel, and I'll be helping to take care of you today."

Filling her glass with water, he says, "Miss Willa, how's your day going so far?"

"Ohhhhh, baby," Willa answers, her voice weak but joyful. "The Lord woke me up this mornin' to a brand-new day. What a blessin', and so are you."

"Well," Angel says, his face lighting up, "I don't think I've ever been greeted with such joy." Quickly looking back at Mimi, he says, "Why, forgive my manners, I'm Angel, and I'm honored to be attending to Miss Willa Mae today."

"I'm Mimi," she chuckles, "and it's so nice to meet you."

He looks toward the window.

"Now, that sun is about to hit you right in the face, Miss Willa. Let me close these blinds a bit for you."

Mimi sits back in her chair, already liking the young man. He's kind, cheerful, and quite the character, with a thick Cajun accent that gives his words a musical quality. He glances out the window, peering over the bayou as if he's about to give a live morning weather report on WBRZ.

"Mais Sha,'" he exclaims theatrically, "the fog's burned off the bayou, and the fishing boats are heading up the channel like ants swarming to a Sunday picnic."

Mimi smiles, enjoying the interaction between them. Angel leans toward Willa, his voice dropping to a playful whisper as he looks around the room like someone about to share a secret.

"Miss Willa, will you please pardon me for a moment? I'm just gonna sneak a little peek at the bayou. I'm looking for the Zydeco Zoomer."

Mimi chuckles softly to herself. *Now that's a name*, she thinks.

"My partner works on that boat," Angel continues, a grin spreading across his face. "His boss runs a zydeco bar and dance hall not far from here. They catch all kinds of fish for the best po' boys you've ever had. I'll bring you one, Miss Willa."

"Mmmm, mmm," Willa hums in delight. "That would be a blessin'."

"Mais' oui," Angel replies enthusiastically. "People come from all over the bayou and across the Atchafalaya Basin for their food and dancing. The bar is famous throughout the parish."

Mimi catches his eye and grins, giving a quick little jitterbug step while nodding subtly toward Willa. Angel picks up on it instantly.

"Miss Willa," Angel asks, leaning closer, "do you like zydeco music? Do you like to dance?"

"Ohhhh, baby, yes," Willa says, her voice lifting with unexpected energy.

Mimi smiles and whispers to him, "Well, the morphine has surely kicked in. Next thing I know, she'll be getting out of bed and bossing us all around."

Angel grins and pulls his phone from his pocket. Within seconds, zydeco music begins to play softly, the upbeat sound of accordions and frottoirs filling the room. It isn't necessarily the song Mimi would have chosen for this moment, but it's too late. The song has already started, and a deep Cajun voice can be heard, almost hard to understand because of the thick accent, "Talk to me, gud whiskey."[14]

Willa doesn't miss a beat. Her hands start clapping. Her head sways side to side, eyes closed as if she's right there on the dance floor. The music reaches a place deep within her, a place untouched by pain or time. Angel steps forward, taking Willa's hands gently, swaying them back and forth. A wide smile spreads across her face, one Mimi hasn't seen in days.

"Laissez les bons temps rouler," says Mimi with a big smile on her face, so happy that Willa was enjoying this moment.

Unable to resist, Mimi joins in, line-dancing around the bed and over to the window. This moment of lightness is just what the doctor ordered.

Mimi glances outside, amused to see her friendly pelican still perched on the cypress knee, staring into the room as if eager to join their spontaneous Fais do-do.

"Hey .... Angel, Willa Mae," Mimi calls out with a laugh, "look at the pelican! I think he's—"

The music cuts off abruptly.

Mimi turns to see the supervising nurse standing in the doorway, hands on her hips, her mouth drawn into her familiar disapproving line.

Glaring at Angel, she huffs, "I didn't ask you to start a dance party in room 108. I simply told you to check on room

108. Could I see you at the nurse's station?" She walks out without saying a word to Mimi or Willa.

Willa is still clapping softly, lost somewhere far away, and for that, Mimi is grateful. Angel turns back toward them, his expression apologetic.

"It was very nice to meet you. Press your button if you need anything."

As though it had slipped in through a back door, darkness had thrown a heavy cloak over the joy, dancing, and light that had filled the room just moments before. *Not something that should happen in a place of such unconditional love*, Mimi thinks sadly. *Something is surely not right here, and I'm going to take care of Willa, just as she did for me all those years growing up.* The coin has been flipped.

Angel turns to leave, but Willa stirs.

"Mr. Angel," she says softly.

He walks back to her bedside, leaning down so he can hear her faint voice.

"You think your friend could catch me some catfish on his boat?" she whispers. "Ohhhh, how I love fried catfish."

Angel smiles, resting his hand gently on hers.

"For you, Miss Willa Mae, I'll ask Andre' to catch the tastiest catfish in the bayou. In fact," he adds, lowering his voice, "legend has it there's a grand Paw-Paw in that bayou, and he's called T-boy. No one's ever been able to catch him, of course. But maybe today's the day."

"What a blessin' that would be," Willa murmurs as her eyes close, a satisfied smile settling on her face, likely dreaming of fried catfish and okra.

Angel gently squeezes her hand and looks back toward Mimi.

"Y'all call me now if you need anything."

He leaves the room, heading to the nurse's station with a look of apprehension on his face.

Mimi picks up her phone and calls Anna Beth.

"Hey, sis," she says quietly. "I just wanted to check in and let you know Willa is resting comfortably. The morphine has really helped."

"Oh, that's good news," Anna Beth replies. "Hey, I talked to Effie, though, she says. Her flight's been canceled because of storms, and she can't get on another one until the morning. She's staying at a hotel for the night, but I know she'll want to call you to talk to her Momma. Also, we're doing our best to find a new place for Willa. We can probably get an ambulance transfer."

"Okay, that's great," Mimi says. "I'm going to talk with the director and let him know there's a good chance we'll be moving her this evening. The issues with this nurse continue to concern me."

After hanging up, Mimi looks back at Willa, still resting peacefully. *When one door closes, another opens,* she thinks.

Sitting down in the chair, exhausted, her gaze lifts toward the window. Raindrops dance on the surface of the bayou.

"Please, Jesus," she whispers in desperation, "let it be a door that flies open wide and illuminates light everywhere around Willa Mae," as she herself dozes off.

MIMI FEELS CAUGHT between a half-dream state and wakefulness; her senses are again overwhelmed by the sharp scent of ammonia. Am I about to faint? Where am I? she wonders, her thoughts spinning.

Sitting up in a state of confusion, having fallen into a deep sleep, she attempts to collect herself. Her heart races as her surroundings slowly come into focus. Turning her head, she sees Willa Mae lying still in the bed.

"Yes ... hospice," she whispers to herself, the words grounding her. "I'm in hospice with Willa."

Mimi rubs her forehead, trying to shake off the lingering daze, and exhales deeply, as though her body is catching up with her mind.

"Miss Mimi, are you okay?"

Startled, she looks toward the doorway and sees Joseph standing there with his mop bucket and a rolling garbage can at his side. His expression, as always, is kind but watchful, as if checking on her is part of his duties.

"Umm, I ..." she begins, her voice uneven as she collects herself. "I guess I fell into a deep sleep, dreaming ... and ... well, yes, thank you, Joseph. I'm fine. Probably just a little worn out."

She manages a small smile.

"This orange chair must be starting to feel like home to me, the way I was sleeping so hard."

They both chuckle.

"You're going through a lot right now," Joseph says gently, his voice steady and full of care. "You need to rest yourself when you can."

Mimi smiles, his words settling over her. *I've heard those words recently*, she thinks, Willa Mae's soft voice echoing in her mind.

"Yes, thank you, Joseph. You are so kind," she says again, her tone sincere. "I will be fine. Did you need to come in? Feel free."

Joseph nods appreciatively, stepping forward with his mop bucket as Mimi settles back, still brushing off the lingering haze of sleep.

Joseph's eyes shift to the side table.

"I couldn't help but notice that ole embroidery there," he says thoughtfully. "I've seen something like that somewhere before."

"You've seen this same embroidery pattern?" Mimi asks as her curiosity piques.

Joseph scratches his head as though trying to remember.

"Well, something similar," he replies. "But my memory isn't so kind to me these days. I just can't, for the life of me, remember where. I sure like what it says, though."

Glancing back at the intricate needlework, "I do too," Mimi says softly. "I just wish I knew who gave it to Willa."

Joseph walks into the bathroom to empty the garbage can, his voice carrying through the quiet room as he continues speaking.

"Well, I'll empty these trash cans and be on my way. Edna, my wife, has a plate of red beans and rice waitin' for me at home."

"Ohhh, Joseph, that's one of my favorite meals! Willa Mae used to make that for us all the time," Mimi says, a smile spreading across her face.

"Yep," Joseph chuckles, "and skillet cornbread?"

"Yes!" Mimi says with growing excitement. "That's another Willa specialty. Now you're making my mouth water, Joseph. You know, Willa also makes prize-winning biscuits with cane syrup."

Joseph grins as he empties the other trash can in the room.

"Miss Mimi, now you're the one making me hungry, and it looks like someone's been to Shrimp Shack and hasn't eaten it yet."

"Anna Beth's Uber Eats must've come while I was dozing," says Mimi.

"Hmmm, now God's gonna give you the strength on this journey, Miss Mimi, but you gonna have to keep your end of the agreement and eat it," he says in a firm yet loving voice. He gives her a warm smile as he finishes his task.

"Well, I best be goin'. You have yourself a blessed one now."

Turning to leave, Joseph pauses at the doorway. His face softens as he looks back at Willa Mae, then at Mimi.

"I'm praying for Miss Willa Mae," he says in a quiet, solemn voice, "and for your family too. My wife and I, we pray for everyone here as they make their final journey from their earthly home to their eternal heavenly home. It's our ministry. I give Edna the names, and she keeps them all in her pretty flowered journal."

The depth of his words takes Mimi aback.

"Why, thank you, Joseph. That's beautiful," she says, her voice full of sincerity. "I can't tell you how much that means to us. And thank you for all the hard work you do to keep everything so clean and fresh here."

Although, she thinks, *I could do without the strong ammonia.*

"You're welcome, Miss Mimi." Joseph turns to go, but Mimi calls after him.

"Joseph," she says, her voice stopping him mid-step.

He turns back, eyebrows raised gently.

"Thank you for the 'lagniappe' of your kind smile, as we Cajuns like to say. That 'little something extra' you share with everyone here means more than you know to those of us going through this difficult time."

Joseph's face lights up with another bright smile.

"Like I said, Miss Mimi, it's my ministry."

With that, he turns and begins walking up the hall, his quiet humming drifting back into the room like a gentle, consoling lullaby, wrapping itself all around Mimi.

She turns her attention to the embroidery on the side table. *How interesting,* she thinks, *that Joseph had seen something similar somewhere in his past. Maybe it was a popular pattern back in the day.* One thing is for sure: Willa Mae is never far from this vintage piece of needlepoint. Mimi can still remember it vividly from childhood, always hanging in the front room of Willa's modest, over-100-year-old, three-room home. But what stands out most to Mimi are the praying hands.

Willa Mae asked Mimi to bring the embroidery to the hospital, and now here to hospice. Only now does she realize just how much it means to Willa. It is the first time it has ever come down from its place on the wall in her home. As Mimi leans in, studying the familiar but age-faded image, something catches her eye. *Is that what I think it is?* She wonders.

"Is that ... a white hand and ... oh my goodness, a brown hand praying together?" she whispers to herself.

She squints, moving even closer. *Yes,* she thinks, *it is subtle, yet undeniably intentional.* Two hands—one pale, the other brown—are clasped together in prayer. Behind the hands, the sky opens up, with brilliant sun rays shooting outward in every direction.

The message above the praying hands reads, "Faith can break the sky in two and let the face of God shine through."

The words, combined with the imagery, strike her deeply. It is as though a hidden message of hope has been placed there, one stitch at a time, decades ago. But, by whom?

Curiosity suddenly burns inside her. She pushes up from the chair, walking quickly to the door and glancing down the hall, looking for Joseph. *Did he also notice that the praying hands are two different colors?* she thinks. But Joseph is nowhere in sight.

Walking back into the room, Mimi checks on Willa Mae. She seems to be sleeping soundly, her breathing steady, the morphine surely easing her pain. Mimi turns toward the window just as the sun slips behind a cluster of clouds, darkening the room.

Resting her crossed arms on the windowpane, she drops her head.

"Please, God," Mimi whispers in prayer, her voice low.

"Make it clear to us what we are supposed to do. I know you love your child, Willa Mae. She has been such a faithful servant for you on this earth. Where do you want her to spend her final days?"

Shaking her head, Mimi whispers, "I feel like it can't be here. I know you want her to be surrounded by love, respect, and kindness. I trust you hear me, God, and will answer my prayer."

Raising her head to the long moan of a distant boat horn, Mimi feels a headache coming on. She rubs her forehead, her mind swirling. *I need to call Effie and Anna Beth,* she thinks. *We need to talk about this.* About to step away from the window, Mimi sees a single ray of sunlight breaking through a small keyhole in the clouds. She turns quickly toward the beams of light streaming across the darkened room, like gentle fingers reaching through the shadows.

Finding their way to Willa, her white nightgown is almost glowing. She looks so peaceful, Mimi thought, like an angel.

"Wow," Mimi whispers to herself, stunned by the brightness. "Just like the needlepoint. Thank you, Jesus, for this surprising and delightful gift of light, a reminder of Your presence here."

This earthly battle, she thinks, is so much more than what we can see. There's so much happening beyond our human sight, yet we can feel it deep within our spirit.

Mimi's mind drifts to Willa Mae's familiar words, ones she has repeated so many times over the years.

'The battle is not ours, Mimi. It's God's. He is the God of mighty angel armies, powerful and faithful. We just need to hold on to our faith. But faith, baby, is not always a feeling.'

"God, I have faith, and I believe," Mimi whispers, her voice wavering. "Please help me overcome any unbelief."

She sits back down in the orange chair, which, oddly enough, has started to feel like a small source of comfort. Picking up the stack of admission paperwork, she quietly fills them out, then sets them back down on the side table. Her eyes again catch sight of the intricate stitching above the praying hands, the words tugging at her heart.

"Faith can break the sky in two and let the face of God shine through," Mimi says aloud, as though she were praying the words themselves. Willa has taught her to pray God's Word aloud. "There's power in it, baby," she would say. "Satan flees when he hears it."

She lets out a breath and looks up, the lingering fingers of sunlight still illuminating the room.

"For our struggle is not against flesh and blood," she continues, "but against the rulers, against the authorities, against the powers of this dark world and against the spiritual forces of evil in the heavenly realms.[15] Amen."

As Mimi pulls out her phone to call Anna Beth and Effie, she hears Willa Mae stirring and immediately cancels the call. She looks over at the bed.

"Mimi," Willa whispers faintly, her voice just above a breath.

Reaching out, Willa's hand brushes against her treasured needlepoint frame on the bedside table. It wobbles, then falls to the floor, breaking the oak frame.

"It's okay, Willa," Mimi says quickly, bending down to pick it up. "I can fix it. What did you need?"

"Is Effie here yet?" Willa asks softly, her eyes searching Mimi's face.

"Not yet," Mimi says gently. "She'll be here soon. You don't need to worry. You just rest now, okay?"

Willa seems comforted by the words, letting her head sink back into the pillow as her eyes close. Mimi crouches down to gather the pieces of the broken frame. As she does, the needlepoint falls out, the edges frayed and wrapped around a piece of crumbling cardboard that looks decades old. She carefully begins to fit everything back together when something catches her eye. A small piece of brown paper peeks out from between the cardboard and the needlepoint.

Curious, Mimi tugs the needlepoint gently away from the cardboard. Hidden beneath it, neatly folded, is a very old piece of brown paper. Her curiosity piques, and she slides it out with great care. Slowly unfolding the paper, she realizes there is something wrapped inside: a photograph. A very old and faded photograph. She hesitates, glancing at Willa to make sure she is still asleep before getting up and moving to the desk.

Under the glow of the desk lamp, Mimi holds the photo closer to the light.

It is faded with age, its edges curled slightly. She can make out two little girls standing together in the image, their small frames outlined against what looks like water … a river, a lake, or perhaps even a bayou. She can tell that one girl is Black, the other White.

Who could this be? Mimi wonders. Is it Willa? But who's the other little girl? It strikes her as odd, almost startling, to see a Black child and a white child standing together like that, especially during a time long ago when such things were rare in the deep South.

Just then, Willa stirs again, her soft voice breaking the silence.

"Mimi, is Effie here yet?" she asks, her words echoing her earlier question.

"No, Willa," Mimi says, her tone calm and soothing. "Just a little weather delay, but she's on her way. Are you feeling a little better?"

Willa gives a small nod. Mimi sets the photo down carefully and brings Willa a glass of water, holding the straw to her lips. Willa sips just a tiny bit.

"I'm putting the frame back together, the one that fell," Mimi explains, glancing back toward the broken pieces. Willa's face clouds with concern.

"It's okay," Mimi reassures her. "I can get it all back together, good as new."

Willa's expression softens. Mimi looks back at the photo on the desk. *Who are these two little girls?* she thinks. *And why has this photo been hidden here for so long? Should I ask her about the photo now? Willa seems much more comfortable, able to talk. This might be as good a time as any.*

Mimi picks up the photo and steps to her bed, sitting down.

"Willa," Mimi says. "This photo fell out from behind the needlepoint. It looks very old."

Mimi holds the photograph up for Willa Mae to see. Willa reaches for it with trembling hands, her fingers brushing the worn edges. Without a word, Mimi quickly grabs Willa's glasses from the side table and slides them gently onto her face. Willa stares at the photo for a long moment, holding it close to her eyes, squinting as though she's looking deep into the past.

Mimi waits, giving her time, but curiosity gets the better of her.

"Willa," she asks softly, "who is this?"

Willa's hand lifts, her frail finger resting on one of the little girls in the photo.

"You?" Mimi asks with a small smile of surprise.

Willa nods faintly, the corners of her lips tugging upward into a smile.

"You were just a little girl," Mimi says, her voice warm. "And so cute."

Willa's gaze lingers on the picture. Her expression shifts. A tear slips slowly down her cheek as she whispers, "Clar ..."

Mimi leans closer, her voice gentle.

"The other little girl is Claire?"

Willa shakes her head faintly.

"Clar-rra," she corrects softly as though that familiar name has been engraved on her heart for decades.

"Clara?" Mimi repeats. "Was she your friend?" Mimi smiles.

Willa doesn't answer immediately. Instead, her eyes fill with a faraway look, distant, as though she's traveled back to another time. She pulls the photograph close to her chest. Her frail hands cling to it as if holding onto something precious, something that still lives deep within her heart.

Mimi sits still, watching in quiet amazement. *Who is Clara? she wonders. Where was this photo taken? How could they have been friends?*

Mimi's gaze shifts briefly to the praying hands in the needlepoint. *One white. One brown. Could they be connected somehow? She thinks.*

After a moment, Willa's eyes softly close. Mimi carefully leans forward and gently takes the glasses from her face and the photograph from her hands. She wants to protect it, keep it safe. As she wraps it back in the paper, she can't resist taking one last look.

The sun, filling the room with a soft light, spills its glow over the photograph, illuminating it in a way she hasn't noticed before. Something faint in the background catches her attention, just barely visible beneath a crease that runs across the photo.

Frowning, she holds it up closer to the window, letting the light pour over it.

"It's an arc," she murmurs. "Could that be ... a rainbow?"

The photo is black and white, but its shape is unmistakable. Mimi squints, feeling a strange certainty that it is, indeed, a rainbow.

Willa has always loved rainbows. Mimi can still hear her voice from years ago: "The colors are always in the same order, baby. Red on top, violet on the bottom. God's promise, painted in the sky."

A small smile touches Mimi's lips as she carefully folds the photo, placing it back safely into what has been its familiar hiding place for decades. She can't wait to show it to Anna Beth and Effie when they arrive. *Maybe Effie can shine more light on this*, she thinks. *So many unknowns.*

MIMI HAD FLOWN in from her home in Denver just two weeks earlier to be with Willa in the hospital. Though she has lived away from Louisiana for over forty years, her roots still run deep here. There is something mysterious and magical about the bayou, the way the cypress trees stretch their knobby knees out of the murky water, the hospitality that is warm and unmatched. The people welcome you as though you are family. Yet, beneath all this charm is another tale of darkness, suffering, and heartache that, as a child, Mimi was never fully aware of—or able to understand the depth of its wounds.

It is a part of her roots that she is not proud of, and no wonder Effie, Willa's daughter, chose to leave. She was part of The Great Migration, as historians call it now, one of the many Blacks who fled the South in the 1960s to escape the world they were born into, in search of freedom, dignity, and opportunity. Effie went to Detroit and never looked back.

She and Mimi's lives were so different growing up. So vastly, achingly different. And now, with Effie returning, Mimi can't stop thinking about it. Maybe this is the time to ask the question that has haunted her for years. Would she dare bring it up? She could just let it lie, leave it as the elephant in the room, and ignore it. But the guilt. The gnawing guilt. It is just too much for her to bear. It has been a captive heaviness behind a locked door in Mimi's heart for too long.

People often ask her, "Where are you from?" Her faint Southern drawl gives her away every time. "Louisiana," she says, but she always says it with reluctance and a pause as if bracing herself for the reaction. There is often a look, subtle, yet it seems loaded with so many other unspoken thoughts, especially if the question comes from an African American.

Truth be told, Mimi admits to herself, *I'm probably creating scenarios in my own mind, things that aren't really there. But are they?* Mimi isn't sure. She always wants to explain herself quickly, to make it clear: I believe in equality. Color doesn't matter to me. And I'm so sorry for the travesties that took place on that native land of mine, at the hands of my people—maybe even my own ancestors.

There is no denying that many of those same ancestors have likely condoned slavery and upheld the laws of Jim Crow. Those people and those times do not define her now, but they leave an aftermath, a burden of brokenness and division, that still reverberates its echoes today. Mimi feels a need and responsibility to face these echoes head-on.

She has never really spoken those thoughts aloud, but maybe it is time. And yet, how could anyone truly understand her world as a child? What it means to be raised by a Black woman who worked for her family for over six decades and became like a mother to her.

"She was a maid and would wait on you?" some asked, their tone feeling judgmental.

"Yes," Mimi would answer softly, her honesty laced with a tinge of shame. "And I'm not always proud of that. That was my world as a child. It's what I knew."

But there is something else Mimi knows, something that outweighs the complexities of her childhood ... Willa Mae's love. The unshakable love and security that exuded from her presence. Even in the unjust South, where wounds run deep and many lie raw and wide open, God's love, light, grace, forgiveness, and redemption shine through.

In Mimi's simple understanding as a child, she saw glimpses of sadness and hurt in that world around her. With a child's earnestness, she wanted to make things right. But how could she? How could any child comprehend the generational trauma and depth of those wounds ... wounds that stretch across decades of hardship for Black families, especially in the deep South?

It was too much. It was as though she wanted justice but didn't know how to achieve it or what that word even meant as a child. The concept was too big for her small heart to hold and her small hands to fix. And yet, what she does know is that she and her sisters received a gift, one of incalculable value, when God placed them in Willa Mae's arms as babies. They were given years of Willa's tender care, her strength, and her unwavering love.

But now, as an adult, Mimi's heart sorely aches. She now understands the burden Willa carried every day of her life, weighed down by the invisible chains of Jim Crow even as she cared so lovingly for Mimi's family. Today, this thought deeply, deeply saddens her.

PART II

SEEN, YET UNSEEN

The world seen through a child's tender eyes leaves an imprint—one we carry into adulthood, quietly shaping how we see ourselves, others, and the world around us. Days are shaped by a lens of innocence, often shielded from life's struggles and harsh realities by those who love and care for them.

Even the most sheltered view cannot fully protect a child from the truths that wait just beyond the edges of what they know. As Mimi looks back on her younger self, she begins to understand just how much she saw—and how much more she didn't.

CHAPTER FOUR

February 13, 1960

In the deep South, there was something unique, perhaps even perplexing to those from other parts of the country. A child could have two mothers, yet often, they were of different colors. Mimi and her sisters had their Mama, and then they had their Willa Mae. In the secure rhythm of their world, like clockwork, Willa Mae would step through the back screen door of their home every day except Sunday.

When Mimi was just a toddler, it was Willa Mae who gave her the nickname that stayed with her for life. Willa Mae loved telling the story of how it happened. Coming into the house from the garden, her apron pockets would be filled with ripe tomatoes, and Mimi, barely able to balance on her tippy toes, would reach into Willa's lace-trimmed pockets and eagerly call out, "me me, mato." Or, if Willa Mae had just made a fresh pitcher of sweet tea, Mimi would tug on her apron, nearly pulling it off, crying, "me me, i-tea." That moment always brought a smile to Willa Mae's face. And from then on, the name Mimi stuck - a simple thread in the fabric of their bond.

IT'S SATURDAY MORNING in Bayou Grande, Louisiana, and a school-free day—seven-year-old Mimi's bare feet pitter-patter down the long wooden hallway of the Benoit home. The comforting aroma draws her toward the kitchen. As she runs in, her eyes catch the familiar crisp white uniform. Willa Mae stands by the oven, peeking in, her melodic voice fills the room.

"You hear the lambs a-cryin', oh Shepherd, feed my sheep. My Saviour spoke those words so sweet, oh, Shepherd, feed my sheep."[17]

It's a song Willa Mae sings often, and Mimi loves the sound of it.

"I see you, peek-a-boo!" Mimi calls from behind the yellow chrome dinette table, her voice playful and full of delight. Willa Mae stops singing and turns, her face lighting up with that warm smile that Mimi knows so well, the one that always makes her feel safe and deeply loved.

"Peek a boo to you, sweet baby. I see you, too."

Willa's face tightens in a grimace.

"Now, Mimi, what are you doin' barefoot? You gonna get a cold. You go right back into your room and put on your fuzzy slippers."

As Mimi runs down the hall, Willa Mae quickly calls out to her, "Don't burn yourself goin' around that floor furnace."

Every morning follows the same pattern, especially when the weather turns cold. Mimi shows up in the kitchen barefoot, and Willa Mae fusses at her without fail.

Mimi, in second grade, and her two older sisters, who all attend the Catholic school just a few blocks away, are thrilled to have the day to themselves. Rain has fallen all night and still lingers in the form of drizzle against the cloudy morning.

Mimi runs back into the kitchen in her pink fuzzy slippers. Willa smiles.

"Now that's better, my baby," she says. "Sit yourself down at this table like a big girl." Her voice is warm but insistent. "Your breakfast is almost ready."

Mimi climbs up and sits with crisscross legs on the vinyl yellow cushion chair, but she can't take her eyes off the olive-green oven. She knows exactly what's about to come out, and the anticipation lights up her face.

The comforting aroma fills the kitchen. Willa Mae places a plate of hot, buttery homemade biscuits in front of her. This is Willa Mae's famous recipe, a treasured favorite of everyone in the family. Mimi picks up a biscuit and reaches for the cane syrup, savoring the ritual of this weekend treat.

One by one, her sisters make their way to the kitchen, drawn from their beds by the enticing, familiar scent drifting through the house. Anna Beth, ten years old, and Mary Grace, thirteen, walk into the kitchen wearing their fuzzy slippers, having learned their lesson one too many times. Groggy, they take their seats, slipping naturally into their own special spots at the table.

"Good morning, my babies," says Willa.

Immediately, Anna Beth asks, "Willa, can I take my biscuits in front of the TV?"

"Now you know you can't do that. You will drip syrup all over your Mama's nice couch. You sit down right here at this table. I don't want to have to be cleanin' spots off that couch today. I have too many other chores to do before I go home and do my own."

At seven years old, Mimi has no concept of Willa Mae's endless list of chores. Beds are magically made when she arrives home from school. Clothes are washed, folded, and neatly tucked away in drawers. Warm meals are always waiting on the table, and the excitement of after-school snacks hidden to be discovered like a tasty treasure hunt always awaits her.

What doesn't cross Mimi's mind is what Willa Mae—or her own daughter Effie—might have had for breakfast that morning. That world, their world, remains invisible to her. All she knows is her own small universe, and in it, Willa Mae is constant and dependable, always there for her and her sisters.

WILLA LIVES WITH HER daughter Effie and her mother, Nellie, in a small wooden home over a century old. It sits on cement blocks, with a small, screened-in porch out front. Well-loved oak rocking chairs, crafted by Willa Mae's great-grandpappy over 90 years ago, invite you to come in, sit, and stay awhile. It started out as a shotgun house and gradually expanded over the years. Generations of her family have called this house home, often with several generations living there all at the same time.

The walls hold countless stories of their lives, marked by love, loss, pain, and resilience. One of those stories is Willa's vivid memory of her grandma Sissy's passing. When Sissy was laid out for viewing in the home, Willa, overcome with grief, climbed into the simple wood coffin, crying and pleading to go with her.

Their home stands in what is called the "colored section" of town. Though only a mile from Mimi's home, it represents a starkly different world, one defined by invisible yet unyielding lines of separation. Willa walks to the Benoit home every day except Sunday. She never learned to drive and calls her feet "her car." She uses them to take her everywhere ... to pay bills, attend church, shop for groceries, and go to work.

On one side of town, Bayou Grande flows gently, while not far on the other side, the mighty and muddy Mississippi River winds its way through the landscape. Mimi's family lives just one block from the levee, a protective barrier against the river's springtime rise caused by snowmelt from northern states and increased rainfall.

WALKING INTO THE KITCHEN, Harriet Benoit, Mimi's mother, is already dressed for the day, displaying her usual poise.

"Good morning, Miss Harriet," Willa says warmly. "Can I get you some breakfast?"

Sitting down at the table, Mrs. Benoit replies, "Just a biscuit and a café au lait will do, thank you."

Without missing a beat, she turns her attention to Mary Grace, seated nearby. "Mary Grace, could you please remove your elbows from the table? We do not live in a barn," she adds, her tone firm but composed.

Anna Beth and Mimi giggle as Mary Grace rolls her eyes.

"Daddy is off to work at the bank today, and I have a morning of errands. Who wants to come with me?" Mama asks.

Anna Beth and Mary Grace are quick to chime in, eager to join her.

"I want to stay with Willa," Mimi says in excitement.

Before long, everyone is dressed for the day. Anna Beth and Mary Grace climb into the family's Oldsmobile 88 sedan with Mama, whispering and giggling as they drive off. Meanwhile, Mimi sits contentedly on the kitchen floor, playing with her Barbie doll near Willa Mae's feet. Willa, as always, wears her yellow apron over her crisp white uniform, its lace pockets neatly stitched on either side. She hums softly to herself as she washes the breakfast dishes. To Mimi, it all feels familiar and safe.

Peering out the window, Willa suddenly turns off the water and dries her hands, moving with a sense of urgency.

"Come on, baby," she says quickly. "We're goin' to the levee. There's a surprise I want to show you. My chores are gonna have to wait."

She hurries to the coat closet and pulls out two raincoats.

"Put on your galoshes. Hurry now," she says in excitement.

Taking Mimi's hand, Willa leads the way, their steps quick along the street under the canopy of live oaks as a squirrel scampers across the road in front of them. Reaching the levee, Mimi catches a glimpse of something up ahead. She lets go of Willa's hand, running forward for a better look.

"Willa!" she calls out, her voice brimming with anticipation. "I see the surprise!"

Willa smiles warmly.

"Let's keep walkin', baby," she says. "We need to get closer to see the whole thing. We don't want to miss God's beautiful show."

A fierce but quick thunderstorm had just rolled through, leaving the air heavy with humidity. The path up the levee is muddy and slippery. Willa slows her pace and holds Mimi's hand tight. The distant rumble of thunder lingers as the storm moves down the river as swiftly as it came in. Dark clouds still hang low on the horizon as the sun begins to reappear.

As they reach the top of the levee, they stop in awe. Arcing to the heavens high above the Mississippi River is the most vivid and breathtaking rainbow Mimi has ever seen. The colors stretch across the sky, brilliant against the backdrop of dark, stormy clouds. They stand together in silence and take in the beauty before them, Willa knowing that they are being given a gift today.

Others stop, drawn to the brilliant brushstrokes of color splashed across the sky's vast canvas. No matter how many times Willa sees a rainbow, it never seems to lose its wonder.

There's something irresistible about it, compelling one to pause and marvel at God's artistic masterpiece. It's always breathtaking, a reminder of a power far greater than anyone can comprehend, a moment to savor and treasure.

"Willa Mae, the colors are so pretty!" exclaims Mimi, jumping up and down.

Willa giggles.

"Come on, baby. Let's go and sit on the bench for a while and watch the rainbow," she says. "But then I've got to get back to my work."

They walk down the rutted road that runs the length of the levee. Willa removes her raincoat, turns it inside out, and carefully lays it on the damp slats of the bench. She sits down and motions for Mimi to join her. As Mimi begins to unbutton her pink, flowered raincoat, Willa's voice interrupts. "You button that back up, baby. You gonna catch a cold," she says firmly.

Always protecting Mimi. Always putting her first. At that young age, Mimi doesn't think twice about it. But as Mimi looks back, the memory carries a different weight. Wasn't Willa chilly without her raincoat? Couldn't she have caught a cold?

Willa points to the rainbow once more.

"The colors are special, baby. God made them perfectly. When I was a little girl like you, my Grandmother Sissy and I would always go outside when there was a rainbow. She'd say, 'Look up, Willa Mae. God put that rainbow there. God first showed it to Noah in the ark, and now we get to see it too. It's a reminder of hope.'"

At this age, Mimi doesn't fully grasp what the word hope means. All she can think about now is getting home to draw a picture of the rainbow with her crayons.

Willa becomes quiet, as she often does when lost in thought. After a moment, her voice rises gently in song. Mimi immediately recognizes the song. It's another one of her favorites, tied to the story her catechism teacher once told about Noah and the rainbow. Willa's voice drifts as she gazes at the vibrant arc in the sky, and without hesitation, Mimi joins in singing, their voices blending as beautifully as the rainbow's colors.

"When God shut Noah in the grand old ark, he put a rainbow in the cloud. When thunder rolled and the sky was dark, God put a rainbow in the cloud. When it looked like the sun wouldn't shine any ..."[18]

Suddenly, a sharp voice cuts through the air from behind the bench, stopping Willa mid-song.

"You gonna need to be gettin' up, 'cause we're needin' a place to sit down," comes a man's voice, his tone firm.

Willa sits still for a moment, not moving, before slowly turning to face him. Mimi turns as well, recognizing the white man and his little girl from church.

"Yes, sir," Willa says softly, her voice subdued. She stands and reaches for Mimi's hand.

"Come on, baby, it's time for us to go."

"But I want to finish the song first," Mimi protests.

"We'll keep singing it as we walk along the levee," Willa says.

"Now let's go," she says with a sense of urgency.

Willa picks up her wet raincoat from the bench and takes Mimi's hand.

As they walk along the levee toward the path that leads down, Mimi looks up at her, confused.

"Willa, why is that man so mean? Why did we have to leave the bench? We were there first. That's what I learned in school."

They start back down the muddy path, with Mimi full of questions, trying hard to make sense of it all.

"Sister Mary Theresa says that if we get to the swings first at recess, we don't have to get off until someone asks nicely for their turn." Her bottom lip juts out, trembling slightly. "He didn't ask you nicely, Willa."

"No, he didn't," says Willa. "Let's just keep walkin.'"

Mimi's words hang in the air, her innocent logic clashing with the unspoken realities of the world around her. Getting a distance away, Willa stops and turns to look at Mimi. The warm smile Mimi knows so well has left her face.

"It's gonna be okay, baby," patting Mimi's hand. "Let's just go home."

Willa stares straight ahead, her eyes fixed on the path as she starts singing again, her voice soft yet filled with conviction.

"When it looks like the sun won't shine anymore, God puts a rainbow in the cloud. When it looks like the sun won't shine anymore ..."

Mimi chimes in alongside Willa.

"God puts a rainbow in the sky."

Mimi stops and tugs on Willa's hand. "Willa, why are you sad?"

Willa glances down at Mimi as her expression, without warning, shifts to a playful sternness.

"You know I'm gonna have to tickle you, or maybe even spank you," she says.

Mimi bursts into laughter, the seriousness of her earlier question forgotten. She darts off the path and into the grass on the side of the levee. Her voice shrieks, "Nooooo," giggling as she runs.

Willa shakes her head while watching Mimi's carefree joy. She would never lay a hand on her, and they both know it. Yet, the teasing game became their tradition, one Willa keeps alive to the day she dies.

Willa Mae remains quiet on the way home. Mimi, ever energetic, rolls down the levee on her side like she always does. This time, the grass is wet, and Willa notices immediately.

"Mimi," Willa fusses, "your clothes are gonna get all wet and grass-stained. And just look at those shoes, already muddy."

Mimi doesn't seem to mind, her laughter filling the air as they walk back. The towering oaks, draped in Spanish moss, create an umbrella of green and gray above them. Willa looks up, her gaze catching something unusual. Nestled on a thick branch covered in moss sit not one, but two doves, their soft feathers blending into the foliage.

"Mimi, look at that," Willa says, looking up, shading her eyes with her hand to block the sun. "Just look at what God did for us."

"These doves are just like the ones in Noah's story," she says.

"God wants us to see this today, baby."

"Why, Willa?" Mimi asks, her eyes fixed on the birds.

"Because it's a reminder of God's peace and hope," Willa replies, seeming calmer now. "That's what my Grandmother Sissy always says. So today, my baby, we saw a rainbow and two doves, and we have hope. God is good all the time. We just have to pray and trust in Jesus, and He will take care of the situation."

Willa stops and turns her head, glancing back up the levee toward the bench, then to the fading brushstrokes of the rainbow. Her father's words echo in her heart as she takes a deep breath and turns to continue walking. His voice feels so near, calling out "number one" to remind her that she is an image bearer of God, a truth he says, never to let anyone take away from her.

Mimi tugs insistently on Willa's uniform, pulling her back from her thoughts. "Willa...Willa! Didn't you hear me? I think you were daydreaming, like you say I do sometimes."

Pausing, "I guess I am," she says, her voice trailing off. "I guess I am."

She stands there watching the doves. "We just gonna keep hoping and prayin' baby," she says firmly.

Mimi is now running ahead of her and yells back, "Okay, Willa, but let's go home now so I can color a rainbow?"

Back at the house, Willa insists Mimi leave her muddy shoes on the porch. Mimi quickly goes in to change out of her wet clothes before getting to work on her drawing. Once settled, Mimi eagerly grabs her crayons and begins to color. Even though Willa has told her many times that the colors of the rainbow always follow the same order, Mimi simply uses whatever crayons she can find.

When she finishes, she holds it up proudly for Willa to see. Willa studies it for a moment and then nods with a smile.

"It's beautiful," she proclaims, reaching for a crayon. Beneath the rainbow, she carefully writes one word: hope.

Years later, Mimi finds the picture tucked in a cardboard box under her bed while packing to leave for college. The memory rushes back, along with a deeper understanding. Willa's love for rainbows was never just about their beauty; it was a quiet declaration of resilience, faith, and, above all, unyielding hope.

CHAPTER FIVE

"The Great Migration would become a turning point in history. It would transform urban America and recast the social and political order of every city it touched. It would force the South to search its soul and finally to lay aside a feudal caste system."[19]

-Isabel Wilkerson

February 26, 1960

Mimi's parents travel often, leaving for a few days at a time. During these trips, Willa Mae stays overnight with the girls. Mimi loves these sleepovers. Willa spreads a pallet of blankets on the den floor, cozy and inviting. Despite Mr. Benoit setting up a small twin bed for her in the upstairs room, Willa always chooses the floor instead. Mimi starts the night in her own bed, with her sister, Anna Beth, sleeping in the other twin bed across the room.

But at some point, in the evening, Mimi inevitably tiptoes out of her bed. The wooden floor of the long hall creaks softly beneath her feet as she carefully steps around the floor furnace and makes her way to the den. There, she always finds Willa Mae on her pallet, lying on her side with one arm tucked under her head.

If it's before midnight, the ambient glow of the TV illuminates the room. The three stations sign off at twelve sharp, playing the national anthem before the screen goes fuzzy. After this, Willa's transistor radio keeps her company, its silver antenna angled upward as she fiddles with the dial to find a clear station. Sometimes music fills the air; other times, a voice cuts through the quiet. Her well-worn Bible always rests nearby on the floor.

Usually, by the time Mimi arrives, Willa Mae is already asleep. Gently, Mimi taps her arm and whispers, asking to join her on the pallet. But tonight is different. Willa Mae isn't sleeping when Mimi tiptoes down the hall. As she nears the den door, Mimi hears a sound she's never heard before—Willa Mae crying. It startles her. She freezes just outside the doorway, unsure what to do.

"Oh, Jesus," Willa whispers through tears, her voice trembling. "Please don't let Effie leave us. You gave her to me seventeen years ago. Please don't let her go from me now ... not up North." She sniffles. "But she's got an itchy foot, like so many others takin' off." Reaching for her blanket and pulling it up, she adds softly, "You know best, Lord ... you know best."

Mimi stands quietly in the hallway, listening. She hears Willa talk about her baby, but she realizes it isn't her or her sisters Willa is speaking of.

"Willa?" Mimi whispers softly, stepping into the doorway.

Willa turns toward her, not really startled, as though she expected Mimi to be there.

"What you doin' up, baby?" she asks, quickly wiping her eyes and tucking her sadness away for another time. Her voice calms. "Can't sleep?"

"No ... Can I sleep with you, Willa?" Mimi asks sweetly.

Willa nods, as she always does, shifting over and grabbing an extra blanket from the couch to tuck around Mimi. Mimi snuggles close, feeling safe in Willa's warmth and comfort.

"Now you go to sleep, baby," Willa says gently.

But Mimi can't let it go.

"Willa, why were you crying? Where is Effie going, and why does she have an itchy foot? Did she get poison ivy?"

Willa bursts into laughter, breaking the weight of the moment.

"Lord Jesus," she says, her smile soft and wide. "Thank you for the innocence of this child."

Mimi doesn't fully understand, she's just happy Willa isn't sad anymore. But as she drifts off to sleep, she realizes something for the first time—she and her sisters aren't Willa's only babies.

GLIMPSES OF MORNING light shine through the window, and a rich aroma fills the air, drawing Mimi from her sleep. Looking over, she sees that Willa is no longer beside her, known for getting up in the early morning hours before dawn. From the den, Mimi hears clattering dishes in the kitchen and Willa's soft singing. She can see that Willa is already dressed in her uniform, her apron tied around her waist, stirring a pot on the stove, and checking the oven.

Mimi stretches, her eyes wide with the promise of a Saturday morning breakfast.

Her two older sisters soon appear in the den, ready for their dance class, and a neighbor soon to pick them up. The three of them gather at the table. Willa sets down a platter of biscuits, each one split and slathered with butter, while the grits gleam with more pools of melted butter on top—and just as much stirred in during cooking. It's an unspoken Southern rule you can never have too much butter in your grits. At least, that's what Willa Mae firmly believes.

A car horn toots outside, and Mimi's sisters jump up from their chairs, grabbing their dance bags as they hurry toward the back door.

"Bye, babies," Willa calls after them. "Dance pretty now, my lil angels. We'll see you for lunch."

Mimi isn't in the same class as her sisters. Her dance lessons are on Thursdays after school, which means she gets to spend another Saturday morning alone with Willa. As she finishes breakfast, Willa turns to her.

"Come on," Willa Mae says. "We're going to the cleaners to drop off the dirty clothes. You'll get to see your MawMaw this morning."

Mimi and Willa Mae walk down the back sidewalk Mr. Benoit once laid by hand, its worn bricks beneath their feet and lined with tufts of grass pushing through the cracks. The girls have fun riding their bikes back and forth on it. It winds through the Benoit property, leading them toward MawMaw's house and the Dry Cleaners. MawMaw, or Miss Jeanne Marie, as she is known by everyone in town, began the cleaners with her husband in their home in 1928. They then built a more formal structure next door to their home in the late 1930s which is now known as Bayou Grande Cleaners. Shortly after that, her husband sadly passed away from tuberculosis. But Miss Jeanne Marie was a true Cajun from a long line of hard-working French-speaking Acadians, a sturdy stock indeed. She was filled with grit, faith, and laughter; as rooted as the cypress trees, bending with the storms but never breaking.

"Let's pick pecans!" Mimi exclaims as she runs toward the tall tree.

Willa puts down the basket of clothes, and her hands go straight to her hips.

"Now you know I have work to do," Willa replies firmly. "Come on now." Waving her arm and reaching back down to pick up the basket. "We don't have time to stop. When your Mama and daddy get home, I have to go to my house and take care of my own chores. I promised Effie I'd be home on time today. Plus, baby, there aren't any good pecans left to pick this time of year."

Disappointed, Mimi trails behind Willa, plucking blossoms from the cherry trees that line the walk. They skirt the edge of the chicken yard and follow the curving path between the two weathered sheds. Mimi and her sisters always race through this narrow stretch—especially at night—half-laughing, half-convinced a possum or raccoon might leap out at them.

As they approach the back of the cleaners, MawMaw's house comes into view—a humble wood-framed home, raised slightly on piers to guard against flooding. A wide porch stretches across the front, furnished with rocking chairs and an old porch swing whose chains always creak with the slightest breeze. Willa Mae first worked for MawMaw years ago. One day, MawMaw tells her, "Willa, the Benoits need your help. Harriet is overwhelmed with raising her first baby and about to have another. Would you be willing to go work for her?" From that day forward, Willa went to work for the Benoits, even before Mimi was born. Willa Mae often recounts the story of the day Mimi came home from the hospital.

"MIMI," WILLA WOULD say, "I remember when your mama and daddy brought you home from the hospital—just three days old. Your mama came right up to me and said, 'Willa Mae, meet Elizabeth Katherine.' Then she put you in my arms—and that was that. Your mama and daddy trusted me. They let me do whatever I thought was best for you girls, and I took good care of you, I sure did. Not one of you ever went out of that house dirty."

To this day, Mimi marvels at how Willa managed it all. She worked tirelessly at their home—cooking, cleaning, washing, ironing, taking care of her and her sisters, and even keeping her daddy's shoes shined—all while raising her daughter Effie as a single mother and caring for her own mother, Grandma Nellie. And yet through it all, unknown to Mimi and her sisters when they were young, Willa lived under a constant shadow of harsh and demeaning laws ... shaping where she could go, what she could do, and how she was seen.

MIMI WALKS THROUGH the side door of the cleaners. Joe Boy, the family collie, trots down the hallway to greet them. Most days, he makes his rounds between the cleaners, Maw-Maw's house for hamburgers and moon pies, the Benoits', and spooking the chickens just for fun. Mimi kneels to pet him while Willa Mae carries the heavy basket of clothes to drop off in the back, scrub a few delicates in the sink, and visit with the pressers, as she knows them all well.

In the hallway, two small bathrooms sit side by side. Willa Mae always uses the one on the left, marked "Colored," just as all the other Black workers do. The bathroom on the right, labeled "White," is used by the White employees working in the front of the cleaners.

Mimi had once asked her grandmother, 'MawMaw, why are there two different potties with signs, and I always have to go in that one?'

MawMaw gently replies, "It's the law here in Louisiana, Mimi. There's something called Jim Crow laws we're supposed to follow."

Mimi's brow furrowed. "So ... Mr. Crow makes those rules?"

MawMaw gave a soft sigh. "Yes, baby. I guess you could say he does."

Mimi's thoughts then drifted to the water fountains at school. Inside the gates, there were no signs above them, because no Black children attended her school. They weren't allowed through those gates. But outside the gates, just behind the convent, there were two fountains, one marked "White" and the other "Colored. Years later, she learned that the nuns and priests had pooled their money to install the "Colored" fountain alongside the "White" one for those hot, sweltering summer months. It seemed to make sense to Mimi, in a way, because it's a rule, and she's a rule follower. Yet, deep down in her young heart, something didn't feel right.

AS MAWMAW COMES DOWN the hall to greet Mimi ... Estelle, one of the Black pressers, steps out of the bathroom marked "White Only," and nearly bumps into MawMaw as she opens the door.

"Oh, Miss Jeanne Marie, I'm so sorry I used the White people's bathroom," Estelle says, eyes wide with worry. "I know I'm not supposed to use the White toilet. I don't want to lose my job here. The Colored one was being used, and I just couldn't–"

Before she can finish, MawMaw gently places a hand on Estelle's arm and tries to make eye contact, though Estelle keeps her gaze lowered.

"Sha', it's alright. You're not going to lose your job here," Miss Jeanne Marie says in her warm, lilting Cajun accent. "Mais', when you gotta go, you gotta go," she chuckles.

This brings a smile to Estelle's face as she slowly looks up at Miss Jeanne Marie, who says, "I cooked up some fried chicken for everyone. It's in the heated drum. And fresh okra too. Now, you go enjoy some," Grace and love are found freely inside these walls.

Looking at Mimi–who stands wide-eyed, having taken in the entire scene–MawMaw smiles.

"Come on now," she says. "I refilled the nickels and dimes in the jar under the front counter. Go get yourself a Coke from the machine. Mimi immediately runs past MawMaw down the hall.

"And be sure to get Willa a Nehi," MawMaw calls out to her.

"Okaaay," is all that could be heard as MawMaw heads back to the front also.

As Mimi walks around the front counter with the two drinks in hand, she sees Miss Lucy in front of the bagging machine. Years ago, MawMaw offered her cousin a job at the cleaners. Mimi had never seen skin and hair so white. Miss Lucy can be nice, but when she's grumpy, she scares Mimi. And today, she is grumpy.

The machine hisses as Miss Lucy pulls the sheet of plastic down over the hanger of the crisp, starched shirt. She yanks it off the conveyor belt as she glares at MawMaw. "Jeanne Marie, did you know Estelle used the white bathroom?" She asks.

"Yes, I did," MawMaw says calmly. "The Colored one was occupied. Sometimes folks just have to sit in the bathroom a little longer, and that's okay. But Estelle couldn't hold it anymore."

"Well, I need to go now myself," Miss Lucy huffs. "And I don't want to clean it. There are probably germs in there."

"Well, I think there are germs in all the bathrooms, Lucy—White and Colored," says Jeanne Marie. "And, I guarantee the germs all look the same."

Reaching under the counter, she hands Lucy a rag and a can of Comet.

"Here you go. And while you're at it, can you be helpful and give all the bathrooms a clean?"

Miss Lucy grabs them and walks away with a scowl. The front door opens and in walks Miss Millie, Bubba Boudreaux's wife, click-clacking toward the counter in her pink high heels and her teased hair reaching to the high heavens.

"Good morning, ladies. I hope my dress is ready," she announces. "My garden party is tomorrow morning." Lucy turns, annoyed even more, and heads toward the conveyor belt to retrieve Millie's dress. As she passes Jeanne Marie, she leans in and mutters, "It's the law that Colored people are supposed to use the Colored bathroom, and Estelle knows that."

She then disappears into the back. Millie's eyebrows lift. Looking her way and quickly trying to change the subject, Jeanne Marie says, "Don't worry, Millie, your dress is all ready for your garden–"

Without warning, a shout rings out from the back. "What's this dog doing under the conveyor belt again, Jeanne Marie? He darn near scared the wits out of me," says Lucy. "And he just might be getting the clothes dirty."

Millie's eyes widen as she poofs up her hair with her freshly painted pink fingernails. Jeanne Marie picks up a complimentary purse calendar for the new year and hands it to Millie, looking for a distraction. Tilting her head toward the back, "It's cool under there, Lucy, and the girls just bathed him."

Miss Lucy returns to the front and hangs Millie's dress on the hook. Millie reaches into her pink patent leather purse and places the money on the counter. Clearing her throat, she says, "What's this I hear, Jeanne Marie? Colored using the White bathrooms? Now you know what the law is," as she lowers her voice, "plus, they carry germs."

Saying nothing, Jeanne Marie walks over to the cash register and presses it open. She pulls out Millie's change and firmly pushes the drawer shut. Calmly walking back over, she looks Millie straight in the eyes.

"Now I'm sure, Millie, when your delicate white bottom sits on a toilet, it leaves the same color germs as Estelle's colored bottom, or the same as Hisako's Japanese bottom from the flower shop down the street. You know I'm Cajun Millie, maybe my bottom ..."

"Why, I never." Millie walks out of the cleaners, gets into her car and slams the door. Within seconds, the car door opens, and she marches back in, firmly retrieving her dress off the hook. With her other hand on her hip and glaring at Jeanne Marie, she says, "This is not the end of all this." She turns and click-clacks as loudly as she can out the door.

"Now, Jeanne Marie," says Lucy, "you're gonna get yourself in trouble."

"Well, someone has to put that prissy, busy body in her place, and Lucy, it was an honor to be the one to do it," Jeanne Marie chuckled.

Before leaving the cleaners, as Willa always does, she uses the bathroom. Mimi never saw Willa use the bathroom at their house. When they were little and too young to be left alone, if Mama wasn't home, Willa would often haul them all to the cleaners just to use the bathroom. One day, Mimi asked Willa why she doesn't use the one at their house. Willa simply answered, "That's just the way it is, baby."

As Mimi heads to the back of the cleaners to find Willa, she passes the garage where the delivery trucks park. She notices a little Colored girl about her age sitting alone in one of the trucks. Mimi stares at her for a moment. It looks like she's reading a book. *Who is she,* Mimi wonders, *and why is she sitting alone in the cleaner's truck?*

Letting it pass, Mimi continues to the back to find Willa, who is chatting with the pressers. The steam from the presses hisses louder as Mimi gets closer. Even in February, the air in the back of the cleaners hangs heavy with heat and humidity. Mimi smiles and greets each of the pressers, noticing the sweat rolling down their faces. In the summer, it's nearly unbearable there, so Miss Jeanne Marie had two big fans installed in the wall to try and keep everyone cool.

As Mimi reflects on those years, she comes to realize that those hard-working, kind pressers, like Willa Mae, also bore the weight of Jim Crow's oppression. It pressed down on them, controlled their lives, and pushed them to the margins of society. As a little White girl living in the South, Mimi didn't know the word oppression. Little colored girls living in the South likely didn't know the word either. Instead, without understanding it, they lived in its harsh reality every single day.

PART III

LET THE BONES SPEAK

The bones rattle. The bones moan. The bones speak. From the Middle Passage to the poplar trees. From unmarked graves to the great marches of peaceful armies–carried on the breath of justice and truth. These bones will never stop speaking–of their pain and perseverance. "Dem bones, dem bones, dem dry bones... Now hear the word of the Lord."[20]

CHAPTER SIX

"A man dies when he refuses to stand up for that which is right. A man dies when he refuses to stand up for justice. A man dies when he refuses to take a stand for that which is true."[21]

-Dr. Martin Luther King

March 4, 1960

Morning

Passing the old oak tree on Magnolia Street, Willa Mae and Effie walk to work, both unusually quiet. It's a wet, chilly Friday morning in early spring. Their usual chattiness has been replaced by a shared silence. With school out today, Effie heads to the Riverside Café, where she has a part-time job in the kitchen, while Willa Mae makes her way to the Benoit home to work.

Both are lost in thought, skirting around the thing neither has dared to bring back up over the past few months. Effie, seventeen and a senior at the all-Colored high school,[22] dreams of leaving the South after graduation to chase opportunities up North. She knows the life she wants isn't here, not in the place that raised her. And now, with graduation drawing near, they both know that this conversation can't be avoided much longer.

"It's nearly quarter to six, baby," Willa says, breaking the silence. "I want to pick up a bag of beignets from the café for the girls' breakfast before school. They look forward to it every Friday! They love Mr. Pierre's beignets. They're so cute when they get that powdered sugar all over their faces."

Effie glances at her mother and forces a small smile.

"I know, Momma. You've told me that story many times about your babies."

Willa stops mid-step. She grabs Effie's hand and looks her in the eyes.

"You know, Effie, you are my most important baby," Willa says, her voice gentle.

Effie's smile tightens.

"I know, Momma," she says again, abruptly letting go of her hand. "Let's keep walking. We're going to be late."

They continue down the path, each weighed down by the heaviness of their own fears.

Willa and Effie make their way up the muddy dirt path toward the back door of the Riverside Café. Only Whites enter through the front, a rule that is not posted but strictly enforced. The air is filled with the sweet, doughy aroma of frying beignets—a small comfort on this dreary morning.

Through the screen door, a familiar voice calls out from the kitchen.

"Got your six beignets, Miss Willa," says a Black teenage boy. "Mr. Pierre made sure they'd be ready for you! He says don't worry about paying today."

Wilton is seventeen, a dishwasher and cook. He also attends school with Effie.

"That's right, Willa," comes a voice from the front. Mr. Pierre, second-generation White owner of Riverside Café, pokes his head through the pass-through window of the kitchen, his broad grin matched by the teasing twinkle in his eyes.

"I'm trying to bribe you to come back and work for me."

Willa laughs, covering her mouth with her hand.

Mr. Pierre continues, his tone playful. "You were one of my hardest workers in your teenage years, except for all that catfish you liked to eat on Fridays. I thought you were gonna put me out of business!"

He winks before shifting his gaze to Wilton and Effie.

"But I guess I'll keep these two. They work hard for their pay."

Lifting his eyebrows, Wilton lets out a sharp "humph" as he aggressively grabs the bag of beignets from the counter. He gently hands it to Willa Mae through the back door, the designated spot for all "Coloreds" to place and pick up their orders, a rule that still grates on him, no matter how routine it has become.

Effie gives Wilton a sharp look. She knows exactly what he's thinking because she's thinking it too. *But it's just the way it is down here,* she reminds herself. *It's the pay we get, and at least we have a job.* Yet the older she gets, the more unsettled she becomes.

Even so, Effie keeps her thoughts to herself, too guarded to voice them aloud. She never knows who might be listening or what trouble her words might stir.

Willa Mae reaches through the door for the bag, her face lighting up.

"Ohhhhh, thank you, thank you, baby," she says to Wilton ... full of gratitude even though surrounded by quiet indignities.

Letting the door slap shut, Willa calls out through the screen.

"By the way, how's your Mama, Mr. Pierre?"

"Ornery as ever but still frying her own beignets at home, sometimes burnin' em, but I don't say a thing."

Willa chuckled, "Well, tell her hello, and I'm missin' seein' her here. Y'all have a blessed day now."

"You too, Willa," comes Mr. Pierre's voice from the front.

"Now don't eat all those beignets before you get to the Benoits'," he chuckled.

"We'll see," laughed Willa as she began her way to work.

"Bye, Momma," Effie calls out. She lingers a moment at the back door, watching her Momma trudge up the muddy path, her white work shoes quickly caking with mud. *Momma works so hard,* Effie thought, *and yet, she never complains.* Lately, Effie finds herself caught between two roads—one leading North to opportunity, the other rooted in the South she's always known.

Effie turns and opens the rickety screen door to the kitchen, the rusty hinge squeaking behind her. The warmth of the kitchen feels good after her chilly walk. Like her momma before her, Effie works as a dishwasher. And now, Momma wants her to follow again, as a maid.

"Hey, Wilton," she says, glancing over to him. When he doesn't respond, she adds with a teasing tone, "Did you wake up on the wrong side of the bed this morning?"

Wilton doesn't look up, but Effie knows him too well to take it personally. They've been best friends for 12 years. Wilton and his daddy had moved to Louisiana from Mississippi after his momma died, and over time, their friendship had only grown stronger.

Without answering her, he throws his broom down, clattering to the floor.

"What in heaven's day is wrong, Wilton?" Effie asks, hanging her purse and sweater on the rusty iron hook by the door.

"I can't do this anymore, Effie," he blurts out with frustration.

"What can't you do? And keep your voice down," she says.

"This job," he snaps. "I can't do this job anymore. The hours are long, and the pay is nothing. Sure, Mr. Pierre treats us fine, gives us free meals, but we're going nowhere here. And even as nice as he is, he still acts like he's superior to us, like we're less."

"Well, he is our boss, Wilton," Effie replies cautiously.

"Stop it, Effie. You always do this."

"Do what?" she asks.

"Conform," he says.

"How do I conform?" Her tone is defensive as she shakes her head, mixed with exasperation and confusion.

Putting on her apron, Effie says, "What I mean is that things stay peaceful ... if we stay in our place."

"Our place?" Wilton's voice rises. "You act like this is just how it is, and we're supposed to go along with it. Well, I'm tired of staying in my place. You say you're a Christian, and that at your church, the Reverend talks about God being a just God. Well, how, Effie?

Pointing towards the front of the café, Wilton says, "Look at the world around you. Does any of this feel just?"

Effie stands silent. She lowers her gaze, knowing he is speaking the truth. Truth that she is fearful to face.

"I want to know where our just God is, Effie," his frustration now boiling over. "I have to get out of this place and go to college. I want to fight for the rights we deserve. My daddy has been stuck since birth in the middle of all this... working like a dog, for little pay, but I've got bigger dreams. I'll make something of my life. I'll make him proud."

He looks out the window above the sink and sighs.

"Not that my daddy doesn't work hard."

He looks over to Effie with fierceness in his voice, "He takes pride in what he does. He's kept us fed and clothed, showing up at that White high school every single day ...

mopping floors, cleaning toilets for White people, moving tables and chairs … and he taught me how to work hard,

Effie. But now, he's getting older, and I swear he's about to work himself to death."

Wilton's gaze falls to the floor, his voice softening.

"My daddy's smart, too. He always wanted to be an engineer. He can build just about anything. They love him at that school, and I think they appreciated him, but he only made it to fifth grade because there wasn't a junior high or high school for Colored children where he lived in Mississippi."

He leans against the sink of dirty dishes, closes his eyes, and shakes his head, trying to compose himself. "Plus," he says, looking out the window again as his voice drifts off, "I can't even make enough money here to save up for college. But that's what my daddy wants for me. He wants me to have what he couldn't."

Pulling away from the sink and standing tall with a renewed determination in his voice, "And you know what, Effie? That's what I want for myself, too. I want to be the first in my family to graduate from college."

"What?" says Effie. "If you don't have the money, how will you even be able to go to college, Wilton?"

Effie begins to nervously wash the dirty breakfast dishes piled on the side of the sink. *So many changes are soon to come*, she thinks.

Wilton turns toward the sink close to Effie.

"I heard about an all-Black school called Fisk University[23] in Nashville," Wilton replies, his voice filled with hope.

"Mr. McKinney at school says they give scholarships. I'm going to go there someday."

Effie glances over at him, her hands submerged in the dishwater.

"Well, you deserve it, Wilton. After all, you'll be graduating first in our class soon."

Grabbing her wet, soapy hand, "And you, salutatorian," Wilton adds with pride in his voice.

Effie smiles faintly, turning her attention back to the dishes.

"I'm just thankful we finally got a Colored high school in our parish," she says.

"The only one," Wilton points out. "And those teachers, man, they take so much time and pride in helping us to learn. They're dedicated to seeing us achieve our goals and dreams."

Effie nods, adding more dishes to the sink.

"I know. Momma had to leave school when she was twelve because there were no Colored schools here back then for her to move on to either. She was so happy when I started high school. She even baked a special cake to celebrate my first day. I will be the first in my family to graduate from 12th grade. I can't wait to wear that cap and gown," her voice trailing off as she keeps scrubbing the dishes.

Wilton leans in, his voice dropping to a whisper.

"I need to tell you something else, Effie," he says. "I've been reading a book."

She looks at him, giggling. "So what's new about that, Wilton? You're always reading a book. Now, could you please pick up a towel and help me before we get into trouble?"

"Sorry, yes," he says, grabbing a towel and moving closer to her. He starts drying the stack of glasses and dishes, but lowers his voice even further.

"But this book is different."

Effie glances at him, curious. "What do you mean?"

"You know about Dr. Martin Luther King, that lady Rosa Parks, and the bus boycott in Montgomery, right?" he asks.

"Of course, I know those names," Effie replies. "We've been told a few things in church, and we overhear plenty at school. You know that, Wilton ... and," she looks around with eyes full of quiet suspicion, "why are you whispering?"

Wilton looks over his shoulder, checking the room.

"Because this book I've been reading talks all about the movement. I'm learning a lot," he whispers, his words barely audible, but his eyes blazing with a fire coming from somewhere deep within.

"What movement, Wilton?"

"I read that there's a 'new Negro in the South. One with a new sense of dignity and destiny.'"[24]

He grabs Effie's hand.

"Look at me, Effie." She slowly and hesitantly turns toward him.

"We are the new Negro. It's our time to stand up for justice, for what's right. Just last month, Negro college students in Nashville sat at White lunch counters in drug stores and asked for service. They were arrested, supposedly for disorderly conduct, and then thrown in jail, but their peaceful actions shouted louder than words."

Effie grips the edge of the sink, holding onto her dishrag.

"How do you even know all this, Wilton?"

Wilton leans in.

"My cousin, Jer, told me. He's over at Southern University in Baton Rouge.[24,25] They get all the news. Being an all-Black college, there aren't any Whites listening in, so people talk freely. We could be a part of this change, Effie! Right here, in this town."

Effie throws her dishrag into the sink. She takes a step back, eyes widening, and looks directly at him.

"Stop right there, Wilton," she whispers. "There are good people in this town, people who give us jobs. For the most part, things stay peaceful."

"That's the problem, Effie," his voice now filled with anger.

"What's the problem?" Effie snaps back.

"Shhhh!" Wilton glances toward the front of the café. "We can't let Mr. Pierre hear us talking about this."

Effie leans closer, her tone now a sharp whisper.

"No, because we're not going to talk about this. Not now. Not ever. We're done. And anyway, if I get involved in any protest or movement and land in jail, Momma could lose her job with the Benoit family. Do you think they'd keep a maid whose daughter is sitting in jail?"

Wilton hurls his dish towel onto the pile of dried dishes. "Effie, don't you see it? Are you blind? You just keep conforming to what we're told to do and be."

Effie takes a deep breath, trying to calm herself. "All this talk just scares me, Wilton."

Her voice softens.

"In church a few Sundays ago," she begins, speaking in a hushed tone, "Reverend Washington shared Dr. King's words. I can't stop thinking about them. 'Protest courageously,' he says, 'with dignity and Christian love.'[26] She hesitates, her voice trembling.

"Those sit-ins in Nashville you heard about, they probably turned violent, and I don't want to be a part of that."

Wilton's frustration softens.

"Effie, that's what I'm trying to tell you about the sit-ins in Nashville. They weren't like that. A lot of those students were from ..."

The swinging doors from the front burst open, cutting Wilton off mid-sentence. "You two gettin' your work done?"

Mr. Pierre glances around the kitchen.

"I'm hearing a lot of chit-chat back here. We've got fresh catfish to fry. It's Friday, and before you know it, those Catholics'll be lined up outside the door like church folks at a potluck—for the Friday special."

"Yes, sir, Mr. Pierre," Wilton replies quickly, straightening up and grabbing the towel again. They work through the morning mostly in silence, Wilton at the fryer, the air thick with seasoned flour and crackling grease, while Effie stays busy at the sink with the steady stream of dishes. Only the sounds of bubbling oil and clinking plates filled the small kitchen.

As Mr. Pierre finishes up in front, Effie and Wilton clean and mop after the lunch rush. Poking his head through the pass-through window, Mr. Pierre calls out, "I see that we have some catfish, tartar sauce, and hushpuppies left over from lunch. You want to take some home?" He asked.

Looking Effie's way, he says, "Your momma loves fresh fried catfish from Bayou Grande. When she worked here, I thought she was gonna turn into a catfish she ate so much of 'em."

Effie giggled, "Yes, sir."

"Well, you two eat your fill and take home what's left to your momma, Grandma Nellie, and to your daddy, too, Wilton."

"Thank you, Mr. Pierre," says Wilton."

Mr. Pierre then calls out to the sheriff who was just walking into the café.

"Your hushpuppies are almost ready, Sheriff. You better save some for your wife now. Don't eat 'em all while you're on patrol."

Chuckling, "can't guarantee that Pierre," calls out the sheriff.

Mr. Pierre goes in the back and bags them up, the seeping grease turning the paper dark as he hands it to him.

Being done with their chores, Wilton gently reaches for Effie's arm.

"Effie, meet me at the levee bench tonight … please. I've got more I need to tell you."

Effie looks back at him with wide eyes but remains silent. She grabs her purse and sweater from the hook, along with the bag of food for her momma. Opening the screen door, she hesitates for a moment before stepping outside.

Turning around, "This scares me, Wilton. I don't know … maybe I'll be there. My momma will be so mad at me if I get involved in any kind of trouble."

As she steps onto the muddy path outside, something catches her eye. The soft crinkling of a bag near the garbage can draws her attention.

"Wilton," she calls out, "that mangy dog is in the trash again. Who does he belong to?"

Wilton replies, "I think he's a stray."

Effie crouches down to get a better look.

"Look how skinny he is; you can see his ribs. And, oh my goodness, he's only got one eye."

The dog looks up at her with a soft whimper, tail wagging timidly. Effie smiles. "He's actually kinda' cute."

"I've been calling him Scrappy," Wilton says, stepping outside to join her.

Effie laughs, shaking her head. "Well, that's a perfect name for him. He's so dirty."

She tilts her head, studying the dog.

"Maybe we should give him some of the hushpuppy scraps," she adds. "Poor lil thing."

Wilton crouches next to her and says with sarcasm. "Just like us, right, Effie? Gettin' scraps at the back door."

Effie doesn't respond. She just stares down at the dog in pensive thought.

Looking up, "Wilton ... I will think about meeting you and hearing what you have to say ... okay? But I don't want us or anyone else to have to suffer from horrible violence like my pappy did years ago, before I was even born. That scares me."

"I thought you said that his death was an accident, Effie."

"It began as an accident, Wilton. It ended tragically in 'hidden violence.' I don't know what it all means, but that is what I overheard my Grandma Nellie say."

Shaking his head, Wilton does not say a word, just looks at her in question and sadness. He then takes her hand.

"But that's exactly why you should want to do this, Effie. You can't live your life in fear. You can't go on as though life is normal here. If you believe so much in God, then trust Him."

Effie lets go of Wilton's hand and turns to continue down the path. A mixture of sadness and anger rises within her as she thinks about the loss of her pappy. *I need to find out the truth of what happened,* she thinks to herself.

"Effie," Wilton calls out.

Raising her right hand in the air, "I can't think about this anymore right now, Wilton, okay?" she says as she walks off.

Effie starts up Magnolia Street toward the White section of town, heading to the Benoit home to check in with her momma. As she makes her way down the sidewalk, she senses someone close behind. Every time she stops, they stop. Her heart quickens, then something bumps her and starts licking her calf.

Startled, she spins around to find Scrappy staring at her with that one sweet eye.

"Goodness gracious, Scrappy! You scared me half to death," Effie exclaims, pressing a hand to her chest.

He whimpers, tilting his head endearingly. Effie finds herself smiling.

"Alright, just one hushpuppy, but you get the broken one," she says, crouching down, handing it to him.

Scrappy snatches the piece, then bolts up Levee Road, disappearing over the top of the levee.

Continuing toward the Benoit home, Effie's mind is swirling. So much to think about. But something bigger was stirring deep within her and relentlessly gnawing at her soul. She's weary of being afraid, always hiding from what she feels God is calling her to do and be. Her hopes and dreams are shouting to be heard, to be free.

Just then, her grandfather's words echo in her mind, passed down through Momma and now to her: "You are an image bearer of God who shines bright, and no one can ever take that away from you."

"I hear you, Pappy," she whispers, gazing upward. "I never knew you, but I feel you're a part of me. I promise I'll make you proud."

CHAPTER SEVEN

-Traditional African American spiritual, adapted
during the Civil Rights Movement of the 1960s

March 4, 1960

Late Afternoon

Willa Mae tries to mimic their dance moves as the laughter of the Benoit girls fills the family room.

Mary Grace can hardly get a word out, giggling so hard. "Swivel your hips more, Willa. When you do 'The Twist,' your arms go right, your feet go left.

Anna Beth throws up her hands in frustration.

"I just can't make my feet and arms go in opposite directions." She turns toward Mimi, who twists effortlessly. "You're just showing off, Mimi."

Mimi giggles, "Maybe you should pay more attention to your teacher in your dance classes."

Willa Mae shakes her head, her hands resting on her hips. "Now you girls know I need to get your supper goin.'"

Mary Grace pouts, "Oh, come on, Willa Mae! We want to keep playing Chubby Checker on the record player and practice some more."

Willa Mae shakes her head but laughs softly.

"Okay, only a few more minutes. But if I don't get started soon, you girls won't have anything to eat tonight."

Mary Grace darts to the record player.

"On *American Bandstand*," she says, "I saw the dancers bend their knees more. Let's try that!"

She sets the needle down, and the room fills with the rhythm of Chubby Checker's "The Twist." The girls and Willa Mae begin twisting, their laughter louder than the music.

"Somebody's knocking at the door!" Anna Beth shouts, her voice rising over the music.

"What did you say?" Mary Grace yells back, her focus still on the dance.

"I'll get it," Willa Mae calls, her knees bending and twisting her way to the back door. The girls burst into uncontrollable laughter. Mary Grace runs to the record player and lifts the needle, silencing the music.

Willa opens the door.

"Hey, baby," Willa Mae says, surprised and out of breath.

Effie stands in the doorway.

"Did I hear Chubby Checker as I was walking up?" asked Effie.

"The girls are teaching me how to twist," says Willa.

Looking at her daughter, "Effie, you know how to twist. I've seen you do it at home. You want to come in and show the girls?"

"I don't think so, Momma," she says, looking toward the den. "Hey, girls."

"Hey, Effie," comes a jovial chorus from the dancers.

"Okay, baby, well, you know I'm stayin' the night, right?" says Willa. "Mr. and Mrs. Benoit are out of town."

"Yes, Momma, I know—that's why I'm here." She holds up the greasy brown bag, pulling out the smaller bag inside and handing it to her momma.

"Mr. Pierre had extra fried catfish and a few hushpuppies leftover. He wanted me to bring you some. I also have a bag for Grandma Nellie."

"Ohhhh," says Willa Mae, "that smells some good. That Mr. Pierre is such a nice White man. You be sure and thank him for me now, you hear?"

"I will, Momma," says Effie, glancing back at the girls as they continue to sing and dance without a care in the world.

Looking back at Momma, "I'll see you tomorrow." says Effie."

With her features drawn and quiet, Effie turns to walk down the back porch steps.

"Effie," Willa calls out.

"You okay, my baby?"

Effie pauses and glances back over her shoulder.

"I'm just tired, Momma. Long day at work. I'm gonna head back home now to check on Grandma Nellie."

Willa Mae watches as Effie takes the shortcut through the Benoit yard, following the brick path—a narrow strip of the White section of town where she'd been allowed to walk, though only by permission.

Effie's feet begin to ache as she makes her way back up Magnolia Street toward home. She swears to herself that, unlike her momma, she'll save enough money to buy an old jalopy and learn to drive it one day.

GRANDMA NELLIE SITS on the porch, sipping her coffee, always with chicory, while a cool afternoon breeze filters through the screen. Growing older, the porch is her favorite spot to sit. Even on chilly days, she can be found there, a simple shawl draped loosely over her shoulders, its burgundy tones faded with age. It once belonged to her mother, Sissy, born into slavery, and still carries the warmth of her hands. She spends most afternoons rocking, greeting neighbors, and gazing out at the sugar cane fields. Her thoughts of the past drift through the parallel rows of young cane stalks, just beginning to stir from their winter dormancy with the promise of a new harvest. Decades of working as a maid had worn down her feet and her body—and could have worn down her spirit too. But her faith and tenacity hold firm. After a recent bout with the flu, Grandma Nellie hasn't been able to attend church, but every Sunday the Reverend visits, and they share a cup of coffee together on the porch.

As a young woman, Grandma Nellie walked the cane fields every morning to the plantation where she worked as a maid for "a nice White family," she would say, though the words do little to soften the backbreaking labor.

Before that, she worked the fields cutting cane, and to this day, her old machete remains safely hidden under her bed. She still asks Effie to gather fallen sugar cane stalks from the roadside, dropped by passing cane trucks during harvest. Grandma Nellie savors chewing on the sugarcane; its earthy juice, with hints of molasses and honey, brings back memories of her childhood.

Grandma Nellie's face lights up, waving as she sees Effie coming down the dirt road toward home. Effie climbs the brick steps, ready to give her feet a needed rest. The screen door creaks open and slams shut with a clap behind her.

"You thinkin' about the old days, Grandma Nellie?" Effie asks, her eyes landing on her grandma, who is still lost in thought.

"Oh yes, baby. I was just thinking about when I used to work down on River Road. Your momma would come with me during the summer months when school was out. She'd play with the little girl who lived there—Miss Charlotte's daughter. Miss Charlotte was the lady of the house. They'd run through those fields all the way down to the bayou, laughin' and carryin' on. Before long, they'd come back to the house, breathless, telling us all about their adventures."

She pauses, shifting her gaze to Effie.

"Now, baby," she says, leaning in with a slight tilt of her head and a sparkle in her eye, "what's in those bags I'm smellin'?"

Grandma clearly knows exactly what's inside the bags.

With a big smile, "Now I bet Mr. Pierre sent that," she says.

"Yep, catfish and hushpuppies just for you, Grandma. That's what he told me," Effie replies, placing them on the side table and then heading into the kitchen for a plate and napkin.

The kitchen is simple, with a small Formica table and four chairs. Once outfitted with a wood stove, the family eventually saved enough for a modest modern stove. Nothing fancy, but functional.

On the small stove sits their slightly worn metal drip-coffee pot, coated in white enamel with red trim, nestled in a pan of simmering water to keep the coffee hot

Coffee in Louisiana is more than just a drink—it's a ritual of hospitality and community. Families often drip a pot in the mid-afternoon, settle onto the porch, and share the day's stories. Sometimes there's even a slice of *gâteau sirop*—syrup cake—sweetened with rich Louisiana Steen's Cane Syrup, to enjoy alongside the conversation.

It's a time to slow down, connect, and savor life together.

Effie returns to the porch, placing grandma's meal on the plate and settling back into her rocking chair. She rocks slowly, hesitating a moment before speaking.

"Can I ask you a question, Grandma?" Effie's voice is filled with apprehension.

As Grandma dips her catfish into the tartar sauce, "Go ahead, baby. What's on your mind?"

Effie attempts to rub the tension from her neck as she says, "I remember you telling me that Pappy died in an accident working on the railroad."

"That's right," she says.

Effie looks at her grandma, waiting for her to say more. Grandma Nellie just chewed in silence, looking out toward the fields.

"But Grandma," Effie says, leaning forward, "I overheard you talking to the neighbors, and you said Pappy died because of the hidden violence of Jim Crow. What does that mean?"

Her eyes innocently search her Grandma Nellie's for answers.

Grandma Nellie places her catfish back on her plate. Her gaze drifts out to the fields. She lets out a deep exhale. Effie waits, knowing her grandma was trying to find the words.

Looking over at Effie, she says, "I think we might just need a cup of coffee for this story, baby." Effie quickly rises, goes into the kitchen, and soon returns, balancing two blue, flower-patterned coffee cups on matching saucers, their edges slightly chipped and the paint gently faded with age. Handing grandma her cup, Effie settles back into her rocker. She waits.

Grandma takes a slow sip, closing her eyes. "Mmmm mmmm, now this is a good cup of coffee."

Grandma Nellie sets her cup and saucer on the side table and looks right at Effie.

"The hidden violence of Jim Crow means that, well, they'll always call it an accident," she begins, her voice heavy with the weight of the memory.

Looking straight at her granddaughter, she says, "Effie, your pappy was a good man, a hard worker on that railroad. Yes, it was an accident at first. The last time I saw him, he was going down those steps you just walked up. He turned around, smiled at me, and I'll never forget what he said to me with that familiar twinkle in his eyes: "You keep those red beans and rice hot for me now, you hear. I won't be late." Her voice cracks slightly. Grandma Nellie pauses, leans back, and begins to rock.

"He never came back home that day. Then I got the awful news. His brother, who worked on the tracks with him, came to tell me. I knew by the look on his face that something was terribly wrong.

'There's been an accident,' he says."

Effie shifts in her rocking chair, wiping away tears.

"Pappy's leg was cut real bad, baby. They put him in the back of a pickup truck. Everybody gave up their shirts to wrap his leg and try to stop the bleedin.'" Grandma Nellie's voice softens, her eyes clouding with emotion as the awful pain of that day returns.

"They took him to the hospital across the river. That's when things started to get real bad, baby. Real bad."

"What happened, Grandma?"

Grandma leaned back in her rocker, the steady creak beneath her seeming to give her strength in the telling, as though each rock carried a bit of the weight. Grandma didn't answer right away.

Effie waited.

The soothing creaks of the rocker suddenly stopped. Grandma crossed her feet, turning her head toward Effie. Without emotion, Grandma says, "They turned him away ... because he was Colored."

Effie gently puts her hand on her grandma's arm.

"His brother begged them to help," says Grandma, "but they wouldn't touch him. They told him that he had to take Pappy to Charity Hospital[29] in New Orleans. Well, you know how far that is. At least an hour and a half away. It's where all the poor people had to go, and the Colored people, too. It's still the same today.

Grandma Nellie's voice becomes soft but resolute. "Yes, Lord," she murmurs, continuing to rock and looking out. "Yes, Lord."

Effie leans in, unable to hold back her question.

"So, what did they do, Grandma?"

Grandma Nellie's rocking slows.

"Well, as they were getting ready to leave in the truck for New Orleans, one of the White nurses ran out. She handed them a box of gauze to help with the bleeding and a blanket to keep him warm. They said it helped some, but by the time they got to Charity, your pappy was losing blood fast."

Grandma grows quiet, picking up her catfish and taking a bite, as if she doesn't want to talk about it anymore.

Effie again waits.

"When they arrived, a crowd of Colored folks was already lined up at the back door, but I'm sure they could see how bad your pappy was. They all stepped aside to let him through. His brother and another man from the truck quickly carried him inside. The doctors took one look at him, his brother says, and they knew he was dying."

Grandma reaches for a hushpuppy and takes a bite, crunching through the golden-brown cornmeal on the outside, then sips her coffee.

"Well, they got to work right away and called for the 'Colored blood,'" she says. "But somehow, they accidentally brought in the 'White blood.' The doctor refused to give it to him. And while they waited for the 'Colored blood' to come, your pappy died."

Her voice trembled.

"That's what I call the hidden violence of Jim Crow laws. And you know, Effie, looking out toward the street, it's still out there today."

Thinking about her and Wilton's conversation earlier in the day, Effie becomes quiet. The church bells ring in the distance ... soft, melodic, and soothing, a moment of calm amid a horrific story.

Effie breaks the silence, "What did you mean by 'Colored blood' and 'White blood,' Grandma?"

Taking the last bite of her hushpuppy, she brushes the crumbs off her dress and shawl.

"Doretha down the street," says Grandma, "who works at Miss Jeanne Marie's cleaners, has a sister who works at Charity Hospital in New Orleans. She told us that the 'White blood' and the 'Colored blood' are kept separate. It's just how things are done down here."

Effie stands, visibly agitated. She walks to the porch screen, staring out as a storm of emotions wells up inside her. Turning back to her grandma, she lifts her hands in frustration.

"Grandma, if they had taken care of Pappy at that first hospital, I know he'd still be alive today! Everything I've heard about him says he was a fighter. And then, having to wait for the 'Colored blood'? It's cruel. It's unjust."

"Sit down, baby, and rest yourself. It's not like you to get so worked up. What's goin' on?" Grandma asks.

"Just doin' a lot of thinking these days, that's all," Effie says.

"So are a lot of youngins, I hear. You want to talk about it, baby?"

"Not now, Grandma, I just can't stop thinking about what a good man you said Pappy was. He deserved to be taken care of and should have gotten that blood. If he had, he could be rockin' on this porch with us right now.

"Well, Effie," she says, "I have heard that in emergencies, some do give the White blood to Colored folks. But it all depends on the doctor workin' that day. They're the ones who make the final decision."

Effie's voice sharpens with conviction.

"But, Grandma, Whites and Blacks have the same blood—the same as Jesus. That's what Reverend Washington always reminds us of in church, ever since I was little. He read from

Genesis, how God created mankind," her voice rises, "in ... His ... own ... image, male and female. And I love hearing the end, 'God saw all that He had made, and it was very good.' That means us, too, Grandma."

Grandma Nellie reaches for Effie's hand, her touch gentle. "That's right, baby. Don't ever forget it, and don't let anyone tell you otherwise." Her voice lowers, just look at this legacy he's left behind," she says, her eyes gleaming with pride. "I see him in you, baby."

Effie nods. *My mind is made up,* she thinks with resolve. *I'm meeting Wilton on the levee bench tonight and hearing what he has to say.* Grandma glances over at Effie, deep in thought, knowing well that her granddaughter's childhood innocence is gone.

She has felt, seen, and heard too much now, Grandma Nellie thinks, then smiles, *but her pappy's strength and courage is clearly in her and will go wherever she goes.* As they sit in silence, dozing off, the only sounds are the familiar, comforting creak of the rocking chairs back and forth and the gentle song of the cicadas.

CHAPTER EIGHT

"The only tired I was, was tired of giving in."[30]

-Rosa Parks, Civil Rights Icon

March 4, 1960

Evening

Effie is startled awake by the low groan of a foghorn echoing from a barge on the river. Beside her, Grandma Nellie is still dozing in her rocking chair. Effie is grateful for the time they shared that evening, talking about her pappy. She glances through the window into the house and catches sight of the clock. It's five minutes past seven and the sun has already set. *Wilton*, she thought. He's waiting at the bench.

Effie grabs her purse from the porch table and leans over, softly tapping Grandma's arm.

"Grandma," she whispers. Grandma gently opens her eyes. "I'm going down to get a malt with Wilton and a few others at the River King."

Looking up with her tender eyes, "Be careful, baby, and don't be too late. Y'all have fun," she murmurs.

Effie doesn't like lying, but she knows neither Momma nor Grandma would understand her reasons for going to meet Wilton at the levee bench alone tonight. They will ask too many questions. Every Friday night, without fail, Effie and her friends all get together at River King for malts and chit-chat, as they like to call it. A couple of tables are set up by the back window, designated Colored. As Effie steps out the porch door, Grandma Nellie watches her intently, her wise eyes following Effie's every move, sensing the turmoil stirring within her granddaughter. *This is your time, Effie Rose,* Grandma thinks, her heart swelling with a mixture of worry and pride as to what the future holds. *It seems like just yesterday,* she thinks, *you were sittin' at my feet makin' clothes for your baby doll with the scraps from my sewin'.* She pulls a handkerchief from her pocket, wiping her eyes. "We did our best to protect you, baby, and to prepare you for this harsh world," she whispers, another tear sliding down her cheek. Grandma Nellie knows in her heart that it is now time for Effie to spread her wings and find her own path. Rising slowly, she reaches to pull the string on the porch light, its soft glow illuminating the growing darkness.

As Effie turns up Magnolia and out of sight, Grandma Nellie whispers, "Be brave. Be courageous, my baby."

She turns and gathers her plate and coffee cups, heading inside.

"Yes, Lord," she murmurs, "yes, Lord."

EFFIE PASSES THEIR CHURCH, all closed up for the evening, and begins her walk up the levee path, the air heavy with patches of lingering fog. Wiping the dampness from her face, she looks toward the bench. It was empty.

"He left," she says to herself, her heart sinking. "I'm too late."

Then, movement near the water's edge catches her eye, accompanied by the occasional flash of light. Squinting, she can't quite make out what it is. She descends the levee further, down the ramp where the cars line up for the ferry.

As she moves closer, she spots Wilton, who is shining a flashlight into the river.

"What in the world?" She whispers as she steps off the road and crosses through a tangle of river bramble.

"Wilton," she calls out, "What are you doing?"

Startled, he looks up.

"Effie, I didn't think you'd show up."

"Well, I'm here, aren't I?" she says. "And what exactly are you doing down here by the river?"

Wilton grins.

"You know the old Black Preacher who baptizes people in the river by the ferry boat landing?"

"Of course I do," she replies, puzzled.

"Well, he was down here tonight," Wilton begins.

Effie, looking at him, confused, "He was baptizing someone after dark?"

"Of course not," Wilton says, shaking his head. "You can't see water moccasins in the river at night, especially with all these patches of fog. You'd have to be a fool to step in that water right now. Preacher was looking for his wooden staff down here with a flashlight, so I came down to help him. He says a dog dragged it off to the riverbank, and he couldn't find it."

Effie teases, holding back more laughter.

"First, we talk," she hears through the dark, "then the malt. You and your sweet tooth. Now, turn it back on!"

With a laugh, Effie flicks the flashlight back on, the beam cutting through the fog. The light catches something bobbing in the water. It looks like the preacher's staff, but there's something coiled around it.

"Wilton," Effie says, her voice low and urgent, "don't go any closer. I think there's a water moccasin on it."

"I see it," Wilton replies. "Just stay where you are, and keep the light steady."

Grabbing a large rock from the ground, Wilton hurls it at the staff.. The snake jerks and slithers off into the muddy waters, disappearing into the murk.

The stick floats closer to the bank, and Wilton reaches out to grab it. He rinses his muddy hands in the water, then turns back to Effie, offering her a hand to help her through the bramble.

"Wilton Ambrose," Effie says with a shake of her head as they make their way back up the levee, "you get us into more trouble than anyone I know."

"I do, don't I?" Wilton says with a chuckle. "And you're too much of a scaredy cat, Effie Rose."

As they reach the bench and sit down, they immediately jump back up, laughing as they look at the damp spot where they had just settled.

"The fog's everywhere tonight," Wilton says, shaking his head.

Pulling a handkerchief from his back pocket, he wipes down the bench as best he can.

"Alright, let's try this again," he says, motioning for Effie to sit.

They both sit back down, the staff resting on the ground beside Wilton as the fog begins to lift off the river.

Across the Mississippi, the lights of Baton Rouge cast a sparkling kaleidoscope of colors over the dark, rippling water.

"It's beautiful, isn't it?" Effie says as she gazes at the shimmering reflections. Wilton turns his head toward her, a gentle smile on his face.

"It sure is," he says, taking her hand.

Effie feels the blood rushing to her cheeks.

"I'm glad you came, Effie."

"I am, too," she says. "After talking with Grandma Nellie, I want to take a stand for my pappy—and for so many others like him. I want to be a voice for him. But I just don't know how."

Effie recounts to Wilton what she just learned from her grandma that evening—how her pappy had been refused care at the local hospital, forced to travel all the way to

New Orleans for treatment, and then died while waiting for 'Colored' blood.

Wilton shakes his head, his grip on her hand tightening.

"Oh, Effie, I can't believe that happened … well," he pauses, "I guess I can."

Effie looks out over the river.

"It's just not right, Wilton," she says, her voice barely above a whisper.

Wilton nods, his heart heavy with the injustice of it all.

"I'm just so sorry, Effie," he says, his voice filled with sincerity. The two sit in silence for a moment, and the soft lapping of the water against the riverbank is all that can be heard.

Wilton draws Effie close, holding her tightly. She feels safe, her fears melting away in his warm embrace. She pulls away slightly, looking at him.

"Wilton," she says in a serious tone, "I don't want to be so fearful anymore. I'm tired of being afraid. I'm ready to be brave. I'm just not sure how."

Wilton nods. "That's what I've been wanting to tell you, Effie. I do know how."

She tilts her head.

"That book I've been reading that I told you about," says Wilton. It's called *Stride Toward Freedom* by Martin Luther King,"[31] he says as excitement grows in his voice.

Effie's eyebrows raise. "Where did you get it?" she asks.

"Mr. Hutton at school," Wilton replies. "He does a lot more than just teach English to us!"

Effie laughs softly.

"I know. Remember how he used to load us all up in that old beat-up station wagon and drive us out to the plantations where the really poor Negro families live? He had us knocking on doors, trying to get them to vote. Talk about being afraid. Those folks were so fearful and reluctant about what we were asking them to do."

"How could I forget?" Wilton says. "Do you remember seeing newspapers covering the cracks in their walls to keep the cold out?"

Effie nods solemnly.

"Yeah, that was hard to see."

"It was," Wilton agrees. "But we were making a difference by going out there and knocking on doors. Mr. Hutton was making a difference, trying to get people to vote. The problem was, and still is, that they give Blacks a literacy test."[32]

Wilton pauses for a moment, then asks, "Effie, did your momma only go up to the fifth grade?"

"Yes," Effie replies. "There wasn't a school for her to go to after that."

"Do you know if she ever tried to take the literacy test to vote?" Wilton asks.

Effie shakes her head. "I'm not sure. Why? What is that?"

"It's a test, like the ones we have at school," Wilton says. "This one tests your reading and writing, but it is really just to keep Colored folks from voting," he explains. "Supposedly, they give it to the Whites too, but in truth, it is meant only for us. Mr. Hutton saw the literacy test when his momma tried to vote. She couldn't prove she had a fifth-grade education, so she had to take the test."

Effie frowns. "I don't think my momma can prove she went to the fifth grade either."

"Exactly," Wilton says, his frustration mounting. "There are no documents to prove that. So, Mr. Hutton's momma had to take this test, twenty-three questions, all to be answered in 10 minutes. If you get even one wrong or don't finish in time, you fail and can't vote."

Effie's eyes widened.

"Did she pass the test?"

Wilton's expression darkens. "It was impossible," he says. "And that was the point. They don't want Blacks to vote. That's why Mr. Hutton started taking carloads of people out to the rural areas. He wanted to encourage them to stand in line at the registrar's office. If enough of us show up, the clerks won't be able to handle it and might give in. It's a way to protest."

Wilton's words came faster now, stirred up by everything he'd been learning. "People have it hard enough as it is. And then get this. Mr. Hutton's momma went back to try and take the test again."

"Did she get registered?"

Wilton clenches his fists.

"No," he says. "They asked for her age and how long she'd lived in town. She wrote her age and said she'd lived here 'all her life.' But they said it wasn't specific enough. She failed again."Effie sits in disbelief as she listens.

"That is so wrong, and it's so demeaning." She says in a tone of defeat.

"It is," Wilton says, in a tone of determination. "These stories make me so angry, Effie. I have to do something. We have to do something. We have to make a difference."

Effie fidgets, shifting uncomfortably as she listens to Wilton.

"Just like in the book I'm reading," Wilton continues with passion in his voice, Dr. King talks about the Montgomery bus boycotts that happened back in 1955. All those people decided to fight back. It all started because of that brave lady, Rosa Parks. She wouldn't give up her seat to a White man. Effie nods slightly, her gaze fixed on Wilton.

"She was just tired, Effie. She had worked hard all day. But to that White man, all he saw was the color of her skin, and he demanded her seat. That moment set everything into motion.

Effie settled onto the bench and got comfortable. She knows her best friend. Wilton lives for this. He is like an Encyclopedia Britannica, except one that reveals all the untold stories.

Wilton continues.

"For one whole year. Do you hear me? One year. Thousands of Negroes, most of them older than us, walked up to twelve miles a day to get to work instead of riding those buses. They wanted justice. They wanted respect. They demanded equality. Isn't that what you want, Effie? I know that I do," he says, leaning back on the bench.

Effie's eyes widen at the thought. Wilton leans in closer, his voice dropping slightly as if sharing a secret.

"Listen to this quote I read in Dr. King's book. He said this at a planning meeting for the Montgomery bus boycott. I think you'll like it, Effie. Let me see if I can get it right."

Wilton pauses, gathering his thoughts, then recites slowly, "If we are wrong, the Supreme Court of this nation is wrong. If we are wrong, the Constitution of the United States is wrong. And if we are wrong, God Almighty is wrong.'"[33]

He looks at her, his eyes searching hers for a reaction.

"So, what do you say, Effie? Are you ready to help make a change?"

Effie hesitates, her hands still fidgeting. Finally, she speaks, her voice soft but resolute.

"I am Wilton. But only if we do it the way Dr. King says: to protest courageously, with dignity and Christian love."

Wilton nods.

"I heard that too, Effie. But listen," as though ignoring the immensity of her comment, "I know where we can start. Mr. Hutton has been talking about picketing the National Food Store."

"The National?" Effie says.

"Yes," Wilton says firmly.

"They refuse to hire Negroes. We can't even get jobs as bag boys there. If we join in, we can make a difference. We can be part of something bigger than ourselves."

Effie exhales slowly, the weight of his words sinking in as she imagines the stares and slurs if she's seen protesting outside the National Food Store in their small town. *What if Mrs. Benoit sees me when she comes to the grocery store?* she thinks.

"But Wilton ... I ... I just don't know if that's me," she stutters. "There's got to be other ways to speak out and make a difference. I'll think about it, Wilton. But also, what if Mr. Pierre finds out? We could lose our jobs."

Wilton stands up abruptly, turning to face her on the bench, looking at her intensely.

"It's the risk we take, Effie. You need to make a choice: risk your job or risk your entire freedom. You can't have both."

He pauses, sitting back down next to her and trying to calm down before he continues. Shifting to the edge of the bench, he faces her.

"You want to talk about risk, Effie? Let me tell you about the risk Black students took in Nashville last month. One night, five hundred Black college students met in the basement of the First Colored Baptist Church there. That's where the sit-in movement was planned."[34]

Effie leans forward, her curiosity piqued.

"Then what?" she asks.

The deep, steady hum of a towboat engine rises up from the river, drawing their attention. Wilton pauses as they both turn to watch a soft white light glowing atop the mast, guiding its barge through the dark waters.

After a moment, Wilton continues.

"Eventually, they marched downtown. White kids threw rocks, spit on them, even hurled lit cigarettes, but those students kept marching, like a brigade of soldiers. Unshakable. Most of them were from Fisk University, where I want to go, but there were others, too. They had been training for months not to react to violence. They sat at the White lunch counters, asking for service." Wilton says.

As the light from the towboat fades into the darkness, Effie leans in, her curiosity still stirring.

"And then what happened after that?" she asks.

"They sat there through it all," Wilton says, "probably pretty scared, but they did not budge."

"How did they know what to do?" Effie asks.

Wilton smiles, just a little. "You'll like this part. The Nashville Christian Leadership Council. It was built on the same principles Dr. King teaches, nonviolence and courage."

Effie tilts her head, intrigued, "Did they ever get served?"

"Of course not," Wilton says, his tone sharpening. "The owners refused, saying it was their moral right. Then, they called the police, accusing the students of trespassing and disorderly conduct. A complete lie. Those students were peaceful, Effie, but about seventy-five of them were arrested."

Effie's mouth falls open. "What happened to them?"

"They were given a choice: pay a fine or go to jail," Wilton says. "I heard that most of them chose jail."

Effie gasps. "Why would they do that? I would've just paid the fine, not that I would have had the money."

"Because paying the fine would fund more of the same treatment, plus it makes a statement," Wilton explains. "They made a choice, Effie. They chose the hard road for something bigger than themselves, and all of us."

Effie takes a deep breath, her eyes drifting to the now clear, moonlit Mississippi. The fog had completely lifted, and the moon glowed brightly against the dark water.

"Alright, Wilton," she says softly. "I'll do it."

Wilton's head jerks back slightly in surprise. "Wait, what did you say?"

"I said I'm ready to take a stand, but maybe not at the National Food Store."

She hesitates, her confidence wavering slightly.

"Well, I mean … I'm at least willing to keep talking about it after I know exactly what we are going to do."

"Are you backing out already?" asked Wilton.

"No, not really. Well, maybe, I don't know. I just don't want to be a part of any violence."

"Well, that's a start," says Wilton with a smile that always melts Effie.

He grabs her hand and holds it tight.

"You are very brave, Effie Rose."

"Now, let's get that staff to Preacher," says Wilton.

"Wait, Wilton, I need you to know something. This doesn't mean I'm necessarily giving up yet on my dreams about moving to Detroit after graduation. I really want to be a seamstress there."

With a smile of determination, "One day, I want to have a business of my own," says Effie.

"Your dreams and your courage to take a stand can work together, you know."

Wilton looks out over the shimmering river, his face contemplative, then turns back to her, almost pleading.

"Stay here with me, Effie. We can make a difference together, be part of these movements happening all over the South. I'm sure you can find good work here. You are such a good seamstress."

Effie reaches for his hand, her voice soft but resolute.

"Wilton, I care for you, and I love you, but if I don't try, I'll regret it for the rest of my life. What if I can do it? What if I succeed? I could show others they can follow in my footsteps. I want to do it for my pappy. He would want me to be brave and have a strong voice wherever I am."

Her voice catches as her eyes well up.

"We're not the little kids we used to be, running barefoot up the levee. Our dreams might be calling us in different directions."

Wilton nods slightly, trying to understand her confusing thoughts. He reaches up to gently wipe her tears and smiles faintly.

"Will you at least join me for now, while we're here?" he asked. "And who knows, maybe your longings will change."

"Maybe," is all that Effie says. He pulls her into a tight hug and presses a gentle kiss to her cheek.

"Now," he says, breaking the silence, "let's get that staff to Preacher."

Wilton bends down to pick up the staff, but his hand meets empty air.

"Where in the world ...?" he mutters, looking around. His gaze shifts to the riverbank, and he bursts into laughter.

"Well, look who it is. That bad one-eyed dog, Scrappy, stole the staff again while we weren't looking. He's just lying down there on the riverbank by the light of the silvery moon, chewing on it."

He chuckles, "My daddy told me that my momma used to sing that song to me all the time." He looks out, lost in thought.

Effie nudges him gently.

"Sorry, Wilton, but no time for reminiscing. Scrappy's going to completely destroy that staff, and Preacher uses it every day, I'm sure."

Wilton snaps out of his thoughts and runs down the levee, calling to Scrappy. After some coaxing, he manages to retrieve the chewed-up staff.

Scrappy, looking utterly unbothered, runs into the bramble and disappears.

Walking back up the levee and shaking his head, Wilton says, "Let's try one more time to get this back to Preacher. Then, I'm going to buy you the biggest malt ever at River King."

Effie raises her eyebrows.

"That'll cost a lot, Wilton."

He stops and turns to her, his expression softening.

"You're worth every penny, Effie Rose."

Sometimes, Wilton surprises her, and she gets a glimpse of what is beyond the anger and hurts of his life. They continued to walk up and over the levee together towards Preacher's house, hand in hand, by the light of the silvery moon.

PREACHER LIVES in a small shack near the levee, a modest structure that seems to mirror the simplicity of the man himself. At eighty years old, he trudges slowly each day up the footpath behind his home, crossing over the levee down to the ferry landing to preach. Everyone in town calls him "Preacher."

His simple, tattered robe, reminiscent of the garments worn by John the Baptist, is made of coarse, camel-colored fabric. It reflects the humble and devout life he lives. A tightly worn bowl-like hat of the same fabric rests on his head, and a rope around his waist. He always carries his staff, a sturdy wooden stick topped with a homemade cross wrapped in rags of the same material. The staff steadies him as he walks and bears his weight when he grows weary.

As cars line up for the ferry, he preaches the gospel, urging passengers to come down to the water to be saved. Some listen, but most ignore him. Those who answer his call wade with him into the mighty, muddy Mississippi, stepping into a quiet eddy near the shore to be dunked and baptized. To the townspeople, his presence is as constant as the river itself—and on the rare days he isn't there, the absence feels almost strange.

WALKING UP TO THE DOOR, Wilton knocks gently. It takes a moment, but soon the door cracks open. Preacher's weathered face appears, his eyes studying his young visitors.

Wilton speaks quickly, holding out the staff.

"I found it, Preacher. This is my friend, Effie, who helped me. I'm so sorry that a stray dog chewed on it, but I think you can still use it."

Preacher stares at Wilton for a few moments without saying a word. Then, he opens the door wider and reaches for the staff.

"Thank you kindly, son," is all he says, his voice hesitant.

As Effie peeks through the door of his humble home, something catches her eye on the wall. It's a photo of Dr. Martin Luther King.

"Oh, we have that same photo," she says, without realizing she is verbalizing her thoughts. He nods again but speaks no words as he walks to the hook on his wall to hang his staff. He is a private man and very to himself except when he is tending to his ministry on the river.

Wilton glances through the door at a side table. Something catches his eye. It's a teacup.

That looks familiar, he thinks, *though he can't say why.*

Breaking the awkward silence, Wilton says, "Well, I guess we better be going. Have a good night, Preacher."

As they turn to leave, his clear voice calls out behind them, stopping them in their tracks.

"Be strong, young people," Preacher commands, his words carrying a weight that makes Effie slip slightly on the muddy path.

They turn back to face him, and Wilton thinks about how to respond to his direct command. Then Preacher speaks again, this time louder and firmer.

"Be courageous," he says. "And go forth in dignity and Christian love."

Wilton freezes, his mind racing. Those words, he'd read in Dr. King's writings. It felt as though Preacher could see directly into his heart, into the fire burning within him.

"Yes, sir," Wilton manages to say. "We will."

"Yes, sir, Preacher," Effie adds quickly and begins to back away, unable to take her eyes off of him.

This must be a sign from God that we're doing the right thing, she thinks. Suddenly, her shoe catches in the mud, and she falls backward.

"Effie!" Wilton exclaims, rushing to help her up. He grabs her hand and pulls her to her feet, both trying to hold back their laughter.

"Are you okay?" asks Wilton, with both concern and amusement.

Preacher was already walking out with an old rag. He hands it to her.

"Thank you," says Effie. She wipes her legs, shoes, and the bottom of her dress. Wilton takes Effie's hand so as not to fall again. She hands the rag back to Preacher, who turns silently and goes back inside.

Wilton holds Effie's hand to steady her on the slippery path until they reach the road. They look at each other and burst into laughter.

"Look at me, I'm a mess!" Effie exclaims, still giggling. "But can you believe that, Wilton? This must be a sign for us. Do you think he knows what we're thinking about doing?"

"How could he?" Wilton asks. "But … I mean, those were Dr. King's words. Like I said, I read those same words in *Stride Toward Freedom*." *There's something about that Preacher that I just can't put my finger on*, he thinks, glancing back at the house.

Turning to Effie, he smiles. "Come on, Effie Rose, let's go. We both deserve a chocolate malt!"

Walking hand in hand, they sense an unsettled world stirring around them, pulling them from childhood's innocence to the uncertainty of what's to come.

CHAPTER NINE

"It was the Sermon on the Mount rather than a doctrine of passive resistance that initially inspired the Negroes of Montgomery to dignified social action. It was Jesus of Nazareth that stirred the Negroes to protest with the creative weapon of love."[35]

~ Dr. Martin Luther King, Jr.

March 5, 1960

The screen door closes behind Wilton as he steps outside, greeted by the sweet aroma of magnolia blossoms. Notes of lemon, vanilla, and jasmine drift from his front yard, carried by a warm spring breeze that sweeps across the porch. He pauses a moment to savor the fragrance of the awakening of spring in southern Louisiana.

Placing his cup of coffee on the table, the events of last night linger as Effie's words replay over and over in his mind. The rocking chair waits for him, its cypress wood polished smooth from years of use. It's Wilton's favorite spot to lose himself in thought or in a good book, of which this morning he brings two. His dad built the chair long ago, crafting it from wood salvaged from deep in the bayou. His handiwork is timeless, able to build just about anything.

Right before he sits, he sees a ruby-throated hummingbird darting around the branches of the pink magnolia blossoms and the red buckeye shrub next to his porch. Its wings hum like the gentle whir of a lawnmower. Suddenly, the bird swoops low, buzzing right past his head. Startled, Wilton ducks and stumbles backward into the rocking chair with a thud.

For a moment, he sits still, catching his breath, before a smile comes across his face. *I feel lucky*, he thinks, recalling a memory his father often shared.

"Son," his dad had said, "when a hummingbird comes close to you, they're bringing positive messages and good thoughts from someone you love who's passed on."

Wilton leans back in the chair, his gaze drifting upward as the hummingbird zips away. His thoughts turn to his momma.

"Could that be you, Momma?" He lovingly calls out. Closing his eyes, he tries hard to remember for a minute what she looked like.

Wilton then places his two books on the side table. The worn cover of his Science 2 textbook sits beneath Martin Luther King's *Stride Toward Freedom*. Picking up his steaming cup of Community Coffee,[37] with chicory ground into the beans, he holds it close. The sweet, tobacco-smoked aroma fills his senses. The scent is a small comfort, one of the few memories left of his momma. Daddy always says she loved her chicory coffee, and now that familiar smell brought Wilton back to a place he felt he knew well and yet didn't.

Setting the cup down, he picks up his Science 2 textbook. Opening to where he left off, he peels back the folded corner that holds his spot and opens to chapter 4, "Observing the Heavenly Bodies." The subject fascinates him. He smiles, knowing Effie also shares his curiosity. Effie's momma has shared stories with her of how much her pappy loved observing the night sky.

Taking another slow sip of coffee, Wilton reads the opening lines about the daytime sky and the sun's role as the closest star to Earth. He pauses and thinks, *ninety-three million miles away from here. That distance seems unfathomable. How could something so far away feel so close, so powerful?* Lifting his head, he squints toward the sun, its heat pressing against his face, and wonders ... *if heaven exists and Momma is there, is it somewhere out there, carried in the same light that reaches across ninety-three million miles to touch me?*

To Wilton, even the eighty-five-mile drive to New Orleans felt like a journey to another world. Of course, the promise of Uncle Ray's red beans and rice with cornbread always made the trip worthwhile, not to mention Aunt Mary's sweet potato pie. Just thinking about it made him hungry.

"Hey, Wilton," a voice calls out from the street, pulling him back to earth. He looks up to see Miss Fannie, one of his favorite neighbors since moving here twelve years ago, walking back from the market, arms full with two overflowing bags of groceries in the heat of the day.

"Whatcha' readin' this time?" she calls out.

Wilton quickly sets the book down and jumps off the porch.

"Let me help you with those, Miss Fannie. They look heavy and that sun's starting to beat down somethin' fierce."

Grabbing her bags, they begin their walk six doors down to her house.

"I'm reading about observing the heavenly bodies," he says.

Miss Fannie chuckles.

"Last week, you were telling me all about what you read in your civics book, and I thought for sure you'd become a lawyer someday. Now, I'm thinking, maybe you'll be one of those folks who teach about the sky. You sure are smart, Wilton. Maybe you can help my Abe with his homework. He's been strugglin' in school. As I'm sure you know, they don't always have enough textbooks to go around, so he has to share his math book with a classmate. He sure seems to be fallin' behind."

Wilton nods. "I'd be happy to, Miss Fannie. Just let me know when."

He sets the grocery bags on her front porch, waves goodbye, and runs back home, eager to dive back into his book. Settling back into the rocking chair, he reads aloud, letting the words fill the quiet porch.

"One million Earths could fit inside the sun." He leans back, closing his eyes again. He tries to comprehend this as the sun's heat again warms his face. He can't wait to share these discoveries with Effie.

Wilton loves it when his dad brings home the new textbooks from the white high school. Mr. McKinny, the science teacher there, enjoys being able to loan books to Wilton's dad at the beginning of each school year. Mr. McKinny knows that Wilton is like a sponge, taking in all he can. Wilton, of course, receives Science books at his school, but they are often ragged older editions leftover from the White high school. Just like their hand-me-down school desks with the White students' names carved all over them, making it difficult to write on.

Startled by the ring, Wilton snaps out of his thoughts. He runs inside, grabbing the phone on the kitchen counter just in time.

"Hello?" he answers breathlessly.

"Hey, bro, it's Jer," comes the familiar voice on the other end.

Jeremiah, or Jer, as everyone calls him, is Wilton's cousin. He is a sophomore at Southern University, the all-Black campus where he lives in the dormitory. Jer and Wilton often share long conversations about their dreams, their admiration for Dr. King, and his philosophies that could change their world.

Jer grew up in Wildwood, Mississippi, a place shadowed by the horrific lynching that happened in nearby Money. The trauma of this, coupled with the heartbreak of what happened to Wilton's mom, was too much for Jer's family. They packed up their belongings and in 1956 moved to New Orleans, where Jer's father, Ray, found work in the kitchen of a prominent, whites-only restaurant.

There, after a chef tasted Uncle Ray's red beans and rice one day, his dish quickly became famous. Under the guidance of a well-known chef, Uncle Ray's beloved home-style recipe–featuring his ham hocks, andouille sausage, and the Creole trinity of onion, celery, and bell pepper–was elevated to restaurant-quality excellence. His uncle's cooking had always been the talk of family gatherings, and now the restaurant's patrons eagerly awaited that weekly specialty on the menu.

"What's up, Jer?" Wilton asks, leaning against the counter.

"I've got something important to tell you," Jer says, his tone serious. "But I don't want to tell you over the phone."

"What's it about?" Wilton presses as he stretches the coiled phone cord out the door, feeling the warm breeze hit his face.

"Can you catch the three o'clock ferry from your side of the river and meet in our usual spot?" Jer asks. "I'll tell you all about it then. Nothing like the charm of the upper segregated level for a deep, possibly life-changing conversation."

They both chuckle, though Wilton still wonders what Jer could possibly want to talk about.

"We'll just ride it back and forth a few times," Jer adds. "We won't have to pay for the ferry fee, since we'll each be getting off on our own sides of the river anyway."

Wilton sinks into the rocking chair, still clutching the phone.

"Alright, I'll see you on the ferry."

"Wait, Wilton, don't hang up!" Jer blurts. "Did you get the book Mr. McKinny had for you?"

"Yeah, I have it right here," Wilton replies, glancing at *Stride Toward Freedom* on the side table. "I'm already halfway through it."

"Good. Write down some of Dr. King's philosophies and bring them with you, but don't bring the book itself. If someone sees the title, it could cause problems."

Wilton frowns.

"Why are you sounding so intense, Jer?"

"This is big," Jer says, his voice tight. "It could stir things up here, big things. I'll explain everything when we meet."

"But Jer, at least tell me..." Wilton starts, but the line clicks, leaving only a dial tone.

Wilton stares at the phone in his hand, his mind racing. *What's so important that Jer only wants to talk about it in person? He thought.*

Just then, the hummingbird reappears, darting back and forth above his head, then disappearing within seconds.

"What an interesting day this has been already," he says to himself.

Walking to the screen door and glancing at the clock, he sees it's already one-thirty.

With little time to spare, he flips through *Stride Toward Freedom*, jotting down key quotes and ideas in his school composition book. Each line he writes fills him with a growing sense of purpose and desire to be a part of this growing freedom movement, which he has been reading about in the book. Something continues to stir within him, as though it's in his blood, determined and unshakable.

Wilton tears the paper from the rings of his composition book, tucking it in his back pocket, and heads out. Arriving early, he can see that the ferry is just pulling away from the dock across the river. He sits on the edge of the levee, watching the ferry captain skillfully navigate the river, steering around strong currents and whirlpools. A *longer route today*, he thinks, only fueling his impatience as to what Jer must tell him.

Wilton spots Preacher, standing almost knee-deep in the muddy river. There's no one else around, no sign of a baptism taking place. Concerned, Wilton gets up and makes his way down the levee toward him, squinting, trying to see what Preacher is doing.

Getting closer, he realizes the old man is struggling to pull a large piece of driftwood from the water, while at the same time trying to hold his robe so as not to get it wet.

"Preacher!" Wilton shouts as he gets closer. "Let me help you. Get out of the water!"

Preacher ignores him, focused on tugging at the driftwood. Wilton hurries to the water's edge and grabs Preacher's arm.

"You're gonna fall in and drown yourself," he says, exasperated. You're going too far out.

Preacher looks up at Wilton.

"Son, I know this river like I know the sure promises of God."

Wilton raises his eyebrows.

"Well, I sure hope God promises to save you, 'cause I don't have that kind of trust in Him."

With a sigh, Wilton rolls up his pants, takes off his shoes and socks, and very carefully wades into the water. Gripping the driftwood, he drags it out of the water and up the bank.

Wilton wipes his hands on his pants and goes back to retrieve his socks and shoes.

"Why do you even want this old log?" Wilton asks, walking back up to where Preacher was standing.

Preacher places his hand on his lower back.

"Well, now that I'm gettin' older, my back's been aching real bad lately. I just need a place to sit and rest myself during the day while I'm out here."

"Thank you, son," he says, grabbing some old rags by his bucket and placing them over the wet log. He lowers himself down with a groan, setting his staff down beside him, leaning on it briefly to catch his breath.

"Sit down beside me, son, and you rest yourself, too." Wilton did as he was told.

"Preacher, why don't you just go inside, take off your wet shoes, and rest in your house? You look tired."

Preacher shakes his head, his voice firm.

"I don't get tired, son. My body just gets a little weary at times."

Wilton chuckles. "I think that's the same thing."

Preacher waves a dismissive hand.

"If I go inside, and someone gets called by the Spirit to be baptized, I wouldn't be here to answer. This is my ministry. This is my work for the Lord."

Both are quiet for a few moments as they watch the ferry approaching the dock. Breaking the silence, Wilton says on a light note.

"Hey Preacher, we're going to my uncle Ray's in New Orleans on Sunday for lunch. He's making his famous red beans and rice. Why don't I bring you some when we get back? He always makes enough for a huge crowd."

"Mmm, mmm, that sounds some good," Preacher says, a slight smile on his lips. "He does make some good red beans and rice." He mumbled

Wilton chuckles. "But you've never had my uncle's red beans and rice."

Without responding, Preacher says, "Now, you get goin', son. You don't want to miss the ferry."

Wilton stands up, brushing off his pants. He heads toward the dock, but before he's gone far, Preacher reaches for his staff to pull himself up. He notices a folded piece of paper sticking out from under the driftwood. It's slightly damp, but he unfolds it and reads over the scribbled words. They're familiar—words he's seen before.

Folding it back up, "Wilton!" Preacher calls out, waving his staff and holding up the paper. "You dropped something."

Wilton turns and runs back, taking the paper from Preacher's outstretched hand and quickly stuffing it into his pocket. As he turns to leave, Preacher's voice stops him again, this time with a commanding tone.

"Be strong and courageous, son. This is your time."

Wilton just stands there staring, realizing it's some of the same words he spoke to them last night, and with the same tone.

"And when you get back, pass by my house," he says, "I have somethin' I want to give you."

Wilton nods. "Sure … I … I'll try to stop back by."

As Wilton walks toward the boat, he hears the consistent thud as each car rolls over the metal ramp onto the ferry deck. He looks back. Preacher is slowly walking toward the final cars in line. He holds his staff to steady himself with every move. *I don't know what it is,* Wilton thinks, *but there's more to that Preacher than meets the eye. He's a mysterious man.*

Wilton walks across the wooden plank and climbs the steps to the Colored section on the top deck. He spots Jer sitting on their usual corner bench, staring out over the water.

"Hey, cuz," Wilton says, giving a quick hug.

"Were you planning on swimming to the other side of the river?" asks Jer, laughing. "The bottom of your pants is soaked."

"Oh, that," says Wilton, looking down at them, chuckling and shaking his head. "It's a story for another time."

The horn blows, signaling the last call. Moments later, the plank is hoisted, and the low rumble of the engine vibrates through the deck as they begin their ride across the river.

"What's this important news?" Wilton asks anxiously.

A strong wind sweeps across the upper deck, causing the ferry to rock more than usual and making the ride noticeably choppy. Wilton slips a hand into his pocket, reassuring himself that the folded paper with his notes is still there.

Looking around, Jer leans forward, his voice dropping to a whisper.

"I was in my dorm room last night and overheard something through the walls. It was muffled, but from what I gathered ... you won't believe it!"

Wilton's eyes narrow.

"What is it?"

Jer looks around once more, checking for anyone nearby.

"Some Southern University students are planning something big on March twenty-eighth, next Monday, around two p.m. They're going to sit at the White lunch counter at Kress Department Store and order something."

Wilton's eyes widened.

"What? I knew sit-ins were happening in Nashville, but here?"

Wilton takes in the news, glancing out at the swirling water as the captain, once again, steers the ferry around the strong currents.

Turning back to Jer, he says, "This is good news, but they'll probably be arrested, or worse."

Shaking his head, "Probably," Jer agrees. "But I heard them talking about Dr. King's words. They kept reminding each other ... no violence ... no confrontation. From what I overheard, it sounds like they're supposed to take whatever comes their way."

"No way," Wilton mutters, shaking his head.

Jer continues, "Then I heard one of them say, 'Let's get to the meeting. We're going to be late. We need the practice.'"

Wilton quickly pulls the folded, damp, and ragged piece of paper from his pocket.

"It's just like I read in *Stride Toward Freedom*," Wilton says. "They had rehearsals and teaching sessions on nonviolent techniques. Let me show you what I wrote down from the book."

"Okay, but keep your voice down," says Jer.

Wilton unfolds the paper and begins reading aloud. "'Meanwhile,' Dr. King says, 'we went to work to prepare people for integrated buses.'"[38]

He pauses and looks at Jer. "He's talking about what came after the Montgomery Bus Boycott in 1956. Folks walked instead of riding segregated buses for 381 days. Then the Supreme Court stepped in, back in November of '56, and said bus segregation was unconstitutional, violating the Fourteenth Amendment. They wanted to prepare the Negroes to bravely get back on the buses and hang on to what was their rights."

Jer raises a hand, half-grinning. "Hold on, counselor. You're talking above my head a little bit. Can you refresh me on the Fourteenth Amendment? Remember, I'm a business major."

Before Wilton can answer, the ferry dips sharply toward the river on their side. "Whoa," Jer mutters, gripping the railing. "Water's really rough today." They steady themselves as a wave splashes onto the upper deck, and the boat rocks as it tries to pull itself out of a strong current.

Wilton wipes his sleeve and gives Jer a nod. "Alright, back to the Fourteenth. Simple version from when it was ratified after the Civil War. It says that states can't treat some people as less than others. Everyone's supposed to get the same protection under the law."

Jer leans against the railing. "So the law says we're equal... but really, only if someone's willing to fight for it?"

Wilton nods. "Exactly. That's why what happened in Montgomery mattered. And it wasn't just about buses. A couple years earlier, in the Brown v. Board of Education case, the Court ruled that segregation in public schools was wrong too—same amendment. That decision opened the door to challenge segregation everywhere."

Wilton looks around the upper deck. "Truth is, we're supposed to be able to sit anywhere on this ferry now. But around here?" He lets out a deep breath. "They still act like separate is just the way it is."

Jer nods slowly, trying to absorb the explanation.

"So, what else did you read from the book?"

Wilton continues, "'If there is violence in word or deed, it must not be our people who commit it. If cursed, do not curse back. If pushed, do not push back. If struck, do not strike back, but always show love and goodwill at all times.'"[39]

Closing the paper, Wilton looks at Jer.

"The more I read this, the more I realize ... I don't think I can do that," he says in a raised tone. "Someone hits me, I hit them back. Especially if it's a White person."

Jer's expression tightens.

"That's the whole point of the movement, Wilton. Don't you understand?"

Wilton turns to stare at the Baton Rouge skyline in the distance.

"I want to go with them on Monday to the sit-in," he says, frustration evident in his voice.

Jer shakes his head.

"You can't just show up, Wilton. These students have planned and practiced for this."

Wilton looks out at the choppy water and becomes silent.

"At least listen to my idea," says Jer. "I know you want so badly to be a part of it. I do too. But we haven't been training for it, and you're still in high school. So, how about we show up at the Colored counter in Kress for a milkshake around that time. We can support those students from the sidelines."

Wilton slams the paper onto the bench beside him.

"I don't want to sit on the sidelines, Jer. I want to be in the middle of it."

Jer sighs, his voice calm but firm.

"Wilton, sometimes the sidelines are the way to learn, to grow. I think your anger is clouding your judgment."

Wilton glares at him, then picks up the paper and shoves it toward Jer.

"You keep it. You're the one who believes in these words."

Jer takes the paper reluctantly.

"Why are you suddenly so angry, Wilton?"

"You wouldn't understand," Wilton mutters, standing abruptly and heading toward the steps.

"Wilton, wait," Jer calls out.

Wilton just keeps walking, heading down the steps to the lower level. As the ferry docks, the plank lowers for pedestrians. Wilton angrily walks off, beginning on the levee path toward home.

"Son," a voice calls out from behind him.

Wilton stops but doesn't turn around.

"I'm not in the mood," he mutters under his breath and keeps walking.

"Wilton," he says.

Wilton stops halfway up the levee path. Preacher has never called him by his name. He looks.

"Don't go," Preacher calls out. "I can tell you're angry. It's okay, let's talk about it, son."

Wilton just stares at him, then slowly begins to walk back his way. He wasn't sure why, but it felt like something stronger was drawing him there.

Wilton stops in front of Preacher.

"What's got you so angry today, son?"

"You wouldn't understand. It's complicated."

"You might be surprised," says Preacher.

"I … I don't know," Wilton says, looking out over the water. "I just want to fight against everything that's wrong out there," his voice rising. "In order to do that, I have to be a part of this protest and movement that's taking place. It seems that God has given justice to the White people, but where is ours? Nowhere! I want to do it for my mother, who was killed when I was only five at the hands of racist Whites who held undeserved power. I'll never forgive them, and I want to somehow get back …"

He stops abruptly and looks down, not even sure why he was sharing this.

Both were quiet.

Preacher breaks the silence, walking towards Wilton and putting his hand on his shoulder.

"I understand, son. I do." He says, with compassion in his voice.

Pulling away, "I'm sorry, Preacher, but you don't understand. How can you understand? They took my mother from me. And her grandmother, my daddy told me, was born into slavery with no rights as a human being. When will it all stop? And I'm supposed to protest in a nonviolent way, like Martin Luther King says? What does that achieve? Where does that get us? Nowhere. You know where else it gets us, Preacher? Right back in the back. Right where God wants us, I guess."

Wilton snatches up a rock and hurls it into the bramble. Then, pressing his hands to his knees, he lets out a deep breath.

"It's okay to be angry and wrestlin' with God, Wilton. I wrestle with Him all the time."

Pointing out towards his home, "Let's go to my house," he says. "I have some fig cookies Miss Mattie brought me, and I'll drip a fresh pot of coffee. You know Miss Mattie's the best baker in town."

A slow, forced smile spreads over Wilton's face.

"And then," says Preacher. "I want to show you somethin'."

When they reach the house, Preacher drips a pot of coffee and slides a steaming cup, its rich aroma comforting, toward Wilton.

That cup again, he thinks. *Where have I seen it?*

As he ponders, a loud scratching breaks the quiet. Wilton looks up, squinting in concern, and glances toward Preacher.

Preacher calmly walks over and says, "That rascal."

Opening the door, Scrappy bounds in.

"What in the world?" says Wilton.

"I figured the Lord had sent him my way since he was probably the one chewin' on my staff and kept ending up back at my house. I think he needs a friend, and he's a nice companion."

Scrappy sees Wilton, runs over, and jumps up with his paws on his pants leg, wagging his tail.

"Looks like he knew you needed a friend, too, and maybe a little love."

This time, Wilton's smile is genuine, and he pats his leg as Scrappy jumps into his lap, muddy paws and all.

"Well, I guess I'm feeling the love, Preacher, from both of you. Did you give him a name?" asks Wilton.

"Not yet."

"Well," says Wilton, "we have met before at my work."

"He showed up at Mr. Pierre's café, too?" asks Preacher with a chuckle. "He sure gets around."

Wilton looks at him in question, "You know where I work?"

"Well, I went once to get a beignet there and saw you workin.' Now help me give him a name," he says.

"I kind of gave him a name when I met him. I call him Scrappy."

"He is pretty scrappy lookin'," Preacher chuckles, "He sure is at that."

Sipping on coffee with Scrappy in his lap, Wilton enjoys a fresh fig cookie. Letting out a deep sigh, he begins to calm down. Preacher takes a sip of his coffee and looks towards Wilton with empathetic eyes.

"I know you're hurtin', son, and I know you're angry. I want you to know that's okay."

They sit quietly for a while. Then, Preacher speaks.

"Let me show you somethin', and somethin' I want you to have."

He goes to the back room and comes out with what looks like a comic book.

With a questioning look, Wilton says, "I know that you preach, but I didn't know that some of your sermons come from a comic book?"

Preacher laughs, "Well, sometimes."

He hands Wilton the comic book.

"I was given this last year by Reverend Washington," He says. "Take a look."

His small home was dark with little light to brighten the space. Wilton walks over to the window. He reads the title aloud.

"*Martin Luther King and The Montgomery Story*.[40] I've never seen this before, and I read a lot but usually not comic books."

"I was told," says Preacher, "they were given out in Black churches, youth groups, and schools all over the South. It helps to inspire nonviolent protest movements.

You see, Rosa Parks chose to not sit in the back of that bus because she knew that would get us one step closer to equality, but she did it peacefully."

"Some people think nonviolence is just passive resistance. From the very beginning of this movement, there's been an overriding theme." His eyes soften toward Wilton's, and he says, "Christian love."

Feeling uncomfortable at where the conversation is going, Wilton says, "Well, thanks, Preacher, for the coffee and cookies, but I need to get going."

He stands up, eyes locking with Preacher, "I really can't listen to this Christian love as a way to fight the battle. In my book, that just doesn't work."

"Don't keep runnin' from God and from your fears," says Preacher.

"Why don't you stay a little longer? Talk about it with me. What's your fear about Christian love? You're safe here. Why not have another cookie?" he holds out the plate.

Wilton looks out the window, wanting to flee this conversation.

"Well, I guess, sure, I'll stay for another one of Miss Mattie's fig cookies." He sits back down.

"Let me tell you a story, son. There was once a man, long ago, who sat on a hill and began to teach. That man's name is Jesus."

Wilton begins shifting uncomfortably in his seat.

Preacher continues.

"His teaching was extraordinary and radical. For days, the multitudes of people could not stop listening and chewing on those sweet, fragrant words of Jesus, upside down from the world's words."

Wilton was having a hard time staying in his seat. He wants to leave, but he reaches for another cookie.

"His words, now called The Sermon on the Mount," Preacher says, "were life-changing." And those same Words inspired the Negroes of the Montgomery Bus Boycott towards dignified social action. Through intense heat, cold, rain, and cruel taunting, they pressed on for justice through nonviolence."

"Yet, I want you to hear me, Wilton, when I say this."

Preacher gets up, pulls his Bible off the shelf, and holds it up.

"These Words. Jesus' Words. They're upside down from what the world tells us to do."

He sits back down, placing the Bible on the table.

"It's just like Miss Mattie's pineapple upside-down cake." He says. "You ever seen her turn that over from the pan after it comes out of the oven? It's not normal to turn a cake ready to eat upside-down. But when you do, ohhh, the treasures you find there.

"The world says to fight violence with violence, but the Bible teaches us to fight violence with love. But that kind of Christian love can only come from the power of God's Word, but to the world, that sure seems upside down."

Preacher places his hand firmly on the Bible.

"That's the only way it can be done. Not in our own power ... no, sir."

Preacher gets up to refill Wilton's coffee cup.

"You see son," placing the cup back down in front of Wilton, "His Word is our weapon, and love is all over his Word. Love has a power, a nonviolent power that is not of this world. But hear me, love also speaks righteous truth and we must stand up to that," looking outside the window, "and speak truth today."

Wilton takes in every word, thinking how eloquently the preacher speaks and how much he knows about the movement. It was unexpected. Preacher reaches for the comic book and hands it to Wilton.

"Read all about it in this comic book. It's yours for the keepin'," he says. "A late Christmas gift."

"Oh, and by the way, be sure to read in your Bible–Matthew 5:43–48. There's treasures to be found there in those pages.

Sometimes Bibles gather dust, son, and the treasures inside stay hidden. But the beauty's still there–waitin' to be found by those willin' to read it. Now, you don't have to. But it's a mighty nice invitation from God, askin' us to sit with Him for a while and chew on His Word."

Preacher continues, "I want to tell you a secret, Wilton."

"That Word," pointing to the Bible on the table, once you find those treasures and let them seep into your heart, then you'll be given the best gift ever.

Wilton waits and listens.

"That gift–that gift is freedom." Now, not always outer freedom, but a sure guarantee of inner freedom, and that's all you need. Everything else works itself out from there."

"Somethin's keepin' you captive deep down inside your soul, son. I can see it. My eyes might be old, but I can see it clearly. And it's got you in bondage, and it's eatin' away at you. Nothin' available to you in this world can ever free you from it. It's just counterfeit. Nothin' can break the chains of bitterness that hold you captive. I have been there, and I see myself in you. There is only one you can trust who holds the key to unlock those chains and free you, and that's Jesus Christ. You just have to choose to invite him in, and when you do, he won't ever leave your side."

He looks straight at Wilton.

"He's waitin' now for that invitation from you."

Wilton looks at Preacher, and his eyes begin to well up. His words were touching something deep down within him. He was beginning to find not only a trust but also a comfort with this mysterious, yet somewhat oddly familiar man.

Preacher gets up and walks around the table to Wilton, gently putting his hand on his shoulder.

"I already wrote the passage number on the back of your comic book," says Preacher. "Do you have a Bible?"

"Yeah," says Wilton. "It hasn't been touched in years. It was my Momma's. I think her daddy gave it to her."

Widening his eyes to not let the tears fall, Wilton speaks in a tone laced with a touch of sarcasm.

"Maybe I'll dust it off and read it one day, who knows. Anyway, I know that it would make my momma happy. I don't remember much, but my daddy told me she loved church, and she loved me. Oh, and she loved chicory coffee," he chuckles.

Preacher stayed silent, just staring at Wilton.

Clearing his throat, Wilton stands up, "Thank you, Preacher, for the coffee, cookies, comic book, and, I guess, for the talk, too."

Looking down at his feet, he says, "And you, too, Scrappy, my friend. Thanks for the love."

Reaching for the door handle, he turns back around.

"Do you think that I could bring my daddy one of Miss Mattie's cookies?"

Preacher picks up the plate and hands Wilton two more cookies.

"One for the both of you," he says.

Wilton heads out the door as Preacher calls out, "Now don't you eat them both on the way home."

"No promises, Preacher," Wilton calls back to him.

Scrappy runs off, trailing behind Wilton.

Deep in thought, Preacher stands at his door and watches Wilton until he is all the way to the top of the levee, heading down the dirt path home.

CHAPTER TEN

"Perhaps nothing about the history of mob violence in the U.S. is more surprising than how quickly an understanding of the full horror of lynching has receded from the nation's collective historical memory."[41]

-W. Fitzhugh Brundage

March 6, 1960

Effie hurries down Magnolia Street, glancing over her shoulder at her mother. "Momma, we're going to be late for coffee and donuts before church," she says, trying to quicken the pace.

Willa chuckles softly, shaking her head. "Now you know you bad, Effie. You're seventeen years old and still acting like you're twelve. You just want me to walk faster so you can have donuts both before and after church."

They both laugh.

"I can't help it, I've always had a sweet tooth."

Their laughter fades as they spot a White couple approaching them on the sidewalk, dressed in their Sunday best. As they come closer, the couple makes no effort to move over.

Without hesitation, Willa and Effie step off the sidewalk.

Effie grimaces as her foot sinks into the muddy, water-soaked grass.

"Good mornin'," the woman says politely as they pass.

"Mornin'," Willa replies with her head and eyes down, her tone subdued.

Once the couple has moved on, they step back onto the sidewalk, and both glance down at their shoes. Effie lets out an exasperated sigh.

"Golly, Momma, our shoes are a mess now with mud and wet grass all over them."

Willa smiles gently.

"It's okay. We're about to pass the old oak tree. Let's sit on those low branches we like, if they're not too wet, and clean off our shoes."

Effie huffs. "We'll never get to church on time."

The sprawling oak tree on Magnolia Street stands tall and proud, its moss-draped branches stretching wide, some touching the ground to form natural benches for weary travelers. Over 200 years old, the tree was once known as the community "bulletin board," where locals posted news for everyone to see. Its massive roots push above the soil, creating a playground for children. Just saying, "Meet me at the old oak tree," was enough to pinpoint the spot. If the tree could talk, it would share tales of joy, sorrow, and perhaps some moments it might rather forget.

As Effie and Willa approach the tree, Effie's eyes light up.

"Look, Momma!" she says, pointing. "Somebody built a bench over our favorite branch."

Willa narrows her eyes and nods.

"Well, will you look at that," Momma says, tilting her head. "This must be new. I guess we'll be even more comfortable sittin' down."

Stepping closer, "It even has a plaque on it," says Effie

Squinting, Willa reads the words.

"May shade and peace be found under these branches."

Willa Mae pauses, her expression darkening as she mumbles something under her breath.

"What did you say, Momma?"

Willa shakes her head as they sit on the bench, picking up sticks to scrape the grass and mud from their shoes.

"Oh, just thinking out loud," Momma says, her voice low.

"Maybe shade from the sun, but it sure is hard sometimes to find peace under this tree."

Effie looks over sharply.

"What are you talking about?"

Willa sighs and glances away, her fingers gripping the stick tighter.

"No matter. Just memories. Let's finish cleanin' up."

But Effie doesn't budge. "Momma, what's wrong?" she asks insistently. "Something's troubling you, I can tell."

Willa sets the stick down and exhales slowly, her shoulders sagging.

"Well, I never told you this before, Effie, but I think you're old enough now to hear the story. We'll probably miss coffee and donuts, but they'll still be there after service."

Effie leans closer, her curiosity overpowering any thought of pastries.

"It's okay," she says gently. "I'd rather hear the story."

Willa looks at Effie.

"Well, I was just a little girl when it happened," she begins, voice trembling. "I must have been around five years old, back in 1926 or '27. I don't remember too much about the story, just bits and pieces. But it was the most awful thing I'd ever seen, and I remember never wanting to think about it again. It haunted me then, and it still does."

Effie's eyes widen. "What was it, Momma? What was so awful?"

Willa takes in a deep breath, her gaze fixed somewhere far away.

"Your grandma Nellie and I were walkin' to church, just like we are today. Magnolia Street looked a lil' different back then, no nice cement sidewalks like these. We just walked along the dirt road. It's funny, the things you remember. We were singing "This Little Light of Mine" when suddenly, I let out a terrible scream. It was so loud I scared myself, but I couldn't stop."

Momma's voice grows quieter.

Looking up through the branches, "There in this tree," Willa Mae says, pointing toward the sprawling oak, "was a man hanging from a rope. Blood was comin' out of his mouth, and he had no shoes on. I remember your grandma grabbing me so fast and turning my face into her dress, holding me there so tight that I could hardly breathe. She cried out in desperation, 'Don't look, Willa Mae. Keep your face in my dress, baby.'"

Effie gasps, "Momma, you saw a lynching?"

Willa nods slowly, staring at the tree as though she can still see the image etched into its branches.

"I guess I did. I didn't know at the time what I was seeing, but I knew I had never seen anything like that before. I think it was one of my first memories as a child."

Willa Mae looks up again, high into the tree.

"Your grandma never said a word about it afterward. I just remember crying all the way to church. And after the service, we took a different street home."

Effie looks up at the tree, as the weight of the story settles over her.

"I just don't understand, Momma. How can our God let something like that happen?"

Willa pats Effie's hand gently, her voice steady but sad.

"Baby, there are just some things we won't understand while we're still standing on this side of glory. "But I do know one thing for sure. "Even in the middle of evil, God is good—all the time." For a moment, Effie considers her mother's words. She's heard her momma say this countless times, but now, hearing it alongside this story, Effie struggles to believe it. They sit quietly together under the tree, reflecting on the horror of it all.

Stepping out from the shade of the old oak, Willa and Effie return to the sidewalk, their thoughts heavy and silent. They turn onto Levee Lane, the road leading toward their church. Just a few feet past the church, the lane ends abruptly at the levee.

The old white wooden church stands steadfast, its presence a testament to nearly ninety years of resilience. Its predecessor, the original church building, was claimed by the shifting waters of the Mississippi River in the late 1800s, taking much of the original town with it. The elders say the old gospel church went down singing, and if you listen closely at night, you can still hear echoes of "Oh freedom, oh freedom, I'll be buried in my grave and go home to the Lord and be free."[42]

Generations of Willa Mae's family have attended this church, a sacred gathering place for their community. Just past it, Levee Lane intersects with a dirt road called Glory Way, a road well-trodden by those making their way to bury their loved ones in the church cemetery. It's a hallowed resting place, reserved for the Black community only.

THIS PARTICULAR MORNING, gospel songs pour out from the church's windows and doors, filling the streets with lively music of praise that carries at least a block away. The service has already begun.

As they pass Mr. Willie's house, Effie waves. Mr. Willie lives just a few doors down from the church and can often be found on his porch, dancing to the soul-stirring gospel music spilling into the neighborhood. His old hound dog seems to sway along with him, tail wagging to the rhythm.

"Hey, Mr. Willie!" Effie calls out, laughing at his lively moves.

"Oh, Mr. Willie," Willa adds with a chuckle. "Now you're really cuttin' the rug with Jesus today, aren't you?"

Mr. Willie waves without missing a beat, his feet still moving and hands clapping in time to the music.

"He's got the church in him," Willa Mae says, "but he sure won't go in the church. I don't think he's ever stepped through those doors—except for his wife Tootie's funeral."

"We'll bring you some collard greens with ham hocks later this afternoon, Mr. Willie," Effie promises. He waves his hand.

As they approach the church steps, Effie hears her name called from a distance. She turns to see Wilton running up Glory Way. He lives down the street with his father in a small house.

"Go on in, Momma," Effie says, motioning toward the church. "I'll meet you in our pew."

Every family at their church has a designated pew, a familiar spot they sit in each week, and everyone respects these sacred seats. Willa disappears through the double doors just as Wilton reaches the steps.

"Wilton, where are you going?" Effie asks, surprised.

"Going to church," he replies, slightly out of breath.

"You never go to church," she says.

"Well, I'm here now, aren't I? Are you glad to see me or not?"

"Yes, of course I am. I'm just … surprised," she admits.

Wilton hesitates, then says, "Daddy told me not long ago that Momma used to take me to church with her all the time in Mississippi. I don't remember much about it, but I thought … why not give it a try? You like it, Effie, and you're my best friend. Maybe I'll feel close to Momma here, too."

Effie's face lights up with a smile, and she reaches for his hand.

"Come on," she says. "Let's go in and sit down."

As they walk through the double doors, Wilton leans close and whispers, "Plus, I have something really important to tell you."

"What?" she whispers back, curious.

"Not now, Effie. After church, we can take a walk on the levee."

She nods, and they walk up the aisle, making their way to the fourth pew from the front, Effie's family pew for decades. Fans are waving all over the church. The choir sways side to side, their flowing white robes adorned with purple stoles draped over their shoulders and cascading down the front. Their voices in harmony, carrying the melody and the hope of "The Storm Is Passing Over" to every corner of the church. She stands next to Momma and joins her in the singing, her hands clapping to the rhythm, her body swaying with the music. Wilton, however, stands still, his arms awkwardly hanging by his side.

"Come on, Wilton, you know you can feel it. You can at least clap your hands," Effie encourages.

Willa Mae, moving so much to the music, knocks right into Wilton, who then bumps into Effie, who falls backwards into the pew. The two look at each other, trying to maintain composure but burst into quiet laughter.

"This sure is a lively place," says Wilton.

Everyone sits down, and Reverend Washington comes to the pulpit. He is a humble, passionate man filled with wisdom. The spirit of the Lord speaks through him with power, sometimes in the most peculiar ways.

"Just give the songs a try," whispers Effie. "It's fun."

Momma looked at Effie, "shhhh," glancing her eyes toward the pulpit.

"And we know," proclaims Reverend Washington, "that we can stand on the firm foundation of a righteous and just God."

Wilton turns toward Effie with a loud whisper, "Well, where is our just God now?"

"Wilton, calm down and for once, try to listen instead of talking."

Reverend continues, "Don't let yourself be worn down and lose hope or the will to fight for that justice. 'Behold, the days are coming, declares the Lord, when I shall raise up for David a righteous branch and He will reign as King and act wisely and do justice in the land.'"[43]

Suddenly, the Reverend's voice intensifies, and he firmly points his finger upward.

"Our citizenship is in heaven with a just God. And we … cannot … lose … hope. I say it again, do not let this world wear you down. This is not our home."

"Look up," he says, "everyone, look up."

The congregation begins to look up at the ceiling.

"What do you see?" He asks.

"What are we supposed to be looking at, Effie?" whispered Wilton.

"Just look up, Wilton. Reverend always has a point he is making. I'm not sure what it is, but let's just listen."

"I know you just see the wooden beams of this old church," says Reverend.

"But up above that, above the roof, into the sky and beyond the veil, there's a place we can't see. It's called heaven. Our loving God is on His throne there, and He is surrounded by his heavenly army of angels that fight for us. There's a mighty battle going on that we can't see. It's all around us out there, but we are not alone."

This moment moves Wilton deeply as he looks back up toward the rafters. Only yesterday, he'd been on the porch, reading about the heavenly bodies in his "Science 2" textbook, imagining the stars and planets—and his mother somewhere up there, now with God. A tender comfort rises within him at the thought of his momma resting at God's heavenly throne. *Maybe God truly is a loving God who sees and cares*, he thinks, *but why does it feel he doesn't see all of us as he looks around the congregation?* A gnawing doubt rises, and Wilton can't seem to get past it in his mind. Reverend pounds his hand on the pulpit, startling Wilton.

"'Do not be afraid or discouraged by this vast army, for the battle is not yours but God's. He goes before you.[44] Pick yourself back up, and fight for justice with the heavenly armies leading the way."

Looking from one end of the congregation to the other, Reverend continues, "We do not fight the darkness with the weapons of this world but with the weapons of God!"

Wilton shifts uncomfortably in the pew, his mind swirling, as Reverend Washington continues.

"A few months ago, a friend and colleague sent me notes from Reverend Martin Luther King's speech last year at Yale University in New Haven, Connecticut. The title of his talk was 'The Future of Integration.'"[45] Amens were heard all over the church.

The Reverend continues, "I was moved by his words. This young man was only 29 years old at the time, yet the spirit of the Lord was upon him."

Hallelujahs break out, reaching up to the rafters.

"He calls his audience to live a life maladjusted. Now, let me explain ..."

"Wilton," Effie leans in and whispers, "what does that word mean?"

She knows that Wilton lives for questions like this.

Whispering back, Wilton says, "It means someone is poorly adjusted. I think what Dr. King was saying is that we shouldn't adjust or settle for injustice or inequality."

"Shhhhh," came from behind. They both look forward.

"So, in the words of Dr. King," says Reverend, "I call us today to be," he pauses and looks at his church family, "maladjusted."

"I want you to be as maladjusted as the Prophet Amos, who in the midst of the injustices of his day cried out in words that echo across the centuries to us today."[46]

He leaves the pulpit and walking down the center aisle of the church, he shouts:

"Let justice roll down like waters and righteousness like a mighty stream.

Do not be adjusted to what is going on around us down here in the South."

Amens were flying around the congregation like bees swarming out of a honeycomb.

"Because who do we have?" asks Reverend.

A shout comes from the back.

"A just God!"

Wilton shakes his head, closing his eyes as the hallelujahs and amens crash into his mind like a hurricane, roaring and twisting through every corner of his thoughts.

God, he thinks, *I know you are out there, but I just can't believe you're a just God. Forgive me, God, but I can't. Why my momma? Why Effie's pappy?* The voices from the church continue to echo, louder and relentless, pressing against his thoughts, making it impossible to find quiet in his own head. Then, right next to him, Willa Mae shouts, "God, you are good all the time."

Wilton sharply turns to Effie and says in a loud whisper, "I can't listen to this anymore. God has forgotten us. I've had enough, Effie, I'm sorry."

Before Effie can respond, he stands up from the pew and angrily walks down the aisle and out the church. Effie begins to get up, and Willa puts a hand on her leg.

"Stay here, baby. Don't go after him. He's angry. He needs time. Let the Holy Spirit do His work in him."

Miss Ella leans forward from the pew behind them and whispers, "Don't go after him, baby. He's wrestlin' with God. And that's okay. Our God can handle that."

The Reverend stands quiet for a moment, his eyes sweeping over the congregation, and then he speaks with power.

"If your life has been complacent with what is happening down here," he pauses, and then shouts: "Wake up!"

Mr. Booker in the first row is startled from his usual Sunday morning nap and slips off the front of his pew. Before he hits the floor, Mrs. Booker catches him and gives her husband an annoyed glare.

"You must not underestimate the power of your prayer," Reverend says. "And you must not ignore your call to action."

He pauses, letting his eyes sweep over the congregation.

"I want to close this morning by calling each of you—not to be spectators, but participants. Do not become adjusted to the evils of segregation and discrimination, as Dr. King has warned."

Pointing to the back, "Let me send you out these doors with God's Word being etched on your hearts and filling your souls with courage. Listen once again, 'Let justice roll down like waters and righteousness like an ever-flowing stream.' May Dr. King's words ring in your ears."

The ushers open the back doors.

"Let us be as maladjusted as Abraham Lincoln, who had the vision to see that this nation could not survive half slave and half free. The world is in desperate need of such maladjustment."[47]

He walks further down the center aisle, "Now, go in peace and take action on God's foundation of love, courage, and power. As we leave, the choir will sing another chorus of 'The Storm is Passing Over.'"

As the choir sings, everyone begins to gather their things from the pew. Effie can't wait to get out the doors to find Wilton.

He should have stayed to hear the rest of the sermon, she thinks. *He would have been encouraged.*

She makes her way through the crowds leaving church, but he is nowhere to be found.

Willa calls out, "Let's get home, Effie, and get those collard greens on the stove."

"I'll be there soon, Momma. I need to find Wilton."

"Do what you think you need to do, baby. I'll see you back at the house."

Having an inkling of where he might be, Effie walks down Glory Way, passing his home, and turns toward the levee above the ferry landing. Sure enough, Wilton sits on their familiar bench, staring out at the river.

"Wilton," she calls out, relieved but a little irritated.

"Why did you leave church so angry and just disappear like that?"

Wilton doesn't turn to look at her. His eyes remain fixed on the water. After a few moments, he turns, looking at the person he trusts and cares for so deeply.

"Do we have a just God, Effie?" His voice was subdued. "Do you really believe that?"

Shrugging her shoulders, she says gently, "I don't know what I believe sometimes, Wilton. One thing I do know is that it's okay to wrestle with God."

"Effie, I need to tell you something ... something that I've never shared with anyone. You remember me telling you that my momma died when I was little, and I told you that she had been sick? She wasn't sick."

Sitting down next to him, Effie's eyes pierce his, searching for the truth.

"What happened, Wilton?"

He exhales deeply, "She was killed by an angry mob of White men. That's all I know. There, I said it." He pauses, "I don't think I've ever said those words out loud before."

"Well, except yesterday to Preacher, and I'm not even sure why. And I've only heard my daddy say them once. He can't talk about it. It's too painful. I still have nightmares, Effie, and I wasn't even there."

Crossing his arms tightly as if shielding himself from pain, he stares back out over the river. Effie gently reaches for his hand, but he keeps his arms tightly folded, holding himself protected. Quietly, she pulls back her hand and sits beside him in silence, letting him grieve.

After a few moments, he speaks again, his voice softer but still raw.

"She's buried where I was born, in Ellisville, Mississippi."

Turning toward Effie, trying to hold back tears, he adds, "I've never been back to visit her grave."

Effie nods, her heart aching for him.

"It's okay, Wilton. I can't imagine how hard that must be. I understand why you wrestle with God, questioning how He can be just."

"I just think I'm angry with God, Effie," he admits.

Taking her hand at last, he says, "Thanks for just sitting here with me."

Wilton stands and watches a barge filled with grain as it moves slowly down the river. He watches it until it vanishes behind the waterfront trees.

"Wilton," Effie says softly, "I'm so sorry about your momma."

He turns back to her, his face tender.

"I know, thanks Effie, but I don't think I want to talk about it anymore right now. My mind keeps making up horrible scenes of how they killed her."

Walking back to the bench, he adds, "The thing is I don't really know much more because Daddy won't talk about it."

"Wilton," Effie speaks up, "Reverend Washington said–"

"Effie," Wilton cuts her off, his tone sharp and his expression stern, "I don't want to hear what Reverend Washington has to say. What I want to do is just go home."

Letting out a sigh, his voice softens.

"I'll call you soon and we can talk more," he says with a gentle smile.

Turning away, he continues along the levee towards home.

Effie just sits there alone, not knowing what she is feeling. She has heard horrific stories of disappearances, murders, and lynchings, but it is just all too traumatizing to think about. Now, someone else close to her has been touched by this violence.

She looks up to the sky and, for a moment, calls out to God.

"God, I guess I'm questioning you now, too. I'm so sorry. I do love you. Momma says you are good all the time. I know you have heavenly armies that fight for us. But God," she cries out, "where were you when my kind pappy, Wilton's loving momma, and the young boy in Money, Mississippi, suffered at the hands of such evil and violence … I don't understand." She whispers, "Help me to understand."

She stands up, and she walks the levee path back to her street. Every step, tears of grief fall, fall … gently being received at the foot of the cross. There, the lamb of God shed His blood for us, for the forgiveness of our sins, and He bore our grief and sorrows, carrying them with Him to that lynching tree one dark Friday 2,000 years ago.

PART IV

A VOICE AWAKENS

Each of us is born with a voice–a God-given voice, uniquely our own. But over time, culture, formative influences, and the weight of life can either distort it or enrich it. Some voices are buried, others silenced. Yet even in the framing of our journey, we're not without choice. Our voice can become an instrument of life, filled with truth, grace, courage, and love–or be a noisy gong or a clanging symbol.[48] "For out of the overflow of the heart, the mouth speaks."[49] This is the awakening: to seek God's voice first, and through it, find our own.

CHAPTER ELEVEN

Shortly after my birth, I became blind. That was a blessing because it allowed me to see the world in the vision of truth. See people in the spirit of them. Not how they look or what color they are. But what color is their spirit?[50]

~ Stevie Wonder

August 6, 2019

Midday

Willa lay in her bed at St. Francis of Assisi Hospice Home, her body frail, yet her spirit strong.

"Ohhhhh, I smell fried catfish," she murmurs.

"If you're hungry, Willa, I'm happy to get you a little something," says Mimi. "Can't guarantee it'll be catfish, though."

But, as she speaks, doubt settles in her mind. *Willa hasn't had an appetite these last few days,* she thinks.

Her body was weakening, retreating inward.

A soft knock interrupts the stillness. The door creaks open just enough for Angel to peek inside, a familiar, mouthwatering aroma coming in with him.

"Unbelievable," Mimi whispers, looking at the bag. "Is that really fried catfish?"

"Miss Willa," Angel says with a grin, stepping inside the room. "I called Andre, and he brought over fresh fried catfish, just for you. Now, it's not T-Boy, the grand PawPaw of them all, but ..."

Before he can finish, Willa interrupts with a sparkle lighting her face.

"Mmmm, mmmm, but I bet that's a kin of his," she says.

Laughter ripples through the room as Angel gently shuts the door behind him.

Angel holds up a paper bag with a grease stain so thick it nearly drips from the bottom.

"They just pulled it out the fryer," he says.

"It smells like heaven," Mimi mumbles, as she glances at her phone. *No wonder*, she thinks. *It's almost one o'clock.*

Willa stirs, attempting to sit up, and Mimi quickly moves to adjust the bed. As the mattress rises, Willa's gaze finds Angel, her eyes gleaming with gratitude.

"Baby, you didn't forget," she says, her voice full of warmth. "What a blessin.'"

Before anyone can respond, another knock sounds at the door.

"Is it okay to come in?" a cheerful voice calls from the hallway.

The door eases open, revealing a young man holding yet another grease-spotted bag. His smile is wide, and when he speaks, his words carry a rich Creole rhythm.

"Bonjour," he greets, the phrase rolling off his tongue like music.

Mimi takes note of his striking features and the way his presence seems to brighten the room.

"Sorry to interrupt," he continues, "but Angel, I forgot to give you the fried okra that we had."

At the mention of okra, Willa's face lights up even more.

"Okra?" she repeats with delight.

Angel glances over at the young man, grinning.

"I think I'll keep you."

"You better," the young man shoots back playfully, "or I won't share any of my Mama's gumbo with you at dinner."

Angel laughs, shaking his head before turning back to Willa and Mimi.

"Mimi, Miss Willa," he says, gesturing toward his companion, "this is my partner, Andre. He works on the fishing boat I told y'all about, the Zydeco Zoomer. It passes by the bayou outside your window all the time."

"Well, baby," Willa replies, "you toot your horn, and we gonna wave at you."

"Okay, Miss Willa," says Andre with a wink, "I promise."

"Thank you, thank you," Willa says.

"Bye-bye, Miss Willa," Andre says as he heads for the door. "Be listenin' for that horn now."

Andre steps toward the door, glancing back at Angel.

"See you at home," he says.

The door closes gently behind him, leaving a lingering warmth in the room.

"Well," Angel says, "if you don't need anything else right now, I will check back soon. But don't hesitate to call if you need me." Mimi watches for a moment as Angel leaves the room before turning back to Willa.

"Willa, would you like a little taste of catfish?" she asks softly.

Willa shakes her head, the motion slow, her eyes already drifting closed.

"I think I'll wait, baby. I'll save it for later."

Mimi exhales, carefully lowering the bed as Willa dozes off.

Just as the room falls quiet again, another knock sounds at the door, the handle turning as it cracks open.

A head peeks in.

"Am I interrupting anything?"

Mimi blinks, taking a moment to put the visitor's face into context.

"Oh my goodness ... AJ!" she exclaims.

Willa's nephew stands in the doorway, taking in the scene. Mimi rises, crossing the room to greet him with a hug.

"Mimi," he says with a grin, "it's been too long."

"It sure has," she replies. "When we were young, we saw each other all the time when I dropped Willa by your momma's house. She sure loved visiting with her sister. Now, just on visits to see Willa. I'm so glad you're here."

His gaze shifts toward Willa, who sleeps peacefully, her breath slow and steady. AJ's face softens.

"I needed to see my Tee," he murmurs.

Only in Louisiana, Mimi thinks, would someone use that affectionate nickname for their auntie.

AJ walks over to the side of the bed, his expression falling as he looks down at her. "She looks so ... so ... frail," he says sadly. "Where did my Tee go?"

"She's still here, AJ," Mimi reassures him gently. "Just a little weaker ... and maybe a little less bossy."

They share a quiet chuckle before AJ's eyes land on the embroidery sitting on the side table. His fingers brush against the fabric.

"Wow," he murmurs. "I haven't seen this in a while. Tee has had this hanging in her house since I was a little boy."

"That reminds me," Mimi says, crossing the room with purpose.

"I wanted to ask if you know anything about a photo I found behind the embroidery earlier today."

She retrieves the picture and hands it to AJ. Taking it curiously, he carefully studies the faded image.

"Willa told me that was her in the photo, but she didn't say much about the other little girl," Mimi explains.

AJ smiles, his expression softening.

"Tee was pretty cute as a little girl."

He squints, bringing the faded image closer, tracing the edges with his thumb.

"Hmm ... I'm not sure who the other girl is," he admits. "I know Tee used to talk about a little White girl she played with when Grandma Nellie worked for a family down River Road. Says they'd run through the sugarcane fields and go on adventures ... but that's about all I know. I guess it could be her, but I'm just not sure."

AJ pauses, tilting the photo at an angle.

"But wait ... this looks like a bayou behind them, even though the picture's so yellowed. Maybe you can ask Tee about it when she wakes."

"I did," Mimi says quickly, exhaling a sigh. "But she teared up and didn't seem to want to talk about it. All she said was that her name is Clara. Then she got tired. I didn't want to push her."

AJ studies the photo a moment longer.

"That could be Bayou Bateaux. It's out near one of the old plantations."

Mimi glances over at Willa.

"It seems pretty important to her."

Then, with a bright smile, she turns back to AJ.

"Come on, sit down. Let's catch up."

She gestures toward the orange faux-leather chair, already reaching to pull the desk chair over for herself.

"I got it, Mimi," AJ says, shaking his head. "You sit in the comfortable one."

She chuckles.

"Not much to choose from for comfort here."

Mimi settles into the orange chair while AJ takes the desk chair. They pull their seats close together, leaning in so they can talk without disturbing Willa.

AJ's expression grows somber as his eyes drift toward his aunt.

"Tee has always been there for me," he says, his voice quiet. "After Momma and Daddy died, she watched out for me. She was strong when I couldn't be."

He wipes his eyes and lets out a shaky breath.

"Sorry, I don't mean to tear up."

Mimi reaches over, placing her hand on AJ's and giving it a gentle squeeze.

"This is a tough time," she says softly. "She's your Tee, but she's also like a mother to you. I know when ..."

The door swings open without a knock. The supervising nurse strides in, her usual grim expression in place, lips pursed as her gaze sweeps across the room. First, she looks at AJ, then at Mimi, and finally, her eyes settle on their clasped hands.

"Well, what's going on here?" she snarls, her tone laced with disgust. Then, with a tilt of her head, she adds, "Is this one of those Black-White situations?"

Mimi goes still, her jaw clenches, fury flickering in her eyes as she locks a glare on the nurse.

AJ looks caught off guard, fumbling for words as he stands.

"I, uh ... I think I better go, Mimi," he mumbles, his voice unsteady. "I need to pick up an old friend from the airport."

He avoids the nurse's gaze as she doesn't flinch, arms crossed, her stare unwavering.

AJ glances around the room, searching for his keys. "He's, uh ... in town for a conference."

Spotting them on the table, he snatches them up, his movements hurried. He turns back toward Mimi, his expression strained.

"We went to high school together," he says. "But yeah ... I'll be back soon. Tell Tee I love her."

AJ forces a tight smile in Mimi's direction and walks out the door as though he couldn't get through it fast enough. A dark cloud has settled over the room, almost feeling an actual chill in the air.

Mimi stands. She levels her gaze at the nurse.

"Is there something you need?" she asks, her voice controlled but icy. "Or something you need to do?"

The nurse smirks, lifting a brow.

"No," she says, eyes fixed on Mimi. "I just wanted to take in what was going on." She turns and leaves the room.

Mimi's eyes follow the nurse as she walks out. She takes a slow, steady breath, then lets it out sharply, trying to process what just happened. She glances toward Willa, relieved to see her still sleeping soundly. *Maybe I've been out West too long,* she thinks. *I keep hoping that more things would've changed down here by now. This just brings back too many bad memories.*

Her eyes drift through the window to the bayou, its waters dark and endless.

Mimi whispers, turning her head back to the door, "This woman is an unapologetic racist."

She had not wanted to believe it at first, not here, not in a place meant for care and dignity. This is always a sacred place. But once again, darkness can enter even the most unexpected places ... lurking ... seeking to extinguish the light.

CHAPTER TWELVE

"Hate is too great a burden to bear. It injures the hater more than it injures the hated."[51]

-Martin Luther King Jr

August 6, 2019

Early Afternoon

Mimi replays the exchange between her, AJ, and the nurse. The weight of it settles over her. A surge of urgency brings her to her feet. Reaching for her cell phone on the side table, she calls Anna Beth, her fingers trembling.

"Please pick up," she says.

Relieved to hear her sister's voice, she steps into the bathroom and shuts the door.

"Anna Beth, how soon can you get here?" she asks with urgency.

Anna Beth's frantic response comes through immediately.

"Is it Willa? Is she okay? I can be there in—"

"No, Willa is stable," Mimi says quickly. "Sorry, I didn't mean to scare you, but have you found a new hospice home for Willa yet? We need to move her. I can explain later, but you and Effie need to know something."

Anna Beth's voice softens. "Take a deep breath and tell me what's going on, Mimi?"

Mimi exhales, pressing a hand to her forehead.

"The supervising nurse here has shown clear signs of racism ... It's brazen."

She paces the small bathroom, her thoughts racing.

"All the other staff I've met have been wonderful. I don't know how this woman ended up here, but we can't let Willa be subjected to her cruelty anymore. No ... I won't let Willa be subjected to her cruelty anymore. She deserves nothing but unconditional love in her final days on this earth."

Before her sister can respond, Mimi cuts in, her voice firm with resolve.

"Anna Beth, I'm going to speak with the director. I'll tell him we're packing up Willa Mae and moving her to another facility tonight. Did you and Andrew find any options?"

"Yes, we found two that can take her today if needed," Anna Beth says. "But ... do you really think she can handle the move? Why don't you wait? Andrew will be home soon, and I'll have him call the director. He knows him, and he can–"

Frustration flares in Mimi.

"No," she interrupts. "I need to do this myself, Anna Beth. I can't be afraid to speak up. I know you remember me as the peace-maker growing up, always running from conflict–but I've come a long way since then, sis. I must be Willa Mae's advocate. I've seen and heard it all firsthand today."

Mimi glances at the door, determined.

"I need to go, but I'll keep you posted. Please confirm one of those places for Willa tonight, and call Effie to fill her in."

As she pulls the phone away from her ear to hang up, she hears Anna Beth's voice start to say, "I'm proud of ..." but the call disconnects before she can finish.

Opening the bathroom door, Mimi steps back into the room and immediately notices Angel by Willa's side.

"Is everything okay, Angel?" she asks, her voice filled with concern.

"Miss Willa's blood pressure is dropping a bit," Angel replies. "I think we should have the nurse come in and check her."

Mimi lowers her voice to a whisper.

"Please, not the supervising nurse. She is not welcome in this room."

Angel's eyes meet hers, filled with understanding. It's as if he knows more than he's willing to say.

"Okay, I'll ask Annie, one of the other nurses down the hall, to check on her," he reassures her. "She is very kind, but if she's not comfortable with where Miss Willa's blood pressure is, we will have to call for the supervising nurse."

He offers her a gentle smile.

"It'll be okay, Miss Mimi."

Mimi nods and sinks into the chair beside Willa, placing her hand over hers. She remembers how this strong hand, this strong woman, once made everything in her world feel right. Now, she holds it in return, hoping to bring the same comfort.

A knock at the door pulls her from her thoughts. A young nurse, probably in her thirties, steps inside, her warm smile immediately easing the tension in the room. Angel follows close behind.

"Hi, Miss Mimi. I'm Annie," the nurse says kindly.

Walking over to Willa, whose eyes are now open, Annie bends down and greets her with a gentle smile. She checks Willa's blood pressure, her movements careful and loving. After a moment, she turns to Mimi.

"Miss Willa seems stable now," she says reassuringly.

Angel grins. "We'll take good care of her. Miss Willa Mae is a pretty special lady!"

As they turn to leave, Mimi calls out, "Angel, can you please keep a close eye on Willa for a few minutes? I need to go to the director's office."

"Of course," Angel replies. "She's been given a little more morphine, so she should be free of pain."

Mimi exhales, giving Willa's hand one last squeeze before rising to her feet.

It's *time*, she thinks.

Mimi and Angel walk towards the door.

"Where's that other nice young man who brought me fried okra?" Willa calls out from the bed, her voice noticeably stronger.

Mimi and Angel turn, surprised by her sudden alertness.

"He's back on the fishing boat, Miss Willa," Angel replies with a grin. "But you and I are going to wait for him to toot his horn when he passes by."

"Ohhhh, that would be a blessin', baby," Willa says. "Now turn my bed a bit and lift up the ..."

As Mimi steps out of the room, Willa's voice trails behind her, already bossing Angel around.

Now that she's feeling better with that morphine, Mimi thought, *Angel's in big trouble.*

She walks down the hall toward the director's office, passing the nurses' station. Relief washes over her when she doesn't see the supervising nurse. Her hands tremble slightly, Willa's words echoing in her mind, "*All you have to do, Mimi, is pray and trust in Jesus, and He will take care of the situation.*"

Mimi sees that the director's door is open. He looks up as she approaches.

"Can I help you?"

"Yes," Mimi replies. "Are you busy?"

"Not at all. Please, come on in and have a seat," he says, gesturing toward an orange chair.

Wow, they're everywhere, she thinks, momentarily distracted by the familiar piece of furniture.

He stands, extending his hand.

"I'm Mr. Rosenbrow, the director here."

They shake hands.

"Hi, I'm Elizabeth Katherine Benoit," she says, settling into the chair, "but you can call me Mimi. I am caregiver and guardian for Miss Willa Mae in room 108."

"What can I help you with, Mimi?" he asks kindly.

Her heart pounds, a storm of emotions swirling inside her. *Be brave, Mimi. Don't let fear control you. Speak truth in love.*

Straightening her back, she presses further into the chair.

"Yes," she says firmly, meeting his gaze. "I'd like to talk with you about a disturbing situation that happened today."

"Of course," Mr. Rosenbrow says, leaning forward in his chair with his focus intently on Mimi. "Please, tell me what has happened."

Mimi senses his genuine concern, the kindness in his voice settling some of her nerves.

"She's been like a second mother to me and my sisters all our lives. Her daughter, Effie, is on her way here soon."

She takes a breath, exhaling softly as she shifts in the chair.

"Well," she begins, choosing her words carefully, "we just arrived this morning, and the supervising nurse has been in our room several times. I have to say ... she's been ... well, quite rude to Willa Mae."

Mimi wrings her hands in her lap. *Come on, Mimi. You can do better.* Willa's words echo in her mind. *Speak out!*

Straightening, she leans forward and places her hands gently on his desk.

"Actually, it's more than rude," she says, her tone growing stronger. "She has clearly shown and voiced a racist attitude, not just toward Willa, but toward others as well."

Mr. Rosenbrow tilts his head, his brow furrowing as he leans forward in his chair. His expression is a mix of disbelief and concern.

"Hmmm ... I'm very sorry to hear this," he says slowly. "This is, um ... quite disturbing. Can you please give me more details?"

Standing, he walks over to close the office door.

"I've only been here a month and am still familiarizing myself with the staff."

He returns to his seat, his focus fully on Mimi.

She takes a deep breath, steadying herself before recounting each ugly confrontation–the supervising nurse's disregard of Willa, the hostility toward AJ, and the way she has spoken to Mimi herself. As she speaks, she sees Mr. Rosenbrow's eyes widen, his jaw tightening.

Mimi feels a shift within her, a quiet yet undeniable strength rising up.

"So," she says, her voice unwavering, "we've decided to remove Willa Mae from this facility tonight." Her throat tightens, but she pushes through. "I'm so sorry that it has to be this way because everyone else here has been so loving, compassionate, and kind, just like my previous experiences with hospice."

Mr. Rosenbrow nods, rubbing his chin in thought.

"I will, of course, look into this immediately," he says. "But may I ask you to possibly wait until tomorrow for ..."

"I'm sorry," Mimi interrupts, her tone firm. "As you know, time is not on our side here, Mr. Rosenbrow. Willa Mae deserves to spend her final days surrounded by love, respect, and dignity."

"Of course," Mr. Rosenbrow says, nodding. "That is in fact, the mission and calling of hospice care. I've never had a complaint of this nature."

"I understand," Mimi replies. "Once again, I've always had incredible experiences with hospice for others in my family. But Willa Mae has endured enough prejudice in her life, and I will simply not stand for her being subjected to it in her final days."

Rising from her chair, preparing to leave, she watches the director intently as he stands.

"Are you from Louisiana, Mr. Rosenbrow?"

"No, I actually just moved here from California. I've never been to the South before."

Mimi studies him for a moment.

"Just a suggestion: you might consider visiting the Louisiana Civil Rights Museum and the Louisiana Civil Rights Trail in New Orleans when you have some time. There's also a Civil Rights trail in Baton Rouge and all over the South. It could help you understand a little better what's happened here over the decades ... and even centuries. There are still, obviously, some ugly echoes that remain today."

He walks around to the front of his desk.

"Yes, thank you for that suggestion. I will definitely try to do that soon. Also, we will help you in any way we can to make sure that Miss Willa Mae's transfer is safe and comfortable."

"Well, I should get back to Willa. Thank you again for your time. And really, everyone else here has been wonderful."

Turning to leave, she suddenly pauses and glances back.

"You know, Mr. Rosenbrow, I was thinking today ... it only takes one person to cast a dark cloud over an entire building."

The weight of her words lingers in the air.

"We'll be packing up soon. My sister will call for a transport for Willa."

Mimi steps out of the office and into the hallway, her heart pounding. As she walks, she grips the handrail, steadying herself against the rush of emotions.

Did those words just come out of me? she wonders. *Thank you, God, for the courage and voice you gave me in there.*

But just as quickly, doubt creeps in. She looks back towards his office. *Maybe I shouldn't have said all of that. What will he think of me for being so outspoken? Silence is sometimes safer.*

As anxiety threatens to overtake her, something catches her eye through the window. A faint rainbow arches over the bayou, soft and barely visible against the afternoon sky.

"Hope," she whispers, Willa's words flooding her mind.

Mimi holds up hope as her banner. She reminds herself ... courage is not the absence of fear. In facing her fears head-on, she overcomes them.

She takes a deep breath, gripping the railing tightly as a wave of lightheadedness sweeps over her.

"Miss Mimi, are you okay?" Angel's voice startles her.

"Yes, um ... I'm fine," she replies, steadying herself. "Thank you for keeping an eye on Willa Mae for a few minutes and for all the love and kindness you've shown her."

Angel chuckles.

"Miss Willa's resting comfortably, though I did see that bossy side you mentioned."

Mimi offers a weak smile.

Angel looks at her with concern.

"Miss Mimi, I think you should go back to the room and rest for a while. You're looking a little pale. I'll bring you some juice and peanut butter crackers," he says, already heading down the hall toward the supply cupboard.

Taking a few deep breaths and feeling a bit steadier, Mimi continues toward the nurses' station, her steps filled with renewed resolve. The supervising nurse looks up, her expression as cold as ever.

"Do you need something?" she asks flatly.

Mimi meets her stare.

"No, thank you, I'm ... I'm fine," she says, continuing to walk past her.

Suddenly, she stops. *No, Mimi. Not this time.*

Turning back, she squares her shoulders.

"Actually, I do need something," she says boldly. Her voice is steady, unshaken. "I need you to show Willa Mae in room 108 the kindness and respect she deserves."

The nurse's expression hardens, caught off guard by Mimi's directness. The other staff at the front desk quickly look down, busying themselves with paperwork.

"We're moving Willa Mae to another facility tonight," Mimi continues. "She deserves dignity, respect, and kindness in her final days."

She starts to walk away, but then glances back.

"And by the way, I let the director know how wonderful and kind the rest of the staff has been."

Walking back towards Willa's room, she catches sight of Joseph in the dimly lit corner of the hall. Their eyes meet. He nods with a gentle smile on his face.

Mimi returns the gesture, watching as he walks away, humming softly.

A choice stands before her: to stay silent on the sidelines or use her God-given voice to stand for what is right. No longer could she ignore a force that had been rising within her over the decades. And she, like the pelican, is spreading her wings, flying higher and higher until gracefully soaring.

Mimi steps into Willa's room and notices crackers and juice waiting on the table. By the window, Willa's bed is slightly turned toward the open air, and Angel stands beside her.

"I see him, Miss Willa," Angel says with a grin. "The Zydeco Zoomer is coming down the bayou."

Willa claps her hands as best she can, her frail movements still filled with excitement. Mimi follows their gaze, looking out to see the boat stop right in front of them. Its horn toots, and the crew is all on deck waving enthusiastically toward the window.

Willa's face radiates pure joy.

Willa softly asks, "You think they'll be catching more of T-Boy's relatives?"

Angel gently pats her hand.

"You can be sure of that, Miss Willa," he replies warmly.

As the sound of the Zydeco Zoomer's horn fills the room, Willa's eyes grow heavy as she begins to doze. Love seems to flow from the bayou, through the open window, and into her heart. Her fading voice whispers, "God is good all the time. What a blessin.'"

Mimi turns to Angel, emotion tightening her throat.

"Thank you, Angel. You and Andre have shown Willa so much love in just one day. I don't know how to thank you."

Angel smiles.

"You can thank me by sitting down," he says gently. "Now drink some of that juice and try to eat a cracker. Miss Willa is stable and doing just fine."

Mimi sinks into the orange faux leather chair, the comforting perch that has become her refuge.

After a quiet moment, Angel speaks.

"We're all sad Miss Willa is leaving tonight."

Mimi glances up. "How did you know that, Angel?"

He shrugs slightly.

"I was walking back with your juice and crackers when I overheard what you said to the supervising nurse."

Mimi exhales, shaking her head.

"I just felt I needed to speak up. I don't even remember everything I said to her."

Angel studies her for a moment, admiration in his eyes.

"I've never heard anyone stand up to her like you did today, Miss Mimi. You spoke truth, and I—we—thank you for that."

Then, with a reassuring nod, he steps toward the door.

"Now, you rest, Miss Mimi."

And with that, he disappears into the hall, leaving Mimi with her thoughts, the sound of the bayou, and the gentle hum of hope.

The phone rings. It's Anna Beth.

"Hey, sis," she says. "Andrew decided he needed to call the director and speak with him, too. You know how much he loves Willa. He's pretty upset about the whole situation. He wanted to back you with support. I hope that's okay."

"It's okay," Mimi says. "We all need to speak out in our own way."

"Well, I'll be there shortly to help you pack up Willa."

As the call ends, Mimi hears the director's voice in the hallway, summoning the supervising nurse to his office.

"Oh, boy," Mimi says quietly. "Here we go."

Needing more paper hand towels in their room, she steps into the bathroom across the hall. As she reaches for them, muffled voices filter through the walls.

Then, the supervising nurse's voice cuts through, sharp and defensive.

"I wouldn't say anything like that."

Mimi's chest tightens.

Returning to Willa's room, she sinks into her chair, trying to process everything that has happened. She glances at Willa, who seems to be sleeping more and more. The weight of time settles heavily on Mimi.

She knows Anna Beth and Effie are finally on their way from the New Orleans airport. Reaching for her phone to call her sister, she hears footsteps coming down the hall.

The supervising nurse walks past the door, her voice loud and cutting.

"It only takes one spark to start a fire, doesn't it?" she says, not bothering to look Mimi's way, but keeps walking.

The words hit their target, but Mimi takes a slow, deep breath. *We'll be leaving soon,* she thinks. But it pains her to think of saying goodbye to Angel and the kind staff who will be left here to endure this toxic person.

Turning toward the window, she searches for the pelican, hoping for a small sign of encouragement.

The cypress knee lies empty.

How odd, she thinks. *He's still not back.*

PART V

"IMAGO DEI"

THE IMAGE MANY TRIED TO ERASE

Eight letters carry the weight of each of our identities and worth. "*Imago Dei.*" These words hold our single holy imprint. They remind us of our shared origin and the unity of our human race. Our shared human dignity and equal value before God. We are "image-bearers of God"—each one of us reflecting the One who made us. That truth can never be erased.

And yet, on December 11, 1967, a document tried—just as many had before it.

The (then) Present-Day Ku Klux Klan Movement Report, issued by men claiming to be rooted "deep in the tenets of the Christian religion"[52]—quoted Scripture in defense of segregation. In that report, they wrote, "God drew the color line and man should so let it remain. Read Acts 17:26 if you please."[53]

But in its true context, Acts 17:26 affirms the exact opposite: that all nations come from one man, and that God determined their times and places so that they might seek Him.[54] It is a verse of unity, not division—of shared humanity, not separation.

Imago Dei.

A holy imprint.

Always was. Always is. Always will be.

CHAPTER THIRTEEN

March 19, 1960

On the murky water's edge of old Bayou Bateau, Mimi and her sisters carefully wrap string around chicken necks, hoping to catch a few crayfish for an afternoon boil. It's one of their favorite Saturday traditions during crawfish season. Mama always drops them off, along with Willa, for a picnic and crawfishing.

Above them, three brown pelicans glide effortlessly over the bayou, their broad wings powerful yet graceful. They move as though in slow motion, each stroke precise, like a well-trained flight team in perfect formation.

Willa watches the majestic birds in quiet wonder, squinting against the sunlight as it dances across the water, making the bayou shimmer like it's filled with thousands of tiny diamonds. The pelicans glide toward the weathered wood pilings, the remains of an old pier lost to a recent hurricane. One by one, they break away from formation, each claiming a piling jutting from the water.

"I feel a tug on my string," Anna Beth whispers, excitement in her voice.

"I see red near your bait," Mary Grace murmurs back. "Bring it up, but not too fast."

"I'm coming with the net," Mimi says in a loud whisper, stepping closer.

As Mary Beth slowly pulls up her catch, bright red flashes beneath the surface, inching closer to the light, and then, with a sudden scurry ... it's gone.

"He got away!" Mary Beth groans, tossing the whole string back into the water in frustration. "They're too fast."

"Wait, look," Mimi says. "He's grabbing it again!" In one swift motion, she swoops the net underneath.

"Got him!" she calls out triumphantly.

Laughter erupts around them.

"Well, that makes three," Mary Grace says, eyeing their small haul in the cooler. "Not much of a crawfish boil."

"I say we just throw 'em back," Anna Beth adds.

With shared nods, they release their tiny catch back into the bayou, watching as the ripples disappear and the crawfish sink back down to rejoin the other bottom-dwellers.

Willa isn't particularly fond of crawfishing, or eating crawfish, but she enjoys the beauty of the bayou, resting beneath the towering cypress trees with moss draping from their branches. She sits on the picnic blanket, grateful for the chance to rest her weary feet after a long week of chores. Keeping an eye on the girls is her main responsibility, but she also cherishes the peace and simple joy of being here.

The bayou gets its name from a French Acadian named Jacque Broussard, who lived deep in the marsh in the early 1800s. Known for his skill in building bateaux, he crafted the shallow-draft, flat-bottomed boats for locals to navigate the endless waterways of Louisiana.

But legend has another story, one that lingers on the misty currents of the bayou. They say Jacque still floats down these waters on nights of a full moon, his bateau gliding silently beneath the cypress trees as he searches for his Chère, his sweetheart who never arrived the night they planned to run away together.

"Mimi, look up at the storm clouds, it's getting dark," whispers Anna Beth, eyes wide with mischief. Look at that old empty bateau across the bayou." Then, with a sudden grin, she adds, "You better watch out! Old Mr. Jacque's ghost is probably in it, looking for his Chère, Jeanne Angelique ... or even better ... maybe ... for you!"

With a sudden shriek, she leaps toward Mimi, laughing as she jumps in her direction.

Mimi runs over to Willa, her eyes wide.

"They're scaring me, Willa."

Willa gives a soft chuckle, shaking her head.

"Oh, don't you let them bother you, baby. Don't believe those stories."

"But, Willa, I just don't think it was very nice of them to say–"

Suddenly, something catches Willa's eye in the distance.

"Mimi," she calls out. "Look up over the bayou, past the trees."

Mimi claps her hands. "It's a rainbow!"

Willa smiles, her eyes warm.

"And do you know who painted that for us today, Mimi?"

Mimi grins. "God did, Willa."

"That's right, baby, the master painter of all creation."

Hand in hand, they walk to the very edge of the water, looking out over the bayou. Storm clouds gather in the distance, but the muted colors of the rainbow still stretch across the sky.

"Willa, I'm going to look for all seven colors and make sure they're in the right order," Mimi says, looking up at the sky. "How many can you count, Willa? You told me there were seven."

Silence.

Mimi gazes up at her, squeezing her hand.

"Willa?" Her voice turns gentle with concern. "Why do you look so sad? Rainbows are pretty. You told me they bring hope."

Without looking down, still gazing at the fading colors, Willa exhales.

"Yes, baby," she murmurs. "That's right, hope."

Mimi brightens. "I always hope, Willa. Like right now, I'm hoping that when we get home, you'll make us some peach cobbler for dessert tonight, even though we don't have crawfish to boil."

Willa finally looks down at her, shaking her head with playful exasperation.

"Now, you know I'm gonna have to spank you for that," she teases. "You better run up to that picnic blanket before the ants get to our M&M cookies for their dessert."

Mimi lets out a squeal and dashes up the bank, laughing as Willa chases after her.

But just before reaching the blanket, Willa slows. She turns back toward the bayou, her gaze lifting to the sky once more. The rainbow is beginning to fade.

She stands still, her heart full.

"I feel you here with me, Clara … and … I miss you. Where are you?"

Willa stands there for a few moments in silence, then slowly turns and walks toward the picnic blanket, softly singing, "God put a rainbow in the sky."

"C'mon, my babies, let's get this picked up. Rain's coming, and I'm sure your mama …"

A horn toots in the distance. Willa looks up.

"Well, there she is," she says.

They quickly gather their picnic supplies and empty cooler, loading everything into the car. No extra passengers coming home today.

As they settle in, Mama glances back at them and shakes her head.

"Goodness, did you girls swim in the bayou today?" she asks. "You're taking a bath as soon as we get home. Daddy and I are going out tonight to a cocktail party."

"Willa, will you be staying with us tonight?" Mimi asks hopefully.

Mama answers before Willa can.

"Willa has a church meeting and can't come over tonight. Mary Margaret from next door is coming instead."

"But Mama," Anna Beth protests, "Willa always walks us down to the River King for ice cream."

"Don't worry," Mama says. "We'll leave money for Mary Margaret to take you. Her friend LuLu will be coming over, too. She's bringing games, and I've already given Mary Margaret permission to take you girls in her car for ice cream."

Mary Grace's eyes light up.

"We get to ride in her red Impala! That's a really cool car, Mama."

Mama nods. "Yes, Mary Grace, I know. She got it for her sixteenth birthday."

"It was her grandparents' car."

"Well, it's still cool," Mary Grace says, crossing her arms.

A thought suddenly pops into Mimi's head. "Willa Mae, have you ever had a red car?" she asks.

Willa chuckles.

"No, baby. The only car I ever had was my two feet. But I did have red shoes once, to put on my feet when I walked to Christmas Eve service."

The girls giggle.

"That's silly, Willa. Your feet can't be your car," Anna Beth says, shaking her head.

"Well, maybe they can if you're the Flintstones," Mary Grace chimes in.

Loud laughter fills the car. Even Mama and Willa can't help but join in.

As they pull into the driveway, Mama glances back at Willa.

"Willa, why don't you go inside and get your things? I'll drive you home. Mr. Benoit is already back, and he can stay with the girls."

Willa nods, stepping out of the car and heading inside. A few minutes later, she returns with her things and settles into the back seat.

They drive toward the other side of town, the road stretching past vast, open cane fields.

"Are you going to spend time with Effie and your momma today and enjoy a nice Saturday afternoon?" Mrs. Benoit asks, glancing at Willa in the rearview mirror.

"Yes, ma'am ... maybe later," Willa replies. "But first, I really need to stop at the grocery store, if you wouldn't mind dropping me off there. Then my car will get me the rest of the way home."

They both laugh, a shared moment of humanity that, for just a second, slightly fades the lines that so often keep their worlds apart.

A KNOCK COMES to the Benoits' front door. Mimi rushes to open it.

Mary Margaret and LuLu step inside, grinning.

"Hey, Mimi! Are you ready for a fun night together?" asked LuLu.

"Yes! And Mama said we could ride in Mary Margaret's red Impala to River King for ice cream."

"We sure can," Mary Margaret replies. "That sounds like fun."

Mama and Daddy give them instructions for the evening before saying their goodbyes. Soon, they pull up to River King, the parking lot overflowing. It's Saturday night, and hardly a parking spot is open.

"Look," LuLu says, nodding toward a group near the entrance. "The basketball team is here hanging out."

Mary Margaret smirks. "And we know what that means, your crush is here."

"Whatever do you mean?" LuLu says, flipping her hair dramatically.

Mary Margaret raises a brow. "You know exactly what, or rather, who ... I mean."

LuLu lets out a laugh.

"Of course I do. Only the most gorgeous boy at Bayou Grande High School."

"Tony might be a hunk, but he's not very nice," Mary Margaret says, crossing her arms.

"Well, he's nice to me," LuLu replies with a shrug. "He always holds the door open for me when I walk into class."

Mary Margaret's expression darkens.

"Maybe he holds the door for you like a Southern gentleman, but I think behind all that handsomeness is something ugly."

She hesitates, lowering her voice. "I've heard stories about his family, Lu."

LuLu sighs. "Well, if I were you, I wouldn't believe everything that ..."

A sudden knock on the car window makes them all jump.

It's Tony.

LuLu quickly rolls down the window, her face lighting up.

Mary Margaret huffs. "Come on, girls. Let's go get our ice cream."

The four of them pile out of the car, leaving LuLu in dreamland.

As Mimi skips toward the front window to get in line, someone catches her eye.

Around the back of River King, she spots Effie, who is standing with Wilton in a long line, waiting to order.

"Effie! Hey, Effie!" she calls out.

Without hesitation, Mimi runs over. She's seen this line many times—seen how everyone in it is colored. She knows it's a rule but she can't quite understand why. Not really. All she knows is, it doesn't feel fair.

"Hi, Mimi," Effie greets her with a smile. "You getting ice cream too tonight?"

"Yes, but our line isn't as long as yours. You want to come get in line with us, Effie?" She asks, looking over to Wilton, who is staring at her.

Effie shakes her head gently. "It's okay, Mimi. We can wait here."

Wilton smiles down at her.

"But at our window, you can get your ice cream faster and I don't think it's fair for you when…"

Having heard enough of the conversation, Wilton looks down in aggravation.

"Because, Mimi," he flares, "our skin is not the same color as yours."

Mimi moves closer to Effie, her lower lip trembling as she stares at the ground.

"Stop it, Wilton," Effie whispers angrily. "She's only seven. She doesn't understand."

Effie softens her voice.

"It's okay, Mimi. We have to wait in this line," Effie says, bending down to whisper. "It's a rule—remember? You know about those from school," she adds with a wink. "But thank you for thinking of us."

Effie shoots Wilton another warning glance.

Wilton shifts uncomfortably. He sighs, glancing down at Mimi.

"Yeah, um … thanks for thinking of us, Mimi." His words sound forced, like they don't quite belong to him.

From the front window, a voice calls out.

"Mimi, come tell me what you want! We're next in line."

She hesitates, looking up at Wilton with sad eyes.

"I gotta go."

Wilton looks at Effie who is still glaring at him, and then back to Mimi. "It's okay, Mimi," he says. "We can still be friends."

Feeling confused, Mimi turns away and walks back toward the front window.

Effie watches Mimi leave, then turns to Wilton, her voice tense.

"Just great, Wilton. Don't take it out on her. It's not her fault. She doesn't understand these rules."

Wilton clenches his jaw.

"Of course, she probably understands. I'm sure she sees things that don't make sense to her, things that confuse her. Like how everyone in this line is colored and standing at the back window. And how everyone in her line is White and getting served faster at the front." He exhales, shaking his head. "Hasn't she ever come with your momma to get ice cream before?"

"Yes, but she probably just waits for them while they get their ice cream. I don't know," Effie murmurs.

Wilton rubs a hand over his face.

"I'm sorry I got so angry, Effie. It kind of comes out of nowhere sometimes."

Effie sighs. "Yeah, I can see that."

"I didn't mean to take it out on sweet little Mimi," Wilton admits. "I'm just tired of it all. Maybe you don't mind picking up your hamburger at the back window, next to the trash cans. Maybe you don't mind climbing up the back steps of the Majestic Theater, entering through the side door, and sitting in the balcony."

His voice is laced with a heavy bitterness that he's been carrying for far too long.

Effie just watches Wilton, trying to understand his anger, but also knowing that tonight, it has already hurt someone who didn't deserve it.

After a moment, Wilton turns to Effie, his voice calmer.

"Do you know what my neighbor had to tell her six-year-old when he asked why they always have to sit in the balcony?" He pauses, shaking his head. "She told him that colored people have better eyesight than White folks. That we need to let White people sit closer so they can see the screen better." His jaw tightens. "She didn't have the heart to tell him the truth."

Effie exhales, looking at Wilton with a deep sigh.

"That's really sad," she says.

"It's more than sad, Effie. It's not right. None of this is right, and it's surely not 'separate but equal.'"

Effie frowns. "What do you mean?"

"Plessy v. Ferguson is what I mean."

"Oh geez, here we go," Effie mutters, taking a deep breath.

"What?" Wilton challenges. "This is a big deal. That Supreme Court decision from 1896 ruled that racial segregation didn't violate the U.S. Constitution—as long as the facilities for each race were equal in quality."

"We're getting the same ice cream as the Whites, Wilton. Just at a different window."

Wilton's voice rises.

"Effie, stop pretending this is okay. You're not seeing the point!"

"Not so loud," Effie says, "you're getting worked up again."

He wipes his forehead with his hand and lets out a sigh.

"Okay. I'm calmer," he says, "but compare our school to the White school. They get brand-new books. We get the old, used ones. They get new desks. We get their broken-down leftovers. They get a new building, and we have a run-down old airport hangar." He then gestures toward the front of River King. "And why are we still standing here while that White line moves twice as fast?"

"Okay, okay, Wilton, I see your point," Effie says, holding up a hand. "But do you have to go off about it tonight? Can't we just have fun? You get so angry these days." She looks up at the night sky. "Look at the stars. The night is beautiful. I just want to walk up the levee with our burgers and shakes, sit on the bench, and watch the full moon."

Wilton takes a long, deep breath, then reaches for her hands. His voice softens. "Okay, Effie. That sounds really good." He pauses. "And I'm sorry—for what I said to Mimi, and then to you." He shakes his head. "And don't get me wrong—I love our school, I love our teachers. It may be separate, but there's nothing equal about it."

Effie smirks.

"You just had to throw that in, didn't you, Wilton?"

Before he can answer, his eyes look past her.

"Unbelievable," he mutters.

Effie turns. "What now?"

"Look who's begging at the back window."

Effie's eyes land on a familiar scruffy figure.

"Scrappy," she laughs.

"And there goes Miss Rosie, putting out a plate of scraps for him," Wilton says. "And here we are, standing right beside him."

Effie shakes her head.

"Really, Wilton? Please do not get started yet again."

From the parking lot, they hear Mimi.

"Bye, Effie! Bye, Wilton!"

They both wave as they step forward in line.

Wilton glances at Effie, lowering his voice.

"I promise, we're going to have fun tonight. But I need to tell you something while we wait."

Effie raises an eyebrow.

"What is it?"

Wilton leans in slightly.

"I spoke with my cousin, Jer, a few days ago. He overheard that there's going to be a sit-in a week from Monday at Kress." His eyes lock onto hers. "Let's go, Effie."

Effie stiffens. "And sit at the White lunch counter?" She shakes her head. "No way I'm doing that, Wilton."

"No. Let's go to support them," he says. We'll sit at the colored counter."

Effie studies his face.

"You're serious?"

Wilton nods. "Jer and I got into it over this. But after cooling down, I changed my mind. I called him and apologized. I want to be there. And I want you to come, too." He squeezes her hand. "For your pappy, Effie."

Effie hesitates, looking to the front at the White line before looking back at Wilton. "I'm scared."

"I know," Wilton says gently.

She exhales. "But ... okay, Wilton. I'll go. But only to sit at the Colored counter. And I'm only doing this for my pappy and because I know Dr. King doesn't want us sitting on the sidelines." She pauses. "He wants us to be maladjusted."

Wilton grins. "Well, look at you, Miss Effie Rose, using your big words."

Effie rolls her eyes. "Now you're just making fun of me." She crosses her arms. "What time should I meet you?"

"How about we meet at the ferry landing at six-thirty that morning? The ferry leaves at seven. We'll meet Jer in Baton Rouge." He glances at her. "I'll give you all the other details then."

Effie bites her lip. "Okay. But I have to think of what to say to my momma."

Wilton shrugs. "Maybe just tell her the truth. You're not doing anything wrong."

"Next!" Miss Rosie calls from the back window.

As they step forward to place their order, Effie exhales.

"I don't know, Wilton. I have to think about it." She manages a small smile. "Let's just go enjoy our supper on the levee."

AS MARY MARGARET pulls out of River King, she glances up at the sky.

"Girls, the stars are so bright tonight. You want to see them even better?"

"Yes!" they all chime in excitedly.

"LuLu says she knows a place where there aren't many lights, and the stars are really bright."

"We're not going to Bayou Bateau, are we?" Mimi asks hesitantly.

"Don't be such a scaredy-cat, Mimi," Mary Grace teases.

"Calm down, everybody," Mary Margaret says. "And don't worry, Mimi. We are not going to Bayou Bateau to see Jacque in his bateau looking for his Chère."

"I'm still scared," Mimi murmurs.

"Nothing to be afraid of," LuLu reassures her. "Wait till you see how bright the stars are out there."

They drive over the railroad tracks, heading out of town.

"Willa says the stars are windows into heaven," Mimi says, leaning forward in excitement. "I can't wait!"

As they drive farther, the night seems to grow darker.

"I'm sure the spot to pull over is just up ahead," LuLu says.

"You've been saying that for almost ten minutes now," Mary Margaret mutters.

Mimi shifts in her seat. "I'm really scared now, Mary Margaret."

Mary Margaret exhales, lowering her voice.

"I don't want to scare the kids or get in trouble for going so far out of town. I'm turning around."

"Well, I know the Boudreaux house is just ahead," LuLu says. "You could turn around in their driveway."

Mary Margaret gives her a side glance.

"Convenient, LuLu. Are you hoping for Tony to see his Chère again?"

LuLu rolls her eyes as Mary Margaret turns onto the long gravel driveway.

But what they see is nothing they expected.

Beyond the house, in the field, a massive bonfire blazes. Silhouetted against it, a group of figures stands in masks and pointed hoods.

"That's a big bonfire," Mary Grace says, her voice uneasy.

"Why do they all have masks on their heads?" Anna Beth asks, eyes widening.

"Is it a party?" Mimi asks.

"It's a big party," Mary Grace murmurs, though something about it feels wrong.

Mary Margaret grips the steering wheel, her pulse racing. She looks at LuLu, her voice shaking.

"We gotta get out of here. Now!"

She slams the car into reverse. The tires spin in the loose gravel, kicking up dust.

"It's the Ku Klux Klan," LuLu whispers. "Hurry, Mary Margaret. Go, go!"

Somewhat out of sight, near the wooden gate leading to the large field, two men in white robes and pointed hoods stand side by side by a parked truck. Within seconds of seeing the girl's car, they strip off their robes, fling them over the gate, pull their hoods off but keep their masks on, and bolt into the pickup.

LuLu gasps. "Back up now," she yells. "I think they're coming after us."

"I am," says Mary Margaret. "I'm trying not to hit the bushes!"

"I'm scared now, too," Anna Beth whimpers.

"We're fine," LuLu says quickly, forcing a calm tone. "It's just a game we're playing."

Mary Margaret finally reaches the road and peels out toward town.

LuLu looks back. Her breath catches in her throat.

"They're coming after us, Mary Margaret. And fast."

Mary Margaret's grip tightens on the wheel. "Girls, get down on the floor."

"I'm scared, too," Mary Grace says, her voice trembling.

"Who's coming after us?" Mimi asks.

"Quiet girls! Just stay down," Mary Margaret says, her voice tight with panic.

"You're fine," she adds quickly. But she doesn't believe her own words.

Mary Margaret glances at LuLu. "I can't believe it's the KKK?" she whispers.

"What's the KKK?" Mimi asks, her small voice barely audible.

"Shhh, quiet," someone from the front murmurs.

The truck picks up speed, pulling alongside them. Mary Margaret tries to slow down to let them pass, but when she does, they slow down too.

The window of the other car rolls down.

An angry voice shouts through the white mask from the dark cab of the truck.

"Stay away, or else."

A chill runs through the car.

Then, just as quickly, the men's car slows, makes a sharp U-turn, and speeds back toward the bonfire.

Mary Margaret's hands tremble on the wheel.

"What just happened?" LuLu whispers.

Mary Margaret exhales sharply. "And I'm sure you know whose house that was?"

LuLu swallows hard.

"Yes. Tony's."

Mary Margaret presses down on the gas.

"Let's just get home."

She takes a shaky breath and turns back toward the back seat.

"Girls, you okay?" she asks. "You can come up now."

Slowly, the girls sit back in their seats, their faces pale, their eyes wide.

"I want to go home," Mimi says, her voice breaking into a sob.

"We're almost there," Mary Margaret assures her. "You're okay, Mimi. We're safe."

Mimi wipes her eyes. "Why were they chasing us?"

Mary Grace stares out the window.

"I think they didn't want us there," she murmurs.

"It was only for grown-ups," LuLu adds.

"Why did they have scary masks on their faces?" Anna Beth whispers.

Mary Margaret's jaw tightens. "Let's just be quiet, girls. Until we get home."

Mary Margaret and LuLu exchange a glance.

Neither says a word.

ONCE THE HOUSE is finally quiet and the girls are asleep, Mary Margaret turns to LuLu as they sit on the couch in the family.

"You know I have to tell the Benoits about this," she says. "I can't keep it from them. The girls will surely say something, too."

LuLu nods.

"Did you lock all the doors?"

Mary Margaret's face is tense.

"Yes."

"I'm a little scared now, too," LuLu admits. "That was really creepy."

Mary Margaret exhales, pressing a hand to her forehead.

"I've heard stories about the KKK, but I've never actually seen them," she says.

"I guess I didn't think they existed here," LuLu whispers. "Not in our little town."

Mary Margaret shakes her head. "From what I've heard, they're everywhere in the South."

She hesitates, lowering her voice. "I've heard my parents talk. My dad says he's shocked at some of the people in town who are involved. Business owners, city leaders. People you'd never expect."

LuLu swallows.

"I don't even want to know."

Mary Margaret's face hardens.

"Well, I do." She pauses. "And my daddy does. He was threatened by them once."

LuLu's head jerks up. "What?"

Mary Margaret nods.

"They warned him because he was hiring too many Colored workers at our Mobile gas station." Her voice drops to a whisper. "But he thinks it had more to do with the fact that we're competitors. The other gas station is owned by the local Klan's second-in-command." That's what my dad said.

LuLu stares at her in disbelief.

The room feels colder now.

The girls hear the door open and a quiet, "Hello... we're home."

Mary Margaret glances at LuLu, her stomach twisting with nerves.

"I need to tell them, Lu," she whispers.

Mrs. Benoit steps into the room, her face warm but observant. "Hi, girls. Is everything okay? How was the night and your trip to River King?"

Mary Margaret and Lulu share a nervous glance.

"Well, umm....," clearing her throat, "the girls enjoyed every last lick of their cones," Mary Margaret says with a forced smile. Then her voice falters.

"But... there's something else I need to tell y'all."

Mr. Benoit, who has just walked in, exchanges a glance with his wife.

"Okay," he says, his voice steady. "Let's sit down. Was there a problem?"

"Kind of," Mary Margaret admits, her hands twisting in her lap. Then, slowly, she begins to tell the whole story, the bonfire, the masked men, the chase.

As she speaks, the Benoits' faces tighten with growing alarm.

When she finishes, Mr. Benoit exhales deeply, his expression unreadable. "Well... that's very concerning," he says.

Mary Margaret's eyes well up.

"I'm so sorry, Mr. and Mrs. Benoit. You don't need to pay me."

"It's not about the money, Mary Margaret," Mr. Benoit says firmly. "Next time, ask before you go anyplace other than where we discussed."

"I wasn't planning to go that far," she insists. "I just wanted to show the girls the stars without the town lights."

"You still should have asked our permission," he says. "You put the girls, and yourselves, in danger."

Tears spill as she nods.

"I never meant to do that," she chokes up. "I was just turning around in a driveway to head back to town."

Mrs. Benoit quietly reaches for a Kleenex and hands it to her.

Mr. Benoit leans forward, his voice softer but firm.

"And what driveway was that? Do you know?"

For the first time, LuLu speaks. Her voice is hesitant.

"It was... the Boudreaux's home."

A brief silence fell over the room.

"I see," Mr. Benoit says, exchanging a look with his wife.

"You know I'll need to talk to your parents about this," he continues.

"I understand," Mary Margaret says, wiping her eyes. "I've just never seen anything like that. I mean... I've heard my parents talk about it."

"It's always kept hidden," Mr. Benoit says. "That's why they had guards by the gate. You two need to get home now. I'm sure this was just as frightening for you both."

Mary Margaret nods.

"I'll talk with the girls tomorrow, and I'll also be speaking with your parents," he adds. "You might want to tell them yourselves before they hear it from me."

Mary Margaret hesitates, then asks in a whisper, "Do you think they'll come after us again, Mr. Benoit?"

"No, Mary Margaret," he says with reassurance. "They just wanted to scare and intimidate you."

He reaches into his pocket and hands her five dollars.

"I can't take that," she says, shaking her head.

He presses it into her palm.

"Take it. Now head home and get some sleep."

Mrs. Benoit walks them to the door and closes it gently behind them.

She stands still for a moment, staring at the door. She turns to her husband.

"Shot," she says, a nickname given to him in high school, "this really concerns me."

Mr. Benoit sighs, running a hand through his hair.

"We knew we wouldn't be able to keep this part of our world from the girls forever, Harriet."

"It's so true, says Mrs. Benoit, "something like this was bound to happen. The girls see it," she continues, "but they don't fully understand it. They hear things at school, but they can't always make sense of it. And now... this."

Mr. Benoit leans against the kitchen table, his expression heavy. "I just don't know," he admits. "But what I do know is that we can't keep pretending it's not happening all around us. Like we're blind to it."

Silence lingers between them.

"I still worry about your Mama at the cleaners," breaking the silence.

Mrs. Benoit folds her arms.

"But how can we stop her? She's not going to stop doing what's right or using her voice to speak up."

"That's more than we can probably say," Mr. Benoit says.

He looks at his wife, his voice almost a whisper.

"How can we teach our girls to have a just voice, Harriet, when sometimes...we can't seem to find our own."

CHAPTER FOURTEEN

~ "What Color is God's Skin" by
Tom Wilkes and David Stevenson

March 20, 1960

"Hi, Willa! Hi, Effie!" Mimi shouts, sticking her head out of the back seat window of the Benoit family's 1959 blue Buick LeSabre.

It's Sunday morning, and the Benoit family is on their way to Mass at Holy Comforter Catholic Church.

"Hey, baby," Willa calls back, waving with a warm smile.

Before Mimi can call out again, her mother's voice cuts through the air.

"Elizabeth Katherine Benoit, put your head back into this car," Mama scolds. "Don't yell out the window at people.

It's not proper. Haven't you learned anything at Sears Charm School? You'll mess up your hair, and we're headed to church. Goodness gracious, what will people think?"

"But Mama, it's just Willa and Effie! I bet they're going to church too."

Ignoring the warning, Mimi keeps waving her hand excitedly out the window–until a gust of wind catches her satin bow.

She gasps as it lifts off her head, twirling through the air before floating down the street.

Before Mimi can react, Effie takes off running, her Sunday shoes tapping against the pavement as she chases after it.

Mimi watches, hopeful, until the bow lands in a puddle of water.

Effie slows to a stop, picks it up, and wrings it out as Willa Mae catches up with her. "You sure do love those Benoit girls, don't you, Momma?"

Willa nods, a soft smile tugging at her lips.

"I sure do, Effie. After all, I've helped raise them from birth."

"Yes, I know, Momma," as they continue walking down Magnolia Street toward church.

INSIDE THE CAR, Anna Beth cannot stop laughing.

Across the seat, Mary Grace tugs on Mimi's dress and yanks her back inside the car. Still distracted, Mimi leans forward.

"Daddy, they look hot. Can we go back and give them a ride to their church?"

Her father shakes his head.

"They'll be okay, baby. They're almost there."

Mimi frowns.

"Mama, why can't I ever go to church with Willa and Effie? They love Jesus, too. And I like the songs they sing at their church. They're better than ours."

Mimi lifts her hands over her head, trying to shape them into a halo as she bursts into song.

"This little light of mine, I'm gonna let it shine, this little …"

"Daddy, can you please make Mimi stop?" Mary Grace groans. "She's being so loud."

She crosses her arms and shoots a glare at her sister. "How do you even know what songs they sing? You've never been to their church. Plus, only Colored people go to that church."

Mimi shrugs.

"She sings them when she's at our house folding clothes and making biscuits. Haven't you heard her? They're fun songs, and we can dance to them. We can't dance at our church."

Mary Grace huffs. "Mimi, if you ever start to dance in church, I will be so embarrassed. I will not …"

"Okay, okay, girls, that's enough," Mrs. Benoit interjects. "Settle down and be quiet. We're almost to church. Help Daddy find a parking place."

As Mrs. Benoit checks her lipstick in her compact mirror, Mr. Benoit's voice lowers.

"Look who's here. If it isn't Mr. Jim Crow himself."

Mrs. Benoit snaps the compact shut, her lips pressing into a thin line.

"I really don't like being around that man," she murmurs, slipping the mirror back into her handbag. I didn't care for him at all when we were in school either.

"So many good people on the city council ... and how did he get there?"

From the back seat, Mimi's ears perk up.

"That's the man who told Willa to get up from the bench on the levee," she says, brow furrowed. "Daddy, why is Mr. Jim Crow so mean?"

Mr. Benoit sighs, shaking his head.

"There's nothing wrong with that child's hearing, that's for sure," he mutters. Then, more firmly, "That's none of your concern, Mimi. And that's not really his name. It's Mr. Boudreaux."

Mr. Benoit parks the car, and everyone pushes open their doors.

"Okay, girls, let's cross the street," Mama instructs. "Watch for cars. Anna Beth and Mimi, you hold Daddy's hands. Mary Grace, you come with me."

The family steps onto Magnolia Street, the paved road that stretches from one end of town to the other, only about a mile long.

Here in the heart of town stands the old white wooden Catholic church, rising high and proud. Its square bell towers flank the entrance, and the central nave roof is crowned with a simple wooden cross. Just below the peak of the front roof rests an ornate, round, flower-shaped, stained-glass window, each pane a vibrant petal of color. Built in 1928, its bells ring several times a day, their tones reverberating across the town. Inside, a grand pipe organ towers in the choir loft, filling the space with commanding yet comforting music. This is the same church where Mr. and Mrs. Benoit were married—high school sweethearts who once walked the halls of the school just up the road. As they approach the church, Mimi grips Daddy's hand even tighter, pressing against his side.

"Mimi, why are you pushing against Daddy so hard, baby?" Mr. Benoit asks, glancing down at her.

Before she can answer, he notices Bubba and his family walking toward them. Bubba Boudreaux was raised in Bayou Grande. He is a successful businessman who owns a large lumber company outside of town and was elected to the city council. He also attended Bayou Grande High School along with Mr. and Mrs. Benoit.

Bubba's gaze locks onto him, and Mr. Benoit straightens his shoulders.

"Morning, Bubba. How are you today?" His tone is polite, but cold.

"Morning, Shot," Bubba replies. Shot was the nickname Mr. Benoit earned back in high school, as he rarely missed a basket. His team had gone all the way to the state championship, and the name had stuck ever since.

Bubba shifts, lowering his voice slightly.

"Millie told me the Colored are using the White bathroom at your mother-in-law's cleaners." He shakes his head. "Now you know that goes against the law. It's just not the way we do things down here."

Mimi hides behind her daddy as Bubba's voice grows firmer.

"Now, we will not continue to give Miss Jeanne Marie our business if this nonsense keeps up," Bubba says. "I'm surprised you allow it, Shot. You know the Colored carry diseases. Further, if this continues, I'm sure it will be stopped ... one way or another."

He crosses his arms, his voice dropping lower.

"Jim Crow laws must be enforced. Did you also know that sometimes the Colored wait on White customers in the front of the cleaners? She treats them like they're equal."

Mr. Benoit waits, unmoved.

"Are you done, Bubba?"

Bubba exhales, adjusting his collar.

"I guess I am."

Without a word, Mrs. Benoit walks up from behind, takes Mimi by the hand, and leads her a few feet away to join the other girls.

Mr. Benoit nods, his voice calm but firm.

"Well, I've got two things to say to you, Bubba, before we're all late for church."

"Miss Jeanne Marie has worked hard since her husband died to keep that business running. Those Colored employees work day in and day out, harder than some White folks I know."

His eyes linger on Bubba for just a second longer than necessary.

"And I'm proud of how she treats them."

He steps forward slightly, lowering his voice just enough for only Bubba to hear.

"Now, we're standing right in front of God's house this morning, about to walk inside. And I've heard many times inside those walls that God is the judge and no other, so why not take this matter up with Him? I'm sure He might just have a few things to say."

Mr. Benoit adjusts his suit jacket.

"Have a nice Sunday with your family, Bubba, and enjoy Mass."

Daddy looks over and says, "Harriet ... girls ... let's go."

"This isn't the end of this Shot," came a stern voice from behind.

Mr. Benoit continues to walk through the church doors without saying a word.

Mimi clutches Daddy's hand as they step into the church. Stopping first at the holy water bowl, Mimi dips her fingers in and makes the sign of the cross, just as Mama taught her.

Out of the corner of her eye, she notices Miss Annabelle, who is Black, at the smaller holy water bowl. She places the tips of her fingers gently into the water.

Mama had often reminded Mimi and her sisters, "We always use the larger bowl."

Mimi never really understood why. It was just another rule.

Miss Annabelle is one of Mimi's favorite lunch ladies at school. She always wears the same black chapel veil on her head, its edges stitched with tiny purple butterflies. Mimi always wanted one just like her. On Fridays, when the cafeteria serves fish sticks, Miss Annabelle sometimes slips Mimi an extra biscuit, though they never quite compare to Willa Mae's.

As if sensing her thoughts, Miss Annabelle glances over and smiles. Mimi grins back, giving a small wave. She watches Miss Annabelle as she joins her friends in their usual seats in the back row, just as they do every Sunday. To Mimi, it was familiar and always comforting to see them there.

She walks beside Daddy, leading the way while the rest of the family follows. They move down the aisle, passing rows of churchgoers fanning themselves, until they reach their usual seats in the front.

Mass begins as Miss Hazel sits on her red bench high in the choir loft, playing the opening hymn. The organ's deep, rich notes flow through the long copper pipes above her, filling the church as the congregation joins in song.

Father Joel moves slowly through the aisles, swinging the burning incense, the heavy scent of smoke and spice trailing behind him.

Mimi wrinkles her nose. It always smells bad.

She tugs at Mama's sleeve, lowering her voice.

"Mama, I don't feel so good. I think I'm gonna faint."

Mama reacts instantly.

"Sit down and put your head between your knees. I'll get you some ammonia."

She rummages through her purse, pulling out her pill case. With practiced ease, she cracks open a smelling salt and holds it under Mimi's nose.

Across the pew, her sisters stare.

Mary Grace leans toward Daddy, whispering.

"Why does Mimi always get faint? It's so embarrassing."

Mr. Benoit looks over to Mimi with love. *She is such a fragile child*, he thinks.

As the ammonia clears her head, Mimi breathes in slowly, waiting for the dizziness to pass.

Father Joel is now speaking from the pulpit as Mimi comes to, the sharp scent of ammonia still lingering in her nose.

"... and we know that love and kindness are two things Jesus calls us to show to others," Father Joel says, his voice steady and clear. "From our scripture today, we see that the Good Samaritan showed kindness, love, and a helping hand to a Jew.

"Now, I am going to use a strong word today. In my extensive research, I read that the Samaritans and Jews hated each other at that time. Two men had already passed by the beaten, stripped, and robbed man who was left for dead on the side of the road. Then the third man, the Samaritan, stopped to care for and bandage the injured Jew.

This is loving your neighbor as yourself, as God calls us to do. And it's not always convenient or maybe even comfortable. But God often nudges us to step out of our comfort zone into a place where He is at work."

Father Joel rubs his chin.

"I'm thinking that maybe it wasn't convenient for the Samaritan to stop that day on the road. He was obviously headed somewhere, maybe even in a hurry. Then, he encountered a 'God interruption.' He chose to do something different that day that the other men did not do. He not only stopped, but he stopped for someone who looked different from him.

"I recently observed something similar on the streets of our town. One day, through my rectory window, I saw a teenage girl walking down Magnolia Street crying. Rushing down the stairs, I headed out the front door to see if I could help. As I walked down the sidewalk towards her, I saw a car pull over to the side of the road."

Mr. and Mrs. Benoit glance at each other.

Father continues, "I could hear him asking her if she was okay. He was White, she was Colored. When I got to the car, I asked if there was anything I could do. She explained to us that she had lost her wallet on the ferry and that all of her money was in it. She thought maybe it had been stolen.

"The man said that he would be happy to go back to the ferry if it was still docked to see what he could do. She seemed comforted by that and extremely appreciative. I invited her back to the rectory for something cool to drink while we waited.

"Unfortunately, she didn't end up finding her wallet. But that day, in a nation and especially here in the South, where cruelty and hate can often prevail, I witnessed a kindness and trust between the two of them as they spoke. When you walk out these doors this morning into the streets of our town, take a look around you to see where there might be oppression and injustice happening in your neighbor's lives. Will you just walk around it, as the Levite and Priest did, pretending you don't see it? Maybe it's just safer to be a bystander. Or will you be courageous enough to be an instrument of God's love?"

The church fell into complete silence. You could hear a pin drop.

Mimi glances across the aisle, her eyes landing on Mr. Bubba sitting in a pew on the other side.

He didn't show love and kindness to Willa on the levee bench, she thinks, *making her get up even though we were there first. And this morning, he wasn't kind to Daddy.*

"So," Father Joel says, "I want to end my homily by leaving you with the most important commandment He has given to us."

He looks down at the large Bible in front of him.

"The most important one, answered Jesus, is this: Hear, O Israel: The Lord our God, the Lord is one. Love the Lord your God with all your heart and with all your soul and with all your mind and with all your strength. The second is this: Love your neighbor as yourself. There is no commandment greater than these." (Mark 12:29-31)[57]

Before she knows it, Mass is over, and the congregation files out of church.

Stepping outside, Mimi instinctively clings to Daddy's leg again.

Mrs. Benoit leans in, whispering into Mr. Benoit's ear.

"She always seems so fearful."

Daddy kneels slightly, looking Mimi in the eyes.

"Mimi, why don't you go say hi to Miss Annabelle? She's your favorite lunchroom lady. You love her! And did you know she and Willa are good friends, too?"

Mimi glances over. Miss Annabelle is chatting with her friends.

Without hesitating, she runs over.

"Excuse me, Miss Annabelle."

Miss Annabelle turns with a warm smile.

"Why, Mimi, you have such nice manners."

Mimi nods proudly.

"That's because Mama makes me go to Charm School."

"Well, you're doing a good job, Mimi."

Miss Annabelle studies her for a second.

"What happened to your bow? You always have a satin bow in your hair."

Mimi sighs, "It flew out the car window and into the water puddle when I was waving to Willa Mae and Effie on their way to church."

The women all laugh.

Standing among them, Mimi feels safe.

She leans in and whispers, "Miss Annabelle, what's for dessert tomorrow?"

"You and your desserts, Mimi. Well, it's a surprise, but I'll tell only you."

She bends down and whispers in Mimi's ear.

But before Mimi can react, her little body stiffens.

Without thinking, she grabs Miss Annabelle's hand and hides behind her.

"What is it, baby?" Miss Annabelle asks, concerned.

She follows Mimi's gaze and spots Mr. Bubba staring at them.

Mimi's voice barely rises above a whisper. "That man scares me."

Just then, Daddy's hand clasps around hers.

"Mornin', Miss Annabelle. Ladies."

His grip on Mimi's hand tightens slightly.

Glaring at Bubba, "Mimi, I think we're gonna head home now."

"You ladies have a good Sunday."

Mimi lets Daddy lead her away, but she can still feel Mr. Bubba's eyes on them as they walk to the car.

On the drive home, Mimi listens from the back seat as Daddy speaks to Mama in a low voice.

"Harriet, I'm a little worried about Jeanne Marie, and the cleaners. I don't want this to get to the point of rocks being thrown through her window … or worse."

Mama exhales softly.

"I understand, Shot. But nothing can stop my mama from doing what she thinks is right. She's strong-willed, and when she sets her mind to something, she follows through. You know that."

She pauses for a moment, glancing out the window.

"I think it's because she can empathize with the Colored people," she continues.

"I used to hear my grandma talk about how the Acadians were forced from their homes and land in Nova Scotia, brutally deported by the British. Families were torn apart, just as the Africans were." She shakes her head. "My mother never forgot those stories. The strong will of the Acadians runs through her blood. She's a survivor, and she gathers survivors around her. She wants to give them a hand up, just as her ancestors were sometimes given a hand up. She works awfully hard to show kindness and love."

Mr. Benoit glances at her, eyebrows slightly raised.

"Wow, Harriet. I've never heard you talk quite this way."

Mama presses her lips together, nodding.

"My mama will stand up to Bubba in her own way, and we can't stop her," she says firmly.

"Just like Father Joel spoke about in his homily at church today, she's that man, only in this case, the Good Samaritan woman who stops on the side of the road to help those in need."

Mr. Benoit lets out a quiet chuckle.

"Sounds like Jeanne Marie could've given that sermon better than Father Joel."

Mama smiles slightly.

"My mama gives that sermon every day. She proclaims it not just with her bold words, which sometimes get her into trouble, but with her courageous actions."For a moment, they sit in silence, both staring ahead through the front windshield. As they pass the cleaners on Magnolia Street, Mr. Benoit finally speaks again, his voice solemn.

"I just still worry about her, Harriet."

CHAPTER FIFTEEN

"I remember feeling excited when I received the letter in the mail—like it was a college acceptance. I was one of seven Black students accepted to integrate Port Allen High School in Louisiana in 1968. We were making history, hoping to pave the way for those who'd come after us. Once we arrived, the white students were anything but kind. Some were cruel—verbally, even physically. They spit on us; others showed disgust with a look or avoided eye contact. Someone even stuck me with a pin in the hallway. It was horrible. And yet one classmate, who refused to participate in the torment, would nod or smile when we passed—that small gesture meant more than he probably knew. Years later, I went to the 50th reunion, with great hesitation. But, many came up to me to say they were sorry and asked for forgiveness. That brought a little healing—for me, and for them. Maybe there is hope for our future."[58]

-Brenda Slack LaMotte, Retired Drug Enforcement Administration

March 22, 1960

A gentle breeze drifts through the open breezeway at Holy Comforter Catholic School as Mimi waves goodbye to her friends, watching them climb onto the bus that will carry them home to the rural stretches of the parish.

She and her sisters attend the only Catholic elementary school in town, nestled right beside the Catholic Church.

Today is choir practice, but Mimi is still too young to join. She'll have to wait until her sisters are finished so they can walk home together.

Being Catholic in 1960s Southern Louisiana means rules... a lot of them.

At seven years old, Mimi knows how to follow those rules. She doesn't always understand them, but she obeys without question.

Still, sometimes, something feels off to her, and today is one of those days.

"Elizabeth Katherine."

Mimi stops, looking up at Sister Agatha, the after-school monitor.

The nuns always use her full name, just like Mama does. But she prefers just Mimi.

"Be sure to stay on the school grounds while you wait for your sisters to finish their practice," says Sister Agatha.

"Yes, Sister," she replies politely.

Clutching the books to her chest, she steps onto the playground, already eager to dive into her latest book,

Mystery Ranch, the fourth in the Boxcar Children series. She loves these stories–she loves to read.

"Mimi, come swing with us," calls Debra from across the playground.

"I want to read," Mimi calls back. "Maybe later."

Mimi walks to the bench against the fence in front of the rectory and settles in for an adventure. She opens to the first chapter, quickly losing herself in the story. She is soon transported to a ranch out West, joining in the hunt to solve a mystery. The rugged Arizona landscape, dotted with cactus and rocky outcrops, unfolds in her mind–until a sudden movement pulls her back to the playground in Southern Louisiana. From the corner of her vision, someone steps out of the side door of the rectory.

A young Colored girl, about Mimi's age, sits in the grass on the outside of the fence. Mimi studies her for a moment. *I've seen her before,* she thinks. Mimi knew it wasn't at school–her school didn't have any Colored children. The girl watches Mimi's friends swinging, her gaze fixed on their playful interactions. Just as Mimi turns back to her book, she notices the girl looking at her.

Mimi smiles. The girl shyly smiles back. And then, it clicks. Mimi remembers where she's seen her before. Without hesitation, she gets up from the bench and walks toward the fence, her book still in hand.

"Hi," Mimi says, stepping closer to the fence. "I think I saw you at my MawMaw's cleaners the other day. You were sitting in the delivery truck."

The girl looks down, her voice barely above a whisper.

"Yes, I saw you, too. My daddy works at the cleaners."

Mimi tilts her head. "Why were you in the truck all by yourself?"

Slowly lifting her head, she shrugs slightly. "Sometimes I walk there after school and do my homework in the truck until my daddy is finished with work. Your MawMaw says it's okay." The little girl smiles, "She's real nice."

Mimi smiles back. "She is."

Mimi shifts the book in her hands. "My name is Elizabeth Katherine, but my friends call me Mimi."

"My name is Dione, but my friends call me DeDe." DeDe's gaze drops to Mimi's book. "Are you reading The Boxcar Children?"

Mimi nods eagerly. "Yes! I have the newest one, *Mystery Ranch*."

DeDe's face lights up with excitement. "I just finished *The Yellow House Mystery*! I can't wait to read *Mystery Ranch*, too, but I haven't been able to find it yet."

"It's silly we're talking through the fence?" Mimi says.

They look at each other and giggle, DeDe covering her mouth with her hand.

"I'm waiting for my sisters, and Sister Agatha says I can't go outside the school grounds," Mimi explains.

DeDe nods. "My momma told me I can't go inside the school grounds. I have to stay on this side of the fence."

Mimi frowns slightly. "Where's your momma?"

"She cleans the priest's house every week," DeDe says. "Sometimes I come with her and watch the children play after school through the fence. If I have homework, Father Joel lets me do it at his kitchen table."

Mimi brightens. "I like Father Joel."

Mimi suddenly remembers the bag of M&Ms in her pocket.

"Hey, I just got some M&Ms from the candy machine. Want to share them with me?"

"Yes," says DeDe with delight.

"I'll hand you some through the fence."

Mimi reaches through the chain-link opening, her hand filled with the colorful candy.

"Oops!" she laughs as a few M&M's slip through her fingers, scattering onto the grass.

DeDe laughs as she begins to pick them up. For a moment, the fence between them is forgotten. With a handful of M&Ms, DeDe reaches out to hand a few back through the chain-link. Suddenly, a ball crashes against the fence right where they're sitting. Mimi jumps.

Across the playground, Ricky, a classmate of Mimi's, and his friend, Joey, run over to retrieve it. DeDe quietly keeps picking up the candy without making eye contact with Ricky or Joey, passing each piece back to Mimi through the fence.

Ricky smirks, nudging Joey. "Hey, Joey, those M&Ms are gonna have germs all over 'em."

Joey shrugs. "So what?"

Ricky's smirk fades, "Well, my pop says they carry diseases."

"Who carries diseases?" Joey calls out with concern.

Mimi feels a chill as Ricky leans in and whispers loud enough for everyone to hear.

"That n–girl does."

Mimi cringes. That word! She knows that word. A word she and her sisters were never, ever allowed to say. They were taught it was wrong. Very wrong. If that word ever came out of their mouths, punishment would be immediate.

Grabbing the ball, he turns to Mimi, eyes gleaming with something mean and ugly.

And then he starts to sing.

"Mimi is an n–lover, Mimi is a …"

"Richard Boudreaux."

The sharp and commanding voice cuts through the air. DeDe and Mimi look up. Sister Agatha stands over them, towering in her black 'habit,' the heavy rosary around her waist still swinging from her swift walk over to him. Her grip on Ricky's arm is firm.

"Come with me, young man."

Without another word, she leads him away. Mimi and DeDe watch in silence as Sister Agatha walks Ricky toward the principal's office. Mimi turns to DeDe, seeing the fear in her wide eyes.

"Hey, DeDe, you want some more M&M's?" she asks, hoping to bring back their lighthearted moment.

DeDe's eyes gloss with unshed tears as she shakes her head.

"I need to go," she murmurs.

Without another word, she turns and runs toward the side door of the rectory, disappearing inside. Mimi sits frozen, clutching the few pieces of candy DeDe had handed her.

Filled with fear and sadness, she wonders, *This was all my fault? I shouldn't have shared my M&Ms.* She glances toward the rectory and thinks, *If I hadn't, Ricky wouldn't have said that really bad word that made DeDe cry.*

Opening her hand, she looks down at the candy DeDe had passed back through the fence to her, her palm colored with melting red, blue, and green.

"*I wonder if maybe DeDe does have germs?*" she thinks.

Passing the trash can on the playground, Mimi looks around and then quickly throws away the M&Ms, wiping her hands on the side of her blue skirt. Confused and heavy-hearted, she walks back to the bench, opens her book, and lets the story carry her away—somewhere very far from here.

She isn't lost in her book for long. A man's loud voice, followed by a child's crying, snaps her attention. Mimi stiffens, glancing across the playground. Beyond the front gate, a truck idles. Ricky is climbing inside, his face streaked with tears, the man shouting at him. Mimi's body tightens—she recognizes the same man who had spoken harshly to Willa on the levee and been mean to her daddy at church.

"I don't care if you use that word—just don't get caught. You hear me?" the man yells, shoving Ricky hard against the truck seat. Mimi sits frozen on the bench, heart pounding, unsure of what to do. She wishes her sisters would hurry so they can go home. She puts her book down on the bench, pulls her knees close to her chest, and begins to cry.

Mimi feels a sharp anger at Ricky for the word he called DeDe—so ugly, so wrong. And yet, beneath that anger, a quiet sadness stirs, and in the soft, tender corners of her young heart, she doesn't yet understand why.

UNSHACKLING THE SOUL

For over four hundred years, shackles took many forms. First, they were made of iron—binding the hands and feet of the enslaved during the horrors of the Middle Passage and slavery. Later, during Jim Crow, the shackles remained, though they looked different. They showed up as signs on water fountains, laws that denied dignity, poll taxes, systems built to oppress and dehumanize. These were both emotional and psychological. Just as real, just as cruel. Yet each generation stood on the perseverance of those who came before—"surrounded by a great cloud of witnesses."[59] They were emboldened by God's hand and upheld by His almighty power. And there were two things no shackle could ever hold: their souls and the mighty wind of the Holy Spirit that blew through them with unrelenting strength.

CHAPTER SIXTEEN

-Tarabu Betserai Kirkland

Monday Morning, March 28, 1960

Effie | Day of the Sit-In

Effie awakes to the sound of the fog horns on the river. It is an uninterrupted chorus of low, hoarse groans finding its way through the thick fog that is hanging over the river this morning. It's always a sure sign that the ferry boats will be running late. Looking through the window, Effie takes in the dark, gloomy sky. She feels it settle inside her too, a heaviness matching the morning's fog. Today is the day of the sit-in at S.H. Kress Department Store in Baton Rouge.

Ignoring the tight knot in her stomach, she focuses on what she'll wear. But uninvited thoughts keep creeping in, nagging at her, making her question if she's really doing the right thing. Since it's a Monday off from school for a teacher's workday, she plans to tell Momma that she's going across the river to town to window-shop with friends.

After all, she thinks, *we're not doing anything wrong. We're just going to provide moral support to the students. At least, that's what she keeps telling herself.*

Effie glances over at the other bed—Momma is still sleeping.

"That's not like her," Effie whispers, concern creeping into her voice.

Momma is always up by now, she thinks, *moving through her morning routine. She never misses work.*

Effie takes a quick glance at the clock. It's five fifty-five. Effie knows it takes Momma almost thirty minutes to walk to the Benoits' house, and they expect her by six-thirty. Effie realizes that she can't let Momma or Gramma Nellie see her leaving for the ferry this early. They will wonder where she's going. But Wilton is waiting, and she can't afford to be late. Effie considers telling Momma that the girls are meeting at a classmate's house for breakfast first.

This is getting complicated, Effie thinks. *I didn't think this through very well.*

I need another plan, one that won't look suspicious.

She gets up and walks over to Momma's bed and leans down.

"Momma, you okay?"

No answer.

Effie gently shakes her.

"Momma," she calls a little louder.

Disoriented, Willa turns quickly towards Effie.

"Ohhhh, baby," Willa says, looking at the clock, "I fell back asleep," she murmurs in alarm. "I gotta get dressed for work, but I felt some bad, and I had to lay back down."

Effie presses a hand to her forehead.

"Momma, you're burnin' up. I'll get you some aspirin."

Willa groans, trying to sit up.

"What time is it, Effie?"

"It's a few minutes after six," Effie says, looking over at the clock again.

Momma pushes back the covers, her voice weak but determined.

"I gotta get up and get to the Benoit house. The girls will be wantin' their breakfast soon."

"Momma, you can't go to work. Mrs. Benoit can cook them breakfast," says Effie.

"Ohhhhh heavens no, that is not a good idea, baby. And the girls would surely not eat it."

"Then those spoiled girls can have cereal," scoffs Effie.

Momma looks out the window and lets out a big sigh.

Looking back at Effie as though ignoring the comment, "Miss Harriet can't take care of things at that house or the girls without me."

"Effie," Momma says, looking her in the eye, "you need to go to the Benoits' and be there for me."

"Me?" questions Effie, with eyes wide, "No ... no, no, no. Last time I was there covering for your doctor's appointment, it was a disaster. The girls are sweet and all, but Mrs. Benoit is so particular about the housework and meals. Momma, I'm supposed to be going across the river to town today with the girls to window shop and get a malt."

"Effie, you can go across that river another day. Helpin' me out is much more important than window shopping.

"Yes, of course it is, Momma."

Effie stares out the window, watching the dampness drip down the glass pane, a remnant of the thick morning fog.

If only Momma knew what I was really doing today, she thought, *and what if ...*

"And the Benoits surely need your help," Willa's voice interrupts her thoughts.

"I know Momma, but ..."

"No buts, Effie," she says, coughing. "Now hand me the phone."

Another hoarse cough echoes through the room as Effie reaches for the phone.

"I need to tell Mrs. Benoit I'm sick and you're on your way. That's all there is to it. I can't go take care of my babies with this cough and fever. I'll get 'em sick."

Effie lets out a deep long sigh as she stretches the phone cord over to Momma's bedside.

Her babies, Effie thinks. *It seems Momma will do anything for those girls.*

Knowing the matter is settled as she hears Momma talking with Miss Harriet, Effie gets dressed quickly, then heads out for the thirty-minute walk to the Benoit home as the patches of fog dampen her face. With every step down Magnolia Street, she thinks of Wilton, waiting for her at the ferry landing.

"He'll probably think I chickened out when I don't show up," she whispers to herself as she hurries on.

As she crosses over Ferry Landing Road, she glances up toward the gravel ramp, cars already lining up for the next ferry. There's no time to take a detour to let Wilton know she won't be going to the sit-in today. She's already late.

In some ways, Effie feels relieved. She isn't even sure she wants to be there. Who knows how dangerous it might be?

She quickens her pace, the familiar sights of town passing in a blur. *Maybe I'm just trying to please Wilton,* she thinks. As she approaches Mr. Tookie's corner grocery store, she sees him unlocking the front door, preparing for the day.

Everyone knows he serves the best snowballs in town, any flavor of syrup you could want. But Effie and her friends have never been able to enjoy one.

His store sits too deep in the White section of town.

JUST ON THE OTHER side of the levee, Wilton waits at the Ferry Landing.

"Where is she?" he grumbles to himself, turning around constantly, glancing toward the footpath, hoping to see her.

He had said six-thirty on the dot, and now it's six forty-five. People are already making their way onto the ferry, the Spirit of the Mississippi. The plank has come down for walk-ons, but Wilton knows it'll be running late because of the fog.

The foghorns were having a heyday, yet Wilton was already having a bad day.

It's sticky, muggy, and his frustration grows by the minute.

I gotta get on, or I'll miss meeting Jer at our spot to talk and make a plan before we head to Kress, he thinks.

"Where is she?" he mutters aloud, his voice swallowed by the mist.

Glancing up the path one more time, he spots someone in the distance.

But the fog is so thick he can't make out who it is.

Hopefully, it's Effie, he thinks.

As the figure emerges through the mist, Wilton's stomach drops. It's not Effie at all. It's Skunky Hebert. Everybody in town knows Skunky.

Wilton shakes his head. *I can't ever let Effie know I mistook her for Skunky,* he thinks, *or she'll never speak to me again.* Despite his nerves being on edge, he lets out a quiet chuckle.

Skunky shuffles down the levee path in his usual coveralls, a slight odor trailing behind him. No surprise there, after all, Skunky de-skunks skunks to sell them as pets. At some point, nearly every child in town has begged their parents for one of Skunky's "pet" skunks—including Mimi.

Resigned to the fact that Effie has chickened out, he lets out a sigh, staring toward the fog-shrouded Baton Rouge skyline, uncertain of what the day will bring. With a final glance up the path, he crosses the narrow wooden plank and boards the ferry.

***

EFFIE FINALLY REACHES the back screen door of the Benoit home. Her mouth falls open as she looks in astonishment through the screen, the girls not yet noticing her. She smelled the burnt toast before even walking up to the porch, but somehow, it looks even worse in person.

On the table, the grits sit horribly dry and stiff, untouched on the plates.

At the table, Mimi sniffles, swinging her legs back and forth with her mama's oversized red high heels dangling from her feet.

"These don't taste like Willa's eggs," she whimpers to herself, lip quivering.

Mary Grace, still in her pajamas, stares at the TV.

Under the table, Anna Beth happily munches on Frosted Flakes straight from the box, sharing handfuls with Joe Boy, their collie dog, who isn't even supposed to be inside the house unless there's a hurricane. Today, the hurricane seems to be happening inside.

And Mrs. Benoit? Nowhere to be found. Effie briefly considers backing up slowly, turning around, and sprinting back up the levee to meet Wilton.

Anything would be easier than this.

She stands frozen for a second, watching the disaster unfold.

Putting her hand to her forehead, she thinks, *How does Momma do this every single day?* Before she can process it all, Mimi glances toward the screen door.

"Hey, Effie!" she shouts. "Will Willa Mae be here soon? Is she feeling better yet?"

Effie struggles for words as she hesitantly opens the door and walks in.

"Umm, Mimi ..." she starts, but Mary Grace cuts her off.

"Of course she isn't feeling better, Mimi," she says, rolling her eyes. "She just got sick today. So stop crying. It's annoying."

Then, with exasperation, she yells down the hall—

"Mama! Can you please make Mimi stop crying?"

"Is that Effie I hear?"

Mama calls from the bedroom.

"Yes, ma'am!" Effie responds. "It's me."

"Oh, thank goodness," Mama shouts up the hall. "I was about to reach my wits' end!"

Really? Effie thinks. *You've been with your own girls for less than an hour.*

Mrs. Benoit appears in the kitchen doorway, wrapped in a pink silk robe and fuzzy pink slippers.

"Thank you, Effie. What would I have done without you today?"

Effie glances around the room and holds back a sigh. *The thought of that actually scares me,* she thinks.

Mama looks around at the chaos before letting out an exasperated sigh.

"For heaven's sake, Anna Beth, stop feeding Joe Boy Frosted Flakes and get that dog out of the house."

Then, turning back to Effie, she hands her a neatly folded piece of paper.

"I made a list of chores for you today that your momma usually takes care of. I thought that you would find it helpful."

Effie glances down at the list written on elegantly monogrammed stationery.

"I'll be back in bed, finishing my coffee," Mama announces, rubbing her temple. "This whole morning has truly given me a headache."

As she starts to leave, she pauses.

"Oh, and your momma's blue plastic cup is behind the sink if you want some sweet tea or lemonade. And of course, feel free to use the bathroom at the cleaners whenever you need it."

Effie stands frozen, still gripping the list, unsure whether to laugh, cry, or walk straight out the door. She shakes her head slightly, the weight of the morning already settling over her.

Really ... How does Momma do this?

Without warning, Mr. Benoit rushes through the hallway kitchen door, suit on, briefcase in hand.

"Bye, girls! I'm late. Be good for Effie."

Effie barely has time to process the whirlwind of movement before he's already heading for the door. She takes in the entire scene–burned toast, barking dog, children in chaos–as if she's suddenly trapped in a *Three Stooges* TV episode. Except this isn't a comedy. This is real. A little too real.

Mr. Benoit stops, taking time to acknowledge Effie.

"Thank you so much for being here, Effie," he says, his voice filled with sincere gratitude.

She nods hesitantly.

"Mrs. Benoit has a bad headache. Try to keep the girls quiet as they get ready for school. It's been a rough morning for her."

He glances toward the bedroom before lowering his voice slightly and handing her a piece of paper.

"Here's my work number if you need me."

Effie stares down at the slip of paper, then back up at him.

"Yes, sir. You're welcome, Mr. Benoit. I'm sure we'll be just ... fine."

Joe Boy lets out a sharp bark, snapping Effie back to reality.

The back door slams as Mr. Benoit hurries out.

Before Effie can even take a breath, she feels a small tug on her dress.

Looking down, she finds yet another piece of paper being placed in her hand.

Mimi looks up at her with tear-streaked cheeks.

"Effie, I colored this rainbow for Willa this morning. She loves rainbows."

She pauses, holding out the drawing.

"But you can have this one. I'll color another one for you to bring home to Willa, so she'll feel better and come back tomorrow to make us breakfast."

Effie softens, taking the drawing.

"I'm sure she'll love that, Mimi. And thank you for mine."

With her purse still hanging on her arm, Effie takes her first step into what is not a movie, but stark reality.

She walks to the closet beneath the stairs and carefully hangs her purse on the hook, right where her momma always puts hers.

For a fleeting moment, she thinks, *Maybe I could hide in here.*

But a stronger voice rises from deep within.

You can do this, Effie Rose. You are strong. Do it for Momma.

A new understanding settles in. She's been here barely ten minutes, and already, she has an entirely new appreciation for how hard her momma works for so little.

Taking a deep breath, Effie straightens and steps into action.

"Okay, Anna Beth," she says firmly. "Close up the Frosted Flakes and take Joe Boy outside."

"Mary Grace, turn off the TV and get your school uniform on."

"Mimi, you're coming with me. I'm sure your teacher wants you wearing your saddle oxfords, not your mama's red high heels."

Mimi pouts slightly.

"I was playing pretend, Effie." She says, click-clacking obediently down the hall behind Effie like a baby chick.

While Mimi switches her shoes, Effie slips two of the three papers into her pocket and glances over the chore list Mrs. Benoit gave her.

1. Help the girls dress for school and see them off.
2. Pick up the kitchen and mop the floor.
3. Make beds.
4. Polish Mr. Benoit's black dress shoes.
5. Prepare a pimento sandwich for Mrs. Benoit's lunch (help yourself to a sandwich too). Paper plates in the drawer.
6. Sweep the back patio, front porch, and sidewalk.
7. Bake an after-school snack for the girls (M&M cookies–recipe in the box).
8. Go to the cleaners and pick up laundry.
9. Polish the silver on the dining room table (silver polish and rag there).
10. Iron the dining room tablecloth for the weekend party.
11. Cook dinner–tuna noodle casserole (recipe in the box under casseroles–the one with crushed potato chips on top).

Ask me if you have any questions. Thank you.

Gripping the list, Effie's hand drops to her side, shaking her head.

"How can Momma do all this in one day?" she whispers.

No wonder her feet need soaking in Epsom salt when she gets home, she thinks.

A firm resolve settles in. *This is not my destiny. I will not do this after I graduate. I have bigger dreams.*

Straightening her shoulders, Effie softly calls out to the girls.

"Okay, time to get to school," she says, feeling her strength return.

She waits with them on the back porch until their thirteen-year-old neighbor arrives to walk with them to school.

As always, they take the shortcut down the back sidewalk, past the pecan tree and chicken yard. When they reach MawMaw's cleaners, they spot her through the side window, scrubbing clothes in the big sink. She smiles and waves with a soapy hand. The girls excitedly wave back before continuing toward Magnolia Street and on to Holy Comforter Catholic School.

Effie walks inside the house, determined to check off every task on Mrs. Benoit's list before the day is over. She will carry on her mother's incredible work ethic, yet Detroit is sounding really good to her right about now.

By mid-afternoon, Mrs. Benoit is feeling better and out the door. Effie finishes making the tuna noodle casserole and places it on the stove, ready to be cooked at supper. She steps out the back door, briskly walking toward the cleaners to use the bathroom. The whole way, her mind stays on Wilton.

Did he go to the sit-in? Is he okay? Is he upset with me?

By the time she returns to the house, she forces herself to refocus.

"Stay on task, Effie," she murmurs.

The girls' after-school snack is baked and hidden, just like Willa always did.

It's a game of hot or cold that Willa plays with the girls every afternoon. The closer they get to their snack, the warmer they are, until they finally find their treat.

Today's prize? Willa Mae's famous M&M cookies.

Effie smiles, picturing their excitement.

She's heard about this game many times from Momma. But no matter how hard she tries, she can't recall a time when Momma ever played it with her. Shaking the thought away, Effie checks the list. Only two tasks remain: polishing the silver and picking up the laundry.

That can wait until after school.

We'll go to the cleaners together, she thinks, *and the girls can visit with their MawMaw.* Effie reaches for Momma's blue plastic cup behind the sink and pours herself some sweet tea. She takes a long sip, letting the cool drink refresh her.

After today, and it's not even over yet, she has a whole new respect for her momma.

CHAPTER SEVENTEEN

"If there is no struggle, there is no progress."[61]

-Frederick Douglass

Monday Afternoon, March 28, 1960

Effie | Day of the Sit-In

Chaos erupts.

The back screen door slams, schoolbooks thud onto the kitchen table, and Joe Boy tears through the house, his paws skidding across the wooden floors.

Effie barely has time to take it in. The house has been so peaceful, with Mrs. Benoit at her Garden Club meeting. Now, school is out and the quiet is gone.

She wipes her hands on a towel, having just finished polishing the silver in the dining room. The girls are home. And by the sound of it, they aren't alone.

Effie remembers what Momma always says—how the neighborhood children love stopping by after school for a "Willa Mae after-school snack." She was known for them.

"Effie, we're home!"

Anna Beth's voice echoes through the house.

Stepping into the kitchen, Effie sees a mix of familiar faces and some new, all brimming with anticipation.

"Hi, Effie! Can we go find our snack?"

Mimi asks, bouncing on her tippy toes.

"Give us a hint," Anna Beth pleads.

"Are we hot or cold standing here?" one of their friends chimes in.

Effie grins, crossing her arms.

"You are very cold," she teases.

With that, all six girls take off down the hall.

"You're getting warmer!"

Effie calls after them, laughing. "Probably even hot at this point."

She knows they're close.

Then, a sudden scream–

"Effie! Effie! Hurry, quick!"

Mary Grace's alarmed voice rings through the house. Effie's heart jumps as she rushes down the hall. Reaching the bedroom, she stops short. There, right in the middle of Mary Grace's bed, sits most of the after-school snack, just where she left it. But someone else has beaten them to it.

Joe Boy lies sprawled across the bed, crumbs scattered around him like evidence at a crime scene. A large cookie is clamped between his teeth as he looks up, wide-eyed, guilt written all over his brown and white furry face.

"Oh my," Effie says, shaking her head.

Laughter erupts around the room. Mary Grace struggles to shove Joe Boy off the bed, but the stubborn collie refuses to part with his tasty treasure. Effie steps in, swiftly retrieving the plate and what's left of the cookies. Joe Boy quickly bounds off the bed and out the bedroom door, clutching his spoils.

"Okay, everybody, back to the kitchen," she orders. "I think there's enough left for each of you to have one."

Mary Grace wrinkles her nose.

"Well, I don't want one. Joe Boy's slobber and germs are all over them. And my bed."

Effie shrugs her shoulders, "Suit yourself."

What a complete disaster, she thinks.

After cleaning up Mary Grace's bed and banishing Joe Boy to the backyard, the neighborhood children trickle back to their homes.

Effie exhales, finally catching a moment of peace.

"Who wants to go to the cleaners with me to pick up the laundry?" she asks. "You can say hi to your MawMaw."

Mimi and Anna Beth immediately perk up, eager to go. Mary Grace stays behind, choosing to work on her homework before Mama returns from her meeting.

As they head down the back sidewalk, the girls chatter beside her, but Effie's mind drifts elsewhere.

Wilton, she thinks. *Will he think she chickened out? Is he okay?* The questions swirl in her head, lingering as they pass the old pecan tree and approach the side door of the cleaners.

Mimi and Anna Beth dart past the conveyor belt, where freshly pressed clothes hang neatly in clear plastic bags, waiting for pickup. They love slipping beneath the line of bags, hiding under the cool shade of the swaying garments. Even Joe Boy has been known to curl up under there, enjoying the breeze whenever the belt moves.

Reaching MawMaw's sewing machine, her usual spot for mending and alterations, they find her chair empty. They hurry to the front counter.

There, standing behind the register, MawMaw is already engaged in conversation with Mr. Pierre's wife, Bunny.

Anna Beth grabs a few nickels from the ceramic cup MawMaw keeps under the counter, her usual stash when the girls want a gumball or Coke.

"Hi, MawMaw! Hi, Miss Bunny!" Mimi chirps as she hurries over to the red-and-white Coca-Cola vending machine. She and Anna Beth love the thrill of pulling the lever and watching the glass bottle clatter down. With their cold, icy drinks in hand, they settle on the bench beside the counter, their feet swinging.

While trying to read the clear letters under their Coke bottles without spilling a drop, Mimi notices movement outside.

Through the large front glass windows, scratched and clouded from being boarded up during countless hurricanes, she spots an older boy—maybe fourteen—peering inside.

"Anna Beth," Mimi whispers, nudging her sister. "Look at that Colored boy outside."

Anna Beth glances up just as he disappears.

"You're seeing things, Mimi," she says, more interested in her drink. "But look, my Coke bottle is from New Orleans! Where's yours from?"

Mimi barely hears her. Just then, the boy's face reappears, looking toward the counter.

"There he is again," she murmurs, watching him closely.

As Miss Bunny finishes her transaction and heads for the door, MawMaw also catches sight of the Colored boy looking through the window.

MawMaw waves her hand for him to come in.

He hesitates, his bare feet shifting against the hot pavement. He quickly steps inside, unsure of what to do next.

MawMaw's voice is gentle as she looks at him.

"Can I help you with something, son? Do you need some water from the fountain?"

Before he can answer, the front door swings open, and in strides Bubba to pick up his clothes. He stops abruptly, eyes narrowing as he takes in the boy standing just inside the front lobby of the cleaners.

"Boy, what are you doing coming in through the front door?" his voice booms. "You need to leave. Right now."

Mimi and Anna Beth don't make a move on the bench, their small hands gripping the cold glass bottles of Coke. They know Mr. Bubba, and he scares them. Neither of them dares to move. Instead, their eyes dart to MawMaw, searching for her reaction. When she speaks, her tone is different from the sweet one they're used to. This one is firm and unwavering.

"He is on my property now, Bubba," she says, gazing at him.

Then she turns back to the boy, her voice softening.

"You don't need to leave, son. Come on in. What is it you need?"

The boy hesitates, his bare feet barely crossing the threshold, his head down, as if too afraid to meet anyone's eyes.

MawMaw walks around the counter to where the boy is standing. Looking at him with gentle eyes, she softens her voice.

"Son, look here at me. Tell me what you need?"

The boy hesitates, "I ... umm ..." wringing his hands in front of him, "I was ..." glancing over to Bubba, now glaring at him with piercing eyes.

His voice now barely rises above a whisper.

"I was wondering if you might have any jobs for me? I heard you hire colored people and give them good jobs. And umm ..."

Bubba shifts his stance, his expression hardening. The boy swallows hard, then blurts out, "I'm a really hard worker."

The words tumble out in a hurry, as if he knows he might lose his chance if he doesn't speak up quickly.

MawMaw doesn't flinch.

"What's your name, son?"

"Alonzo," he mumbles, still staring at the floor. "But my family calls me Brother."

A sharp voice cuts over him.

"Boy, I told you to leave. You don't belong here," says Bubba, lowering his voice and staring right at Alonzo. "Enough troubles been goin' on today from you Colored, we don't need more."

On the bench, Mimi moves closer to Anna Beth. The tension in the front lobby is thick. The girl's eyes dart to MawMaw again, searching for reassurance.

She nods at them with a calm smile before turning back to Bubba, lifting her chin high.

"I assume you are here to pick up your clothes, Bubba."

His mouth tightens. "I am."

Without missing a beat, she turns back to Alonzo.

"You sit right here in this chair, son. We'll talk in a minute."

Alonzo does as he is told, quickly seeking the haven of the chair, eyes still looking down.

Bubba huffs, shifting his weight, but MawMaw ignores it. She commands the room now, her presence palpable.

"Mimi, get Alonzo a Coke," she instructs, her tone leaving no room for question. "Anna Beth, get him a gumball from the machine."

The girls scramble to their feet, eager to obey.

MawMaw moves behind the counter and to the back to retrieve Bubba's clothes, but before she can reach for them, Miss Lucy has already pulled them from the conveyor belt.

As MawMaw takes the bundle, her eyes glance toward the back of the shop.

Effie stands frozen, eyes wide. Doretha and the other pressers peek through the rows of hanging garments, watching the standoff unfolding before them.

Everyone is watching.

Miss Lucy hands MawMaw the clothes, her eyes filled with apprehension.

Without the slightest hesitation, MawMaw takes them and turns to Bubba. She holds his gaze as she places the bundle in his arms. He pays, with a continued angry scowl on his face.

The room stays silent.

The only sound is the sharp ring of the cash register drawer sliding open, followed by a resounding click as it slams shut beneath MawMaw's firm hand, an unspoken message that echoes through the room, loud enough for everyone to hear.

MawMaw drops the change into his hand, her eyes locked on his, making it clear she's not intimidated. Bubba's jaw tightens, his eyes dark with indignation.

"This is not the last of this, Jeanne Marie," he mutters.

Then, without another word, he turns and marches out the door.

Mimi watches him go, pushing even closer to Anna Beth, a knot tightening in her stomach. She knows that he is not a nice man, not the way Father Joel says people should be.

Anna Beth speaks up.

"He's a mean man, MawMaw."

Without flinching and with a firm tone, she says, "God is the judge of us all, Anna Beth."

She walks through the pass-through of the front counter toward Alonzo, who sits safely in his lobby chair staring down at the floor, as if afraid to move.

MawMaw bends down towards him and gently asks, "Can we call you Brother like your family does?"

"Yes, ma'am," he murmurs, still looking down.

MawMaw nods.

"Do you go to school?"

He shifts in his seat.

"No, ma'am. I need to work to help my family out."

MawMaw takes a deep breath, adjusting her glasses as she looks over him out the window.

"Well, how old are you, son?" she asks.

"I just turned fourteen. I help when it's sugarcane harvest with bundling the cane, and Mr. Pierre gives me jobs sweepin' out front the café and cleanin' his windows."

MawMaw smiles, "Well, it sounds like you are a hard worker.

"Yes, ma'am, I am," with more confidence in his voice.

She gently pats his hand, "Well, I probably have some jobs for you to do. I could sure use the help."

In a moment of excitement, Brother stands and lifts his eyes to hers, a glimmer of a smile as his shoulders ease. The weight he carries seems just a little lighter.

"I would really like that," he says.

MawMaw looks down, noticing his bare feet, calloused and raw against the floor. She exhales slowly, a deep ache settling for a moment in her heart, a familiar reminder of the hardships around her. Then, just as quickly, she lifts herself from the weight of what she sees. With a strong resolve and a cheerful voice, she says, "But first, there's something real important we need to take care of."

Brother glances up, confused.

"We're going down to Henry's Shoe Store. You need some work shoes, son. I don't want you hurting yourself walking around here barefoot."

Reaching for her purse, "I'll get my car. You sit right back down here and wait. I'll pick you up out front."

As MawMaw turns to leave the cleaners heading to her house, she sees Effie, Doretha, Estelle, and all the pressers just staring at her.

"Come on, now," she says, "we're not gathering for a fais-dodo here this afternoon. We have work to do. And be sure to get yourself some chicken gumbo from the heating drum when you need a snack."

"Miss Jeanne Marie," Doreatha calls out as she passes her.

MawMaw pauses.

"You done a good thing, you know. That young boy's daddy went up North like so many other Colored folk to find work, only to get himself killed. Now he's left a wife with four children to tend to on her own."

MawMaw glances back at Brother, shaking her head as she walks toward the hall.

"All those little lambs of God we've turned our backs on."

From that day on, Brother spent many years working in the back, pressing clothes and helping with other odd jobs for MawMaw and the family.

"Let's go, girls," Effie calls out to the girls on the lobby bench. "We gotta get back to the house."

Mimi and Anna Beth race past her, darting between the presses, bursting through the back door of the cleaners and into the chicken yard, with Mimi shouting back over her shoulder.

"Okay, Effie, but first we need to check Henrietta's eggs! She always lays the prettiest ones!"

Anna Beth suddenly stops, spinning back around toward Effie, a Coke bottle in her hand, spilling soda with every step.

"Oh! I forgot, here's your Coke, Effie! We got you one, too." she says, breathless, handing it over.

Effie takes the sticky glass bottle, eyeing the half-empty drink.

"Thanks for getting me one, I think," she says with a small smile.

"And look, Effie," Anna Beth adds, as she takes off back to the chicken yard. "Your bottle's from Jackson, Michigan ... wherever that is."

Effie stares at the label, her mind drifting. *How far is that from Detroit?* She wonders.

Suddenly, something seems off as she turns toward the back of the cleaners.

It is too quiet. There is no hissing of the presses.

Where is everyone? She thinks. *They were just here.*

Looking to the far back, a quiet group huddles around the biggest press, the one that hisses the loudest when steam releases. Today, it's silent. Only whispers fill the space.

Effie moves closer, spotting Doretha among the group. Concern is written on every face.

"What's going on?" Effie asks, her voice uneasy.

Doretha steps forward, her expression heavy.

"My husband, Louis, just came from the ferry landing. He heard about something big happening in Baton Rouge at Kress. Some kind of protest."

Effie's stomach tightens.

"Was anyone hurt? What else did he hear?"

Doretha sighs.

"The police broke it up. Some were injured. Some were arrested."

Wilton, she thinks, a surge of panic washing over Effie.

"Come on, Effie!" Mimi's voice rings through the open window, jolting her.

"We got Henrietta's eggs! Let's go home. We want to ride our bikes down the boulevard!"

Effie swallows hard, trying to pull herself together.

"Okay, I'm coming, girls," she says with a shaky voice.

She turns back to Doretha, eyes welling up.

"Wilton went to Kress today … I need to find out if he's okay."

Doretha places a gentle hand on Effie's arm.

"We gonna put our trust in Jesus, as your momma always says, and He will take care of the situation. Things are stirring, baby. And I feel it's only just begun."

As Doretha heads back to her press, her voice, filled with both heaviness and hope, can be heard throughout the back of the cleaners.

"Some things we can't stop because they're meant to happen. Maybe, just maybe, this is all part of God's plan. Like I've heard Preacher say when waiting for the ferry, 'justice flows like a mighty river. You can't stop it when it's from the hand of God.'"

Amens could be heard coming from the presses.

Effie looks away as tears slip down her cheeks. She walks home in silence, her heart heavy with thoughts of Wilton. Anna Beth and Mimi walk beside her, cradling Henrietta's soft white and pale blue eggs. They don't speak either.

They had seen a different side of MawMaw today, something quiet, yet powerful, something that touched the depths of their innocent souls. Something that would stay imprinted on their hearts long after she was gone.

CHAPTER EIGHTEEN

~ Days That Shook the World,
"The Dream of Martin Luther King"

Monday Morning, March 28, 1960

Wilton | Day of the Sit-In

Wilton arrives at the appointed time, eight in the morning, standing in the back parking lot of Our Lady of the Lake Sanitarium,[63] the Catholic hospital in Baton Rouge. It's a practical meeting spot, not far from Third Street downtown, where Kress is located. There is still a lot of time before the sit-in takes place. He surveys the area. No sign of Jer.

Maybe, like Effie this morning, he isn't going to show up either, Wilton wonders.

The last time they spoke, on the ferry, it hadn't ended well. Later, Wilton called to apologize, making plans to meet here.

He shifts on his feet, his concern growing.

"Where is he?" Wilton whispers to himself.

Just then, a car slows to a stop across the lawn. A hand waves out the window.

Wilton turns to look behind him, assuming they're waving at someone else.

No one's there.

Me? he wonders.

Then he hears his name.

"Wilton!"

As he squints towards the car with his hand above his eyes to block the sun, he recognizes Jer's head poking out the window, waving his hand with great vigor.

This isn't what they had planned. He was supposed to meet Jer here and then walk together to Kress.

Why is Jer in that car? he thinks. Wilton doesn't hesitate. He moves quickly across the lawn.

As he reaches the curb, Jer calls out, "Get in! Hurry, I'll explain once you're inside."

The door swings open, and Wilton climbs into the back seat of the old Buick, instantly hit by a warm, familiar aroma, rich and comforting.

Pulling away from the curb, Wilton takes in the faces around him. Three others sit in the car, but the only one he recognizes is Jer.

Leaning closer, he whispers, "What's going on?"

"I want you to meet my friend, JoJo, from Southern University and his momma, Miss Pearl," says Jer. "This is my cousin, Wilton."

"Well, hey baby," comes a kind but rather loud voice from the front seat.

"How you doin', Miss Pearl?" Wilton says cautiously as he looks at Jer with confusion, as if to say, "Who are these people, and why are we in their car?"

"Jer, please tell me what's going on," Wilton whispers.

Looking at Wilton, Jer raises his voice just enough to be heard over the hum of the road.

"JoJo wanted to join us at Kress today. When he told his momma last night about our plans, she offered to drive us downtown."

Wilton glances toward the front seat, surprised.

"And … uh … Miss Pearl, you okay with what we're doin' today?"

Miss Pearl chuckles softly, keeping her eyes on the road.

"Just sit back, baby," she says. "Since we're early, we're takin' a little detour."

She nods toward JoJo.

"Now, go on and pass around that basket of biscuits. I bet you boys are hungry."

JoJo grabs it from the front seat and hands it back. Wilton willingly reaches for one, the warm butter dripping down the sides of the flaky crust onto his hand.

"We're commemoratin' somethin' today," Miss Pearl announces.

JoJo sits up straighter, looking over to her. "Momma, where you takin' us?"

Miss Pearl just smiles.

"I know that smile," JoJo mutters, shaking his head. "That means you're up to somethin.'"

With one hand on the wheel, she leans over and pats his leg.

"Trust me, baby."

JoJo exhales, turning toward the back seat, and shrugs. Jer and Wilton exchange uncertain glances. Miss Pearl keeps driving, following the road along the riverfront. She passes the ferry landing, then turns east toward the Old State Capitol, perched on a bluff overlooking the Mississippi River.

Its castle-like appearance and tall turrets illuminated at night make for a stunning view, especially from the river. The wrought iron fence, its black metal, tipped with fleur-de-lis, wraps around the stately building. Towering oaks stretch their limbs overhead, their branches forming a canopy that casts shadows onto the sidewalk below.

Miss Pearl slows to a stop and shifts the car into park.

"Look out your window, boys," she says. "See that oak tree stretchin' its shade over us?"

They follow her gaze.

"If it could talk, you know it would have some things to say." She pauses, letting her words settle over them. "You boys wanna hear a story?"

With questioning looks, Wilton and Jer hesitantly say, "Yes ma'am," not being sure if they even have a choice. Miss Pearl seems to be in charge, and it's best to just listen.

She nods, satisfied.

"I wanted to bring you here today before y'all go watch more history bein' made. 'Cause right here, right on this very spot, only seven years ago, somethin' happened that changed everything."

She lets the moment hang in the air as she stares out at the sidewalk.

"In 1953, the Baton Rouge bus boycott took place."

She turns in her seat, looking at them with pride.

"And I was right there in the middle of it."

She reaches for the basket and holds it toward them. "Here, have another biscuit while I tell you all about what happened."

Turning off the car, she shifts and stretches her arm across the back of the seat, turning so everyone could hear.

"The people who were there ... they will never forget. We gotta keep this story alive through the generations. You young people need to know this. From our efforts in that boycott, they say we were an example to cities all over the South of what could be done to begin change, including the Montgomery bus boycott only two years later in '55."

Miss Pearl reaches for a biscuit, takes a slow bite, and savors the buttery warmth. She chews thoughtfully, her eyes distant for a moment, as if tasting not just the food but the memories tied to it.

Her thoughts turn back to the story at hand.

"Now, can you boys guess how long that Montgomery Bus boycott lasted? 'Cause they walked for days."

JoJo was the first to speak.

"I don't know, Mama, maybe a few weeks?"

"Now you know you wrong," says Miss Pearl.

"When we folks set our minds to somethin'," she continues, "we stand together and see it through ... no matter what."

Jer speaks up.

"I remember hearing my parents talk about it, but I was young."

"So how long was the boycott, Miss Pearl?" asks Wilton. "I'm thinkin' maybe a month or two?" he says.

Turning toward the back seat, she speaks slowly yet firmly.

"Three hundred and eighty-one days they walked. That's right. It wasn't easy for 'em. Through rain, cold, and heat, they kept walking. It took courage, determination, and like I said, workin' together."

Chuckling, "But there sure were a lot of shoes bought that year."

"It's just like those young men and women from Southern University, right here in this town, takin' a seat for justice this very day at Kress. I know they're scared. I don't see how they couldn't be. But let me tell ya'll, you can be sure they'll have God's mighty wind against their backs, but the evil one will try to blow harsh winds in their face to turn them back. If we are doing what God is calling us to do, we are never to give up hope. They are puttin' their lives on the line today, but they are doin' it on the winds of change, and it's blowin' hard, boys. It's blowin' hard."

Just then, a warm spring breeze moves through the car windows, rustling the oak tree's leaves above. Everyone glances at one another, eyes wide.

"Look at that," Miss Pearl says, her voice full of knowing.

"Now you know God is good. That was surely a sign."

"Yes, Lord," she responds, her voice filled with conviction.

"That wind of change has been blowin' a loooong time now, through the streets of our city and cities all over the South. And I see no signs of it lettin' up. Do you know who's directing the power of that steady wind?"

JoJo exhales, shaking his head. "Well, I'm sure you gonna tell us, Momma."

Miss Pearl chuckles, giving his knee another pat. "You know I am, baby."

Looking up through the dashboard window, her tone raised in praise.

"It's the Lord Almighty, the God of the mighty angel armies, sittin' on His throne of justice. And today, He's callin' those boys and girls to boldly sit at those White lunch counters for what's right."

She pauses, her eyes glancing in the rearview mirror, meeting Wilton's gaze.

"And don't you think for a second they're doin' it in their own strength. No indeed."

Her voice softens. "It has to be done through God's power. Why everything we do has to be done through Him; because His power is made perfect in our weakness." She taps the top of the seat. "That's right. And it has to be done in nonviolence. And that, boys,"–she pauses–"has a power all its own."

Wilton begins to shift uncomfortably in the back seat, thinking of things he had heard from Reverend Washington and Preacher. This time, though, he can't flee. Plus, Miss Pearl wouldn't have it.

"Amen, Momma," says JoJo, then tilts his head toward her.

"But what's this got to do with us being parked here today?" he pauses. "And ... how do you know all of this anyway?"

Miss Pearl leans forward, adjusting herself, gripping the steering wheel with one hand, looking out the window.

"Son, you were just a young boy, not fully understanding all that was going on. But I wasn't just there in the middle of it. I was there through it all, with your daddy cheering me on.

JoJo was beginning to see his momma through new eyes, mature eyes, realizing that there was so much he witnessed as a child but never comprehended the magnitude, the impact her actions made on his future and that of the South.

Reaching for her hand, he whispers, "I'm proud of you, Momma."

Miss Pearl smiles, squeezing his hand as her eyes well up, feeling as though she were passing a baton of courage and hope to her son, now a grown man.

Miss Pearl gives her son's hand a strong pat before continuing on with her message for the young men.

"The reason I'm telling y'all this today is because it had to be said right here, under this very oak tree, in front of the Old State Capitol. Look out the window, boys. This is where the winds began to stir up that day. They began to pick up strength like Hurricane Audrey back in '53 as she rolled in off the Gulf of Mexico. Nothin' could stop her, and nothin' can stop the Holy Spirit on the move.

Her voice lowers in soft reverence.

"Can you feel it?"

The car falls still. The only sound is the distant hum of traffic and the rustling of the trees above.

"Be quiet for a minute. Just listen."

Wilton was beginning to wonder if Miss Pearl was related to Reverend Washington?

Breaking the silence, she says, "And those gusts of wind and rumblings aren't gonna stop anytime soon. You boys are about to witness it today."

She turns to look at each of them.

"This isn't about you," Miss Pearl says. "It's about something much bigger that you are a part of. You see, I felt the same way as you seven years ago. I sure did," she says, shaking her head.

"I wanted to help make a change. So, I joined in on the bus boycott, right here in Baton Rouge. As the days went on, we all began to realize that we were a part of somethin' really important."

She settles back in her seat with a sober tone as she passes the basket back around again.

"Have another biscuit. Momma Pearl has more to say."

She waits for them to take one before continuing.

"Y'all know that big church up the street from here, Mount Zion Baptist?"

They all nod.

"Well, their new pastor, Reverend T.J. Jemison, he didn't just step into his pulpit to preach; he stepped right into the middle of the fight. In February of '53, he walked into an all-White city council meeting, stood tall, and spoke to them in brotherly love. He asked that Black folks be treated fairly on the buses, seein' as how they pay the same fare as the White folks. And we sure did," says Miss Pearl, "every penny."

She rubs her head, remembering.

"And sure enough, two weeks later, the council decided yes. An ordinance was passed. I know it by heart," Miss Pearl speaks it loud, filling the car with its reverberations.

"All city buses should be filled on a first-come, first-served basis. Whites would board from the front, Black folks from the back, and we would fill up with no seats left empty."

She pauses, her voice lowering with conviction.

"Because, boys, we know that all are welcome at God's table and that includes buses too."

Wilton frowns. "So how did it go?"

Miss Pearl sighs, shaking her head. "Well ... not so good."

Jer and Wilton lean in, listening closely.

"The bus drivers refused to enforce it," she explains. "Didn't matter what the city council said. So for three more months, nothin' changed. Same ol' cruel system of Colored folks havin' to give up their seats to the White folks. Then, something amazing happened, only God could orchestrate."

Miss Pearl reaches under her seat to retrieve a thermos of water.

"Here, boys, quench your thirst. It sure is gettin' hot today."

Miss Pearl continues on.

"It was the beginning of summer and a hot, muggy day, almost like this one but worse. A woman named Martha White,[64] who worked as a maid, was just worn out that day. She boarded the bus, and her eyes caught sight of one of those empty seats. The only problem was that it was in the White section. She sat down, and an elderly Black lady sat down beside her. See, nobody ever talks about how hard these women work."

Miss Pearl glances at them, letting her words sink in.

"Now, why don't y'all guess what that bus driver said to them?"

"Probably told them to get up," Wilton mutters.

Miss Pearl nods.

"You right, baby. And he said it real mean. But listen to what happened next, and this is where God just stepped right in."

Wilton and Jer shift to the edge of their seats, hanging on now to her every word.

Miss Pearl's voice softens.

"Miss Martha refused to give up her seat. She looked at that driver square in the eye and said, 'I'm just so tired. I'll get up if White folks get on the bus, but I am soooo tired.'"

Miss Pearl leans in, her voice low.

"That bus driver didn't like that and shouted, 'I said, get up.'" Miss Pearl points her finger at the boys. "But then, boys, somethin' miraculous happened."

Jer and Wilton exchange a glance, drawn in.

"A woman named Pearl, just like me, stood up from the back. She looked around that bus and says, 'Now, everybody's gonna stick together this mornin', and nobody's gettin' off this bus.' And do you know what she did?"

The boys shake their heads.

Miss Pearl smiles. That lady Pearl faced that bus driver with bravery.

"She linked arms with the others on that bus. All of 'em. And they held strong. She kept up their spirits that morning. Wouldn't let fear break 'em down."

Miss Pearl pauses, her voice turning almost reverent. "And do you know what Miss Martha later said? She said she never remembered seein' that lady, Miss Pearl, before that day. Not once."

Wilton swallows hard.

"What do you think that means?" he asks.

Miss Pearl exhales, looking out toward the towering oak tree.

"I think, boys … no … I know … that she was one of God's angels, placed on that bus to get things rollin'."

"What happened then?" Asks Jer.

Well, because of the courage of these women, all the bus drivers walked out and had a four-day strike. The union leaders ended up saying the new ordinance violated Louisiana's segregation law and got it overturned. We were right back to where we started."

Wilton leans back in his seat, arms crossed.

"Humph, we'll never move forward, will we?"

"Well, hold on now," says Miss Pearl. "We were discouraged for sure, and there was some anger. But we weren't gonna give up that easily."

Looking again through the rearview window straight at Wilton, she says, "And we can't today."

Wilton shakes his head, not budging.

Miss Pearl continues.

"Many of the maids who worked for White families all over Baton Rouge wanted to protest. They said, 'We are not gettin' back on those buses. There's nothin' wrong with our feet. They can be our transportation.'"

The ferry horn blows loudly in the distance, as Miss Pearl's voice rises.

"Their voices were heard loud and clear that day. They were ready to walk for justice. An announcement went out to the Black community. A big meeting was called for that night. Black churches and civic leaders came together and formed the United Defense League. Reverend Jemison was chosen to lead. And boys, let me tell you ... the winds kept blowin'."

She glances at them.

"That night," just up the road from where we are right now, "the meeting was packed. I was happy to get inside. People were standing outside the doors. It was so crowded and hot."

JoJo shakes his head in awe. "Wow, Momma, I didn't know you went to all those meetings."

Miss Pearl smiles.

"I know, baby, but remember, you were just an innocent youngin' wantin' to ride your bike and be with your friends."

Looking at JoJo with gleaming eyes, she says, "But look at you today, son. You takin' after me."

Jer spoke up. "What happened at the meeting, Miss Pearl?"

"Well, Reverend Jemison spoke about solidarity, peace, and lawfulness. There was hope in that room that hot summer night in June, and we felt it. We were ready to fight back. When the meeting was almost over, Reverend Jemison said something that stuck with me. 'Do not go home until you knock on somebody's door and tell them not to take the bus tomorrow.' Not one Black person was to ride."

Miss Pearl shakes her head, chuckling.

"My friend Beulah and I got back to our neighborhood that night and went door to door. We woke folks up, but they didn't mind. They were glad to hear the news. One woman even invited us in for coffee and sweet potato pie. Even though it was nine o'clock at night, they wanted to know everything that happened at that meetin'. This was big boys."

She exhales, eyes distant.

"Lying in bed that night, I was too excited to sleep. I knew by not gettin' on those buses, I'd be makin' a difference."

She looks at JoJo.

"You and your daddy were probably already snorin'."

JoJo grins.

Miss Pearl continues.

"I remember turning on WLCS radio. And do you know what I heard? Mr. Raymond Scott, the secretary of the United Defense League, was on the air, urging every Black citizen to stay off the buses. He said the old ordinance was back in place and that carpools were being organized for the morning."

Her voice drops, filled with emotion.

"And the next morning? The streets were filled with cars picking up folks who needed rides to work. And I was one of 'em."

Wilton leans back toward the front seat, becoming interested again.

"Many of the drivers made signs that read 'Free Rides'. The sight of all those cars. My heart swells thinkin' about it."

"I was working for the Landry family back then, and I had to get from Scotlandville to the White part of Baton Rouge. I was picked up and brought right here to this spot at the Old State Capitol."

She gestures around them.

"This was our hub."

She throws open the car door.

"Mercy me, it's hot in this car. Come on, boys. Let's step into the shade under this old oak tree."

They happily step onto the sidewalk in front of the wrought-iron fence. Miss Pearl leans against the oak tree, looking up at it, as though saying hello to an old friend.

"That day in June of '53, car after car lined up on this street," she says. "The boycott had begun. I stood right here, waitin' my turn."

She shakes her head, chuckling.

"It was raining that morning. I was standin' with my umbrella, my feet soaked. Then, finally, a Buick sedan pulled up. I was so relieved."

She turns to them, eyes bright.

"I climbed in quickly, along with the others, and as I shut the door, I looked over. And there, sittin' right next to me was a White man. He smiled and said, 'Good mornin'. Now wasn't that somethin'? A White man was our driver."

Wilton blinks in surprise.

"But wait," she says, raising a hand. "There's more. That man stepped back out into the rain, went around to his trunk, and came back with a covered basket."

She grins.

"'I almost forgot about these,' that nice White man said to everyone in the car. 'My wife got up early this morning and baked biscuits. She told me to give them to whoever God puts in my car. She said to tell you that each of you are brave for what you're doin.'"

Miss Pearl presses a hand to her heart.

God wanted me—and all the others that day—to see this. He wanted us to know He was in the battle with us, going before us, behind us, and all around us. I'll never forget that moment. And let me tell you, I sure was glad God put me in that car," she chuckles. "I was some hungry."

She breaks into laughter.

Miss Pearl then draws a solemn look on her face, "Something special happened that rainy day in 1953, boys. That morning, we sat shoulder to shoulder, Black and White, sharin' hot buttered biscuits, ridin' together on the winds of change."

A quiet settles over the group. *Maybe*, Wilton thinks, *the same winds of change Miss Pearl once rode are now calling us to jump on.*

He finally spoke.

"But, Miss Pearl ... how did you really know God was there?"

Miss Pearl turns to him, voice firm yet warm.

"Baby, you gotta be alert. Ready to see, hear, taste, and feel what God is doin' all around you. You couldn't help but taste the sweetness of those biscuits that day, biscuits made with hands of kindness and the love of Jesus."

She nods toward the oak tree.

"Just like that gust of wind that blew through these leaves and into the car earlier. Didn't you feel it? God was speakin'."

The boys exchange glances, unsure what to say. Miss Pearl folds her arms.

"Now, do y'all know how many cars and trucks showed up right here to take us to work on that mornin'?"

Wilton shrugs.

"I mean ... I don't see how y'all could've gotten more than a couple dozen in that short of time."

Miss Pearl smirks.

"Humph. We had one hundred and twenty-five."

Jer's eyes widened. "What?"

"That's what I mean, baby," Miss Pearl says. "That could only have been orchestrated by the hand of God.

Pointing to the street, she says, "Anytime a city bus rolled by while we waited, they slowed down, hopin' we'd get on."

Miss Pearl lifts her chin.

"We just turned our backs to 'em. That's right—we turned our backs on injustice and our hearts toward the God of justice."

The boys stare at her.

"The buses moved on," she finishes.

"Empty. Without us in those seats, they weren't gonna last."

JoJo frowns.

"But who paid for all that gas to drive you around?"

Miss Pearl's eyes twinkle.

"God provided, son. They took up offerings at the meetings. Everybody gave what they could. We worked together. Nobody complained."

Jer shakes his head.

"That still doesn't sound like enough."

She grins.

"You know Horatio Thompson's Esso station?"[65]

Jer nods.

"Well, Mr. Horatio let all the carpool drivers fill up at cost, just the cost of what he paid for gas."

She gives them a knowing look.

"That's what I mean about bein' alert to see what God's up to. He stirred generosity in Mr. Horatio's heart. God equips those He calls."

Miss Pearl looks down at her watch, knowing their time is running short.

"Before we go, I want to tell y'all one last thing about Miss Martha White that she shared with us."

She pauses, making sure they're listening.

"One day, while takin' the carpool during the bus boycott, she was late to work and had to explain why. Her employer wasn't happy about it and told her that it was just not going to work out for her."

Wilton moves in closer, curious to hear what's next. Miss Pearl's voice softens. "This is the part I want you to hear, boys, because Miss Martha White, who seemed to only be in her early twenties, found her voice that day and boldly spoke up."

Waiting for the car horn to pass by, Miss Pearl continues, "This is exactly what Miss Martha said," as Miss Pearl clears her throat.

"'And then, something came up from my toes, all the way up, out of my mouth. And I said, it will work, long as it will work. That's all I told her, and that's all that was ever said.'"

The boys sit in stunned silence. Miss Pearl shakes her head.

"She found her voice that day. And so did hundreds of other Colored folks. People took action, too. Reverend Jemison risked everything, speakin' out in brotherly love to the city council. And yet, he still found a cross burnin' in his yard."

She lets out a slow breath.

"Boys, it's easy to sit in the eye of the hurricane. It's calm, it's safe there. But change happens where the winds are strongest."

She looks each of them in the eye.

"Y'all are about to step into the storm. But don't be afraid. You got God's mighty wind at your back."

The boys nod.

"Now," she says, "stay in solidarity. You hear me?"

Nodding, they speak in unison: "Yes, ma'am."

"Be respectful. Nonviolent. And always, always stand firm on God's truth. Now, let's get goin'."

Wilton swallows hard, looking out toward Third Street and the possibilities the day might bring.

"Come on, Wilton, we gotta load up," says Jer. "We don't want to be late."

The car stays quiet as Miss Pearl pulls away, heading toward Third Street and Kress. Finally, Wilton speaks.

"Miss Pearl?"

"Yes, baby?"

"What is God's truth anyway? How can I stand on it if I don't even know what it is?"

Miss Pearl meets his eyes through the rearview mirror.

"God's truth is His spoken Word. And His Word is the sword we fight with."

She takes another quick glance back at him.

"But son, you can't trust somebody's words unless you get to know 'em."

She lets the question settle before asking, "Wilton ... have you spent some time with God to get to know Him?"

"My momma used to, and my daddy told me that she was teaching me all about Him. But I was only five when she died. I don't really remember much anyway."

Miss Pearl suddenly pulls the car over to the side of the road. The boys did not question her. They sat quietly. She turns around and looks right at Wilton.

With a voice of compassion, she says, "Wilton, it's in you, baby. It's still there. Your momma planted that seed in you. You just need to water it a bit. And when you do, it will produce a great harvest."

For a moment, you could have heard a pin drop in the car. Miss Pearl simply turns back around, pulls out, and drives on. Wilton is taken aback to think that something of his momma is still within him.

CHAPTER NINETEEN

"While sitting at that (White lunch) counter, I was completely wet with perspiration. That's exactly how afraid I was. But, we had to do what we had to do."[66]

-Kenneth Johnson, Kress sit-in,
Baton Rouge, 1960, Southern University student,
Associate Judge, Baltimore City
Circuit Court (1982-2001)

Monday Midday, March 28, 1960

Wilton | Day of Sit-In

The boys sit in the car, silent. Their nervous anticipation hangs heavy around them as Miss Pearl pulls over on Third Street, just a couple of blocks from Kress Department Store.

"Alright, hop out fast," she says. "Be safe, and know my prayers go with you."

Doors open, and Wilton is the last to get out. But before he joins the others, he turns back, leaning in through the passenger window.

"Miss Pearl," he says, hesitating, "thank you for telling us those stories. But if I'm gonna stand for justice, I need to believe it's really out there."

"Come on, Wilton, we gotta go," Jer calls out impatiently.

"Look at me, son," she says, firmly pointing at him. "Justice is all around you. And it's within you because you are one of God's warriors, fighting for what is right and just. Open your eyes to see. Keep your ears alert to hear. God is on the move."

Wilton swallows hard.

"You just heard it in my stories," Miss Pearl says, "and today, you're about to witness it with your own eyes. It's blowin' in on the wind by the breath of our most powerful and just God. Now go out there and make a difference. God's inviting you to ride those winds of change with Him.

Nodding firmly with vigor in her voice. "Get ready to hold on."

"Wilton, come on!" Jer urges in frustration.

Wilton shuts the car door, hesitating for only a moment before turning back once more. He looks at Miss Pearl through the window, voice catching in his throat.

"And Miss Pearl," he says, his words softer now, "thank you for the biscuits."

His eyes glisten.

"They tasted just like I think I remember my momma's." Exhaling, he continues, "I think it might be time for me to start watering those seeds."

Miss Pearl's face warms with a knowing smile.

"You go find that watering can, son," she says gently. "God's with you. And so is your momma."

As Wilton, JoJo, and Jer walk down Third Street, a quiet sense of empowerment settles over them. Each step forward feels like they're marching into something bigger than themselves.

Then, an unexpected voice calls from behind.

"What you boys dressed up so nice for? Gonna have a hot night on the town later?"

They don't need to turn around to know trouble is following.

"Just keep walking," Jer mutters under his breath. "Don't say a thing."

Wilton clenches his jaw but keeps moving.

Then, one of the White boys says the word, the one that cuts deep, the one that sets his blood on fire.

Wilton spins around, fists tight, ready to strike.

JoJo grabs his arm before he can throw a punch.

"Solidarity, Wilton," he says firmly. "It's the only way. No violence."

Jer steps in, and together, they pull Wilton into the shaded breezeway of a department store.

"Cool down," Jer warns, keeping his voice low but firm. "Or you're not coming in with us."

The White boys pass by, spitting into the breezeway as they go.

Wilton's chest rises and falls, his anger still smoldering.

"Let it go, Wilton," Jer says. "They're not worth it. We got more important places to be and things to do. You cool?"

Silence.

"Wilton." Jer's voice sharpens. "You cool?"

Wilton exhales, unclenching his fists.

"Yeah," he mutters, "I'm cool. Let's go."

The entrance to Kress Department Store was just up ahead. The three White boys had already gone in before them. JoJo stops on the sidewalk just before they get to the front door of Kress. "Okay, guys, are we together in this?" he says. "We are here to support those Southern students, and as Momma says, 'Who knows what God is preparing and equipping for us later on?'"

"JoJo," says Jer, "you seem to know more about all this than we do. "You lead the way."

JoJo nods.

"Okay, we ready?" asks Jer. "We will stick together. Be respectful."

Jer looks over to his cousin, "Wilton?"

"I'm cool, I told you. Let's go," he says.

Stepping into Kress, Wilton, JoJo, and Jer look toward the White section of the lunch counter. The Southern students have not yet arrived, but they noticed something troubling. JoJo leads them toward the colored section of the counter. As they pass, the three White boys from earlier sit perched on their stools, smirking.

Jer watches Wilton carefully, giving him a subtle nudge forward. "Keep moving," he whispers.

They reach the Colored counter where JoJo slides onto a stool, motioning for the others to do the same.

A moment later, the White manager approaches. "How you boys doin' today?"

"We're doin' good," JoJo replies with a polite nod. "Just tryin' to cool off a bit."

The manager wipes his hands on a rag. "It's startin' to heat up out there, that's for sure."

"Yes, sir," JoJo says without looking up.

"Well, enjoy."

"Yes, sir," they say in unison.

An older Black waitress steps over, pulling the pencil from behind her ear and pad in hand. "What can I get for y'all?" she asks, her voice kind.

JoJo doesn't hesitate. "How about a Coke float?"

"Sounds good to me," Jer adds.

Wilton nods. "Yeah, I'll take one too, please." As he speaks, his eyes sweep the lunch counter, searching for any sign of the Southern students.

"I don't see anyone," Jer whispers.

"No, I think I heard they weren't coming until two o'clock," JoJo says, glancing at the clock on the wall. "It's only one thirty-five."

A minute later, the waitress returns, setting three Coke floats in front of them.

"Here you go, boys. Enjoy," she says with a small smile before stepping away.

JoJo picks up his straw but pauses. He looks over at Jer and Wilton, who are already slurping theirs down.

"Drink slowly," he whispers. "We don't know how long we'll be sitting here."

Right about then, JoJo looks over. "I think they're here," he says quietly, "but I only see two."

Wilton and Jer follow his gaze as two Black students approach the White lunch counter, their movements careful, deliberate. They slide onto the red stools, their backs straight, their hands resting on their laps. Nervous tension clings to them like the Southern humidity.

A moment later, more students appear, coming from different directions. Then more.

They are dressed in suits and ties, the girls in pressed dresses. Their presence is quiet, their posture dignified.

Wilton watches as one young man takes a seat, his forehead slick with sweat, his hands trembling slightly.

As the White waitress just stares at them, one of the students politely addresses her.

"May I have a cup of coffee, please?"

The White waitress doesn't budge. Her expression hardens. "Boy, you know we can't serve you in this section."

No one moves.

She places a hand on her hip.

"Now, you go on around to the Colored side. Miss Fannie will be happy to serve you there."

Still, not a single student shifts.

The waitress exhales sharply before disappearing through the swinging door.

Moments later, she returns, her lips pressed into a thin line.

"The manager is eatin' his lunch. He says to tell you that when he's done, he'll be calling the police if you haven't gone to your proper place."

The students nod politely, acknowledging her words.

Yet, no one moves.

Some quietly pull out books, flipping them open, their eyes focused on the pages.

Across the room, the three White boys who had harassed Wilton, Jer, and JoJo earlier sneer loud enough for all to hear.

"We ain't stayin' here with all these n––."

They slam their soda glasses on the counter. As they turn in their stools to leave, one of them spits onto the back of a young Black woman.

She does not flinch.

None of the students reacts.

They remain still, steadfast, and unmoved.

"If I were them, I'd knock that White boy right to the floor," Wilton mutters under his breath.

"Quiet, Wilton," Jer whispers sharply. "They've been training and practicing for weeks. They're ready for this kind of treatment. Now, let it go."

Wilton clenches his jaw, forcing himself to stay quiet.

As the last White boy walks out, he grabs a glass of water from the counter. With a smirk, he tips it forward, dumping it down the back of one of the male students. Laughing, he shoves the glass onto the counter and strolls out.

The student doesn't flinch.

No one reacts.

The room stays silent.

The young man who had been sweating earlier now looks even more tense. His hands clench slightly in his lap.

His eyes catch JoJo's.

JoJo gives him a slight nod, a clear yet silent message: You can do this! We're with you!

From the other side of the counter, the Colored waitress wipes down the counter with slow, deliberate strokes, shaking her head.

Not taking her eyes off the Black students sitting at the White counter, she mutters under her breath. "Now you know ... that's enough of this."

Setting her rag down, she straightens her apron and marches toward the students.

Leaning in, she lowers her voice, but her words are sharp.

"Y'all have no business being here. You're just bringin' trouble to the rest of us."

The students say nothing. Their silence seems to frustrate her more. Huffing, she turns and heads back to the Colored section of the counter. Looking at Wilton, Jer, and JoJo, she gestures toward the empty stools in front of her.

"Now, this is where they should be sittin'. You boys are doin' the right thing. We don't need trouble around here."

Wilton watches her for a moment, then speaks up.

"Ma'am, if I could be sittin' over on that side of the counter, I would. And I probably will someday."

Wilton looks toward the students and then back at the waitress. "Aren't you tired of being treated like this? Are you just gonna keep accepting it?"

The waitress stops wiping the counter. Slowly, she leans in, looking Wilton straight in the eyes.

"Son, I've learned to keep my head down and stay in my place by followin' the rules." Her voice is quieter now, but firm. "That way, we all get along just fine."

Wilton shakes his head, but she isn't done.

"You young folks don't know what you're gettin' yourselves into," she continues. "You just wanna shake things up. But I've seen what happens when folks stir the pot. I've seen some bad things."

She exhales, setting her rag down.

"I'm just tryin' to keep the peace."

Without another word, she turns and walks away.

Wilton shakes his head, frustration bubbling inside him as he looks at Jer and JoJo.

"How can she not want to fight for what's right?"

His eyes shift back to the White counter. One stool sits empty.

His chest tightens.

"I'm joining them," he says suddenly, determination in his voice. "I have to do this. I'm doin' it for my momma. She didn't deserve what she got, and they're about to get what they deserve the minute they lay a hand on me."

Jer stiffens. "No, you are not, Wilton," he says firmly. "You have no idea what you're getting yourself into. This isn't a game. You're not ready for this."

Wilton doesn't seem to hear him. Without hesitation, he swivels his stool around and stands, eyes locked on the empty seat at the counter.

Jer and JoJo move in an instant. Slamming a few coins on the counter, they scramble after him. Just as Wilton takes his first step toward the White counter, they each grab an arm. Without a word, they steer him toward the door. Wilton tries to resist, but they're stronger.

As the door swings open, several police officers push past them, heading inside.

"Keep walking, Wilton," Jer commands under his breath.

They don't stop.

Hands still gripping Wilton's back, Jer and JoJo lead him away from Kress, down the sidewalk toward the other end of the building. Only when they're out of sight do they release him.

Jer turns to him, voice low but fierce.

"What were you thinking?"

Wilton's jaw tightens, but Jer doesn't stop.

"I told you … this isn't a game. I shouldn't have invited you to come with us."

Wilton exhales sharply, rubbing the back of his neck, but before he can respond, a lot of activity on the street draws their attention.

More police officers descend on Kress.

The boys step to the side, blending into the crowd gathering on the sidewalk, White and Black onlookers watching the scene unfold.

One by one, the students are led out the door.

The police pat down each of them before loading them into the paddy wagon parked on the street.

Not a single student resists.

They do exactly as they are told.

Their silence is louder than any protest Wilton has ever heard.

Wilton steps back, trying to get a clearer view through the crowd.

"You too scared to sit at the White lunch counter?" comes a sneer from behind.

Wilton stiffens. He knows that voice. It's as though a volcano had been boiling within him just beneath the surface, and is now ready to erupt. Before he even realizes what he's doing, he whirls around, spewing anger, and knocks the White boy to the ground.

Before Jer or JoJo can reach him, the White boy gets up, blood dripping from his lip, and slams Wilton against the brick wall. Pain shoots through his head as the rough surface cuts into his skin.

Jer rushes toward Wilton just as JoJo throws up his hands between them and the three White boys. "Stay cool," he warns. "We don't want trouble."

The other two White boys grab their friend.

"Come on, Dennis, cool down," one of them urges. "Let's get out of here. A cop's headed this way."

As they turn to leave, Dennis pulls a lit cigarette from his friend's mouth and presses it into Wilton's arm. Then, the three disappear.

Jer hurries to Wilton's side, crouching down on the sidewalk next to him, blood trickling down his face, holding his burned arm.

A uniformed officer steps up to them, eyes sharp with suspicion.

"You boys gettin' yourselves into trouble? Were you sitting at that White lunch counter too?"

He jerks his head toward the paddy wagon. "There's still room for three more. Maybe we oughta take y'all down to the station too."

Jer leans in close to Wilton.

"Don't say a word," he whispers.

JoJo straightens, his voice calm and respectful.

"No, sir. We're not looking for trouble. With all these people crowding the sidewalk, our friend got pushed against the wall."

Another officer strides over.

"Everything okay here, Joe?" he asks. "We need you back at the paddy wagon."

The first officer hesitates, his gaze hard on the boys, as if daring them to give him a reason. Then, after a long moment, he exhales sharply.

"Consider yourselves lucky today," he snarls before turning and walking away.

Jer focuses on Wilton, pulling a handkerchief from his back pocket and pressing it against the bloody cut on his forehead.

"You okay, Wilton?" JoJo asks, eyeing the burn on his skin. "That's gotta hurt."

"I'm fine," Wilton mutters.

JoJo doesn't look convinced.

"Well, you don't look fine."

"I said I'm fine," Wilton snaps.

The three of them sit in tense silence, eyes fixed on the paddy wagon as the last of the Southern students are loaded inside.

Breaking the silence, Jer asks, "What happened in there?"

Wilton keeps his gaze ahead.

"I said ... I don't want to talk about it."

Jer exhales sharply.

"Fine. But at least sit for a minute until the bleeding stops."

JoJo stands, noticing the growing police presence.

"I think we need to get out of here before we end up in that paddy wagon, too," he says.

From down the sidewalk, a familiar voice calls out.

"JoJo!"

They turn to see Miss Pearl hurrying toward them.

"Momma, what are you doing here?" JoJo asks.

"I've been driving around downtown for a while," she says, breathless. "Then I saw all these police and got worried about you boys." Her eyes land on Wilton.

"Wilton, you're bleeding! Mercy sakes, what happened to you, son? And oh my gracious," she exclaims, "Look at that burn on your arm."

"We'll explain later, Momma," JoJo says. "Let's just get him to the car."

As they walk, they watch the paddy wagon roll down Third Street, lights on, heading toward the police station.

At the car, Miss Pearl points to the trunk.

"JoJo, grab two rags from back there, quick. That handkerchief is soaked something bad."

JoJo hands her the rags, and she pours water from her cup over one before gently wiping the blood from Wilton's forehead and face.

"Here," she says, "hold this tight against the cut to stop the bleedin' and put this butter leftover from the biscuits on that burn."

"Let's get you to our house, Wilton," she says, her voice filled with urgency.

"No, just take me to the ferry, please," Wilton insists. "I'll be fine. I don't live far from the other ferry landing."

Jer looks over, taking charge.

"I'm coming with you," he says.

Wilton shakes his head.

"No. I said ... I'm fine. The bleeding's not so bad now."

"You are so stubborn," Jer huffs.

Wilton stares out the window as Miss Pearl drives over the levee and down to the ferry landing. The horn blows, signaling the last call for passengers. She pulls over.

Miss Pearl turns in her seat.

"Baby, let me see that cut before you go."

"I really need to catch the ferry before the plank goes up," Wilton says, easing out of the car. "It's fine now."

Miss Pearl sighs. "Be careful. Get straight home now, you hear?"

Wilton nods.

"Yes, ma'am. And ... thank you."

"Call me," Jer says through the window. "Let me know how you're doing."

Wilton just gives a small nod and heads toward the plank. They watch as he steps safely onto the ferry. The plank lifts, and the boat pulls away.

Miss Pearl shifts the car into gear.

"Alright, let's get you boys back to Southern. I want to hear everything on the way."

Wilton climbs the steps to the colored side of the ferry and heads straight to the snack shop window, ordering a Coke. The Black woman behind the counter watches him closely, her expression filled with concern.

"You okay, baby?" she asks gently.

"I'm fine, thank you," he replies, though the words don't feel entirely true.

She hands him the Coke and waves away his attempt to pay.

"Don't worry about paying. Now, you go sit down and rest yourself."

Wilton nods in gratitude and takes a seat on one of the benches. The gentle rocking of the ferry and the hum of the river lull him into an exhausted sleep.

A sudden jolt awakens him. The ferry has bumped against the dock, signaling their arrival on the other side. The ropes are already being thrown to shore, anchoring them in place. Wilton blinks a few times, gathers his bearings, then stands and returns his empty Coke bottle.

The woman watches him closely.

"You get on home now and get some rest," she says.

"Yes, ma'am." He says as he walks toward the stairs. Then, stopping, he turns. "And thank you for the Coke. I'm feelin' better," he says.

As he steps onto the plank, a sudden wobble nearly throws him off balance. Catching himself on the rope, he steadies himself. Then, through the stillness of the afternoon, a familiar voice echoes through the air.

Down by the water, Preacher is preaching to the line of cars waiting to board the ferry back to Baton Rouge. His deep and fervent voice rolls over the crowd.

"In faithfulness, He shall bring justice," Preacher proclaims. "He will not falter or be discouraged until He establishes justice on the earth. Come down to the water and be baptized into the family of a just and loving God."

Wilton exhales. The sound of Preacher's voice feels oddly comforting. But before he can take another step, Preacher catches sight of him.

His sermon stops mid-sentence.

Preacher grips his staff and hurries across the gravel toward Wilton.

"Son, what happened?" he asks, his eyes immediately catching the blood-stained rag pressed to Wilton's forehead. His voice grows more anxious.

"Why are you bleeding? Come on, let's get you to the house and clean you up."

Wilton meets Preacher's gaze. Something in him softens.

"Maybe so," he murmurs, his voice almost childlike.

Wilton steps into Preacher's house, his eyes drifting toward the teacup on the corner table. Scrappy lies curled up on a blanket, sound asleep. The sight calms him. A small comfort in the midst of everything. After washing the blood from his cut and giving him a bandage, Preacher applies salve to his burn and hands him a glass of cold sweet tea. Then, he encourages Wilton to lie down and rest on his bed.

"You stay here and get your strength back," Preacher says. "You seem weak. I'll be back soon, and we can talk."

Wilton, already beginning to doze, feels Scrappy jump into bed, snuggling next to him. Together they drift off to sleep.

Not knowing how much time had passed, he awakens to his name being called out.

"Wilton ... Wilton ... are you okay?" He thinks for a minute that he was dreaming, then he feels a horrible ache in his head. Looking up, he sees his daddy standing there by the bed with Preacher.

"Daddy, what ... where ... why are you here?"

"It's okay, Moses," says his daddy, looking at Preacher. "I can stay with him now."

Wilton stares at his daddy, brows lifting with quiet confusion. "And why are you calling the preacher, Moses?" Wilton asked.

On that note, Preacher turns to walk out of the room. Stopping at the door and turning around with a somber face, he looked right at Wilton. Without saying a word, he leaves the house. Wilton's heart is racing. He sits up, wincing at the throbbing pain in his head.

"Daddy, what's goin' on?"

His father moves closer, standing at the edge of the bed, his face hard to read.

"We got some things to talk about, son," he says in a solemn tone. "But first … rest."

CHAPTER TWENTY

Monday Late Afternoon, March 28, 1960

Effie | Day of Sit-In

"Why isn't anyone picking up the phone? I need to know if Wilton's okay." Effie murmurs in frustration as it keeps ringing. Exhausted, she has just returned from a long day at the Benoits', her thoughts heavy with worry over the unknown— what might have happened to Wilton at the sit-in." Stretching the coiled phone cord out onto the front porch, she closes the door behind her, ensuring Momma and Grandma Nellie won't overhear.

He's always home this time in the late afternoon. Effie thinks. *He never misses dinner. What if he got arrested ... or worse?* She imagines. The fear gnaws at her. She had knocked on his door on the way home from the Benoits', but there was no answer.

Even his daddy isn't picking up. Something's not right, she worries. *I won't be able to sleep tonight until I talk to him.*

With a defeated sigh, she walks inside and quietly rests the phone's receiver back on the cradle.

From the back room, her momma's voice carries forward.

"Now you know I can tell when somethin's wrong, Effie Rose. Come sit in here and talk with me."

Effie sinks onto the bed across from her momma.

"You're trying to reach Wilton," Willa knowingly says, "and he's not answering his phone, is he?"

Effie hesitates, then sighs.

"I think he might be in trouble, Momma."

Willa Mae's expression changes.

"What do you mean?" asks Momma.

"There was a protest across the river today," says Effie hesitantly.

"I know," Willa Mae says.

Effie's eyes widen as she lifts her head sharply.

"You know? What do you know, Momma?"

"Bootsie from next door brought over soup for me this afternoon," Willa Mae explains. "There's talk on the street about Southern University students sittin' at the White lunch counter at Kress. It doesn't sound like it ended well."

Effie stands.

"It didn't?"

She walks over to sit on the edge of her momma's bed. "What happened?"

"No one knows for sure yet," Willa Mae says carefully. "But I heard many of 'em were arrested and taken to jail."

The words hit Effie like a punch to the gut.

"Momma … Wilton was there."

"He was there?"

Willa Mae says with alarm as she sits straight up in bed.

"Did he sit at the White lunch counter?"

"I don't know," Effie admits.

"He was supposed to go with his cousin from Southern University, just to support them. But knowing Wilton …" Her voice trails off.

Her momma's eyes narrow.

"So have you talked to him?"

"No, that's the problem. No one's at his house, and that's not normal for dinner time."

Willa Mae stares out the window in silence. Taking a sip of water from her cup on the bedside table, she lets out a worried sigh and then turns, looking straight at Effie.

"Did you know about this, Effie?"

Effie shifts on the bed uncomfortably, the worn bed springs groaning beneath her.

"I knew a little of it, and …"

"And what?" Willa Mae presses.

Effie hesitates, then swallows hard.

"He kinda wanted me to go with him."

With lips pursed, her momma shakes her head.

"Effie Rose, what are you tryin' to do, get yourself arrested?"

Rubbing her forehead and avoiding her momma's stare, Effie is silent.

Willa Mae gets up to sit next to Effie. She puts her arm around her. Effie continues to look down as she fidgets with her hands.

Holding Effie tighter, she says, "Thank goodness I needed you at the Benoits' today."

Then, the mood in the room took a sharp turn. Her momma abruptly turns to face her, the bed springs letting out an even sharper rattle.

"Effie, were you really gonna go with him?"

Effie finally turns to face her momma, eyes welling up.

"Yes ... maybe ... I don't know," Effie admits. "We were just going to sit on the colored side of the lunch counter to show support."

Slowly lowering her gaze, "I'm sorry I lied to you, Momma ... about going shopping across the river."

Willa Mae lets out a deep breath.

"Well... I'm glad you told me the truth now, Effie. I knew somethin' was goin' on. You haven't been yourself lately."

Effie's jaw tightens as she rubs her temples. "I don't know, Momma. I feel confused. It's so hard sometimes living here. Why can't we sit at any seat we want to at the lunch counters? From what I've heard, things sound much better up North."

Silence falls between them.

Breaking it, Willa Mae says, "I know we have to follow laws, but it's not all bad. There's some good people here."

Effie lets out another sigh, this one heavier. "I know, Momma, but that's just it. Wilton says I'm just accepting how we're treated down here. And maybe I am. Maybe you are too."

Momma straightens.

"Let me tell you somethin', Effie. We have a roof over our head, we have food, and we have our church family. The Benoits—they're good people, and I have a good job there. You can do the same. After high school, you can find a good job like me or like Grandma Nellie, who worked for years for a nice White family outside of town."

"That's just it, Momma. I don't want to be a maid or a housekeeper or whatever they call you."

Willa Mae grows quiet, looking out the window.

Effie's voice softens.

"I'm sorry, Momma. I didn't mean it like that. You work so hard, and you're on your feet all day, for so little. I just experienced it at the Benoits' and now I have an even greater respect for you."

Momma turns back to her, eyes filled with something Effie can't quite name. "Maybe it looks like I'm just acceptin' the way things are down here," she says, her voice firm. "But

I'm not. I'm fightin' it on my knees, baby. That's how I speak out for what's right, Effie. I speak out to God."

Willa Mae gets up from the bed and goes over to the window, looking out.

"There's a battle goin' on between darkness and light, a battle we can't see."

Closing the curtains, she turns back toward Effie.

"I know it might seem like I'm standin' on the sidelines, like Reverend Washington talked about at church," Willa Mae continues, "but I'm right in the middle of the fight too, baby. I'm prayin' to a just God who cares about how we're being treated ... pushed to the side ... how we haven't been able to have a voice or respect."

Effie looks at her momma. She had not heard her talk quite like this before.

Willa Mae throws up her hands, "I don't know, baby, maybe what those young people did today is an answer to my prayers, and so many others. But that's my voice. To pray. Prayers are the keys to heaven," she says with conviction in her voice, "And faith unlocks the door."

Before Effie can answer, Grandma Nellie enters, leaning on the doorjamb.

"Baby," she says, settling into the conversation as though she's been there the whole time, "I think your pappy would be proud of those students who spoke out today with their actions. What they did today gave your pappy... and so many others, who felt they never had a voice ... a voice.

Grandma turns to Momma with a knowing look.

"And what your momma does on her knees, that's her voice. That's what God calls her to do."

Then, her gaze lands on Effie. "Now, what are you gonna do, Effie Rose?"

Effie shifts, unsure.

Gramma Nellie nods, already knowing.

"I know you don't wanna be a maid, baby," she says. "But let me tell you somethin'. It might not've seemed like much–workin' as maids for White folks–but I was good at what I did, and your momma's good at what she does. We worked hard and earned respect in our jobs. We didn't complain. And God? He was always faithful, establishin' the work of our hands–and our feet–every single day."

Grandma continues with a voice full of wisdom earned through years of hardship. "Because of that work, God provided for us, even in a world where the rules and laws are just plain wrong. But, we answer to a higher Master, baby, and He sees everything that's happenin' to us. The time is comin' for justice. It's rollin' like a mighty river. It sure is. Yes, baby, it sure is."

With that, Gramma Nellie turns and walks back into the front room, humming a hymn as she goes.

Then, Grandma Nellie calls out through the doorway. "Effie, come in here for a minute. I wanna show you somethin'."

"Grandma, I really need to try to call Wilton again and–"

"Now you come with me, Effie Rose, you hear?" Grandma Nellie interrupts, her voice firm. "You can call after this. This is important for you to hear."

Effie hesitates, but something in her grandma's tone tells her she better listen. She gets up and follows.

Looking at her momma and giggling, she says, "Coming, Grandma."

Turning back quickly, she adds, "And Momma, I'm glad you're feeling better today. You lay down now and get some more rest."

Effie steps into the front room, where her grandma is waiting.

"See that framed embroidery up there on the wall?" Grandma asks.

"Sure, Grandma, it's been there forever."

"Get it down for me, will you?"

Effie reaches up over the couch, carefully lifting the old frame from its hook.

"Phew, this is really dirty," she says, blowing a cloud of dust into the air.

Grandma chuckles. "Now, hand it here to me, baby. Look closely. What do you see?"

Effie studies it, tilting the frame toward the light.

"I see embroidered words that say, 'Faith can break the sky in two and let the face of God shine through.'"

"And what else?" Grandma presses.

"Well ... of course I see praying hands, and it looks like they're breaking the sky in two," she says with a small laugh.

"Look closer at the hands," Grandma instructs.

Effie steps closer to the lamp, bringing the embroidery beneath its glow. She squints, then gasps.

"Wait … is that a white hand and a brown hand praying together?" She shakes her head.

"It's been up there forever, and I've never noticed that."

Turning back to Grandma, she asks, "Why are there two different-colored hands praying? And where did this come from?"

Grandma pats the couch beside her.

"Sit down here for a minute, baby. I want to tell you a story. See those sugarcane fields out there?"

Effie glances toward the window.

"Well, it's dark, Grandma, but yes," she says, smiling, "I see them every day. And you know how I used to love to play in them when I was little."

Grandma nods, a soft smile tugging at her lips.

"You sure did, and so did your momma. I used to cut cane in those fields, baby. I still have my machete under the bed."

Her eyes drift toward the window.

"And those same fields … those are where your pappy used to take your momma when the sky was clear at night. He'd show her the stars, and they'd always watch for the shootin' ones."

She pauses, her voice tinged with remembrance.

"Lookin' up at those stars, he taught her about life, about all she needed to be prepared for in this world. It can be cruel, baby. He wanted your momma to understand that her faith didn't belong to this world but to another. That's right. The one we can't see. The one that is truly our home. Don't forget that, Effie."

Her voice lowers. "And that's where your pappy is," Grandma says, looking out the window, lost in time.

Effie studies her grandma, her curiosity growing.

"Grandma, what does this have to do with the framed embroidery?"

Grandma Nellie's eyes soften.

"I want you to see the big picture, Effie Rose. If this piece of embroidery could talk, now you know it would have some things to say. There's a bigger story behind it of how God works in our lives. Just like the light beams you see in that embroidery, His light reaches down. And that light of His? It's been invadin' the darkness of injustice in so many ways over the years. You just have to open your eyes to see it. And when you do, it gives you hope. Helps you press on."

She exhales, her gaze drifting for a moment before settling back on Effie.

"Your pappy prepared your momma for the suffering she was bound to face. The heartache, the struggles, the cruelty. And if you keep going through those cane fields, you'll find more of God's mighty hand at work. Beyond those fields, there was once a plantation. That's where I worked, and this embroidery has a history there.

Effie listens intently. She's heard about that plantation before.

"I walked through those cane fields every day to get there," Grandma continues. "It's where I spent years workin' for a nice White family. Your momma was just a little girl, and they let me bring her with me when she wasn't in school. Even when there was no school for her to go to anymore, she came to work with me."

Effie sits up straighter, almost stiffening.

"I've heard about that place, Grandma. They owned slaves."

Grandma nods solemnly.

"Yes, baby, they did. As did most plantations before emancipation back in 1865.

Her voice lowers, her tone edged with something unspoken.

"I knew of the things that took place there decades before, some not so good things. But there were good things too. The lady of the house, Miss Peavy, was one of them. When I was there, I felt hope. I felt God's presence."

She turns to Effie. "The plantation house eventually burned down. Maybe in some ways, that was a good thing. But God ... He can turn ashes into beauty. And from those ashes, His presence still remains out there in those fields."

Effie frowns.

"But Grandma, how? Some of the people who lived there enslaved others. Who knows what they did to them."

"Yes, baby, and that sure is painful to think about," Grandma nods.

"Our ancestors were slaves. But I believe that God made His presence known to them in ways we'll never understand."

Grandma Nellie takes a deep breath.

"But Effie? I felt God's Spirit when I worked there. And this is what I want you to hear."

Effie swallows, intrigued.

"What happened to the family?"

Grandma sighs, her eyes clouding with memory.

"Before the tragedy, it was a peaceful place. Miss Peavy, the lady of the house, she was kind. Quiet. Spent a lot of time in her sittin' room, readin' her Bible, drinkin' her coffee. Her husband was gone a lot, either in the fields or at the sugar mill."

She folds her hands in her lap.

"They kept to themselves, never saw them much in town. My work was simple, cleanin', cookin', and lookin' after their little girl, Clara. She and your momma were the same age."

Effie's eyes widen. "Momma knew her?"

Grandma smiles wistfully.

"Oh yes, baby. Those two were inseparable. Loved playin' together. Spent afternoons in the sittin' room while Miss Peavy read her Bible and embroidered."

She chuckles.

"Now, the Peavys weren't Catholic like most folks in the parish. You didn't see many Catholics readin' their Bible at home, still don't. Only time they opened it was at Mass.

It's just the way they did things. But the Peavys? They were Baptists and read their Bible daily."

Effie listens closely as Grandma continues, taking her away from the worries of Wilton.

"The girls loved hearin' Bible stories. Their favorite was the one about the sick man who got lowered on a mat through the roof by his friends." She chuckles, "That was the only way they could think of to get him in front of Jesus to be healed. Now you know they were determined."

Grandma's eyes twinkle with remembrance.

"Well, anyway, one day, while I was outside hangin' clothes on the line, I saw those two girls in the barn. Your momma and Clara were always up to somethin'," she grins.

"That day, they were pretendin' they were lowerin' the sick man through the roof." Grandma claps her hands and laughs. "Those girls tied an old piece of wood to a rope and were lowerin' all of Clara's baby dolls through a hole in the hayloft. Then, they started yellin' through the hole, 'Jesus our friend needs you.'" Grandma puts her hand to her heart. "It just made my heart full that day. They had the best time together, those two. That's right, they sure did." Her voice trailing off.

"That is the cutest story, Grandma," says Effie

She looks right at her granddaughter.

"They didn't see color, Effie. No one gave 'em trouble for being best friends, either. Not out in the countryside, where no one was around to notice or care. Everybody had too much work to do."

She exhales.

"I often heard Miss Peavy prayin' the same prayer while the girls sat at her feet. I can still hear her words. I remember them well, I sure do."

"Well, what were they, Grandma?" Effie asks.

Grandma Nellie sits up, folding her hands, her voice lowering with reverence.

She prayed, "Heavenly Father, may our faith break the sky in two and let the face of God shine through. And when it does, please, please bring people of all colors together in peace, just like these two little ones at my feet."

Grandma closes her eyes for a moment, then sighs.

"I can still picture 'em, sittin' there, holdin' Clara's dolls so they could pray too."

Effie reaches for Grandma Nellie's hand. "That's beautiful, Grandma."

Grandma Nellie looks out across the room.

"I still pray that, baby," she says. "Then, when the girls got a little older, they were allowed to go down to the bayou by themselves behind their property. They had built a little house out of sticks and branches and old wood they hauled from the barn. They called it WC's Playhouse, standing for Willia and Clara's Playhouse. They had put their names together because they told me one day that they were sisters and would always be together.

Her voice catches.

"As they got even older, around 13 or 14, things changed. Clara spent more time with her White friends. Less time with Willa Mae. I think that was hard on your momma."

Effie leans in. "What happened after that, and what about this embroidery?"

"I'm gettin' there, baby. It's all a part of the story."

Grandma's face darkens, a shadow passing over her features.

"One Christmas Eve … everything changed."

Grandma's voice cracks with emotion.

"It was bitter cold that night, like ones we don't often get down here. I remember because we were freezin' in this house, huddled around the fire. We stayed by that fire all night to keep warm, sleepin' on pallets on the floor. I remember hearing the old hoot owl hootin' in the tall oak tree down the street. Maybe it was an omen."

She glances toward the window, as if looking into the past. "The way the story goes is that the Peavys were headed to Christmas Eve service. The roads were icy."

Effie tightly grips the embroidery frame.

"What happened, Grandma?"

"Well, the sleet got worse, and then the car …"

Before she can finish, a voice calls from the screen door, pulling them back to the present.

"Hey, it's me!"

Bootsie steps inside, balancing a pan with a towel draped over it.

"The biscuits just came out of the oven to go with the soup I brought earlier. I had to bring them over while they were hot."

She sets the pan down and holds up a glass jar.

"Didn't know if you had any cane syrup, so I brought some of that too."

She greeted Grandma Nellie and Effie, her presence filling the house with love and familiarity. Bootsie and Willa Mae always popped in and out of each other's houses daily.

"Effie, baby, take these to the kitchen for me, will ya. I want to go check in on your momma."

Bootsie places them on the side table and disappears to the bedroom.

Grandma Nellie pats Effie's leg.

"Well," she says with a smile, "seems like the rest of this story is for later ... or maybe even for another day."

"That's alright, Grandma," Effie says, though her mind lingered on the unfinished story.

Effie takes the biscuits and cane syrup into the kitchen, but as soon as they are set down, she turns straight for the phone, her thoughts no longer on the story but on Wilton.

She dials his number, Dickens 2-1913, without hesitation. She knows it by heart.

Ring.

Ring.

Ring.

Nothing.

"Where are they?" she whispers.

Putting the phone back onto the hook, she walks into the front room sinking into the couch, tears spilling out before she can stop them.

From the bedroom, Bootsie's voice carries through the house.

"Effie Rose, you better set your alarm clock. Your momma still has a fever. You need to go to the Benoits' for her again tomorrow."

Effie lifts her head, wiping the tears away, trying to disguise the crack in her voice.

"Momma, I have school."

Bootsie steps into the doorway, hands on her hips.

"Now, Effie, you know that after Wilton, you're one of the smartest students. You can miss one day. Wilton can get your papers from school."

Effie drops her head back onto the cushion, fresh tears slipping down her cheeks.

"No," she whispers, her voice barely audible. "I don't think he can."

With that, she falls sound asleep on the couch.

PART VII

CRUCIFORM HEALING

Where the Wounds We Carry Meet the Cross

Wounds run deep—some passed down, some inflicted by others, and some we've carried without even knowing their origins. Mixed in with our own experiences, they weave through our DNA like an invisible thread. But, healing comes not just through time, but through truth—and through Jesus Christ. The cross is where injustice met mercy, where sorrow met redemption. There, in the dust beneath the splintered cross, transformation begins. This is cruciform healing: Arms wide, heart exposed—where the weight of our wounds is met by the weight of God's glory.

CHAPTER TWENTY-ONE

Monday Night, March 28, 1960

Wilton | Day of Sit-In

Wilton awakes. It's dark. He tries to place where he is, but all that comes to him is a deep ache, throbbing between his temples. As he stirs, the pain sharpens, slicing through his head. Panic rises. Where am I? Sitting up too quickly, the room tilts and spins around him. He closes his eyes, trying–desperately–to steady himself.

Like pieces of a puzzle snapping into place, it all rushes back. Miss Pearl. The sit-in. The White boy. The ferry ride home with his head bleeding. The kind lady at the snack bar pressing a Coke into his hands. As the room stills, his eyes are drawn to the one small lit lamp on the table outside the bedroom door ... sitting there is the familiar teacup. Yes, he thinks, calm washing over him. *I'm still at Preacher's house.*

His gaze shifts to something else sitting on the table, something familiar. He would know it anywhere ... the olive-green work hat that his dad wears every day to the school. Unease creeps back in. He remembers now that his daddy had been here, standing in this very room, telling him they had things to talk about. *What could be so important?* He thinks. *And why was he even here, at Preacher's house?*

Suddenly, he feels a gentle weight pressing against his leg. Looking down, he sees Scrappy curled up on the covers, his one sweet eye gazing up at him.

"Scrappy boy," Wilton says in a whisper as he reaches over to scratch behind his ears. "You stayed here with me."

His tail thumps against the bed cover.

Hearing voices from the next room, Wilton looks up.

"I'm back, Moses. Is he awake?"

"It's been quiet in there," Preacher says. "I checked on him a few times."

Wilton hears the rustle of a paper bag.

"Well," his father replies, "I brought the red beans and rice for supper."

Preacher chuckles. "Now you know I haven't had Clyde's red beans and rice in years."

A pot clangs against the stove. "I'll heat 'em up."

Wilton lies still, listening. His head pounds. His mind races with questions.

Why is Daddy calling Preacher, "Moses," like he knows him well? And why is Preacher talking about Uncle Ray from New Orleans?

The thoughts swirl in his head, spinning like a top.

Just then, his daddy appears in the doorway.

"You awake, son? How you feelin'?"

Wilton shifts, wincing at the lingering pain in his head.

"Like I got hit by a truckload of bricks, but I think I'll live."

His daddy exhales, relief in his eyes.

"You had us worried. I brought some red beans and rice from your uncle for supper. Moses ... uhh, I mean ... Preacher is heating them up. Says he made some cornbread yesterday we can have with it. I'm thankful he saw you coming off the ferry and took good care of you."

"Dadd—"

"Son—"

Speaking at the same time, both voices hesitate.

"You go first," his daddy says.

Sitting up in bed, Wilton looks through the door into the other room, then to his daddy.

"Why did you call Preacher ... I mean ... you talk to him like ... well, like you know him really well."

His daddy stays quiet, looking through the bedroom door.

"You called him Moses," Wilton blurts out. "In all my years here, I've never even seen you talk to Preacher. I didn't even know his name was Moses."

His daddy pulls up a chair next to the bed, sitting down with a heavy sigh. The warm, savory aroma of red beans and rice drifts from the kitchen right into the bedroom.

"Son," his voice low, "I've been keepin' somethin' from you for a very long time, and I'm not proud of that."

"What?" Wilton's voice rises as he gets up, standing on the side of the bed. Almost losing his balance, he grips the iron headboard.

"What have you been hiding from me?"

"Wilton," his father jumps up from the chair and steadies him. "I need you to get back in bed and try to settle yourself so we can talk. This isn't easy for me, and I don't think it's gonna be easy for you either."

Wilton watches his daddy for a moment, sensing the gravity in his face, then slowly sits back down on the bed.

From the next room, Preacher opens the front door to leave. He calls back to them. "The red beans and rice are heatin' on the stove, whenever y'all are ready." He nods toward Wilton's father before stepping outside, leaving them alone.

Wilton's daddy lets out a slow breath, rubbing his hands together before speaking again.

"Wilton, you know I love you. And I loved your momma so much, too."

"I know that, Daddy," Wilton swallows hard. "But why don't you ever talk about her? The only thing you ever told me was that she had a strong faith–that she was teaching me all about God before she died, I mean ... before she was ... murdered."

He pauses, looking out the window, then sharply turns back to face his daddy.

"But that's all I know," he says in a tone filled with frustration. "I've always wanted to know more about her. I want to remember her. All I do is spend time making up stories in my mind of how she died."

"I'm gonna change that," Daddy says. "And it starts now. I've never really told you the whole story."

Wilton tenses.

"You once told me something about an angry White mob."

His father exhales, rubbing a hand over his face.

"That's not the full story, son. You were too young to understand it all. I had to protect you."

"Daddy, I need to know the truth now," Wilton says, his voice firm. "I'm not a child anymore."

His father leans forward in his chair, resting his elbows on his knees.

"Back when we lived outside of Ellisville, Mississippi, we stayed in the same house with your granny and pap. They were your momma's momma and daddy. I don't even know how much you remember of them."

Wilton shrugs his shoulders. "I have a few memories," he admits. "But not much. I know you said we left there when I was only five."

His daddy nods.

"Well, when we lived in Mississippi, out there in the country, I worked in the back of one of the feed stores, loadin' up supplies for customers. Your momma helped your granny iron for several White families in town. We were poor, but we did okay."

A faint smile crosses his daddy's face.

"Let me tell you something about your momma, son. She was the sweetest and prettiest lady you'd ever meet, but she had a strong-willed streak in her."

He pauses, meeting Wilton's gaze.

"Just like someone else I know."

Wilton gives a knowing smile.

"Your momma knew right from wrong, and she was willing to fight for it," his father continues. "Her daddy—your pap—was a pastor at a little church not far from our house. A small one-room church, but let me tell you, he sure spoke powerful sermons to those country folks."

Leaning back, he warmly chuckles.

"Your momma used to say he always had a little fire and brimstone in him."

Then, his expression darkens.

"But as Granny told the story, in 1919, just a few years before your momma and I were born, something happened that changed him. Something that made him start preaching about more than just heaven and hell.

"That's when he started preaching about the injustices against our people. And that, son," his father swallows hard, his voice dropping lower, "is when everything started to change."

Wilton's father gets up and walks over to the window, staring into the darkness. He lingers there. Pensive. Silent. After a long moment, he turns, leaning against the windowsill, pushing his sleeves up from the heat. Crossing his arms, his eyes settle firmly on Wilton.

"Let me explain something to you, son," he says, his voice heavy. "Back then, all it took was a wrong look, a wrong word. And before you knew it, a mob of White men were at your door, dragging you out, deciding your fate before the sun even set."

Wilton reaches for the cup on the nightstand and takes a slow sip of water. He doesn't speak.

His father exhales, rubbing his jaw. "But let me get back to 1919 when it all happened. The town still talks about it." He shakes his head, jaw tightening. "A young Colored man, John Hartfield,[69] only twenty-six years old, was hanged from a tree."

Wilton lets out a gasp. His father doesn't flinch, allowing his son to feel the horror of the story.

"He was accused of assaulting a White girl. Now, many say that the two of them had a consensual relationship. False accusations were placed on Black people all the time. We often became the scapegoats. The law didn't give that young man any kind of fair trial. He never had a chance.

His father shakes his head. "Your pap ... he saved the newspaper from that day. I saw it with my own eyes."

His father leans forward.

"The headline read: John Hartfield Will Be Lynched By Ellisville Mob at Five O'Clock."[70]

Wilton swallows hard.

"The governor himself said he was powerless to stop it." His father's voice darkens. "Thousands came to watch. Brought their children. Took pictures and turned them into postcards. Some even cut pieces from his body ... sold them off like trophies." He shakes his head. "Pure evil."

Pushing off the windowsill, he walks back to the chair and lowers himself into it. Wilton sits on the edge of the bed, his body feeling stronger.

His father watches him carefully, then reaches a hand toward him, but Wilton shifts away.

"I'm okay," Wilton mutters. "Just ... keep going."

His father nods. "I'm telling you this story, son, because I want you to understand how your momma ended up being ... murdered.

They both let the vileness of the word sink in, feeling its weight settle between them—opening a wound that has lain raw, never healed.

"That next Sunday after the lynching," Wilton's father says, "I was told your pap, filled with anger, stood in that pulpit and preached about justice. He condemned the evil of what had happened, called it out for what it was. Got his congregation all worked up." His voice tightens. "White folks didn't like that. Word spread fast, and suddenly, they saw your pap as a rabble-rouser, a threat."

Scrappy stirs from his curled-up spot on the blanket, stretches, then shakes himself off before padding over to Wilton and curling up beside him. As Wilton strokes the dog's soft fur, a small wave of calm settles over him. He looks up.

"What happened after that, Daddy?"

His father exhales. "Years went by, and your pap kept on preachin', fierce, bold, almost ... angry. Like your momma used to say, fire and brimstone."

He pauses, rubbing a hand over his jaw, lost in thought.

"I remember the day rocks came flyin' through the church windows while the choir was singin'. White folks tried to burn the place down more than once, but somehow, it always stood." His expression softens. "When I was growing up, my family went to Pap's church, too. That's where your momma and I met as kids. We grew up together. And in that same little country church, we got married."

Wilton shakes his head. "I can't believe you never told me any of this." A rumble of thunder could be heard in the distance. "And what happened to Granny and Pap?"

His father shifts in his chair. "Let me finish, son. We'll get to that."

Wilton nods, leaning in.

His father takes a slow breath. "Then, in 1943, you were born." He lets out a soft chuckle. "You were the light of your pap's life. After you came along, that fire and brimstone preachin' settled. He changed. The last thing he wanted was for harm to come your way."

The pitter-patter of rain can be heard clinking on the tin roof. Wilton's father stands, crosses the room, and turns on a lamp. Its soft glow flickers against the walls as he returns, this time sitting on the bed beside his son. Scrappy nestles between them and rests his head between his paws..

"Then one day," his father says, his voice heavier now, "everything changed."

Wilton stiffens.

"Pap was in town, waitin' for me outside the feed store. We were pickin' up supplies—like we always did. We were buildin' a little house for the three of us, just behind theirs. You were almost five." He shakes his head. "Then, right in front of the store, two White boys sat on a bench, laughin', like something was funny."

His father's expression darkens.

"Pap heard them talkin'. He looked down and saw what they were holdin'. A postcard." He swallows hard. "It was a picture of a Black man, lynched—hangin' from a tree." His voice drops lower. "It was John Hartfield."

Wilton pulls Scrappy in closer to him, his pulse pounding.

"The boys laughed, proud to own that card. One of them started braggin' about how his granddaddy kept one of the man's fingers … as a souvenir."

Wilton's stomach twists.

His father's jaw clenches. "Pap couldn't take it. He grabbed the postcard right outta that boy's hands and tore it to pieces. Told them, 'I'm not the judge, but God Almighty is. And He will judge you, your grandaddy, and everyone who had a hand in that wickedness.'"

Silence swallows the room, except for the thunder, which now seems to be just above the house.

"That night, those boys ran home and told their daddies." His father exhales shakily. "And that same night … a mob came lookin' for Pap."

A flash of lightning comes through the window, illuminating the room.

"They came to the house, we found out later—angry, drunk, ready to kill. But Pap wasn't home." His father's voice catches. "But your momma was."

Wilton's breath stills.

"Her name was Belle," Daddy says, looking down. "I'm so sorry, son, I just couldn't speak her name until now. I wasn't there … able to protect her.

Looking back up at his son, he says, "It's nice to say her name again."

Clearing his throat, Daddy continues.

"She'd stayed behind to finish the ironing for the White families. You, your granny, and Pap were at Wednesday night church. I was workin' late at the feed store." He swallows. "She was all alone," his voice choking up. "I wasn't there to protect her."

"Oh my gosh, Daddy, what did they do to her?" asks Wilton.

His father presses a hand to his forehead, squeezing his eyes shut. When he looks back at Wilton, his expression is cold.

Grabbing his father's arm, he says, "Daddy, I need to know. Please."

Tears roll down his daddy's cheeks as he shakes his head, his words barely audible.

"They chose her, son ... they chose her."

Wilton says nothing. The lines of his face caught between anger and sorrow. His hand covers his mouth, shaking his head.

"She tried to run. We found her out back, in that little house we were buildin'." His voice breaks. "We found her."

Wilton's hands tremble.

"What did they do to her?" Wilton's voice is sharp now, edged with desperation. "Don't try to protect me, Daddy."

His father meets his gaze.

"Son," he says, his voice thick with grief, "it doesn't matter how old you get. A parent always wants to protect their child." But as he looks at Wilton, something shifts in his face.

His son isn't a child anymore. He's a man now. A man who deserves to know the truth.

"I'm sorry I never told you," he says. "Maybe I was tryin' to protect myself, too."

Scrappy moves closer, as if sensing the weight in the room. He rests his head gently on Wilton's knee, tail still for once, eyes watching the two of them with quiet empathy.

Wilton's dad swallows hard.

"They beat her bad," his father says. "She lived for two days."

Wilton's eyes well up.

"We stayed with her. Cared for her the best we could." His father's voice is trembling. "We tried to keep you from seein' her like that. You were just a little boy. You didn't understand what was happenin.'"

Wilton stares ahead, unblinking, as though his mind has shut it all out, even as he strains to remember.

"On the second day," his father continues, "you came inside, holding a handful of wildflowers. You said they were for Momma."

Wilton's chest tightens.

"We let you go to her." His daddy wipes his eyes. "You climbed onto a stool beside her bed. Tried to put the flowers in her hand, but she was too weak to hold them."

Wilton's heart pounds.

"So you just ... laid them on her." His father looks down. "And you held her hand."

Wilton's vision blurs.

"You told her, 'I love you, Momma.'" His father's voice breaks. "That was the only time she opened her eyes. Just a little. Just enough to let you know she heard you."

Tears flow down Wilton's cheeks.

"She died that night," his father says softly. "We placed your flowers in the casket with her."

Wilton stares at the floor, his whole body trembling.

"Daddy," he whispers. "I don't remember any of it."

His father nods. "I know, son. It was just too much for you. You were so young."

Wilton looks out the window, squinting, "It's like I don't remember anything about that part of my life. I do remember comforting smells and tastes." He looks toward the door to the kitchen "... that teacup ..."

A long silence stretches between them. Then, Wilton lifts his head, his voice stronger now.

"But I'll hold on to that precious moment as long as I live."

"Son," he says, looking at Wilton. "I'm sorry I didn't tell you these things sooner. I think it's hard for me to talk about it, too. It brings up too much. So ... let's try to get through this together."

He reaches for his hand. "We've got some healin' to do. And I wanna tell you lots more stories about your momma while we sit in the rockin' chairs on the porch. Maybe it'll help bring back more memories to you."

Scrapp begins to lick their hands.

"He knows we need his love right now," Daddy says with a soft smile.

They both begin to pet Scrappy, but Daddy's face turns solemn again.

"There's more I need to tell you, son." His voice heaving with regret.

"I never forgave your pap. I blamed him for what happened to your momma." He pauses, rubbing the back of his neck. "That's why we left Ellisville. You and I started over here, and not long after ... your granny passed."

His voice softens. "I think it was just too much for her heart to bear."

Wilton looks up in anticipation of one more piece of the puzzle.

"Then what happened to my pap?" His voice is uncertain. "How did he die?"

His daddy looks at him, a deep sadness in his eyes. "I should never have lied to you," he says slowly. "You see ... your pap didn't die."

Just about then, the door creaks open, and Preacher steps inside. Wilton's eyes snap toward the doorway.

Wilton's daddy turns toward him.

"It's okay, Moses," he says. "Come on in. You should be part of this conversation, too."

Wilton looks from his father to Preacher, confusion flashing across his face, his heart racing.

"Is Preacher my ..." He can't even finish the sentence.

Preacher takes a step forward.

Wilton's daddy gently places a hand on Wilton's back.

"Wilton, meet your pap."

Wilton jumps to his feet, his breath coming fast. He looks between them, searching their faces as if trying to make sense of something impossible.

"I don't understand." His voice is edged with disbelief. "All this time ... all these years in this town? I must've passed Preacher a hundred times when I was getting on the ferry."

His stomach clenches. "And yet, you told me my pap was dead." His voice catches. "Daddy, you lied to me."

His daddy gets up from the bed, his shoulders heavy with guilt.

"I wanted to tell you so many times, son," he says. "But I couldn't. I made your pap swear never to say a word to you. To me, he was dead, and I wanted him to be dead to you also."

Silence fills the room. He looks up at Wilton. "And for that," his voice a whisper now, "I am truly sorry."

Wilton turns sharply toward Preacher, his eyes burning with hurt. "You let me sit here in this house, talk to you like you were just another person in town, and yet you wouldn't tell me the truth?"

Preacher meets his gaze.

"I swore to your daddy, Wilton."

Wilton shakes his head, stepping back. "Why, Daddy?" His voice rises, raw with pain. "By taking my pap away, you took part of my momma away from me."

His daddy's expression twists with remorse. "I know," he murmurs. "It wasn't right. But I was angry. I blamed Moses, your pap, for her death. For all of it."

Daddy turns to Preacher. "Moses," his voice filled with pain, "And for that, I ask your forgiveness."

Preacher steps closer, his eyes fixed on the man he once called his son-in-law. Resting a hand on Daddy's shoulder, his voice is calm. Filled with kindness, he says, "Albert, I've been given more grace than I could ever deserve from our mighty Creator. Grace that covered all the guilt I held for years. How could I not pass that same grace to you?

Albert nods, feeling a weight lifted.

Turning to Wilton, his voice low and full of remorse, "I'm so sorry, son. Will you forgive me?"

Silence lingers between them.

"I'll understand if you can't," his voice filled with emotion. "Or if you need time."

Wilton doesn't speak. He stares at the floor.

Then, looking up, he murmurs, "Daddy ... Pap was right here."

Wilton's eyes are now brimming with tears.

"Right here. Where I was growing up." His voice cracks. "How could you do that to me?"

His daddy lowers his head.

"I know, son. And I'm sorry that you lost all these years with your pap," He exhales, voice raw. "I was hurting so bad. I needed someone to blame."

His gaze shifts to Moses, holding it steady. "So I blamed your pap."

Wilton takes a few steps closer to his daddy.

"How could I not forgive you, Daddy? I love you—and I know now that you were hurtin' too."

He reaches out, and they hug for a long, quiet minute, both crying. Still reeling from the weight of it all, Wilton glances at Preacher. When he speaks again, his voice is softer.

"Well," he says, shaking his head slightly, "I think Preacher and I ... I mean ... my pap and I... we've already started making up for lost time."

Preacher steps closer, his eyes glistening. "Would you be willing to give your pap a hug?" he asks gently.

Wilton hesitates only a moment before stepping forward. As they embrace, Preacher, his pap, whispers, "You got my fire in you, son. And I'm so proud of that."

Wilton lets out a breath that feels like it's been trapped inside him for years.

"I knew there was something about you," he says, pulling back slightly to meet his pap's eyes. "Something I couldn't put my finger on, but it was stirring in me." He glances at the table, his expression shifting as realization dawns. "And that teacup, I know now. It was my momma's. I remember."

A small smile tugs at Preacher's lips.

"You got your momma's smile, son," he says, his voice thick with emotion. "I've been waiting years to tell you that."

Daddy steps closer, his hands clenching, unclenching at his sides. Finally, he looks Moses in the eye.

"I'd like to give you a hug, too, Moses. If you'll have it." His voice wavers. "Belle would want me to. And I want to, also."

Moses doesn't hesitate. He pulls Daddy into a strong embrace, his voice barely above a whisper.

"I already feel closer to Belle again," says Daddy.

"She's here with us, Albert," Moses murmurs. "I feel her."

Daddy nods, his throat tightening. "She and Granny, too," he says.

A moment passes, thick with unspoken words, slowly giving way to the first stirrings of healing.

Preacher clears his throat.

"Well," he says, his voice filled with hope, "I think we all need to eat."

He and Daddy serve up the red beans and rice, the rich aroma filling the small house. Preacher sets a plate of hot cornbread in the center of the table, the butter melting in the night shadows. The thunder had rolled down the river. The moon is high in the sky.

They sit. They bless the food.

As they begin to eat, Daddy looks over at Moses.

"Thank you," he says quietly, his voice barely above a whisper, "for coming to get me today. I know that couldn't have been easy for you."

Moses meets his gaze. "I've learned something," he says, pausing for a moment. "When you feel God's nudges, you better pay attention."

CHAPTER TWENTY-TWO

"If we do not transform our pain, we will most assuredly transmit it."[71]

-Richard Rohr

March 29, 1960

Effie wakes to the familiar smell of Community Coffee dripping from the old enamel drip pot on the stove. It is a ritual. Effie has watched her momma and Grandma Nellie make coffee this way every morning since she was a little girl, the deep, roasted aroma filling the house. After last night, the scent brings a small sense of comfort. The phone is gone from the couch where she slept, her shoes neatly set aside, and Great-Grandma Rose's quilted blanket is tucked around her.

Hearing cups clink in the kitchen, Effie sits up, rubbing the sleep from her eyes. "Grandma?" she whispers, careful not to wake Momma.

"I'm here, baby, gettin' your coffee ready," Grandma Nellie calls back from the kitchen.

"You got fifteen minutes before you need to leave for the Benoits."

No time to try Wilton, Effie thinks. I'm already late. If I don't get there soon, it'll be a repeat of yesterday's catastrophe.

She moves quickly ... bathing, dressing, and gulping down her coffee in a matter of minutes. Snatching one of Bootsie's biscuits from the kitchen, she heads for the door.

"Have a blessed day, baby," comes Momma's voice, a little bit stronger from the back bedroom.

"You too, Momma. Feel better."

Effie opens the door. She suddenly stops.

"Oh, and Momma, I almost forgot." Effie pauses, digging into her purse.

"Mimi drew you a picture of a rainbow. She says it would help you feel better."

She steps back into the room and hands Willa Mae the small drawing.

"That sweet baby girl," Momma says, running her fingers over the colors. "Always thinkin' about her Willa. You thank her for me now, you hear? And tell her it's real pretty, and that these colors cheered me up."

"I'll be sure to, Momma."

Effie turns and steps onto the porch and out the screen door, creaking as it swings shut behind her. The air is filled with the scent of spring. Her pappy's magnolia tree, planted years ago by the front porch, is beginning to bloom. She pauses, closes her eyes, and takes a deep breath. The sweet fragrance lingers, taking her back to her childhood when she would pick the biggest white magnolia blossoms, put each one in a cup of water, and present them to Momma and Grandma Nellie ... until her thoughts drift back to Wilton.

Letting out a sigh, she mutters, "I need to talk to him."

From the next yard over, Bootsie calls out through her open kitchen window, where pink-flowered curtains blow gracefully in the spring breeze.

"I see you got one of my biscuits, Effie."

Her voice carries a teasing note.

"You oughta go and make some of your momma's biscuits for those Benoit girls. You know that recipe just as well as she does."

Effie smirks and calls back. "They'd probably take one bite and say, 'This isn't how Willa Mae makes them!'"

Bootsie lets out a hearty laugh.

"You got that right!"

With a grin, Effie shakes her head, making her way through the yard, already bracing herself for the day ahead.

A faint voice drifts through the bedroom window behind her.

"I heard that, Effie Rose," Momma calls out.

Effie looks over her shoulder, shaking her head.

"Golly, Momma, your ears are everywhere."

"You know that's the truth," Bootsie chimes in from her kitchen window as she's busy washing dishes.

Halfway down Magnolia, just as she's about to cross Levee Road, Effie hesitates. *Should I just run to his house real quick and check on him? I know he hasn't left for school yet.* The thought nags at her. Before she can decide, a familiar voice interrupts.

"Morning, Effie." She turns to see Mr. Benoit slowing his car beside her, his elbow resting out the driver's side window.

"Thanks for coming to the house again today," he says.

"Yes, sir," Effie replies with a polite nod.

"Your momma feeling any better?" he asks. "Maybe we'll see her back at work tomorrow?"

Effie lets out a sigh.

"Oh, I sure do hope so … I mean, yes, sir, she's … feeling much better! I'm sure she'll be there tomorrow. Don't you worry about a thing," she adds quickly. "I'm headed over now to make breakfast."

Another car approaches from behind, and Mr. Benoit gives a quick wave before rolling up his window and driving off down Magnolia toward work.

No chance to check on Wilton now, she thinks with a sigh. *I'll have to wait.*

When she reaches the Benoits' house, she pauses before stepping up onto the back porch, unsure what kind of scene she's about to walk into after yesterday's chaos. Joe Boy is stretched out in the shade and barely lifts his head.

"Hey, boy," she murmurs sweetly, crouching to give him a scratch behind the ears. "No Frosted Flakes today?"

His tail gives a half-hearted wag, but he doesn't budge.

"You were a bad, bad boy yesterday, and I bet your belly's paying for it now."

Joe Boy's eyes look up, then his eyes drift closed as if to say I don't wanna talk about it. Effie chuckles, shaking her head as she stands up and steps onto the porch.

Effie knocks on the door, then pushes open the screen and peeks inside.

It's so quiet, she thinks. *A good sign. Or ... It could also be a bad one.*

"Hellooo?" she calls out, stepping inside. "I'm here. I'm starting on breakfast."

"We're down the hall, Effie," Mrs. Benoit calls out in a cheerful tone. "Come on down."

"Be there in a minute," Effie replies. *Well, this is quite the change from yesterday*, she thinks.

She hangs her purse on the hook under the stairs, then rushes into the kitchen to turn on the oven. It isn't Saturday, but she decides to surprise the girls. Today, she'll prove she can make biscuits just as good as Willa Mae's.

Heading down the hall, she stops at the doorway to the Benoits' bedroom.

"Effie!" The girls call out in unison, genuinely excited to see her.

All three of them are curled up in bed with their mother, taking turns sipping from her cup of café au lait. In Louisiana, they say, babies start drinking coffee in their milk bottles.

"Effie," Anna Beth pipes up, her stomach clearly leading the conversation, "what's for breakfast? I'm really hungry."

"It's a surprise," Effie teases. "So I'd better get back to the kitchen and get it started."

"Oh, Effie," Mrs. Benoit says, shifting under the pile of her daughters. "Would you mind bringing us another café au lait to share? The milk is already heated on the stove. And with a little sugar, please."

"Yes, ma'am."

Walking back toward the kitchen, Effie shakes her head in thought. *This is quite the change from yesterday. Momma was right, you never know what kind of mood Mrs. Benoit will be in.*

After fetching Mrs. Benoits' coffee, she returns to the kitchen, pulling out the Crisco, milk, and flour to quickly make the biscuit dough. Welcoming the peace and quiet, she rolls it out, cutting perfect rounds before sliding them into the oven. Turning back toward the sink, she nearly jumps.

Mimi stands there, quiet and wide-eyed, already dressed for school.

"Is Willa feeling better?" she asks. "I miss her. But I like you too, Effie."

Effie softens.

"Well, you're about to like me even more. Look at what's in the oven."

Mimi stretches onto her tiptoes, peering into the high oven.

"I knew it was biscuits!" she squeals. "I could smell them. But it's not Saturday."

"I know," Effie says with a smile.

"I wanted to surprise y'all cuz I probably won't be here tomorrow."

Mimi throws her arms around Effie's waist.

"Thank you, Effie."

"Aww, you're welcome, Mimi, and you know what? I like you, too."

"And oh!" Effie's face lights up. "Momma loved her rainbow you made for her. She says the colors were real pretty and it made her feel much better."

Mimi beamed, knowing how much it meant to her Willa.

As Effie stirs the grits, along with the scrambled eggs that she is making to go with the biscuits, she feels a satisfied warmth going through her. *The girls really are quite sweet,* she thinks. The oven timer dings. She pulls out the steaming biscuits, cuts them in half, butters them, then sets them on the table.

"Girls," she calls out, "breakfast!"

Anna Beth and Mary Grace rush in, sliding into their chairs, while Mimi is already waiting, hands folded, eyes on the biscuits. Effie looks at the girls and grins. *Maybe this morning will turn out just fine after all,* she thinks. But she can't keep her mind off Wilton.

"Oh boy, biscuits!" Anna Beth exclaims.

"Yep, that's my surprise," Effie says. "I made grits and eggs, too."

"Thank you, Effie," the girls chime in together.

Mimi, eyes hopeful, turns to Anna Beth.

"I'll trade you the top of my biscuit for your bottom."

Anna Beth shakes her head. "No way, Mimi. Everybody likes the crispy bottoms."

Mimi pouts.

"Anyways, these bottoms aren't quite as crispy as Willa's," she whispers.

And there it is, Effie thinks to herself. *I knew that was coming.* She lets out a quiet giggle, shaking her head.

"But they're still really yummy, Effie!" Mimi adds quickly, as she jumps up from the table and runs over to give her a hug.

"Is Willa Mae coming back tomorrow?" Mimi asks.

"I'm sure she will," Effie reassures her. "She misses you girls."

Mimi nods. "Daddy missed her too this morning. He says nobody knows how to polish his shoes like Willa Mae."

"Now I'm sure that is true," says Effie.

Mimi suddenly hops down from her chair and runs over, clutching a piece of paper in her hands.

"I made this for you, Effie!" She beams. "It's a pink flower for spring. You can hang it up in your bedroom when you get home."

Effie takes the picture, reading the careful, wobbly handwriting: To Effie, Love Mimi.

Effie's heart softens.

"I love it, Mimi. I share a room with Momma, so she'll get to enjoy it too."

Mimi's face lights up.

"Tell her I said hi, okay?"

Then, in a flash, she's dashing down the hall, calling out, "Mama, Mama! Willa will be back tomorrow!"

Effie smiles as she watches her go, then turns back to the counter. Willa's blue plastic cup sits just behind the sink. She picks it up and pours in the last of the morning's coffee. As she sips, she stares out the window at the weeping willows swaying in the breeze.

Her thoughts drift to Wilton.

Is he in jail? At the hospital? A lump forms in her throat. *Or something even worse, something she hasn't even wanted to imagine? If that was the case, surely his daddy would have gotten in touch with me by now.*

Once the girls are off to school, Effie spots Mrs. Benoit's list of chores on the counter. One task stands out: Take Mimi's Easter dress to Miss Jeanne Marie at the cleaners for hemming.

Miss Jeanne Marie is known for her sewing. She's been busy making dresses for the girls with Easter coming up. Effie tucks the dress under her arm and heads out.

At the back door of the cleaners, the hum of the sewing machine and bursts of steam from the presses fill the air. Miss Jeanne Marie sits at her machine, pedaling away, her hands skillfully guiding the fabric.

Effie loves that sound, the smooth, rhythmic stitching, like a song without words.

Spotting Doretha at her press, she makes her way over to her. Doretha looks up and says something, but the hiss of the steam drowns it out. Effie quickens her pace. When she reaches her, Doretha's face is tight with worry.

"Tell me you've got some news on Wilton," Doretha says.

Effie shakes her head.

"I don't. I thought you might."

Doretha's lips press together, shaking her head.

"No, nothing since yesterday. The news just says students were arrested and jailed. That's all I know."

Effie swallows hard.

"No one's answering the phone at his house."

"Lord have mercy," says Doretha.

Effie grips the dress in her hands.

"I gotta get this to Miss Jeanne Marie."

"Go, baby," Doretha says gently. "It'll all be okay."

Effie nods, but as she turns, her heart tells her she won't believe that until she sees Wilton for herself.

Effie walks toward the front of the cleaners. She stops as Miss Jeanne Marie comes into view. Effie watches, admiring her as she sits at her Singer treadle machine, her movements with beauty and ease. Her feet gracefully glide over the iron foot pedal, rocking back and forth in a steady rhythm, knowing just the right touch to set the speed. The leather belt hums as it spins the wheel, the needle dancing up and down with a melodic whirr through the fabric.

Every few stitches, she leans in, eyes narrowed in concentration, her hands guiding the fabric like she's done a thousand times before. Effie knows this passion well, for she carries the same love for careful hands and meaningful work, for the gentle rhythm that sings a beautiful song without words.

She makes her way over to the sewing machine. "Hi, Miss Jeanne Marie, says Effie.

"Well, hi, Effie," she says, as her foot lifts from the pedal and the song stills. "Looks like you're at the house again today. Is your momma feeling any better?" she asks.

"Better by the day," says Effie. "I think she'll be back tomorrow."

"Well, that was so kind of you to step in for your momma, especially on a school day," says Miss Jeanne Marie. "But, what I hear from your momma, you won't have any problem catching up."

They both chuckle.

"Looks like you have something for me there," says Miss Jeanne Marie.

"Mrs. Benoit asked me to bring Mimi's new dress to hem," she says, handing it over.

As she does, her eyes catch a familiar pattern draped over the worktable.

"Is that remnant fabric from Mimi's dress?"

Miss Jeanne Marie nods.

"It sure is. Would you like it?

Effie's face lights up.

"Oh, that would be wonderful! Thank you!"

"You sew, Effie?" Miss Jeanne Marie asks, passing her the leftover fabric.

"Yes, ma'am, I do! I love to sew! We have an old sewing machine at home that someone from church gave to us. One day, I'd like to be a seamstress like you."

Miss Jeanne Marie chuckles.

"Well, I sew when I can, but this cleaners keeps me runnin'. Your momma told me you're graduating this year. If you're interested, I'd be happy to give you a job here at the cleaners helping with alterations."

Effie hesitates.

"Thank you, Miss Jeanne Marie," she says carefully. "That's real nice of you. I know everybody here loves working for you."

Trying to change the subject, Effie glances down at the fabric in her hand.

"I could make a cute bow out of this for Mimi," she says. "And attach it to a bobby pin for her hair. She loves bows."

Miss Jeanne Marie's face softens.

"Oh, now I know she'd love that."

After leaving the cleaners and finishing up her last chore from the list, sweeping the front walk and porch, Mrs. Benoit approaches her with a new request.

"Effie, would you mind walking the girls home from school this afternoon?" she asks.

"Our neighbor girl, an eighth grader who usually walks with them, can't today. They also wanted to stop by the library to return their books and pick out a few new ones. I need to go to a last-minute committee meeting for the Garden Club, but I'll be back in about an hour.

She hands Effie a small stack of books.

"These are the ones that need to be returned. Willa usually waits for the girls outside the doors of the library."

Not really giving her a choice, she continues, "I hope you have time to stay a little bit longer? It would be so helpful."

"Yes, ma'am, that's … that's just fine," Effie replies, gathering the books in her hands.

"Once you get them back to the house, feel free to head on home," Mrs. Benoit adds. "They'll be fine for a few minutes until I get back home. Just have them start on their homework after their after-school snack and tell them not to leave the house."

Effie nods, but her mind is elsewhere.

Mrs. Benoit grabs her purse.

"And, Effie, thank you for everything these past two days. Yesterday was a rough start for me. I don't know what I would've done without you."

Effie forces a polite smile, watching as Mrs. Benoit steps out. *I don't know what you would have done without me either,* she thinks.

The moment she hears the car pull out of the driveway, she goes straight to the phone. *Wilton should be home from school by now,* she thinks, dialing quickly.

The line rings.

"Come on," she mutters, tapping her fingers against the counter.

"Answer."

"Answer."

Nothing.

The ringing goes on and on.

Slamming the receiver down in frustration, she grabs her purse from under the stairs and heads out the door.

She needs to get to school. Now.

Waiting at the gate of Holy Comforter, Effie shifts anxiously, a prickling sensation crawling up her neck. *Someone's watching me*, she feels.

She glances over her shoulder. A truck idles behind her. *Mr. Bubba.*

Everyone knows his reputation.

Effie, books in hand, slowly inches toward the far side of the gate, putting as much space between herself and the truck as possible.

Thank goodness, she thinks. The girls are coming down the front sidewalk, chattering away with one another.

"Hey, Effie!" Mimi calls, running up to hug her.

Just then, Bubba's son passes.

A sharp bump to Effie's shoulder sends the books flying from her arms.

"Oops, sorry," Ricky sneers, not bothering to look back. "Guess you better pick them up."

A cruel chuckle follows as he strides toward the truck.

"That's not nice," Mimi whispers, her small hand slipping into Effie's. Anna Beth and Mary Grace shoot glares toward Ricky.

Effie exhales, trying to maintain her composure.

"Don't say anything, girls. Just ignore him."

The truck rumbles. Bubba watches, smirking, before rolling away down the street.

A younger White man, about to walk through the gate, stops. He glances sharply toward the truck, then back at Effie.

"Here, let me help you," he says, crouching to gather the scattered books.

Relief washes over Effie.

"Thank you," she says softly, keeping her gaze down.

He smiles, nods, and walks through the school gate.

Holding on tightly to the books, Effie straightens and brushes off her dress.

"Alright, girls," she says, cautiously looking around. "Let's get these books dropped off."

Heading down Magnolia Street, Effie stops at the front door of the library.

"You girls go on in and return your books. Then pick out whatever you'd like," she says. "I'll be right here waiting. Afterward, we'll head home for your after-school snack."

Anna Beth tilts her head with a mysterious smile.

"What is it?"

Effie grins.

"Not telling. It's a surprise. But I will say, it's one of your favorites."

Mimi bounces on her toes.

"Now we gotta hurry!"

Effie watches them disappear inside. Through the large window, she sees them return their books, then scatter in different directions down the aisles, eager to find new ones.

She shifts her gaze, wondering what kind of sewing books the White library might have, knowing she can't check out any of them.

A tap on her shoulder startles her.

She quickly turns. Her hand goes to her heart as her eyes widen and shoulders drop, letting out a loud sigh of relief.

"Wilton!" She exclaims with a smile. Then, remembering how worried she had been, her expression just as quickly turns to a scowl.

"Where have you been?" Her words spill out in a rush. "I've been calling your house for two days! I thought you were in jail, or at the hospital, or maybe even..."

Wilton gently grips her arms with both of his hands.

"Calm down, Effie. I'm fine."

She exhales sharply. "Well, I didn't know you were fine."

"Well, I didn't know you were fine either," he counters.

"You weren't at school today. You didn't meet me at the ferry landing yesterday," he says, narrowing his eyes. "You chickened out, didn't you?"

Effie folds her arms. "I had a good reason. I needed to be at the Benoits."

Wilton shakes his head. "Well, that sounds safe ...You always need to comply."

"And you're always looking for trouble, Wilton."

He turns away, folding his arms, trying to compose himself.

Turning back to face her, he says abruptly, "I'm not looking for trouble. I'm looking to stand for what is right. I'm tired of standing in the shadows," he snaps. His eyes turn toward the library doors.

"Like you are right now, Effie. Standing in the shadow of this building because you can't go in. And you seem fine with it."

Effie stiffens. "Well, I'm not fine with it."

"Then why didn't you show up at the ferry landing?"

"Because Momma got sick, and I had to help her out."

She tilts her head and stares at him, allowing the silence to make him feel uncomfortable.

"Okay, I'm sorry, I didn't mean to make it sound that way. I hope your mom is feeling better. You did the right thing."

"You know, Wilton ... maybe I didn't really want to go to the sit-in. I can make that choice, you know."

Wilton huffs, shaking his head.

"That's your prerogative, Effie, but look at you. Here you are standing outside this White library not being able to go in, and I don't think you really mind. Just like you don't seem to mind picking up a hamburger around the back of River King, where stray dogs wait for scraps."

He steps closer, voice low but firm.

"But I can't. And I won't. I've got to call out what is wrong when I see it. Like your reverend says, fight for justice. That's why I went yesterday."

They move to the side as a White lady and her daughter step out of the library doors and continue down the sidewalk.

"Wilton," she says, her voice surrendering, "just tell me what happened. I don't want to argue or have a debate with you. I mean, all I know is that people got arrested and thrown in jail." Her words began to tumble out quickly with rising emotion. "And I didn't know if you were dead or alive or ..."

"Effie, stop." He gently holds on to her arms. "Look at me," Wilton says, his voice soft. "Try to calm down."

Effie's eyes well up, the worry from the past two days has taken a toll on her. Wilton takes her hand.

"I'm sorry I had you worried. But you had me worried, too. I didn't know why you weren't at school today. A lot has happened since I last saw you, some of it you won't believe."

"Well, what is it, for heaven's sake?" Effie presses, eyes searching his face. "And is that a cut on your head?"

Wilton rubs the side of his head, as if noticing the wound for the first time.

"It's too much to tell you here," he says. "Let's talk tomorrow during lunch at school."

His gaze shifts past her.

"And why are you standing out here by yourself, anyway?"

"The Benoit girls are inside," she says, nodding toward the library.

Just then, through the large front window, Effie sees a boy roughly yank a book from Mimi's hands. Before Mimi can react, he pushes her, and she falls to the floor.

Effie doesn't think, she moves. The library door swings open as she rushes inside, Wilton right behind her.

Effie runs to Mimi, bending down beside her, tears streaming down her face.

"He took my book, Effie, and pushed me down!"

Mimi, hardly able to catch her breath from crying, looks straight at Ricky and says, "And that wasn't kind, Ricky! Jesus wants us to be kind."

The librarian rushes over, flustered.

"I can handle this," she says sharply, cutting a glance at Effie and then to Wilton.

"These girls are my responsibility," Effie responds.

"I understand, but you need to please leave and wait outside. You know the rules, and I don't want any trouble here."

Trouble? Effie thinks, staring at the librarian in disbelief. *You're looking at the wrong people.*

The library doors swing open. Bubba barges through the doors, his presence engulfing the room. The librarian seems at a loss as to how to handle the situation. Everyone in the library now—Anna Beth, Mary Grace, the handful of Whites—

all fall silent. Effie doesn't wait to see what Bubba will say. She bends down, brushing a tear from Mimi's cheek.

"Girls," she says, looking over to Anna Beth and Mary Grace, "let's go."

"You better leave," Bubba growls at Effie and Wilton. "You don't belong in here."

Without flinching, she looks at Wilton and points to the door. She takes Mimi's hand, guiding her out of the library, Anna Beth and Mary Grace close behind. Wilton glares at Bubba as he walks out the door.

Outside, Mimi buries her face against Effie's skirt.

"I didn't do anything wrong."

"I know," Effie soothes, squeezing her hand. "That boy was not being nice at all."

"I saw Ricky take your book and push you," Anna Beth says, her voice trembling. "He is so mean."

Effie leads them around the corner of the building, kneeling beside Mimi. Wilton joins them.

"Listen to me," she says to Mimi gently. "You did nothing wrong. Are you hurt?"

Mimi sniffles, wiping her face.

"I think I'm okay. But ... he took my Boxcar Children book. I was getting it for DeDe."

Mary Grace steps closer. "Who's DeDe?" she asks.

"She's my friend I met through the fence at school," Mimi explains.

Anna Beth and Mary Grace look at each other, confused.

"She really wanted the newest Boxcar Children book, but she couldn't find it anywhere. I wanted to surprise her."

Looking up at Effie with teary eyes, she says, "Mama told me that there's a bookmobile just for the Colored children. Maybe they have the *Yellow House Mystery* there?"

Wilton exhales hard.

"I wouldn't get my hopes up, Mimi. You really think the Colored bookmobile has the newest Boxcar Children book? We just get leftovers—old, torn books nobody else wants."

Mimi's lip quivers.

"And you don't want to go inside there. It's not always safe."

Wilton continues, "I was in there when a rock came flying through the door. I heard someone yell, 'You're just a …'"

"That's enough, Wilton," Effie cuts in sharply. "You're scaring the girls." Wilton closes his eyes, regretting his words.

"Mimi was just wondering about the bookmobile," Effie says, softer this time. "She didn't need a whole essay from you. Did you even hear what she was asking, or do you just want to stay worked up?"

Pausing, taking a deep breath, Wilton crouches down to Mimi's level. Smiling and looking her in the eyes, he says, "I'm sorry I got a little angry, Mimi. Now try to dry those tears and tell me what happened. I want to hear the whole story."

Mimi hesitates, then mumbles.

"I don't understand why Ricky is so mean. His daddy is, too. Ricky just looked at me and said he wanted the book.

He grabbed it from me, and when I tried to get it back, he pushed me." She sniffles. "Father Joel says we should be kind to everybody, and Ricky wasn't, and I told him Jesus wants us to be kind."

Wilton nods. "Well, it sounds like Father Joel is a pretty smart man, and you did the right thing, Mimi, by speaking out and telling Ricky that Jesus wants us to be kind. And I tell you what, next time I'm at the bookmobile, I'll ask if they have *Yellow House Mystery* for your friend. I like books too."

Effie watches him closely. *Sometimes he can be so tender-hearted and sweet,* she thinks.

Just then, Mimi gasps, "Oh no," and hides behind Wilton.

Anna Beth and Mary Grace instinctively move back, eyes wide and faces stiff.

Looking back at them, Wilton says, "It's okay, girls. Just stay there, everything will be fine."

Ricky heads over to Mimi with Bubba close behind.

Effie and Wilton move in a protective stance in front of Mimi and the girls.

"I'm not gonna do nothin'," Ricky mutters. "My daddy's makin' me give the book back because she's Mr. Shot's little girl.

Mimi looks up at Effie, "Is he going to say he's sorry for pushing me?"

"I don't have to tell her I'm sorry," Ricky snaps. "I'm just givin' her the book back. It's on the library desk."

Saying nothing, Bubba grabs his son's arm roughly. He shoves him across the street toward the truck. Mimi watches.

Something tugs at her heart, sending a strange ache to her stomach.

Effie exhales, looking at Wilton relieved.

"I think it's time we go home."

Anna Beth chimes in. "That was scary."

"I know," says Effie, "It was. And we'll need to tell your mama and daddy what happened."

"Now, let's get home and have our after-school snack!"

Effie looks over to Mimi, who is still watching Mr. Bubba and Ricky.

"Come on, Mimi, it's time to go. Don't you want your snack?"

Mimi turns and runs over to join her sisters.

"I bet it's peach cobbler," Mary Grace says.

"No way," Anna Beth says.

"I bet it's banana pudding with vanilla wafers because Effie doesn't know how to make Willa Mae's peach cobbler."

"Bet you it's not!"

"Bet you it is!"

Their argument fades as Wilton crouches again beside Mimi.

"If it's Miss Willa Mae's peach cobbler, save me some," he whispers with a wink and stands up to leave.

Mimi giggles, tugging on his sleeve.

"Wilton?"

He bends down.

"Yeah, Mimi?"

"Thank you for listening to me," she says shyly. "I needed you to know that it wasn't my fault."

He glances up at Effie, who has her hand over her mouth, hiding her smile.

"You're welcome, Mimi," giving her a wink.

Getting up, he turns to Effie.

"You know, what you did in the library—you were standing up for what was right. You were very brave, Effie Rose."

"I guess I was," she smiles at him proudly.

Turning to the girls, she says, "Let's get home. I have banana pudding with vanilla wafers waiting for you ... if you can find it."

Anna Beth grins. "Told you so."

Mary Grace rolls her eyes.

As Wilton heads toward Levee Road, he calls back, "Hey Effie, I'll call you later. I need to fill you in on everything that's happened."

"Great, and Wilton," Effie calls back to him. "Will you come to church Sunday?"

He stops, glancing over his shoulder.

"It's covered dish Sunday," she adds with a teasing grin. "Good food. Momma's making her peach cobbler."

Wilton tilts his head, a glimmer of amusement in his eyes.

"I'll think about it."

"You know where we sit. We'll save you a spot," Effie says.

"I said maybe," he calls out as he continues to walk toward Levee Road.

As Effie watches him go, Mimi tugs on her hand.

"Effie, my book!"

"Oh, my goodness! I nearly forgot," says Effie.

I'll get it, Anna Beth says as she runs back inside, grabbing it off the librarian's desk.

As the girls head home down Magnolia, Mimi walks quietly, trying to make sense of the swirl of emotions. She notices the hurt, the anger, the cruelty—and the kindness—around her and within her, seeing it all through a child's eyes, but not yet knowing the complexity of their roots or how deep they run. As she grows and looks back, Mimi begins to understand that genetics, intertwined with behavioral influences and wounds passed down through generations, shape a child's path and frame their future.

CHAPTER TWENTY-THREE

"Let there be no further discrimination or segregation in the pews, at the Communion rail, at the confessional, and in parish meetings, just as there will be no segregation in the kingdom of Heaven."[72]

-Pastoral letter, "Blessed are the Peacemakers" (1953), Archbishop Joseph Rummel of the Catholic Diocese of New Orleans

April 1, 1960

A blast of hot, sticky air blows in through the front door of the Cleaners along with Sister Mary Carolyn on her weekly pick-up for the Sisters of Holy Comforter. As she steps into Bayou Grande Cleaners' lobby, she immediately lifts her long black robe to her knees and fans her legs with it.

"It's like an oven out there, girls. They need to come up with some different outfits for us nuns in this deep South," Sister says.

Jeanne Marie laughs as she finishes putting clothes from the last customer into a laundry bag.

"Now, Sister, that's a prayer I wouldn't hold my breath for."

Continuing to fan her legs, she counters, "Well, I might just have to talk to the bishop."

"Wouldn't I like to be a fly on the wall to hear that conversation," says Jeanne Marie.

Sister Mary Carolyn was known to be outspoken; after all, she was from up North.

"We'll bring up the 'habits' in a minute," Miss Lucy calls out from the back.

Sister Mary Carolyn steps up to the counter, letting go of her robe, and a large wooden rosary attached to her belt drops back down to her side.

"Thank you so much, Miss Jeanne Marie," she says, "for your kindness and generosity in always cleaning our 'habits.'"

Lowering her voice, she continues, "even though it's one of the deadly sins, the sisters in the other parishes are very jealous that we have our own personal cleaners," she winks.

Miss Lucy and Doretha shuffle in from the back, nearly swallowed by a sea of black 'habits.' They wrangle to get them hung on the large clothes hooks.

"Well," says Jeanne Marie, "And I always appreciate the sisters' extra prayers over at the convent."

"Prayers we all need," says Sister Mary Carolyn. "Did you hear about the sit-in at Kress a few days ago? They also happened at Sitcoms Drug Store and the Greyhound bus station."

"I did," says Jeanne Marie. "The workers in the back have been talking about it most of the day."

"Yes," Sister continues, "And did you hear on the news that after the sit-ins, thousands of Black students walked out of their classes at Southern University to march in protest to the Louisiana State Capitol? You hear me, thousands! And it was all very peaceful, they say."

"Must have been a sight to see," says Miss Jeanne Marie as she pulls the tickets off the plastic bags covering the 'habits' and writes on each one: Donation.

"Do you know Mr. Paul?" asks Sister. "He's one of our parishioners who works over at the State Capitol in maintenance?"

Jeanne Marie nods as she continues to sort the tickets and place them on the receipt spike sitting on the counter.

"Well, he says that there was an orderly stream of protesters, many holding signs that said '*Justice For All*' *and* '*End Segregation Now*.' God is up to something, Miss Jeanne Marie, and I think he's calling us to all pay attention."

Doretha hung the last veil on the hook. "Amen to that," she says, as she disappears to the back.

"And I heard, too, that Governor Davis refused to meet with those students. Now you know he's not paying much attention, or he's blind."

Miss Lucy, bagging clothes, pokes her head out from around the bagging machine. "Well, I don't like it one bit," she says. "Things just need to stay as they are. Everybody seems to be getting along just fine in my opinion, until all this started up with this young Colored generation."

Sister Mary Carolyn chimes in, "Well, I don't think that's gonna happen."

"Humph," grunts Miss Lucy, as she returns to her bagging in the back.

"Well, in my opinion," says Sister, "things are already set in motion. I think the Lord Almighty is in this movement, and there's no stopping it. In the Bible, he talks all about justice. How can we not support it?"

"As a novitiate, I did my final paper on justice. And let me tell you, justice is not just an idea or suggestion in the Bible, or even a political debate ... it's God's command."

Miss Jeanne Marie watches Sister as she heads over to the gumball machine. *She sure is one rebel of a nun,* she thinks.

Standing in front of the gumball machine, Sister digs into the pocket of her black robe for some change.

"There's not many places where I can enjoy a good gumball," she says, putting a penny in the machine and popping it in her mouth.

Chewing briskly, she continues, "Do you remember what Archbishop Rummel's Pastoral letter to the church was a few years ago? It gave me a good visual for how wrong segregation is in our nation."

"Vaguely ... what was it he said?" asks Jeanne Marie, knowing that she was about to be told anyway.

"He says that 'racial segregation draws a color line across God's plan for redemption.'[73] Now that's something, isn't it?" says Sister.

"Just picture it now, Jeanne Marie. It would be like taking a stick and drawing a line through that sacred dirt at the foot of the cross on Calvary and having colored in the back and Whites in the front. I don't think Jesus has any rules about who gets to kneel in the front at the foot of the cross and who needs to kneel in the back."

Hearing the door open, Miss Lucy comes from the back to the front counter.

Nodding his head, Bubba says, "Ladies. Sister."

"Hello, Mr. Bubba," says Sister. "How's your mama? Is she feeling better? We have been praying for her at the convent."

"Yes, thank you, Sister," he says politely as he places his dirty clothes on the counter. "She is now out of the hospital. I know that she appreciates those prayers."

Jeanne Marie turns, going to the back to grab his clothes. She mumbles under her breath, "He needs more prayers than his mama does."

Lucy looks at Jeanne Marie, giving her the eye.

"I'll go get his clothes," Miss Lucy says in an annoyed voice.

Bubba walks over to get a Coke from the machine. Sister Mary Carolyn loudly continues.

"But I completely agree, Jeanne Marie, with Archbishop Rummell. It's finally time to integrate the parochial schools."

Pulling the bottle from the machine with a clunk, Bubba interjects, "Pardon me, Sister, but I wouldn't count on that. I know that you came from up North to teach here, and the children sure seem to enjoy you, but that's just not how things work down here."

Straightening the bottom of her robe, she says, "I do believe that I have been here long enough, Mr. Bubba, to see what's going on."

Things get quiet. Bubba begins to drink his Coke as Lucy comes from the back, carrying his shirts and hanging them on the hook.

"Why, I happen to have a newspaper article I saved from a few years ago," says Miss Jeanne Marie, glancing over to Bubba. "My sister-in-law sent it to me from New York, saying that we had made the national news down here in Louisiana because of Archbishop Rummel. I was going to frame it. You might be interested in it, Sister."

Jeanne Marie looks through a stack of papers under the counter.

"It's in here somewhere." Papers fly up onto the counter. "What a mess ... Ah, here it is."

She takes it out of the envelope and opens the folded newspaper article.

"I will be happy to read it word for word."

She looks toward Bubba to command his attention.

"Yep, it's from the big newspaper, the *New York Times*. It says ... 'Archbishop Rummel will integrate the parochial schools of the Roman Catholic Archdiocese of New Orleans at the earliest possible opportunity and definitely not later than when the public schools are integrated.'[74]

Looking over at Bubba. "I agree with every word the Archbishop says, Sister, don't you?" asks Miss Jeanne Marie.

"Every word," says Sister, as she adjusts the oversized wooden-bead rosary hanging from her waist.

With an air of superiority, Bubba slams his half-finished Coca-Cola bottle on the counter and says, "Jeanne Marie, the business you run here in this cleaners is unacceptable." His voice lowers and points at Jeanne Marie, "and you hire way too many n-----s, and I've even seen some working up front as though they're in charge."

Without a word, Miss Jeanne Marie walks around the counter, steps firm and deliberate. She stops just inches away from Bubba. "That word," she points back at him, "is not used here. And those Colored employees," pointing to the back, "who work hard ... harder than some people I know ... they are family."

Sister Mary Carolyn moves aside as she picks up one of the Bayou Grande Cleaners calendars and begins fanning herself nervously, taking in every moment of this encounter.

"Bubba, I believe this is a good time to let you know"–she now points toward the doors–"you're not welcome through these doors anymore. Now, your mama is a good and sweet person, but I've been wanting to ask you something for a long time. Where did you get that mean streak of yours? Now, you can pay for your shirts, take your dirty clothes, and leave my property now."

Glaring at Jeanne Marie with spiteful eyes, Bubba turns to Sister.

"Sister, I'd be happy to help you get your 'habits' to the car," he says in a forced, courteous tone.

"Why, I would so appreciate that, Mr. Bubba. If you help me with one load, I can surely carry the rest myself."

After paying, he reaches for his two clean shirts, grabs the ones out of the dirty clothes bag, then lifts the 'habits' off the hook and heads toward the door.

"Mr. Bubba," Sister says, "I'm praying for you and your family."

He nods, then briefly glances back at Jeanne Marie with a look of disdain, then turns and leaves.

Miss Lucy aggressively pulls the drawstring on the empty dirty clothes bag and tosses it in the basket. "Jeanne Marie, I told you once before," says Miss Lucy, "and I'm gonna tell you again, you need to watch what you say and do. You're gonna get yourself in trouble one day.

"Lucy," says Jeanne Marie, "sometimes things just need to be said as they are."

Lucy grunts, "and sometimes, you just say exactly what you're thinking. You and Sister Mary Carolyn are two peas in a pod."

Jeanne Marie glances over at Sister. "Aren't we, though?"

The two chuckle.

Lucy walks away, mumbling, "That's one pod of peas I don't wanna be around."

MIMI BURSTS THROUGH the back door of the Cleaners, tossing her school books onto the counter by the scrubbing sink before racing toward the front to greet her MawMaw. She stops suddenly, eyes catching the Cleaners' delivery truck parked in the covered garage. Mimi clasps her hands together, barely able to keep still. She dashes toward the front.

"MawMaw!" she calls out, finding her at the counter. Without taking a breath, "Oh, and hi, Sister Mary Carolyn." Mimi turns back to her MawMaw and continues. "DeDe is in the truck! I think she's doing her homework. Can we do our homework together in PawPaw's pirogue?"

PawPaw has been gone for years now, but his beloved pirogue still rests on wood blocks under the shed in the chicken yard, cherished and untouched.

MawMaw shakes her head with a knowing smile.

"You and that pirogue, Mimi." MawMaw looks toward the back of the cleaners. "Make sure her daddy knows. Go on now."

As Mimi turns to run toward the delivery trucks. MawMaw calls out to her.

"Does your mama know you're here?"

"Willa knows!" Mimi shouts over her shoulder.

"Well," MawMaw says, looking back at Sister, "that's all that's needed."

Mimi hurries to the side door, waving wildly for DeDe to come inside. Through the truck window, DeDe gives a big grin before hopping out.

"I have the best place for us to do our homework!" Mimi announces. "Are you doing homework or just reading?"

"I have to finish my math homework so we can drop the book off to my friend, Sharon," DeDe says, gathering her book, pencil, and paper.

"Did she lose her book?" Mimi asks.

"No, we share it."

Mimi tilts her head in question. "You share your math book? Why?"

DeDe shrugs. "I don't know. It's just what we do. Sometimes there aren't enough books for everyone. So usually the smarter kids–" she pauses, lowering her voice, "that's what the teacher told me I was–use it first and get it done fast."

"We don't do that," Mimi says. "We all get a book."

"Oh," DeDe murmurs, as if satisfied with the answer for now.

Mimi leads the way toward the back door leading to the chicken yard. DeDe waves to her daddy before stepping out the door. They pass the girl's two-story tree house with a big oak tree coming out of the top. DeDe stops just staring at it. "Come on, DeDe, let's climb into the pirogue! There are two seats. You sit on this one, and I'll sit across from you."

Settling into the old wooden flat-bottom boat, they work on their assignments in peaceful concentration, occasionally giggling as the chickens peck and cluck around them.

Before long, their imaginations take over, and they pretend the chickens are giant alligators circling the boat, waiting to eat them.

From inside the Cleaners, by the press machine, DeDe's father, Norman, watches them through the back window. Beside him, Estelle folds a freshly pressed garment and shakes her head with a soft smile.

"Those two are so innocent right now," Norman says, his voice thick with emotion. "Look how much fun they're havin' together. Their young eyes don't see any difference between them. If only I could protect my DeDe from the ugly this world is bound to bring her."

Estelle puts down the shirt and pats him gently on the back.

"You can only protect her for so long, Norman. She sighs, watching the girls outside. "We can only pray and hope that our children and grandchildren will have a better life."

Norman doesn't respond. His gaze stays fixed out the window, but his mind drifts to the lingering memories of his childhood, ones that left deep, unrelenting scars. He will never forget the summer day his mother told him he couldn't play at the new community center playground with the White children or swim with them in the parish pool. That summer, the innocence of youth was taken from him, and the sting of bigotry took its place. To this day, Norman has not learned to swim.

"Let's go get some water, DeDe. I'm thirsty."

As the girls climb out of the pirogue, Mimi spots her mother driving past the chicken yard in their car. Mimi waves excitedly.

"That's my mama! Let's wave."

DeDe hesitates but lifts her hand in a shy wave. Mrs. Benoit slows down, lips pressed together in a way that reminds Mimi of the look her mother gives when she's done something wrong. Then, she drives off.

They take off running, racing through the Cleaners toward the hallway water fountains. Breathless and giggling, they reach the fountains and gulp down the cold water, slurping loudly.

A harsh voice cuts through their laughter.

"What you doin', child?"

DeDe flinches, nearly choking on her water. She looks up to see Doretha standing over her, arms crossed, eyes stern.

"Don't you ever drink from this fountain again," Doretha says, her voice firm. "You gonna get yourself in trouble."

Mimi straightens, eyes wide, wiping her mouth with the back of her hand. They were so thirsty, all they could think about was the cold water—not which fountain they were using—and Mimi knew exactly which one her MawMaw had told her not to drink from.

DeDe's eyes welled up with tears. She doesn't say a word, just turns and runs to the back of the Cleaners, straight to her daddy's press.

Mimi watches, heart thudding. She knows there's a rule about the two fountains. She has heard it enough times, but she still doesn't fully understand why. *It was just one sip, just one time.* She thought. *Why did Doretha get so mad?*

Mimi carefully watches DeDe's daddy kneel in front of her, gently wiping her tears.

Norman takes his daughter's hand and leads her toward the truck. DeDe climbs in and sits, her small shoulders hunched. Through the window, her tear-streaked face sees Mimi now walking toward the front of the cleaners. Mimi slows down, her heart heavy. Their eyes meet.

Mimi slowly raises her hand in a small wave.

DeDe hesitates, then lifts her own, barely moving her fingers.

Something shifts inside of Mimi—something she doesn't yet have words for.

Mimi finds MawMaw at her sewing machine, where she is bent over, working on an alteration. MawMaw looks up, noticing her wet eyes.

"Now what are you crying about, Sha?"

Mimi sniffles.

"Doretha fussed at us for drinking out of the water fountains."

MawMaw touches the hand wheel, slows down her foot on the treadle, and the pulsating whirr of the sewing machine comes to a stop.

She looks at Mimi. "Now, were you drinking from the one I told you to?"

"No, but we were just so thirsty we drank out of any fountain." Mimi swallows. "Doretha fussed at DeDe real bad."

MawMaw sighs, looking into her granddaughter's eyes.

"Come on now, Sha. Let's go sit in the rocking chairs on the porch." She leans in, voice dropping to a whisper. "How 'bout I make you a café au lait with just a little bit of coffee in it?" she says.

Mimi nods with a small smile.

"But don't you tell your mama now," MawMaw teases, wagging a finger as she laughs, muttering something in French.

MawMaw's home was just next to the Cleaners. Hand in hand, they walk the short distance through her garden of lilies and hibiscus. MawMaw's cat, Chrissie, scampers across the walk in front of them, disappearing high into the magnolia tree. The wooden porch on the front of the house creaks as they settle into their rocking chairs. Mimi lets out a breath. She feels safe here, like the world is as it should be.

The warm café au lait soothes Mimi as she sips, the creamy taste comforting.

She proceeds to explain the whole story of what had happened at the water fountains. MawMaw just listens, rocking beside her. Placing her cup and saucer on the porch table, she then speaks.

"I want to tell you a story, baby."

Mimi puts her cup and saucer on the table and crosses her legs as she rocks.

"When your mama was a little girl, she used to hear me and your PawPaw speaking French, just like you hear me sometimes, don't you?"

Mimi chuckles. "Mama says it's because you don't want me and my sisters to know what you're saying."

MawMaw laughs, her head tilting back. "Well, part of that is true, Sha."

Her smile loosens as a solemn look comes across her face.

"So when your mama started going to school, she spoke French because that's what she heard at home. We are French people, Acadian people, and we came from a place called Nova Scotia."

Mimi's eyes widened. "Can we visit there on one of our Sunday drives, MawMaw?"

"Oh, how I wish we could, Sha. But it's far, far away."

Picking up her café au lait from the table, MawMaw takes a slow sip, then looks out over the yard, gathering her words.

"The teachers at your mama's school didn't like the Acadian children who spoke French. They would look down on them as though it was a bad thing and because they were so different from everyone else. Some of the children made fun of her and teased her because of it. She would come home sad and confused.

"So, to protect her, we had to tell her to stop speaking French at school. We helped her with more English. Mimi puts her feet down to stop rocking. "Just so she wouldn't get teased anymore and fussed at by the teacher? MawMaw nods with a soft smile.

Mimi glances back up. "Was Doretha being mean to DeDe for that reason?"

MawMaw reaches over and tucks a loose curl behind Mimi's ear.

"Oh, Sha. Doretha wasn't trying to be mean. She just wanted to protect DeDe, like your PawPaw, and I wanted to protect your mama."

Mimi sits back in the rocker, trying to understand her MawMaw's words, then looking over, she says, "Mama must have been sad like DeDe."

Before MawMaw can answer, Mimi speaks up again.

"MawMaw," Mimi looks up at her grandmother as she takes another sip of her café au lait. "I heard some boys at school say that … well, they used that bad word … anyway, they say the Colored people have germs and diseases. Do they? I wasn't sure if I could eat the M&M's DeDe touched, so I threw them away. And Willa has to drink from a different cup from us. Is that why?"

"Let me tell you something, baby, there are people who aren't nice to Colored folks, especially if they try to drink from the same water fountain as White folks do. They have to use different bathrooms and go to different schools. It's not right, but that's what the law says. So, your MawMaw has to have separate water fountains and bathrooms at the Cleaners. Doretha didn't want DeDe to get into trouble."

MawMaw leans forward in her rocking chair.

"Mimi, you gonna hear a lot of things at school and on the playground, but listen carefully. You carry germs and DeDe carries germs. We all carry germs, Sha. Germs and diseases don't care about the color of your skin. "So," she continues, smiling at her granddaughter, "you and DeDe just keep sharing M&M's–that's what your MawMaw says."

"From around the corner of the house, Brother calls out.

"Miss Jeanne Marie, my work is done today. Can I head home now? Oh, and I brought the pot back from the cleaners that held the grits this mornin'. It was some good. I put it on your side steps."

"Well, tomorrow morning I'm makin' some sauce piquant' to put over the grits. Don't be late, or you'll miss out. It always goes fast. And tell your momma hi now."

Mimi watches and listens, taking it all in.

Waving, Brother heads up Magnolia Street.

MawMaw turns back to her granddaughter.

"Now, my sweet Sha, you just keep being kind to DeDe and all the colored people who work in the cleaners and …"

Mimi breaks in. "And Willa Mae, too."

MawMaw chuckles and nods.

"And especially Willa Mae."

The two rock in silence for a while, finishing their café au laits.

"MawMaw?"

"What is it, Sha?"

Mimi lifts her head, her young eyes filled with something deeper than before.

"I think all of that makes God sad. Don't you?"

MawMaw lets out a slow breath, setting her cup down on the porch railing.

She nods.

"I think you're right, baby," she whispers. "In fact … I know you are."

As Mimi walks home along the family's sidewalk, her heart hurts for DeDe. Suddenly, an idea comes to her.

She'll ask Willa if they can bake M&M cookies to bring to DeDe tomorrow, to cheer her up. And maybe they can make enough for Norman, Doretha, Estelle, and all the Colored workers in the back of the Cleaners.

Excited about her plan, she races into the house, where Willa Mae is folding clothes and watching one of her shows.

"Willa, can we make cookies and bring …"

"Elizabeth Katherine! Echoes a voice from down the hall. "Come into my room, please. I need to talk to you, right now."

Mimi freezes. Mama only calls her by her full name when she's mad.

"Yes, ma'am," she answers, walking down the hall into her parents' room.

Stepping through the bedroom door, Mimi sees her daddy sitting on the edge of the bed, home early, taking off his shoes. He looks up as Mimi enters, but it's her mother who speaks first.

"Did I see you playing with a Colored girl out in the chicken yard?"

"Yes, ma'am. That's my new friend, DeDe, and we were doing our homework together in PawPaw's pirogue. Her daddy is Norman, and she waits for him to finish work. MawMaw said it was okay."

Mrs. Benoit exhales, smoothing her dress. "I'm sure she's a very nice little girl, Mimi, but I don't want you playing with her again."

"But Mama, why?" She sits on the bed, tears well up in her eyes. "Is it because she's a different color? MawMaw says some people think that Colored people carry germs and diseases, but she says we all do, and it doesn't matter your color."

Before her mother can answer, Mr. Benoit gets up from the bed and crouches down to her level. His voice is soft. "It's complicated, baby."

Looking up at his wife, he adds, "I think we should talk about this, Harriet. There's no harm in the children doing their homework and playing together out in the chicken yard."

Looking out the bedroom window, Mrs. Benoit's arms fold across her chest as she lowers her voice.

"But what will the neighbors think, Shot?"

Raising his arm toward the window.

"They can think what they want. Say what they want," he replies firmly.

Mrs. Benoit takes a deep breath, considering his words. After a long pause, she sighs.

"Well ... I guess it's okay," she says, looking over at Mimi. "As long as you stay at the cleaners or in the chicken yard. Don't bring her here to our house."

"But you let Willa come into our house, and she's a different color from us."

Mr. Benoit rubs his forehead.

"Always from the mouths of babes," he murmurs.

Harriet exhales sharply, shaking her head.

"She surely has a point, Harriet," he says, meeting his wife's eyes.

Mr. Benoit looks down at Mimi.

"Like I said, baby, it's complicated." He dries the tears from her eyes. "Now go on and finish your homework. You didn't do anything wrong, and like I said, DeDe is welcome to play with you at the cleaners or in the chicken yard."

Mimi hesitates, searching her mother's face, but Mrs. Benoit has nothing more to say.

As Mimi leaves the room, Willa Mae comes walking down the hall with a handful of folded bathroom towels. Mr. Benoit gently shuts the door.

"Harriet, remember what we talked about last week. We know what's right. We know what God calls us to do and be. But when it comes down to it—are we bold enough in this climate—this tense, turbulent climate—to actually say it? And ... do it?"

He sighs, rubbing his chin.

"How can we expect our children to find their voice in all of this, when we can't seem to find our own?"

A silence settles between them.

After a moment, he speaks again.

"I haven't been able to stop thinking about what Father Joel said in his homily a few weeks ago. He says we can't let ourselves be tossed back and forth by every thought, every opinion," he releases a deep breath," or pretty soon we will start mistaking it for truth."

He looks up at Harriet. "Are we going to be influenced by people ... or be influencers of people?"

"It's not an easy choice, Harriet. But let's try to make the right one. For us ... and for our girls."

CHAPTER TWENTY-FOUR

"The spirit of the Sovereign Lord is on me to preach good news to the poor...to proclaim the year of the Lord's favor and the day of vengeance of our God, to comfort all who mourn, and provide for those who grieve in Zion - to bestow on them a crown of beauty instead of ashes, the oil of gladness instead of mourning, and a garment of praise instead of a spirit of despair. They will be called oaks of righteousness, a planting of the Lord for the display of His splendor."[75]

-Isaiah 61:1-3

April 3, 1960

The fog hangs low and thick. A slight chill lingers in the air, settling into the fabric of their Sunday best. From the river, the constant call of foghorns drifts through the mist, their deep, long groans carrying a melancholy note with them. As Effie and Willa Mae walk the familiar path to church, they pass the old oak tree. Its sprawling branches reach out eerily through the fog, as though calling out to them.

Effie glances toward the tree, then quickly looks away.

"I'll never look at this tree the same," she says, her voice uneasy. "It's such a horrible story."

She pauses, looking at her mother. "Momma, did you know who it was ... the man they hung in this tree that day?"

Willa exhaled, buttoning her sweater against the damp morning air.

"I never knew," she admits. "I was too young, and your Grandma Nellie never would talk about it."

Her voice softens. "It sure is hard to think about it, though."

Crossing her arms, trying to keep warm from the morning chill, Willa Mae steps closer to the tree and stares up at it—its branches above her swaying in the breeze.

"But even though we don't know his name, baby," She turns to Effie. "We must never forget."

She gestures toward the tree's outstretched limbs.

"See those, Effie?"

Effie closes her eyes, shaking her head with a grim look on her face.

"Momma," she says, anxiety rising in her voice, "I told you, I don't want to think about it again. I want to forget that terrible story."

Willa's expression darkens, long-ago memories flashing through her mind.

"It was bad, baby. And the picture of those Black, bare feet dangling from this tree will always be in my mind."

She looks up, tracing the grueling, embedded images of that day, then speaks with a firm resolve.

"But Effie," she implores again. "We must never forget."

Willa Mae turned fully to face Effie, her eyes intent, her voice urgent.

"You hear me, baby? Never!"

A hush falls between them, broken only by the chasm of the distant groaning foghorns and the heavenly song of mockingbirds perched high in the branches. Willa's gaze remains fixed on the tree.

"God can cause beauty to rise even from the ashes of sorrow, pain, and evil," she says.

Willa Mae stands straighter, shifting her purse and holding her Bible up between them.

"I found it right here in these pages. I sure did. Jesus' light is brighter than the darkness from that horrible day, and let me tell you somethin', Effie Rose. That darkness can never put out that light. God's light just keeps bringin' on His grace, love, redemption, and healing. We'll see it. It's soon comin'."

She exhales, as if releasing a prayer into the heavens.

Effie shakes her head.

"But, Momma, a man was left dead, hanging in this tree. How can there be beauty in that?"

Willa turns to her daughter, her eyes filled with quiet strength.

"Oh no, Effie Rose, there was no beauty in what happened here that day," she says, her voice firm. "It was evil, baby. Pure evil."

She pauses, looking toward the rising sun breaking through the mist.

"But there's beauty and justice in what God can bring from it. It's all the things the Reverend preached on Wednesday night at the Baptist church."

She gestures gently toward the tree, her tone filled with hope.

"I believe that the beauty will one day be children of all colors playing together under those branches."

She turns, looking up and down Magnolia, and continues.

"God's healing oil will be sprinkled all over this town, bringing people together with no Jim Crow laws separatin' us. God's mighty hand of redemption can do that, baby, but we can never stop prayin.'"

She grows quiet, bringing her Bible close.

"Now, do you think the day that my daddy died, there was beauty in what happened?" Willa Mae asks.

"No, indeed, I just wanted to die and go be with him. But years later, I could see the beauty from the ashes. I began to remember all he taught me about God's promises. That kept me going, and I want them to keep you going too, baby."

She smiles at her daughter and adds with conviction, "So remember, my little image bearer of God, we must never forget all these ashes...and the beauty rising up from it."

Effie smiles back.

"I will, Momma. But you know I'm not your little image bearer of God anymore. I'm seventeen."

Willa takes Effie's hand and gives it a gentle squeeze.

"Now you know I'm gonna have to spank you."

They both laugh as they walk on down Magnolia.

Pulling her hand away, Effie says, "Momma, you know you have to stop goin' to two churches at one time. You're either Baptist or Methodist."

"Now, baby, don't you know we're all God's one big family!" says Willa Mae.

"I love going to the Wednesday night revival at the Baptist church," she says. "It's lively!"

Effie shakes her head with a smile, knowing there wasn't a thing she could do to change her momma's stubbornness.

As they pass the Catholic church, Willa Mae waves at Miss Annabelle heading into Mass. She slows, glancing at the parishioners, hoping to catch sight of the Benoits. When she doesn't, she picks up her pace, focusing on getting to her own church.

"Now you know, Effie, maybe one day I'll have to go to the Catholic church too and sit with all my friends."

Glancing over to Holy Comforter, Effie mutters, "In the back, of course."

Ignoring her daughter's comment, Willa says, "Even though I belong to the Methodist Church, the choir at the Baptist church made me an honorary member. I'm proud of that, you know."

"Now, Momma, what is Reverend Washington going to say about that when he hears it from someone in our church?"

"Well, I guess he'll say, 'Miss Willa Mae, you go on for a third,'" she replies, raising three fingers with a big smile.

Effie just shakes her head again, without saying a word.

As they make their way up Levee Road toward the Methodist church, the sound of the choir finishing the early service drifts through the air. This service is always small, mostly folks who have to work on Sunday but want to be sure they still get to church.

Without warning, Effie stops in the street.

"Momma, look," she says, pointing to Mr. Willie's porch. "That's strange. Where is Mr. Willie? He's always on his porch when we pass."

"Well," says Willa Mae, "go knock on the door and make sure he's okay."

Effie runs up the front steps and knocks.

"No answer," she calls back.

From the backyard, the hound dog let out a low, lonesome howl.

Knocking harder, Effie calls, "Mr. Willie, you there? You okay?"

Still no answer.

"It's okay, baby," Willa Mae says. "We'll check on him on the way home."

"It's just not like him to not be there," Effie replies, worry in her voice.

"We just gonna pray and trust in Jesus," Willa Mae says calmly. "He will take care of the situation."

The small congregation from the first service is walking out the church doors as they arrive. There is always coffee and donuts in the church hall afterwards. Willa Mae and Effie visit with folks for a bit before heading into the sanctuary. The second service is already filling up. This one is always full.

As they walk up the side aisle, Effie taps her momma on the shoulder.

"Momma ... Momma."

"What is it, Effie?"

"Look in the last pew. Look who's there," she says, eyes wide as her mouth falls open.

"Why, if it isn't Mr. Willie," Willa Mae says, her face lighting up.

She walks over to him.

"Now, you know it's good to see you here, Mr. Willie. Tootie would be so happy."

"You right about that," he says with a twinkle in his eyes. "I guarantee she's lookin' down at me right now. I already been to the first service and I'm ready for the second," he whispers loudly. "Tootie always wanted me to walk through these doors, and I finally did. It was time, Miss Willa Mae."

Willa Mae glances around, and a frown crosses her face.

"Well, this just won't do," says Willa Mae, shaking her head. "You can't be sittin' here in the last row. You come with us right now to our seats. We gonna sing and worship together."

Feeling proud of the invitation, Mr. Willie stands and follows Willa Mae and Effie to their fourth-row seats. As they are about to make their way into the pew, a voice calls out from behind.

"You mind if I join you?"

"Wilton!" Effie exclaimed. "You came!"

"Come on, baby," says Willa Mae. "There's always room for one more."

From the pew behind comes another voice.

"You've got a ministry going on right here in your pew," says Miss Ella, whose family has sat behind Willa Mae's for decades."

She leans over the pew toward Wilton and whispers, "It's okay to wrestle with God, baby. I'm just glad you heard His call—and came back."

Wilton thanks her with a smile and sits down. Reverend Washington steps up to the pulpit and welcomes everyone, giving a few announcements, then sits back down. The choir begins to sing, and soon the whole congregation joins in. Wilton still isn't completely comfortable with the whole church thing ... Yet, at the same time, there was something oddly comforting about being there.

"Come on, Wilton," says Mr. Willie. "Clap your hands, son. There's no time to waste on this earth."

He grabs Wilton's hand and shakes it playfully, trying to get him going. Wilton's eyes stretch wide as he looks at Effie as though to say, "Do something!"

Effie giggles, thoroughly enjoying the scene playing out beside her.

All around them, the church is alive with singing. Women begin pulling out their fans, fluttering them in front of their faces like hummingbird wings to chase away the heat. Ushers move to the back, propping open the double doors with the usual rocks, letting a faint cross breeze drift through the open windows. Men reach for their handkerchiefs, dabbing at the beads of sweat forming on their brows. As the choir and congregation take their seats, the whoosh-whoosh of fans rises into its own chorus, a rhythm almost as old as the church itself. Reverend Washington steps back up to the pulpit, his own handkerchief in hand, his expression somber as he looks across the congregation.

"I think that we all know there has been a lot going on with the young people in our own community."

Wilton straightens in his seat, just like many others, unsure of where the pastor is headed with this.

"I know that some of you sitting here today support their actions."

With those words, a hush settles, soft and invisible, but impossible to ignore.

The Reverend's voice breaks through the silence.

"A few weeks ago, I spoke about an important word," he continues. "And that word was 'maladjusted.' If you choose today to be maladjusted like those young people … I'm going to ask you to do something, and that is … to stand up."

People look around, uncertain. Is this a trick question? Is standing good? Or bad? Silence hangs in the sanctuary. Only a single sharp cough is heard from the back.

Wilton looks around, still seated.

"Or," says the Reverend, "maybe you are adjusted to what is going on around us. Maybe it feels comfortable to be adjusted. Safe."

Wilton glances at Effie. Then at the Reverend. He didn't plan it. But somehow—he stands.

All eyes go on Wilton.

"Amen, son," Reverend Washington calls out.

It was as though the entire congregation let out a collective sigh of relief. Someone has finally stood. But how will the Reverend respond?

He continues on, almost as if Wilton has been planted in the service for this very moment.

"This young man is bold. He's the first to take a stand."

Looking straight at Wilton, the Reverend asks, "Son, do you know what you are standing for?"

Everyone waits. Effie holds her breath, unsure of what might come out of Wilton's mouth.

"Yes, sir, I do," comes Wilton's strong, assured voice.

It was as though he had finally been given the opportunity to speak his calling aloud. All eyes remain fixed on him.

Wilton swallows hard, clears his throat, and looks out over the church congregation.

"I am standing because I refuse to sit by and watch the injustices that are taking place around us every day. I'm tired of it."

A few bold Amens ring out across the sanctuary.

"If you say that we have a just God, Reverend," Wilton continues, "then I don't think that He is happy with it either. So, I choose to be maladjusted to it—just like those students were at Kress."

Now came a sudden outburst—claps, Amens, voices lifting. Wilton nudges Effie to stand. She pressed herself back into the pew, as if trying to disappear. But people were rising to their feet, Willa Mae among them, her voice rising up with the others.

"God is good all the time," she proclaims.

"Yes He is—all the time!" shouts Mr. Willie.

Effie's heart pounds. She knows what this means. She needs, no, she wants—to stand. And then, she did. Wilton grabs her hand and squeezes it tight. The Reverend speaks again, his voice calm and reassuring.

"If you can't take a stand today, it's okay. You go home and pray about it."

Someone in the choir softly begins a chorus of "We Shall Overcome." Slowly, others join in as the Reverend motions for everyone to stand. For a few sacred minutes, the church slipped into another realm—beyond the veil—right into the throne room, with an army of angels all around them.

The song ends. The Reverend lifts his hand, signaling the congregation to now be seated.

"We are called to be children of light," he says. "We cannot—I repeat, we cannot—stand in the shade of apathy. Don't just leave here today with a good feeling. No. You are being called to do something. You are called to be maladjusted."

He lets the words settle over the congregation.

"Maladjusted looks different for everyone. What is God calling you to do? To be a voice? To act? To sign a petition? Take a bold step? Feed and care for those in the trenches. Or to be on your knees, praying?"

Effie looks over to her momma and smiles.

Reverend pauses, his gaze resting on the quiet expectancy in the church.

"Ask God what your part is. Then, be bold enough, courageous enough, to step into it. Being a spectator is easy. But it takes courage to be a participant. God bless each of you ... and go forth in God's power, love, and non-violence."

From the open doors, sunlight pours in, casting long beams up the aisle and setting the cross on the altar aglow. One by one, people walked through the light as if being anointed—God's messengers. His warriors. Called and ready.

As everyone filters outside beyond the walls of the safe haven, the congregation feels equipped to do what God is calling them to do. Outside, the ringing of the Catholic church bells drifts through the air, mingling with the distant notes of a calliope from a steamboat winding its way up the river. It could not have been a more beautiful day filled with God's hope.

"Willa! Willa!" a voice calls out with urgency through the crowd. Doretha, Willa's friend from the Cleaners, pushes through, looking frantic.

"What is it, Doretha?" Willa calls out, worry in her voice.

"Somethin's happened down Magnolia Street, near where the Benoits' live. It looks like there was a fire."

"What?" Willa asks. "Do you know anything else?"

"No, just talk—people saying something happened in the White section of town."

Wilton and Effie overhear the exchange.

"We gotta get down there," Willa says.

"Miss Willa, I'll get my daddy's truck and be right back to pick you up," Wilton offers.

"Thank you, baby, but my feet are just fine and will get me there quickly," Willa replies.

"Momma, you've got your church heels on," Effie says. "Let Wilton take us. Please? He's already headed to get the truck."

Moments later, Wilton pulls up in front of the church in his daddy's red pickup.

"C'mon, Momma, let's go," Effie urges.

They climb into the front seat—Effie first, then Willa—and Wilton heads down Levee Road, turning onto Magnolia toward the White section of town.

They pass the Snowball stand, with the Cleaners in sight.

"Oh Lord," Willa says. "I see police cars in front of Miss Jeanne Marie's cleaners."

"It's okay, Miss Willa. It's gonna be okay," Wilton replies, trying to keep his voice calm.

Effie leans in closer to Wilton, comforted by the calm strength he carries. As they approach, the scent of burned wood fills the air.

"Oh Lord Jesus," Willa says, her voice low. "They don' burned a cross in front of Miss Jeanne Marie's cleaners."

Wilton pulls the truck to a stop across the street. He and Effie slide out together, circling around quickly to help Miss Willa down, steadying her as her heels touch the pavement.

"Now what are those girls doing here?" Willa says, looking through the crowd. "They don't need to be seein' this."

She hurries across the street. Mimi runs to meet her, throwing her arms around Willa's waist.

"Willa, look what some bad people did!"

"It's gonna be okay, baby," Willa says, trying to calm her voice and wrapping her arms around Mimi.

Mr. Benoit spots Willa and comes quickly to her side.

"Thank you for coming, Willa. Mary Margaret came over to help the girls dress for church, and they went with her family to Mass. They just got dropped back off here. Miss Harriet and I have been with Miss Jeanne Marie since early this morning."

"I'll get these girls home and make sure they get a decent breakfast," Willa Mae says.

"Don't worry yourself about a thing," she adds.

"Momma, can I help?" Effie asks.

"Yes, baby. Help me get these girls home and fed," Willa replies.

Effie turns to Wilton. "Thank you for all your help," she says in a tender voice. "I'll see you later on."

Wilton nods, but his eyes remain fixed on the still-smoking cross and the scorched ground. He just can't stop staring at the destruction... or thinking about who might have done it. The word 'maladjusted' echoes in his mind.

Maybe it isn't just the Blacks in this fight, he thinks.

As though by instinct, Wilton walks over to where Mr. Benoit is inspecting the smashed front windows for damage.

"Mr. Benoit, I'm Wilton—Effie's good friend. I can help you clean up this glass."

"Thank you, Wilton. Effie mentioned you and how you helped out at the library that day. Thank you. And I could sure use the help. I so appreciate it," Mr. Benoit replies.

"Also," Wilton adds, "my daddy's got a lot of wood at our house. He can bring some to board up the window until you get a new one."

"Well, that would be so helpful too. Are you sure your daddy will be okay with that?"

"I know he will," Wilton says. "I'll head home and get him. We can help you get this all cleaned up."

Out of the corner of his eye, Mr. Benoit sees a familiar truck passing. Bubba and his family were probably coming from church. Their eyes meet for a brief moment, and then he disappears up the street.

"I'm sorry, Wilton, what was that you said?"

Oh, just that I'll go ahead and get my daddy, and we can help you get this all cleaned up."

"Yes, thank you again, Wilton," Mr. Benoit says as he brushes his hand through his hair. "We will have to wait a little longer until the sheriff is done investigating."

"Sounds good, Mr. Benoit," says Wilton. "I'll be back soon."

The image of Bubba driving past the cleaners still lingers in Mr. Benoit's mind. *Did I see a smirk?* he wonders. He walks over to the sheriff, who is standing near the ashes and remains of the burned cross.

"Hey, Shot, you doing okay?"

"Long morning, Ace," says Mr. Benoit.

Since high school, the sheriff has gone by the nickname "Ace"–he could outplay nearly anyone at the card table. He and Mr. Benoit had grown up together and were like brothers.

"I've been examining this cross," Sheriff says. "Look closely, Shot. It's classic Klan. A six-foot high cross with a three-foot crosspiece."

"Exactly like this one," Mr. Benoit says, examining it closely.

"Yep," Sheriff nods. "And, as usual, they wrap kerosene-soaked burlap or rags around it. Now look at the bottom—see that iron rod," says the sheriff. "That's how they drive it quickly into the ground."

He crouches slightly, pointing toward the base.

"Oh—and another thing. They usually use two-by-fours. That matches, too. Now the last piece of the puzzle: what exactly happened here?"

"What do you mean?" Mr. Benoit asked.

"It's intimidation, plain and simple," Sheriff says. "Typical KKK play. They're trying to scare Miss Jeanne Marie—and those Colored folks that she employs, too. I hear she pays them well, treats them right. The Klan doesn't like that."

Mr. Benoit runs his hand through his thick hair, his jaw tight.

"To my mother-in-law," Mr. Benoit says, shaking his head, "this burning cross only adds more fuel to her fire."

Sheriff takes a deep puff of his cigarette and exhales slowly.

"You gotta talk to her, Shot," he says. "Come with me. One of my deputies brought us some coffee. Let's sit in my patrol car and talk."

"That sounds good," Mr. Benoit says. "Let me check in with Jeanne Marie and Harriet first—they've been here all morning."

After speaking with them, he returns and climbs into the patrol car beside the sheriff.

Looking over, he says quietly, "I know who did this, Ace. And I think you do too."

"Slow down now," Sheriff says, lifting a hand. "Don't go accusing."

"Look, Ace," says Mr. Benoit. "We've known each other for a long time. I know you. You're trying to keep things calm, but I'm telling you—I'm upset. And I know," raising his voice, "it was ..."

Sheriff again puts up his hand, looking around the car to see who is near.

"Okay, okay," Mr. Benoit takes his voice down to an angry whisper. "I know that it was Bubba. He's the one who's been threatening Jeanne Marie for weeks, and to be honest, threatening me too."

Letting out a deep sigh and rubbing his chin, "Do you have proof, Shot?" Sheriff asks.

"Aren't threats enough, Ace?" His voice again rises.

Ace speaks with caution.

"Shot, you know that the Klan carries a code of silence. Between you and me—you're probably right. But I don't think we'll ever be able to prove it. That code protects every last one of them."

He pauses, then adds, "I used to think it was just scum of the earth who joined groups like this. But over the years, I've had informants tell me different. They are businessmen and often respected men in their communities—some of them pouring money into it. Oilmen. Politicians. Men from all walks of life."

Mr. Benoit looks straight at his good friend.

"I don't care who they are, Ace. If they're a part of this foul, evil group—they're scum. All of them."

Sheriff lights another cigarette, lowering his voice further.

"I've heard the FBI might be getting involved soon—here in Louisiana and over in Mississippi. Let's keep that quiet for now."

Sheriff glances past Mr. Benoit, out the window.

"Looks like your help is back."

Mr. Benoit turns to see Wilton and his father pulling up in their truck.

"Can we begin to clean up yet, Ace?"

"Give me a few more minutes," Sheriff replies. "I want to check the premises one last time. See if there's anything else we can gather for evidence."

Wilton and his daddy work alongside Mr. Benoit to board up the two broken windows. Shoulder to shoulder, a quiet mutual respect passes between them. Amid the crisis, their hands dusty and slick with sweat, something deeply human unfolds. Invisible boundaries seem to fade as they pause beneath the oak tree beside the Cleaners, sharing fried chicken and sweet tea that Miss Jeanne' Marie has brought over. It isn't just a meal—it's a breaking of bread, a moment of grace among men who might not have shared a table just a day before.

When the job is done, Wilton leaves with his daddy to head back home.

"You quiet, son."

Letting out a deep sigh, Wilton turns his head and looks over at his daddy.

"Daddy, I need to tell you something."

"What's on your mind?"

"For a long time, I've got to admit ... I've been carrying hate in my heart toward White people. When I see someone who's White, all I can see is their skin—and their skin is the same color as the ones who murdered my momma."

He stares out the front windshield.

"But lately ... I've been seeing good in a lot of White people, like Mr. Benoit, Mr. Pierre, and Mr. McKinnly, who works with you at the high school. He doesn't have to give those books to me you know ...but he does."

His daddy breaks in.

"I think he does that because he knows it's not right what's being kept from the Colored schools. He knows you get the hand-me-downs. He sees it."

Wilton's father glances over at him as they pull into the dirt driveway in front of their house. He turns off the car.

"It's hard for me to talk about your momma's death. But like I said at your pap's house, it's time. Just like it was time to let you know who your pap was."

Your pap, Wilton thought. *I like how that sounds.*

"As you know now, I blamed your pap for your momma's death. I made him suffer enough all these years, and I'm sorry for that. I want to do what I can to mend things in the time we have. We lost your momma, but he lost his daughter. Back in Ellisville, Mississippi, we were happy together. You were young, of course, and I took you away from there when you were five."

He pauses before continuing.

Sitting in the truck, they both stare out the front window. Children could be heard playing on the levee in the distance.

Turning to Wilton, "Let me tell you about your momma, son. She was somethin' else, one of a kind. She helped your grammy iron clothes for several families in town and would deliver them."

"You had a car, Daddy?"

"No indeed. Old Mr. Sam, our neighbor, had a truck. When he'd go into town, she'd catch a ride. He was happy to stop by the houses so she could drop the clothes off."

He smiles warmly.

"All he asked for was a few of her homemade pies now and then. Your momma was some kind of pie maker. She was known clear across the county. People would pay her for those pies. She made everyone smile. When she'd drop the ironed clothes off, several of the White folks would give her a little extra because she was a hard worker and did such a good job. Now, not all of them were nice to her, but most were."

"Let's go sit on the porch, son. This truck's gettin' some hot."

Walking up to the porch, they settle into the rocking chairs. They feel good after working so hard.

"Daddy, tell me more."

"Well, at Christmas ... Now that was special. When she delivered their ironed tablecloths and napkins for their Christmas tables, she always brought them one of her sweet potato pies—even to the ones who weren't so kind. Your momma tried to see good in people."

He grows quiet, then his daddy adds, "Well, the day after that horrible thing happened that changed our lives forever, somethin' unexpected came.

Wilton angles his rocker toward his daddy, eager to catch every word, every thread of memory he could hold onto about his momma.

"You and I were back at the house grievin' somethin' bad with your granny and pap. Neighbors were there too, comforting us. Cookin' for us."

"Then, a knock came to the door. It was a White lady—I hadn't seen her before. A man waited for her in a real nice car outside. She stood on the steps and looked at me with kind eyes.

'You have my deepest condolences for this terrible thing that happened to Belle and your family,' she says to me. She explained that your momma had ironed for her family for six years. Said your momma was always kind, always a hard worker, and she'd be missed."

"Then, she handed me an envelope. Said they wanted to help us out with any burial costs. They knew we were poor. We were all poor on that side of town—but we were poor together, we kept our dignity, and we helped each other out."

He pauses again.

"Then, she did somethin' that surprised me. She reached out and patted my hand. Said they'd be praying for our family. Just before leaving, she added, 'I know your Belle was a strong Christian lady. My husband is the pastor at the

Baptist church in town.' Then she reached into her purse and pulled out something wrapped in pretty paper. 'He wants you and your family to have this,' she said. 'A gift from us to remember Belle.' She turned to go, then looked back. 'We'll miss Belle's sweet smile. And, we'll sure miss her wonderful sweet potato pies.'"

"Well, what was it, Daddy? What was the gift?" Wilton asks.

"I'll do better than tell you," his daddy says. "I'll show you."

They walk inside. His father reaches under the coffee table and pulls out the Bible.

"It was this, son. Her gift has been sitting here all these years. Open it to the front page."

Wilton opens the cover and reads aloud.

"In memory of Belle, a beautiful reflection of God." Wilton clears his throat as he tries to continue, voice cracking.

"May she dwell in the house of the Lord forever."

His father exhales softly.

"I didn't expect that comin' from White folks. But there are good people out there, Wilton—White and Black. And all along, God's been sending people to walk this journey with us. People to lend a hand. To stand up for what's right. To fight for what is right and just in the eyes of God."

Wilton just stares at the man who had faithfully and lovingly raised him all these years on his own. A quiet, renewed gratefulness rose up within him.

"Daddy, I never heard you talk like this before."

Wilton's daddy begins to rock slowly, both of their gazes drawn upward toward a hummingbird fluttering over the tree, its wings a blur against the light as it disappears.

"Humph," he says, continuing to gaze out at the tree. "I guess it was just time."

They rock in silence for a while, the spring breeze and the words they'd shared settling over them like a healing balm after the morning they'd had.

Daddy turns to Wilton, rubbing his chin, the way he does when something is stirring inside of him.

"You know, son, I been thinkin', your momma and I—we loved going to church together." He chuckles. "Loved taking you with us, too. We enjoyed hearing your pap preach. Maybe ... just maybe, it's time for both of us to find God again. We done pushed Him away for too long. I let a bitter root grow inside me 'cause I refused to forgive."

He looks over at Wilton, his voice lower now.

"I think you got one of those in you, too, son. If we don't tend to it, it'll take over—it'll grow right into our hearts and harden 'em. Forgivin' your pap, asking for his forgiveness—that was a start. But there's more. I got more forgivin' I gotta do. And this one ... this one might be even harder."

Wilton looks at him in question.

"Who is it, Daddy?"

His father holds his gaze.

"Myself," he says.

CHAPTER TWENTY-FIVE

"I am a Negro and proud of its color too... I am a Ne-gro and I want to be free as any other child. To wander about the house and the woods and be wild. I want to be Free, Free, Free."[76]

-Poem by Rosalyn Waterhouse,
11 years old, Meridian, MS Freedom School, 1964

April 10, 1960

As the Benoits drive past the church on their way home from Mass, palm branches waved out of the back seat window like it's a Mardi Gras parade instead of Palm Sunday. Parishioners spilling out of church stop and stare, some laughing as they watch the scene unfold—the supposedly proper Benoit girls, putting on a show without even knowing it.

"Mimi and Anna Beth, those have been blessed by Father," Mama says. "Can you please be respectful of that and pull them back into the car?"

"But Mama, that's what the people did when Jesus rode into town on his donkey. They waved them! I learned that in Catechism class."

"Well, that's just not proper. It looks like we have a carload of hooligans in our back seat dressed in their Sunday best. What will people think?"

"Harriet, calm down," Mr. Benoit says gently. "Mimi has a point. Let her and Anna Beth pretend."

Mary Grace, completely embarrassed by her little sisters' antics, reaches across the backseat and out the window to grab the palm branch from her sister's hands. A tussle begins, and off flies Mimi's palm frond. By this time, they are beyond the sanctuary building and now passing the church parking lot. Mimi searches out the back window to see where it has gone.

"Oh no," she cries out, "that mean man is picking it up."

"His name is Mr. Bubba," corrected Mary Grace, "and he is staring at us now."

"Daddy, please go back," Mimi asks. "I want my palm leaf."

"It's a palm branch," says Mary Grace, "not a leaf."

Mrs. Benoit grips the front dashboard, turning to Mr. Benoit with urgency.

"Shot, keep going. This has been embarrassing enough. Do not go back. And, I don't want anyone in our family to have any more encounters with that man, even over a palm branch," Mrs. Benoit says, sitting back. "I don't know how he can even go to church with a clean conscience. I just know that he is the one behind the burning cross at ..."

Quickly turning her way, "Harriet!" Mr. Benoit says firmly, then lowers his voice to a whisper, "Not here. Not now."

The girls become quiet.

Anna Beth shifts in her seat, leaning forward, and places a hand on her daddy's shoulder.

"Daddy?" asks Anna Beth, "Is Mr. Bubba the one who burned that cross at MawMaw's cleaners?"

"Is he, Daddy?" asks Mary Grace.

Mimi sits quietly listening, eyes wide, twisting the edge of her sister's palm branch between her fingers until it nearly tears.

Mr. Benoit looks up at them through the rearview mirror.

"Let's everyone sit back and settle down," says Mr. Benoit. "Why don't we stop for hot donuts at the bakery? I wonder what Mr. Jacque baked today?"

As he parks the car, he asks, "Who wants to come in and pick them out?"

The doors fly open, and the girls flood out of the car into the bakery. Mr. Benoit holds back for a moment.

"We need to talk with the girls, Harriet. Things are heating up, and we need to tell them at least what they're able to understand. They keep overhearing us and are confused."

Looking at him with concern, Mrs. Benoit says, "I guess you're right."

Mr. Benoit gets out of the car and follows the girls into the bakery. They are already up at the counter, pressing their hands to the glass and pointing excitedly at the trays behind it—eclairs, cream puffs, and rows of hot donuts with glaze dripping into the pan.

A few people stand ahead of him in line, including the sheriff, hat in hand, rhythmically tapping his fingers against his thigh. When the bell above the door jingles, he turns slightly, glancing over his shoulder, and spots Mr. Benoit.

Walking over to stand with him in line, Sherriff speaks quietly.

"I need to talk with you, Shot. I have some news."

"Come by the house later, Ace," Mr. Benoit replies. "I'll be home."

Walking through the back door of the Benoit home, the girls carry two boxes with great anticipation. They spread them out on the table like a feast—plain donuts hot from the oven, some with chocolate and strawberry icing, eclairs, and cream puffs. The smell is intoxicating.

Crisco and butter are staples in the South. On Sunday mornings, it is all about butter for the Benoit family. Come Sunday afternoon, Crisco takes the spotlight for a fried chicken dinner at MawMaw's house.

Now, Mimi and her daddy have their own Sunday morning ritual that everyone around the table has come to expect. "I'll get the butter, Daddy," Mimi says, already hopping up. "There those two go again," Mrs. Benoit says, shaking her head. "Eww," groans Mary Grace.

With knife in hand, Mimi and her daddy carefully place a thick, creamy slab of butter on each bite of their donut, letting it melt into the warm, sugary glaze.

Everyone sits quietly, enjoying their special Sunday treat—until Daddy speaks.

"Girls, there's something that your mama and I want to talk to you about. Things are beginning to change here."

"What do you mean, Daddy? What's changing?" asks Mimi with apprehension filling her voice.

Looking over to Mimi, seeing the fear in her face, he reaches to pat her hand.

"There's nothing to worry about, baby," Mr. Benoit says in a reassuring voice. "It doesn't mean it's a bad thing. It's just going to look ... a little different."

He glances over to Mrs. Benoit, nervously stacking the dirty plates on the table and closing the box lids.

Clearing his throat, he continues, "Let Daddy explain."

"First of all, I know that you've heard us and Father Joel talk about Archbishop Rummel in New Orleans. He's in charge of all our parish Catholic churches and schools, including your school, Holy Comforter."

"I remember he came to our church one time," says Anna Beth. "He wore a really tall white hat on his head," she chuckled.

Mimi giggled, "I remember, too. He had lots of sparkly things on it."

"Yes ... well," says Mr. Benoit, "it's called a miter. But what I want to say about him is that he sent out a letter saying that soon our schools will be desegregated. Now, I know that's a big word, and I don't expect you to know—"

"I know what it means," says Mary Grace proudly. "It means the Colored children will come to our schools. My friends were talking about it."

"Yay!" says Mimi. "Then DeDe and I can be in the same class. When, Daddy, when?"

"Well, it's a little complicated, Mimi," says Mama.

Mimi leans back in her chair, throwing her hands up to her head.

"Why does everything have to always be complicated?" she asks, exasperated.

Mr. and Mrs. Benoit exchange a glance—one of shared helplessness, the kind that says they wished they had an easy answer.

"Let me try to help you understand," says Daddy.

"A lot of people who live here don't want schools to be integrated, meaning they don't want Colored children going to their schools.

"Why?" asks Anna Beth.

Again, Mary Grace speaks up. "Because they think that Colored people carry diseases and don't want to be–"

"Mary Grace, that's enough. Don't say such a thing. Where did you hear this?"

"At school. Kids talk about it, Mama. That's why the Colored have to sit in the balcony at the Majestic Theater, they say."

"That's not what DeDe told me," says Mimi. "She said it was because they can see better than we do. They have better eyes," she adds, "so we need to sit closer."

"That's ridiculous," says Mary Grace.

"Okay, okay, girls," says Mrs. Benoit. "It's all very compli-cated."

Letting out a sigh, Mimi mutters, "That word again."

"Mary Grace, everything you hear at school is not always true. Don't fall for gossip, and please do not be part of spreading rumors like that," her mama cautions.

"Daddy, is that why DeDe got in trouble for drinking out of the water fountain at MawMaw's cleaners that say it's only for White people? Mimi asks. "Is that why she can't come to our house and Willa has to drink from the blue plastic cup behind the sink … because they're a different color from us?

Anna Beth reopens the lid of the pastry box and pulls out another eclair, licking the chocolate from her fingers.

"Well, Sister Mary Theresa says that we are all the same and God loves us all the same," says Mimi.

Mr. and Mrs. Benoit look at each other, shaking their heads as though regretting even starting this conversation.

"Mary Margaret said that's probably why a cross was burned in front of MawMaw's cleaners," says Mary Grace. "Because she has lots of colored people working for her, and some people don't like it."

"But DeDe's daddy, who works there, is really nice," says Mimi. "He's nicer than Ricky's daddy, who's White. Will someone burn a cross in our yard because Willa works for us?"

"Okay, let's all settle down, girls. And no, Mimi, that's not going to happen. But, these are all good questions," says Mr. Benoit.

Mrs. Benoit stands up, holding the stack of dirty plates.

"I think we should stop talking about all this for now," she says. "They don't need to know all of this, Shot. It's too much."

"If not now," says Mr. Benoit, "then when? We can't keep hiding everything from them."

"What are you hiding from us, Daddy?" asks Anna Beth, mouth full of eclair.

Mrs. Benoit becomes quiet, and the girls all stare at their daddy as though waiting for him to make everything right—to make everything okay, just like he always does.

Mr. Benoit calmly signals for Mrs. Benoit to sit back down.

"I want us to go back to the one thing Sister Mary Theresa said. 'God loves all people the same, no matter what their color.' He loves you, Mary Grace, just as much as He loves Willa Mae. He loves you, Mimi, just as much as He loves DeDe. And He loves Daddy just as much as He loves Mr. Bubba.

"Now, that doesn't mean God is happy with the way Mr. Bubba treats people—but maybe, one day, he'll ask for forgiveness."

Mr. Benoit leans forward.

"I've been thinking about the story you told us, Mimi," he says. "Mr. Bubba wasn't very kind to Willa Mae at the levee bench, was he?"

"Well, I don't see how God can love somebody so mean," Anna Beth says with a frown.

"Once again, Anna Beth—we're not the judge of people. God is," Mr. Benoit replies firmly.

"That's what MawMaw told us, too, Daddy," Mimi adds.

"Your MawMaw is right," he says with a nod. "And to be honest … I guess I need to hear that, too."

"Right now, all we can do is show love, treat people with kindness, and always do the right thing. And maybe, some of our actions will rub off on others."

"Meanwhile, you can ask Mama or Daddy anything you want. Things you might be scared about or not understand. I know sometimes at school you hear classmates saying things that are not kind about Colored people or even calling them that bad word we talked about. You can do the right thing by speaking out and telling them that God loves all people, no matter what color. That's a good start. That's a way you can make a difference."

A knock sounds at the front door.

I'll get that," says Mr. Benoit. "You girls help Mama pick up the kitchen."

Opening the front door, Sheriff stands there on the porch.

"You got a minute, Shot? I need to talk with you."

"Sure, come on in, Ace," he says. "It's perfect timing. A teaching moment at the table over donuts was getting a little too complicated."

Going into the garden room, they sit down in the two rocking chairs.

With a troubling look, Ace begins.

"I have heard again from sources that the FBI is going to be cracking down soon on the Klan."

The garden room doors suddenly open.

"How you doin', Sheriff?" says Jeanne Marie. "I didn't expect to see you here, but I'm glad you are. I was coming over to show something to Shot."

"What do you have there in your hand, Jeanne Marie?" asks Mr. Benoit.

She hands him a torn piece of paper and sits in the rocking chair next to them.

"I found this in the cleaners today while I was cleaning up."

He reads it with concern and hands it to Sheriff, who reads it aloud.

"Know your place."

"Hmmm, sounds like a warning to you, Miss Jeanne Marie," says Sheriff. "Where did you find this?"

"It was on the floor under the front counter," says Jeanne Marie.

"I can see that it has tape on it," he says. "Maybe it was taped to one of the rocks that came through the glass window. Jeanne Marie, I think you need to back off a bit. I heard you now have a colored girl at the front counter every now and then to wait on customers. You might be stirring up some trouble."

Jeanne Marie's face tightens with a renewed spark of conviction.

"You already employ quite a lot of Colored people, and that has raised some eyebrows," Sheriff says.

"Now, I appreciate you trying to watch out for me, but I'm not gonna back off, Sheriff," says Jeanne Marie.

"Estelle is good with people. She is smart and a hard worker. It's my property and my business, Sheriff. I'm gonna do what is right and what the good Lord tells me to do. Now, I think I'm going to going in the kitchen to visit with Harriet and the girls."

Holding up the note, Sheriff says, "I'd like to keep this piece of paper for evidence."

"It's all yours," says Jeanne Marie. "I was just gonna throw it in the trash where it belongs."

Walking away, she says something in French and makes her way through the kitchen door.

"She is one tough lady," says Sheriff.

"She is that," says Mr. Benoit, "and, as good as they come."

IT'S MONDAY MORNING, and the girls walk into the kitchen for breakfast, wondering why they smell the aroma of home-made biscuits.

"Willa," says Mary Grace, "you're doing what Effie did. We don't usually have biscuits on Mondays. It's supposed to be egg in a hole."

"Well," says Willa Mae, "I can't make biscuits on Saturday. I'll be busy cooking your Easter dinner. Then I have to get home and make Easter dinner for my own family. Your mama said I could stop by Mr. Jacque's bakery and bring you girls some donuts on Saturday instead?"

Their eyes light up.

"Thank you, Willa Mae," they say in unison.

"That's right, girls," says Mrs. Benoit as she rushes through the kitchen door, running late for her breakfast with the ladies.

"Willa has a lot to do on Saturday, so you can't bother her."

Opening her compact and quickly applying lipstick, she continues calling out instructions.

"Girls, Willa Mae will be with you tonight. Your daddy and I have a dinner to attend, and we'll be home late."

Snapping the compact shut, she throws open the door as she calls back over her shoulder, "Be good at school! And Willa Mae, I'll be home later this afternoon to get ready for our dinner out."

COMING IN FROM SCHOOL, the girls drop their books on the table.

"Willa," Mimi calls out, "we're home." Do we have an after-school snack? Do we need to find it?" asks Mimi.

"Well, I guess you better try, my babies," says Willa.

Anna Beth and Mimi begin to hunt, but Mary Grace, feeling too old for such games these days, just sits down and lets them do all the work.

"Anna Beth, you are getting warm," says Willa. "Mimi, you are cold."

Mimi runs over to where Anna Beth is and walks into the dining room.

"You are about to burn up, Mimi."

There on the buffet table sit M&M cookies.

Mimi stops, runs to the window, and listens.

"I hear something," says Mimi. "Everybody, be quiet. Do you hear it?"

"It's the calliope on the river!" Anna Beth calls out.

"Willa Mae, can we go to the levee to hear the calliope?" she asks.

Mary Grace calls out from the other room.

"I've heard it a hundred times, I'm staying here to do my homework."

Before they know it, Willa Mae is packing their after-school snack into a cookie tin, and they're walking as fast as they can to the levee, hoping to get there before the steamboat paddles its way down the river. Wildflowers bloom at the bottom of the slope, and purple wild irises are just beginning to peek out along the levee path. As the loud steam-whistle organ blares in the distance, Mimi races to their favorite bench. Anna Beth and Willa Mae sit down beside her just as the steamboat begins to appear from upriver.

They all watch as the massive red paddle wheel turns, scooping up water and flinging it behind the boat as it glides down the Mighty Mississippi with such grace. The music makes it feel like a circus has come to town. People are drawn to the river from all directions to catch a glimpse of the steamboat and hear the calliope. The high-pitched tune of "Camptown Races" whistles out through towering brass pipes, powered by high-pressure steam—it echoes for miles up and down the river.

"Willa, I wish we could see a rainbow, too, and then it would be the best day ever," says Mimi with excitement. "The calliope, a rainbow, and M&M cookies!"

Willa laughs. Then she thinks to herself, *these girls don't go wantin' for anything. They have everything a heart could ever desire.*

Without warning, Mimi grabs Willa's arm tightly. Willa looks up. Walking toward them are Ricky, two of his friends, and his daddy, Bubba.

"Willa, I'm scared," Mimi whispers.

Anna Beth pushes closer to Willa Mae.

"It's okay, girls. Let's just sit still and keep eatin' our cookies. Look at the people waving to us from the steamboat." But Willa's eyes continue glancing down the path as they approach.

Bubba marches past, glaring down at Willa and the girls, but doesn't stop or say a word. Willa holds her breath in apprehension, not wanting the girls to notice—then finally exhales. Ricky and his buddies trail behind him, snickering and whispering among themselves. They drift farther down the levee until Bubba stops, flicks a match, and lights a cigarette. The sharp scent of tobacco cuts through the warm, river air as he stands listening to the distant, whimsical tune of the calliope. Growing restless, the boys begin chasing each other up and down the levee, their childhood laughter filling the air.

With everyone feeling a sense of relief on the bench, Mimi asks quietly, "Willa, why does Mr. Bubba always look so mad and seem so mean?" Mimi looks out toward the boys playing. "And Ricky is mean, too."

Willa sighs softly. "Well, baby, I think Mr. Bubba has a hurt heart. And because he has a hurt heart, his little boy probably has one too."

"How do you fix a hurt heart, Willa?"

"My daddy always told me that we should pray to Jesus—that He can heal hurt hearts."

Willa gazes out toward the steamboat, then looks back at Mimi and Anna Beth. "You know what I think, my babies?"

She pauses. "Kindness. That's right. If we are kind as best we can, we're showin' God's love. And God's love can heal that hurtin' heart."

"Like the Good Samaritan did?" Mimi asks.

"Yeah, he showed love," adds Anna Beth.

Mimi stands, looking straight at Willa. "And he even gave the hurt man a Band-Aid. And Father Joel said they didn't even like each other."

Willa chuckles. "He sure did give him a Band-Aid. He sure did."

Just then, Bubba, Ricky, and the other boys pass by the bench again. Mimi quickly sits down close to Willa. Bubba again walks by without looking at them or saying a word—but this time, the boys stop.

"We could sit here if we wanted," Ricky says, trying to sound tough, "but we have to go."

Ricky's daddy turns around and snaps, "I told you—it's time to leave. Get movin', or you gonna get the belt when we get home."

Mimi reaches for the tin of cookies in Willa's hands. Willa's eyes gleam, handing it to her with a smile.

"You want one of Willa Mae's special cookies with M&M's?" she asks.

The boys go quiet, glancing at each other, unsure of what to do.

Ricky stares down at the tempting cookies for a moment, then quickly glances toward his daddy's back as he walks down the levee path, cigarette dangling from his fingers.

Ricky speaks up, his tone shifting. "Sure, I mean ... why not." He hesitantly walks over, the other two boys following. Each one cautiously reaches into the tin for a cookie—then takes off running.

Ricky stops and turns. "Thanks!" he shouts, then keeps running.

Willa looks at Mimi and gently pats her hand. "That was very kind, baby. That's a good way to begin to heal a hurt heart."

Anna Beth looks over with wide eyes. "And that was brave, too, Mimi."

Listening to the strains of music as it fades down the river, Willa puts the lid on the cookie tin. Then, in a quiet voice looking out on the river, she says, "God's presence was here today, yes he was, through a child's innocent tender heart."

Willa Mae stands, filled with a new strength. "Let's go home, girls. Even though we didn't see a rainbow, we can always keep God's promise of hope in our hearts. Don't ever forget—faith can break the sky in two and let the face of God shine through."

Looking back, Mimi will remember that day clearly. She found a new strength rising up through her innocence—and a voice. Willa saw it too, one that will continue to take root and grow through the years.

CHAPTER TWENTY-SIX

> *"In Him was life, and that life was the light of all mankind. The light shines in the darkness, and the darkness has not overcome it."*[77]
>
> -John 1:4-5

April 17, 1960

Easter Sunday

The pungent, sweet fragrance of Easter lilies filled the church as the choir and congregation clap to the final verse of the opening hymn, "He Lives." Willa, Effie, Wilton, and his daddy, Albert, stand together singing in their usual fourth pew. Mr. Willie rushed in late, dressed in his Easter Sunday suit.

With not much room left in Willa's pew, a welcoming invitation comes from behind.

"Come on, Mr. Willie, sit back here with us," says Miss Ella. "We're all family."

The morning sun streamed through the large stained-glass windows, lighting up the church with a mosaic of colors.

"He is risen. The tomb is empty!" proclaims Reverend Washington as he stands on the steps of the altar with his hands raised.

"He is risen indeed!" Everyone shouts back. "The tomb is empty!"

The jubilant voices ring through the open windows and the church doors and echo down the streets of the Colored section of Bayou Grande. Their resurrection joy flows on the wind like a trumpet blast!

The Reverend walks up the steps into the pulpit and calls on everyone to be seated.

"I want to take you back a few days before the resurrection," he says, "so that we can feel and know the miraculous impact it continues to have on our lives and on all of humanity."

The Reverend then sets the scene.

"Far away and long ago, in a moment the world still remembers, there stood an old rugged cross," he continues. "And there," he turns and raises his hand toward the wooden cross above the altar, "Jesus paid the ultimate price, acting as our substitute on the cross. Paying the penalty for our sins. He was arrested, mocked, beaten, humiliated, and spit on ... for my sins, for your sins, and yours, and yours." He slowly points throughout the congregation, his eyes filled with hope.

"His body was broken so that we could be made whole."

Stomping his foot, he says, "This is a promise we can stand on."

Hallelujahs burst from the pews with a contagious hope riding strong on its tailwinds.

Reverend steps down from the pulpit and into the center aisle, his manner turning solemn.

"Much has happened over the past few weeks. Just last month, we watched as students courageously answered the call to take a stand for justice. But on that day—March 28th—they didn't stand. No, they took a seat for justice. Boldly, they sat at the White lunch counter inside Kress Department Store. And the next day … more students did the same at Sitman Drug Store and the Greyhound bus station."

He pauses, stroking his chin, looking out over the congregation.

"They, too, were mocked. Spit on. Kicked. Insulted. Arrested. Does this sound like a familiar story?"

The Reverend lets the weight of the words settle over the sanctuary.

"Some say they broke the law—I say … they broke the chains."

"That's resurrection power!" someone hollered from the back.

"Tell it, preacher," comes a cry from the front.

Then, from somewhere in the middle, a strong voice shouts, "He lives!"

"Amen, brothers and sisters, but as many of you know, that wasn't the end. On the third day—March 30th—more students rose up. Two thousand strong. They walked for miles from Southern University to the Louisiana State

Capitol. Their feet were fitted and ready with the gospel of peace, and they marched with dignity down Scenic Highway and onto Spanish Town Road."

Wiping his brow with his handkerchief, he glances toward one of the families still bearing the weight of it all.

"But," he says softly, "there was again a cost."

Quietly, he turns again to the cross, takes a breath, and turns back to face his beloved congregation.

Reverend says in a heavy tone, "We must press on."

Raising his voice, he shouts, "Because we are a people who have always pressed on. Jesus pressed on, too. He saw the cross before Him, and He knew what He had to do. I don't know about you, but when I looked at those students on the news ... I saw a reflection of Jesus in them. They brought God's light into the darkness to shine on the injustices around them."

Just then, Wilton turns to Effie.

"I see it now, Effie," he whispers.

"What?" asks Effie. "What do you see?"

"From all the stories I have heard," he says with urgency in his voice, "my momma was a reflection of Jesus, too. She brought His light. And now I know ... that light lives on in me. I'm called to carry on what she began."

Effie squeezes his hand. "She'd be so proud, Wilton."

The Reverend's voice rises with even more conviction.

"For you see, Jesus himself is peace. And Jesus Christ, on that cross, offers universal peace—peace to all people—

through the reconciling work He did for us. Reconciliation of humanity with God ... and reconciliation with one another."

"We are each called to be agents of reconciliation. But this Kingdom work that Jesus did on the cross was not easy, no."

Reverend shouts toward the heavens.

"'My God, My God, why have you forsaken me?' Jesus cried out from the cross. I personally think that Jesus was wrestling with His Father in those final moments, feeling alone and abandoned. And Jesus cried out again with a loud voice and after that... gave up His spirit, He was gone. Then, something unbelievable happened," Reverend preached. "I will read it from His Word. But I want you to picture this scene in your mind that happened the moment Jesus died on the cross. It's a miraculous event that affects each of us today."

Picking up his Bible, he reads, "'And behold, the curtain of the temple was torn in two, from top to bottom. And the earth shook, and the rocks were split' (Matthew 27:51)."[78]

Reverend looks up, shaking his head in amazement.

"Picture it. The 60-foot-high and 30-foot-wide temple curtain into the Holy of Holies—which only the high priest could enter only once a year, on the Day of Atonement, to offer a blood sacrifice for the sins of the people—was torn from top to bottom," he says. "The barrier between God and humanity had been removed. The barrier between God and each of us has been removed."

He looks at Mr. Booker in the front row, uncharacter-istically wide awake. "Do you even know how tall a curtain that would have been?" The Reverend points straight up to the ceiling. "Six stories high." He glances back at Mr. Booker, shaking his head, eyes wide with disbelief. "No human could have done this—only God Almighty Himself."

"This moment in time was both deeply human and profoundly divine. And in one sacred collision, heaven met earth."

The whole church stills as though they have been transported in time to the foot of the cross on Calvary Hill 2,000 years ago.

Reverend continues, "Everyone standing under the cross that day waited to see if God would save His Son, Jesus. But, without hearing a voice from heaven, Jesus gave up His spirit. He was gone. Those standing there witnessing this horrific crucifixion must have felt that darkness had finally won and they, too, had been abandoned."

Suddenly, the lights go out in the church. At that same moment, the sun disappears behind the clouds and the church darkens even more. Everyone is silent, looking around and shifting uncomfortably in their seats.

Wilton whispered to Effie, "I'm beginning to believe that this is not coincidence."

A voice comes from the darkened altar.

"The darkness can make us fearful, can't it?" says the Reverend. "It makes me fearful, too. At those times, we begin to wrestle with God, thinking He has forsaken us through the hardships we face. Some of those students fighting for justice and dignity maybe felt alone and wondered, 'Where are you, Jesus?' Are you sometimes ready to throw in the towel? Are you willing to give up that easily?"

"No!" Startling everyone, a loud voice booms from the fourth row back.

"That's right, baby," says Miss Ella, patting Wilton's back. "You done with wrestlin'."

Grabbing Wilton's hand and squeezing it, Effie can't believe what she is hearing. Willa Mae reaches over and pats Wilton's leg. "You speak it, baby."

"That's right, Brother," says Reverend. "The devil wants us to believe that he has finally won the battle and extinguished God's light. At those times, we might cry out, 'My God, my God, why have you forsaken us!'"

"Then," Reverend says in a hushed voice, "that's Satan's cue. Like a prowling lion he moves in and without warning comes knocking at your back door. Don't let him in, no matter how hard he knocks. He wants to come in with a rusty bucket of overused lies; Jesus comes in with a cup of fresh living water, overflowing.[79] Not half full, do you hear me, but overflowing! Because you see, your cry of desperation and abandonment is not the absence of faith, but the evidence of it."

Continuing down the aisle of the church, he says, "But you are probably wondering, why, Reverend, on Easter Sunday, would you share this? Because there would be no Easter Sunday without a Good Friday and I want you to know and feel the miracle and the power of the Resurrection. I want you to look around. Look carefully. What do you see?"

Everyone looks around.

A shout comes from the front row.

"I see some sunlight comin' back in through the stained glass."

"Amen, Brother Booker, because there was more to come from that cross than just death and sorrow. And that's why we celebrate today."

"The light."

"The light of the world."

"The light of the world is Jesus."

"His light is all around us and it will never go out. Even if you lose all hope, a flicker of Jesus' light is still there. Never, I say, never give up hope because the light shines in the darkness, and the darkness cannot extinguish it."[80]

As amens are heard around the church, the lights come back on, and the choir begins to sing another chorus of "He Lives." When the song ends, the Reverend looks up to the rafters, gathering his thoughts. The congregation waits in anticipation.

"I want each of you to do one more thing for me today to remind us of the power of the resurrection on this glorious Easter morning.

"Look around at the folks here today. You have known many of them all your life. The first thing I see," says Reverend, "is everyone dressed in their Easter best."

"But I want you to look past that, look further. Do you see it? Look hard now," he says.

Everyone looks around, not seeming to see anything different than what they have known all these years. Mr.

Booker is somehow dozing off again. Mrs. Grey, as always, wears the brightest hat in the room. And, Miss Lillie, now 97—the matriarch of the church—sits in silence, wisdom in her eyes.

He walks back up to the pulpit.

"No," he says, "I don't think we do see it, do we? It's because often we keep it hidden. I do, too, at times. So, what is it I'm speaking of?"

The church holds their breath so as not to miss what Reverend is about to say.

He opens his arms wide, glancing from one side of the congregation to the next.

"Wounds," he calls out.

"Scars. Not necessarily the ones you can see."

Effie looks at Wilton and to the cut on his head. He winks and smiles.

"No, I'm speaking of the wounds and scars that can't be seen. They're the ones that we carry deep within our hearts and souls ... grief, bitterness, heartbreak, pain from injustices, and scars that can go back generations."

He points to the cross once again. In Reverend's eyes, it can never be too many times.

"Scars come from healing and can become a witness to others. As scripture has it, you will be able to overcome Satan through the blood of the Lamb and the Word of your testimony to others."[81]

Lowering his voice, he says, "Now some of us might still have open wounds. The ones that fester ... keeping us captive and making us soul-sick."

Pointing back to the cross, the Reverend continues.

"Go to the foot of the cross. Fall to your knees. Surrender to the One who still carries the scars—scars He bore for our sins and our wounds."

Preacher continues, but Wilton just stares, not able to take his eyes off the cross. A prayer comes from somewhere within as Preacher's voice fades into the distance. *Jesus, I can't let go of my anger and bitterness. It has me captive. I hate it. It's eating away at me.* He glances at Effie. *It's coming in the middle of my relationships. How do I surrender to you? My momma would want that. I want that.*

Reverend's voice draws Wilton back.

"Then, on that glorious Sunday morning, when that stone was pushed away from the tomb, out flowed streams of living water, washing away our sins and healing our wounds. Jesus is that living water who brings eternal life. The tempter has been defeated, and we know ..."

Reverend suddenly begins to clap, "Look at those beams of light comin' in from the open doors. Let's applaud God!"

Everyone stands up, erupting with applause, amens, and hallelujahs.

"Oh, we are having good church today! What a celebration! The power of praise lifts the heaviest of hearts. But, there's more in store for you," the Reverend calls out. "Let's all be seated for a few minutes."

The church is on fire, and there is a sense of the Holy Spirit hovering over them.

"Before we go out and continue with fellowship, coffee, donuts, and an Easter Egg hunt for the youngins', I would like you to welcome our special guest who is going to end our service for us on this powerful and glorious Easter morning." Reverend gestures toward the back of the church.

Everyone shifts in their seats, surprised to see Preacher coming through the double doors dressed in his white garment, staff in hand. He dons a rose-colored sash around his waist, a color that speaks of new beginnings and joyful hope. It's a shade that often greets the dawn of a new day.

Preacher looks out over the congregation. His eyes catch Wilton's.

"I invite you this Easter morning," he calls out, "to accept Jesus' invitation to you as He waits knocking at the door of your life ... invite Him to come in and be your Lord and Savior. To fill the dark rooms of your heart with His light. Surrender at the foot of the old rugged cross. Jesus is waiting. The tomb is empty, and He is here living among us. He waits for you to ask Him into your heart and life. Let's all bow our heads and take a moment with God."

Wilton bows his head. *If you are here, Jesus, I ask you to please come into my heart and my life. I don't think ... no, I can't ... do it alone.* With those words, he feels his shoulders relax as though his body is being released from something that has had hold of him for longer than he wants to admit.

"Now proclaim before this church family your commitment to follow Jesus and," pointing behind him through the doors, Preacher says, "the river is flowing mighty on this Easter morning, and it's invitin' you to come and be baptized, washed clean by the water. Join us down by the river. Don't worry," he smiles, "I've been told that the pastries and festivities will still be here when you get back."

The choir begins to sing, and the clapping explodes. The children come in from Sunday school and begin dancing in the aisles. Mr. Willie is the first to make his way to Preacher. Wilton's heart is beating fast as though it is going to burst right out of his chest. He feels a calling from deep within, like something he has never felt before.

Whispering, he says, "Come with me, Effie. I need you to be there."

He grabs her hand and pulls her out into the aisle with him, his daddy close behind. Preacher places his hand of reassurance on Wilton and Mr. Willie's shoulders.

Mr. Willie, Wilton, his dad, and Effie follow behind Preacher as he leaves the church and starts the walk down Glory Way towards the river. Many from the congregation follow behind them—heels, hats, and all—along with the choir, their voices continuing to sing out the door. Wilton holds Effie's hand tight.

Feeling a gentle tug on his shirt, he turns to see little Ruth Ann, one of his neighbors, holding a cross made of sticks. Wilton bends down, smiling.

"What is it, Ruth Ann?"

"I want you to have my cross, Wilton. I made it in Easter Sunday School today. Jesus told me to give it to you. Maybe you need it."

Looking up at Effie, he smiles and then back at Ruth Ann.

"I think Jesus knew exactly what I needed today, and thank you for being His special messenger," he says to her.

Smiling, she runs back to her momma as the crowd continues their Easter procession.

Hearing commotion behind them, Wilton and Effie turn around once again. Scrappy is making his way to the front of the procession with a whole strawberry frosted donut clenched tightly in his mouth.

"I guess he doesn't want to miss out on this glorious day either, and especially the donuts," says Effie.

As the congregation reaches the river's edge, the sun is sparkling on the water like diamonds. Only a few cars are in line for the ferry, but those that were there watch the events being played out before them.

Wilton and Mr. Willie take off their shoes and roll up their pants.

"You know you are going to be completely dunked, Wilton," warns Effie.

"It's okay, I live close," he smiles.

"And so do I," says Mr. Willie as he takes off his suit jacket. "I know Tootie is watching from above. She'd be some upset that I'm gettin' my new suit pants wet." He chuckles.

There is a safe eddy of still water about waist deep that the river has naturally cut out towards the shore. It makes for an ideal baptismal pool.

"Are you ready to be immersed into the water and brought back up to new life in Jesus?" calls out Preacher loudly.

"Yes," they say in unison, Wilton's eyes meeting Effie's.

Wilton is first.

"Wilton, as you step into this river, may it symbolize the living water of Jesus. May it always flow around you, through you and out of you to others. God freely gives you this gift. You are not saved by works, but you are saved for works. Have you accepted Jesus as your personal savior?"

"I have," he says solemnly.

"Because of your faith and obedience to Jesus, I baptize you in the name of the Father and of the Son and of the Holy Spirit. Cross your hands over your chest, Wilton."

Preacher and Wilton's daddy helped to fully immerse him backwards into the water. As he comes up with water dripping from head to toe, there were shouts and claps. There are even honks coming from the waiting cars.

Preacher touches his head to Wilton's and whispers, "God's got a mission for you, son. I've always known it. You have my spirit and your momma's courage in you. Lean on Jesus and not yourself. Be courageous and go in peace."

Something stirs in Wilton, and he smiles ear to ear at his pap.

Mr. Willie is next and steps into the water. His baptism is completed with more cheers. Towels are given out, and everyone congratulates Mr. Willie and Wilton.

"Now, let's pray," he calls out to all who are gathered.

Raising his hand high, he continues, "Jesus, may we recommit our lives to you. If there are any embers in our lives, let us fan into flame the gift of God.[82] May our lives become a bonfire for you, just like the ones on this levee every Christmas Eve lighting the way, the day before we celebrate your birth."

Shouts of Amen fill the air.

Little by little, groups of people head back to church. Wilton and Mr. Willie walk home to change.

"I'll see you back at church, Effie. Save a seat for me at the festivities," he winks.

"You know I will," she says. "We have a lot to talk about. Graduation is soon."

On their stroll back to church, Willa Mae and Effie are filled with excitement about Wilton's baptism.

"He's a fine young man, Effie."

"He sure is, Momma. I have always known that. And even though he can be mighty strong-willed at times, he's got a tender heart."

Willa Mae smiles. "God can use that strong-will, Effie, for His good and His glory."

Turning thoughtful, Effie says, "Momma, I really don't know what to do after graduation."

Willa Mae doesn't speak—just waits.

"I mean ... I want to stay here, I do. Be close to you and Grandma Nellie."

Effie struggles to find the right words. She wants to speak her heart, but she doesn't want to break her momma's.

Effie stops to pick up a pink Azalea bloom that has fallen onto the road from its bush. She lifts it to her nose, and the sweet, familiar fragrance sweeps her back to childhood–barefoot mornings, porch swings, and the way her momma and Grandma Nellie used to hum hymns while snapping beans.

Effie continues, "But ... I don't know if there's anything here for what I want to do. I ... I just feel ... confused."

She glances at her momma, then away again.

"You know, Momma, Wilton's got his heart set on Fisk University, up in Nashville. Some of the teachers here think he's got a real good chance at a scholarship. They've helped him apply."

Her voice cracks.

"I want to be happy for him, I really do, but ..."

Her voice trails off. She gives a little shrug.

"I don't know what's gonna happen. And I don't know what I'm supposed to do. I'm just ... confused. I've heard about so many people, and many my age, moving up North or out West, chasing opportunities we just don't have around here. You know I want to be a seamstress, Momma. I dream of opening my own shop one day."

She looks over, searching her momma's eyes.

"And you know I'm good at it," she states with enthusiasm in her voice.

"You sure are," says Willa Mae.

She gently reaches for Effie's hand and stops on the road. Their eyes meet. "Effie Rose, all any momma wants for her child is for them to be happy and follow their heart and their dreams." Swallowing hard, she continues, "and that's what I want for you, baby."

Effie wraps her arms around her momma. No words are needed as Willa Mae does the same.

They continue toward the church.

"Now, don't forget, Miss Jeanne Marie says that you could work for her. Maybe you could start out there at the cleaners and then see where that takes you."

Taking a deep breath and looking at the church just up ahead, Effie says, "I know, Momma, and that was really so nice of Miss Jeanne Marie. I just don't know what to do."

"Well, I do," says Willa Mae. "We're just gonna enjoy Easter, and we can keep talkin' more about it next week."

Coming down the road toward them trots Scrappy.

"Now look at that dog. He has another donut in his mouth." They both laugh and then Momma says something to Effie that she will remember long after her momma is gone.

"Effie, God knows the plans He has for you. All you need to do is pray and trust in Jesus, and He will take care of the situation."

Putting her arm around her baby, they walk down Glory Way back to church.

CHAPTER TWENTY-SEVEN

May 13, 1960

Graduation mortarboards soar high above the heads of the jubilant graduates. The white caps sail toward the clouds, filling the sky with celebration, dreams, possibilities, and new beginnings. The day is warm, yet deeper warmth fills the hearts of the graduates and their families.

"Ohhhh, what a beautiful sight. Thank you, Jesus," Willa Mae exclaims to Grandma Nellie.

Willa Mae beams from ear to ear, eyes locked on her baby girl–reaching, giggling, and filled with excitement as she tries to catch her cap midair. The moment holds more than joy–it is a momentous occasion. Effie is the first in Willa Mae's family to graduate from high school.

Willa's thoughts drifted to the past, her heart tugged by memories long buried. At Effie's age, she had yearned to attend high school, to sit in a classroom and learn. But there were no Colored schools nearby–only McKinley High in Baton Rouge, a world away when you couldn't afford the ferry fare or a bus ticket. So at fourteen, she traded textbooks for dirty dishes, stepping into a kitchen instead of a classroom, her dreams dashed by circumstance.

What a redemptive day, Willa thinks.

Effie runs over, arms outstretched, and throws them around her momma, then Grandma Nellie.

"Congratulations, my baby. Your momma's heart is so full right now," Willa says, pulling her close again before reaching into her purse.

She pulls out two small boxes wrapped in bright, multi-colored floral paper, pretty enough that Effie might have wanted to turn it into a dress if it had been a bolt of fabric. Willa Mae hands them to her with a smile.

"Here are your graduation presents. This first one is from your grandma."

Grandma Nellie waits in excitement for her grand-daughter to see the gift inside. Wanting to save the pretty paper, Effie peels it back carefully, with a mixture of antici-pation and delight. Folding back the tissue paper, she finds a crisp white handkerchief beneath it, with her name–Effie Rose–embroidered in soft pink thread.

"Oh, Grandma Nellie," she exclaims, holding it to her chest. "I love it and will treasure it always."

She leans in, embracing her grandmother in a warm hug.

"Now this one is from me," Willa Mae says, handing her the second box wrapped in the same paper. Again, carefully opening it, Effie's face lights up.

"Momma! I've never had a watch of my own. It's so beautiful. You shouldn't have..."

"It's a very special day, Effie," Willa Mae says, eyes shining. "We are so proud to have a high school graduate in our family. I want to give you something you can keep for a long time."

"Forever," Effie says, hugging her tightly. "It will be treasured and kept safe right along with Grandma's handkerchief."

"Thank you both," she says, "for all your support and love through high school."

She takes a step back, her face glowing.

"I'm excited to show the gifts to my friends. If that's okay, I'll see you later on!"

Smiling, Willa Mae shakes her head. Now you go on and enjoy your classmates."

As Effie turns to go, Willa calls after her.

"Effie! Remember, I have to be with the girls tonight–I won't be able to go to the graduation party."

"I know, Momma, it's okay!" Effie calls back with a wave. "I'll see you tomorrow!"

All Willa Mae and Grandma Nellie see is the back of Effie's white robe billowing in the wind as she runs off to find her friends, her laughter blending into the joyful chorus of graduates.

THE EVENING IS WARM, and not a cloud is the sky as Effie and her girlfriends walk toward school for their graduation party. Everyone is bubbling over with joy and anticipation. The air is filled with the distinct scents of jasmine, honeysuckle, and magnolia, drifting from the yards of houses along the way. Above them, Spanish moss sways from the oak branches as it catches the intermittent gentle breeze. The sunset stretches across the horizon in layers of golden yellow, peach, and amber—a painting waiting to be framed, glowing with promise. Louisiana in spring is like no other place.

The girls had gone home to change after the ceremony and are now dressed in their finest, ready for an evening of celebration. Effie has sewn her dress from a stunning, yellow-flowered cotton fabric, with a ruched waist that accentuated her slender figure. She found a Butterick pattern and worked tirelessly on her creation for months.

Opening the doors, they step into the auditorium—an old army hangar hauled across the river from the airport. It had been the first building placed on the school grounds back in 1948. Its weathered walls steeped in stories of years gone by.

But tonight, the space is transformed. Festive decorations hang from every corner, and the rhythm of a local band—led by two proud dads of graduating seniors—fills the room, setting the mood for a night to remember.

Across the floor, Wilton stands, surrounded by classmates and parents congratulating him on his achievement of class Valedictorian. It is tradition to include family in the beginning, then let the young folks have their fun once the music picks up. Effie catches his eye, and he meets her gaze with a smile.

Wilton makes his way across the dance floor, weaving through the crowd, with more congratulations along the way. Effie keeps talking to friends, pretending she doesn't see him coming. Feeling a gentle tap on her shoulder, she turns. At first, Wilton is speechless, struck by Effie's smile that lights up the room and by how beautiful she looks in her stunning yellow dress.

"You ... you look beautiful, Miss Effie Rose."

Smoothing her dress, she blushes. "Why, thank you, Mr. Wilton Ambrose."

Taking her hand, he says, "May I have the honor of your first dance?"

Hand in hand, they make their way to the dance floor as the band puts their own spin on popular hits.

The music softens. They draw close, as the saxophone carries the melody like a lullaby. Effie puts her head on his shoulder.

"I love the Drifters," she says softly, "and especially their new song."

"Well," Wilton says, "what do you say—think you might save the last dance for me?"

They chuckle.

"You know I will," as they finish the song in silence.

Parents and siblings have long left for home, and the music flows on. The band picks up the beat as the first notes of Chubby Checker's "The Twist" fly off the stage and the floor comes alive. Girls kick off their shoes, boys shed their jackets, and laughter echoes beneath the lights as hips begin to swing.

As the song ends, Wilton shouts over the music, "Let's get some punch and go outside to cool off."

They step into the night air, the stars above sparkling. A night filled with wonder.

Effie turns to Wilton, her eyes shining.

"Did you know that all the stars are little windows into heaven?" she asks. "That's what Momma always told me as a little girl," she smiles, "and I think it's true!"

"It's a nice thought," Wilton replies, "but what they really are is a body of gas that–"

"Okay, okay, Mr. Valedictorian," Effie says with a laugh. "You don't have to be so technical. Can we just pretend and dream on such a beautiful evening?"

"Sorry," Wilton says, grinning. "Sometimes I can't help myself."

A symphony of frogs echoes from the nearby bayou, their raspy calls carrying a ballad unique only to Louisiana.

Wilton takes her hand, then looks into her eyes.

"Can I kiss you, Effie?"

"If I can kiss you back?" she asks, smiling shyly.

They draw close, their lips meeting in a tender kiss beneath a crescent moon, framed by a canopy of stars like windows into heaven. The night holds its breath–it is now quiet, still, and magical.

Gently pulling away, Wilton's voice is barely above a whisper, "I have something for you," he says, his eyes searching hers.

"Come sit with me a while."

He reaches for her hand, guiding her toward the old school bench beneath the magnolia tree, its white blossoms faintly glowing in the moonlight.

Sitting down, Wilton pulls out a small black velvet box from his pocket and hands it to Effie. The box is a bit worn, its corners dulled with time.

Looking at him shyly, she asks, "What is this, Wilton?"

"Just open it."

As she lifts the velvet top, her breath catches. Inside rests a delicate gold locket on a golden chain. Effie lifts it carefully, opening the locket to reveal a small piece of a dried rose petal, pressed and preserved. "It's so beautiful," Effie whispers.

"Let me explain," says Wilton.

"Years ago, Daddy gave a red rose and this locket to my momma for her birthday." As Wilton looks up at the stars, he sniffles. "Her name was Belle."

Placing her hand softly on his, she murmurs, "What a beautiful name to remember, Wilton."

Shaking his head, he wipes his eyes.

He said he had to save up a long time to buy it for her. He wanted me to hold onto it until I found someone special to give it to.

Looking at her, he says, "This rose symbolizes our long friendship and love that will live on forever."

He looks deep into her eyes.

"I love you, Effie Rose."

"I love you too, Wilton," she replies as she carefully places the locket in the box and holds it close.

"I just want to hold it for a while, and then will you clasp it around my neck?"

"I would love nothing more," he says.

Effie rests her head on Wilton's shoulder as they sit quietly, watching the stars and listening to the rising chorus of frogs behind them.

"I still can't believe what you told me on the phone the other night, that Preacher is your pap," says Effie. "How are you doing with all that?"

"I think it's still sinking in," he says. "Especially the part about my mom."

"Well, I'm always here with a listening ear," she says, looking up at him with eyes that carry more comfort than words ever could.

Wilton gently kisses her on her forehead.

"I want to tell you something pretty special, Effie, that happened the other afternoon. I pulled out our Bible, the one given to us after Momma was," he swallows hard, "murdered." Effie takes his hand and squeezes it.

"You know what," he says, "I think it helps me to heal to be able to say out loud the truth of what happened that night.

The two sit in silence for a while looking up at the stars. Sitting up, he looks at Effie and continues. "I took the Bible to the porch, well, you know the spot."

Effie gives him a warm smile.

"The hummingbirds were everywhere that day. As I was looking through the Bible, I found a treasure. The people who gave it to Daddy that night must have slipped it in. It was a piece of brown paper, cut into a heart, and it said, 'Enjoy the pie and Merry Christmas, Belle.' Effie, it was my momma who wrote it. I have her handwriting—and that's not all. Below her name was a Bible passage. Isaiah 9:6. I looked it up, and Effie, I want to know the Jesus my mom knew. I read he's a wonderful counselor, a mighty God, and a Prince of Peace. Those are powerful words. I know that Jesus is with me, and my momma is too. I feel it. And I know," he says quietly, "what I'm about to tell you, my momma would be so proud of."

He tenderly takes the box from her and places it on the bench. Taking both her hands in his, he looks into her deep brown eyes.

"Effie?" Wilton says hesitantly.

"What is it?" she asks, sensing a change in his tone.

"I ... I've got some news." His eyes shift, watching her face. "I've been accepted to Fisk University on scholarship," he smiles. "I'm going to be heading to Nashville soon."

"Wilton ... that's ... that's wonderful," she says, forcing a smile she wants to mean. "It's ... the answer to your dreams."

"I know," Wilton says. "Ever since Easter Sunday when I was baptized, I sense something changing in me. I have been doing a lot of talking with God, and like I said, reading some of the Bible. I've asked Him to show me what to do. This is an answer to my prayer, Effie."

Effie pauses. "I'm so happy for you, Wilton. Really. And I guess I thought something like this might happen. But ... where does that leave us?"

Wilton takes Effie's hands again, this time with vigor. "Come with me, Effie," Wilton pleads. "I've been thinking about it a lot. We can start our lives there together. I can go to school, and you can find a job at something you love. This is a perfect plan for us."

"Us?" Effie asks, pulling her hands away and standing up. "Wilton, could we have talked about this? What about ... my dreams? You know I've been thinking about moving to Detroit.

"But you can do seamstress work in Nashville. I'm sure there's opportunities for you there," he says.

"Not like in the North, Wilton. My aunt has invited me to work alongside her at her seamstress shop. My dream is to one day open a dress shop of my own."

"But I can help you look for jobs," he says. "I plan to start summer school in a couple of weeks. I can check things out, then you could meet me there later in the summer."

"Did you even consider coming with me to Detroit?" she asks, looking at Wilton.

"You know why, Effie. It's not just going to college in Nashville. I also feel called to be a part of the Nashville Student Leadership Movement. There are a lot of student leaders there who are challenging segregation. Don't you want to be a part of that?" Wilton asks.

"Right now, I feel my opportunity is in Detroit, not Nashville," she says, her voice rising.

Wilton gets up and walks away, staring into the starlit sky, then turns back to her.

"I always thought we would be together, Effie."

Sitting back down on the bench, Effie says quietly, "I did, too, but I guess we're not those two little kids kicking cans down the street and sitting on the levee in summer with our popsicles anymore. Life doesn't feel as simple as it used to."

"Yeah," Wilton says, rubbing the back of his neck and walking toward the bench. "I guess, at least right now, what we each want is different." He pauses, then looks down at Effie, his voice filled with conviction.

"But Effie, I have to stay here in the South. I need to get my degree and find a way to make a difference. It's something I feel deep inside of me. I have to join the fight for justice ... to be a light, like Reverend Washington says—and to carry on my momma's legacy. And I thought you wanted to carry on your pappy's, too."

Shaking his head, "It feels like, I mean ... I guess if you want to run away to Detroit and pretend like none of this is happening down here, then I say go. But don't forget, you're leaving your momma and Grandma Nellie sitting right here in the middle of it."

Effie stands up, not believing what she is hearing.

"Wilton, how can you say such a mean and hurtful thing to me. You know I care about my momma and Grandma Nellie more than anything else. I thought you knew me better than that."

Standing up, she turns her back to him.

"Just go, Wilton," she says, "please," raising her hand and breaking down in tears.

She quickly turns to face him. "Right now, Wilton, the way I feel," her voice cracks, "I don't care if I ever see you again. Go off and do your protest. It's what you have always wanted to do anyway."

She turns and heads down the street for home.

"Effie, wait. Effie, please. I didn't mean for it to come out that way."

Effie keeps walking with tears streaming down her face.

Arriving home, heartbroken, Effie walks into the house and falls onto her bed, her yellow-flowered dress crumpling beneath her.

Grandma Nellie walks in and leans over her bed.

"Baby, what happened?" she whispers. "You're home so early."

"It's Wilton. I don't want to talk about it, Grandma."

Well, let's at least get you out of your pretty dress."

"No, I just want to be alone."

Effie lies there and cries herself to sleep, her heart broken, her hopes and dreams shattered.

"EFFIE, EFFIE!"

A gentle shake. Her eyes try to open, still puffy from last night.

Grandma leans over her bed.

"Effie, it's Saturday morning. Wilton keeps calling–he wants to talk to you."

Effie's voice trembles, "I don't want to talk to him, Grandma. He said hurtful things to me last night." Her face falls into the pillow.

She can hear Grandma quietly talking with Wilton and hanging up.

Coming back into the room, Grandma Nellie says, "I think you will want to know what he told me, Effie. He is packing. He has found a ride to Nashville and needs to leave today. He is catching the 10:30 ferry and really wants you to meet him there." She pauses. "He seems to be very remorseful."

Lifting her head from the pillow, she looks at her grandma.

"He's leaving? Today?"

SATURDAY MORNING, AND THE GIRLS are dressed for the day, finishing up their biscuits and eggs on TV trays, a special treat that Willa usually does not let them do. Mr. and Mrs. Benoit will not be home from their overnight trip until after lunch. Willa Mae stands at the sink. Laughter comes from the den as the girls watch the end of The Flintstones.

Suddenly, a loud knock comes from the back door.

"Momma!"

More knocking.

"Momma!" comes a panicked voice.

Willa turns off the water, dries her hands on her apron, and rushes to the door. She opens it to find a frantic Effie, her face streaked with tears.

"What happened, baby?" Willa asks with alarm. "What is it? Are you okay?"

"Wilton is leaving, Momma. Leaving for good."

"What?" Willa says, with a confused look on her face. "Slow down."

Willa steps outside to the back porch and closes the door behind her, shielding the moment from the inquisitive eyes and ears inside.

"Now, try to calm down and tell me exactly what happened."

"We had a terrible fight last night at the graduation party, and I told him I never want to see him again. Now he called this morning and told Grandma to tell me he's leaving… today! He got into Fisk University in Nashville and–at the last minute–he's got a ride to get there to start summer classes." Effie draws a shaky breath, "It's kind of what our fight was about last night."

With eyes red from crying, Effie looks out toward the levee.

"Have you talked with him since?" Willa Mae asks.

"No, but he's home with his dad, packing and saying his goodbyes. He's catching the 10:30 ferry this morning and wants me to meet him there."

Willa glances down at her watch.

"It's ten minutes after ten right now," Willa Mae says with urgency.

Willa turns back toward the house, spotting Mimi and Anna Beth peeking through the open window and hearing every word.

"Go! Go down to the ferry now—you don't have much time."

Mimi runs from the window to her bedroom, Anna Beth still listening.

"Y'all have been the closest of friends, and probably more, for way too long. Don't let it end like this. You'll regret it. Now go. Take the shortcut down the back sidewalk past the cleaners. That'll get you to the levee faster. Now hurry, baby."

"Momma, you sure this is the right ..."

Mimi runs through the back door.

"Wait, Effie. I have something for you to give Wilton before he leaves. I made it for him because he was so nice to me at the library."

Wiping her eyes, Effie bends down to Mimi and says, "He will love this, Mimi, thank you," and gives her a hug.

Willa Mae puts her arm around Mimi. "Now hurry, Effie."

Her heart racing, Effie rushes down the back sidewalk, past the old pecan tree, around the corner by the cleaners, and on toward the levee. Just then, the ferry's 10:30 horn echoes through the humid air. She breaks into a run, out of breath, up the levee path. Catching her foot in the thick grass, she stumbles, landing hard on her hands. Quickly, she pushes herself up and keeps going.

Reaching the top of the levee, she steadies herself, looking out toward the river.

"No..." she gasps, desperation catching in her throat.

The ferry had just pulled away from the shore, its engine groaning as it rocked gently, headed toward the Baton Rouge landing.

"I missed him," she cries, her voice breaking as she fights to catch her breath.

Sinking into the grass, she pulls her knees to her chest and sobs. *I should've talked to him,* she thought. *He tried to talk to me. I shouldn't have said those words to him ... it's all my fault.*

She pulls out Grandma's graduation gift from her dress pocket and dabs her eyes. A pelican swoops overhead and lands on a row of old wooden pilings near the bank.

That's where Wilton was baptized, she reflects. Fresh tears slip down her face.

How could I let him leave like this? She thinks, her thoughts unraveling, feeling helpless as to what to do next.

Then, something catches her eye. There are two figures sitting on Preacher's log. She stands and squints through her tears to see better.

"Wilton!" she says aloud, barely believing her own voice. "He's still here."

She takes off running down the levee, heart pounding with renewed hope. But as she gets closer, she slows, suddenly unsure and afraid of how he might respond.

"Wilton!" she calls out hesitantly.

He turns at the sound of her voice, a wide smile breaking across his face. He stands and runs to meet her, Scrappy trotting at his heels.

"I didn't think you would come," Wilton says.

"I thought I missed you," Effie replies, wrapping him in a hug.

Preacher joins them with a knowing smile.

"I think you two youngins have some talkin' to do. I'll be leavin' you alone."

He touches Wilton's arm and nods with quiet encouragement. Wilton smiles back, understanding what his pap has given him in just that small gesture.

"Let's go up to our bench for old time's sake, Effie."

They walk side by side and sit down on the worn wooden bench where they'd spent so much time growing up together. It feels like a warm blanket wrapping around them—familiar, comforting. But now, it seems to be releasing them.

"Why didn't you catch the 10:30 ferry?" Effie asks.

"I wanted to spend a little time with my pap, and to be honest, I wanted to wait a little longer ... just in case you might come. Effie, I apologize for my words last night. I never meant for them to come out like that."

"I know," Effie replies softly. "And I'm sorry too, for what I said. I don't think I can go through life without ever seeing you again."

Wilton smiles.

"Effie, do you remember what Reverend Washington said in church a month or so ago? His words stuck with me. He said, 'Maladjusted looks different for everyone.'"

Wilton looks out over the familiar, mighty, and muddy Mississippi River, his safe haven for so many years.

"And then today, Preacher," Wilton chuckles, "I mean Pap, reminded me that we all have different callings and gifts from God, and we need to honor those," he looks at Effie, "and not hold each other back."

Effie smiles and puts her hand over his.

"Wilton continues, "And then Reverend asked, 'What is God calling each of you to do? To be a voice, to take action, to be on your knees praying?' I can't really remember all he said, but then he told us to ask God what our part is—and to be courageous enough to step into it."

Wilton holds Effie's hand as though not wanting to ever let it go. "I'm sorry for ever trying to hold you back from what God is calling you to do."

He smiles gently.

"You looked so pretty in your yellow dress last night. And you made that, Effie Rose. It looked like something from a New York designer. That's a gift you have. Now go and use it. And if God's calling you to Detroit, then you take that bold step and go. I'll be looking for your dresses in one of those fancy magazines one day."

Effie blushes.

"I don't know about that, Wilton," she says with a laugh. "But I do want to go and give it a try. I'll miss you so much, but we'll find a way to see each other," she says. "I think our callings and dreams are something we both need to follow for ourselves right now."

"I'm cheering you on, Effie. We'll see each other. We can figure all this out. There's always the Greyhound bus to connect us, but yes, we each have to be bold and follow our dreams."

"We do," says Effie. "Reverend Washington also said that being a spectator is easy, but it takes courage to be a participant."

"Oh," he says, reaching into his coat pocket. "You left pretty upset last night and forgot this."

He pulls out the small black velvet box, opens it, and carefully takes out the locket. He fastens it around her neck. Effie puts her hand on the locket and holds it tight for a few moments.

"And Wilton Ambrose," she says, "I don't think you're capable of being a spectator. God has put a fire in you. When you stood up in church that day, I was holding my breath, afraid of what you might say. But after you spoke, I was so proud."

She smiles through tears. "I'll always remember your words. Always. You said, 'I am standing because I refuse to sit by and watch the injustice taking place around us every day. I'm tired of it.'" She taps her fingers against her chin, trying to remember. "Oh yes," she says, "'if you say that we have a just God, Reverend, then I don't think He is happy with it either. So, I choose to be maladjusted to it—just like those students.'"

Wilton blinks. "Wow, Effie. You remember it word for word."

"It's because it was so powerful. When I got home, I wrote it down. God gave you a voice, Wilton, and it needs to be heard. Your calling is here in the South. You can make a difference—I know you can. And I'm cheering you on, too. Just... don't get yourself hurt."

"I'll try not to, Effie," he says, "but I've been reading more about Dr. King's teachings on nonviolence. I want to learn how to do this the right way."

The ferry horn bellows across the river.

"I need to catch this one," he says. "It'll be here soon."

"Where are your things?" Effie asks.

"Daddy, Uncle Ray, and Jer took them to the landing across the river to wait for me. Will you ride with me to the other side to say goodbye?"

"One last ride together," says Effie, "until we see each other again."

Standing up, he grins. "Last one down the levee gets eaten by the alligators."

"What are we, ten years old?" Effie laughs.

"It's fun to reminisce," he calls over his shoulder. "Life's too serious." And he takes off running.

"Wilton Ambrose, you're cheating!" she shouts, racing after him down the levee.

She watches as Wilton throws his arms around his pap in a long, silent hug. Then he bends down and scoops up

Scrappy for one last squeeze. "No more begging for scraps around the back. You go to that front window, you hear me."

Effie and Wilton walk together up the wooden plank onto the ferry, then climb the stairs to their usual side. Sitting down on the weathered bench, they turn to watch Pap and Scrappy, who stand at the edge of the water watching the ferry as it undocks.

Pap lifts his arm high in the air and waves.

Wilton leans over the railing, waving back. He watches as Pap and Scrappy turn and walk toward the landing as a new row of waiting cars queues up..

As they fade into the distance, Wilton turns his head, brushing a tear from his cheek.

"I just met my pap a short time ago ... and now I have to say goodbye," he says quietly.

Effie reaches over and places her hand on his, giving it a gentle squeeze. They sit in silence, watching the muddy water roll past them.

"Oh, I almost forgot," says Effie. "Mimi asked me to give this to you." Effie pulls the folded paper from her pocket and hands it to Wilton.

Wilton carefully unfolds it. It is a piece of light brown-lined school paper. Wilton reads it aloud.

"Thank you, Wilton! I will always tell people that Jesus wants us to be kind, and you do that too."

Wilton smiles tenderly.

"That's really sweet," he says. "Please tell Mimi I'll keep this where I can see it—and that I'll never forget her smile or the kindness she showed me." He pauses, emotion tugging at his voice.

"That little girl ... there's something in her no one can teach—something only God could've placed there, for His purpose."

The ferry bumps gently against the other shore. Effie and Wilton stand and hold each other in silence. Their arms slowly slip away from one another, and Wilton walks down the stairs onto the dock and down the plank to the landing. He turns for one last look.

"Effie Rose, follow your dreams. I love you," he shouts.

She waves back, her voice catching.

"Wilton Ambrose ... go change our world. Love you more."

As she watches him walk up the landing, she clutches the locket resting softly on her neck, feeling a heavy tug in her heart—the ache of not knowing when or if she might see him again.

Old Man River had brought these two together. Its strength seems to flow through their veins. The shadows of the moonlight over the Mississippi will always hold a piece of their innocence. The joy and pain of their journey will live on in them, shaping who they are and laying the foundation for who they will become.

PART VIII

A MAGNUM OPUS

Humanity has a story told in a ballad. Every generation adds its verse. Each of our lives contributes a passage. It is beautifully orchestrated at the foot of the cross. This great work is unfinished.

Every act of justice, every cry for truth, every bold voice, every heart turned toward healing adds a new note. Together, they rise in crescendos of lament, reconciliation, and hope—creating a soul-filled, transcendent harmony. God's unchanging promises form the refrain, giving us strength to persevere and courage to find our voice. A Magnum Opus.

CHAPTER TWENTY-EIGHT

"In order to heal the deep wounds of our present, we must face the truth of our past."[84]

-Equal Justice Initiative

August 6, 2019

Later Afternoon

Mimi stands on the small pier at the bayou's edge just outside St. Francis of Assisi Hospice Home. Looking out over the water, everything around her feels untouched by time. Sadly, too much remains the same.

A soft toot from a passing fishing boat catches her attention. The captain, his face dark and leathered by years on the bayou, waves as he heads home from a day's catch. Moss drapes from the cypress trees, a living emblem of Louisiana's beauty, reaching down towards Mimi in all its quiet glory.

The Louisiana summer wraps itself around Mimi—thick, sticky, and humming with the sound of cicadas, as if the bayou itself is pulling up a porch rocker and saying, *Welcome home.* Decades ago, in this untamed land with its enduring spirit,

Mimi's voice had begun to find its strength, her courage had taken root, before she knew it was even there. She looks back toward Willa Mae's window, knowing that her second mother had been a big part of this nurturing.

Mimi glances back at the time on her phone, not wanting to be away from Willa too long. It's already late afternoon, but she needed a few minutes in a quiet spot over the bayou to pray. She sits, letting her feet dangle over the water. Both hands grip the edge of the pier as she leans forward and looks up.

"Dear God," she whispers. "Please give me, Effie, and Anna Beth the guidance on what to do. We do not want Willa to spend her final days here without respect and dignity—even if it's just one person subjecting her to this. We want her to feel nothing ... nothing ... but love, respect, and light surrounding her. Amen."

Lifting her head, something soars above—wings stretched wide against the pale blue sky. He was back ... her pelican.

Coming in for a graceful landing, he glides with power and ease before settling onto the wide knuckle of a cypress knee. Mimi watches as she holds her breath. It is him. She is sure of it. The same one she'd seen yesterday with the distinct dark mark on the top of his beak. *He has a story, too,* she thinks.

Her peace is quickly chased away by thoughts of the supervising nurse—one who had made the hospice halls feel cold, not because of the austere rooms, or the smell of disinfectant, but because of the ugliness she carried in her entire demeanor. *One person,* Mimi thinks, *and yet her bitter toxin seems to spread through the entire place like a black cloud.*

Still, Willa's words echo. *Baby, we don't know what wounds or scars people are carrying deep within them. We can't see them with our eyes. We don't know their life story. All we see is what's on the outside, and sometimes, it can be a bitter cup.* Willa would always pause here before gently adding, *but we are called to give them a cup of God's sweet grace.*

Mimi glances back toward Willa's window.

"Well, Willa Mae," she murmurs, "this is a tough person to give that cup to."

The pelican, now with his wings tucked neatly in, shifts on his perch and stares straight at Mimi—eyes intense and unblinking. Mimi looks away, suddenly uneasy under his gaze. When she glances back, he is still watching, his eyes locked on hers.

Okay, okay, she thinks. *I'll try. I guess grace comes in all different forms. My prayers for her will be my cup of grace.*

Mimi slips off her sandals, letting her toes dip into the bayou's cool water, sending little ripples through the surface. It feels just as it had when she was a little girl, most of the time with her shoes off during the summer. She always cherishes the bit of Cajun she still carries within her.

Her body relaxes into the sounds of the swamp's age-old lullaby, a cacophony of cicadas, chirping crickets, grunts of a spoonbill somewhere in the reeds, and cricket-frogs clicking like marbles tapping together.

She closes her eyes to take it in. And in the stillness, memories rise ... crawfishing with Willa and her sisters on Bayou Bateaux and fishing with her PawPaw in the pirogue at daybreak on Bayou Grande. In those quiet mornings, it had always felt like the bayou creatures were warming up for a song they had sung for centuries.

Her phone rings, jarring the moment. She lifts her feet from the water and stands, retrieving the phone from her pocket. It is Anna Beth.

"Hey, sis, any update on a new facility for Willa?" she asks, not even giving her sister a chance to say hi.

"Yes," Anna Beth says. "We found a great place. A friend of mine is a hospice nurse there. I've arranged for a private ambulance to pick up Willa Mae tonight at eight."

Mimi takes a deep breath of relief. "That's great news," she says. "This is an answer to prayer."

"I know. I'm so relieved," says Anna Beth.

Then, she pauses. "Mimi, do you think we're doing the right thing? I just don't want this move to take a toll on Willa."

"I know," Mimi says softly. "But we have to remember what Willa Mae always reminds us of. We just need to..." she begins, and Anna Beth joins in unison, "...pray and trust in Jesus, and He will take care of the situation."

They both chuckle through the emotions.

"Thanks for that reminder, sis," Anna Beth says. "Gosh, I'm going to miss hearing her say those words."

"Don't get us started," Mimi says, her throat tight. "We have lots to do before tonight."

"We need to be strong for Willa," Anna Beth says. "Love you, sis."

"Love you too," Mimi replies, hanging up.

As Mimi steps back into Willa's room, a young Black nurse is taking her vitals.

"Hi," Mimi says. "How is Willa Mae doing?"

"She is stable right now and seems to be resting comfortably," the nurse replies. I will check back soon.

"Thank you," says Mimi, as she walks the nurse to the door."

Opening the door, the nurse glances both ways down the hall. Then she quietly stands there looking at Mimi. There is an awkward moment of silence as the two women stare at each other.

"Did you forget something?" Mimi asks.

"I ... well, I just wanted to say thank you," the nurse says, her voice dropping to a whisper. "I—and others who work here—want to thank you for speaking out.

Mimi is surprised, not realizing that word had already gotten out.

"There has been discrimination here," the nurse says quietly, "but it's only coming from that one person. She intimidates everyone, and because we have a new director, I don't think he has seen all of this yet."

She looks back down the hall nervously.

"She's very prejudiced, and not just toward Black patients and nurses, like me. What you said brought it out into the open, so ... thank you."

The nurse looks over to Willa Mae.

"We are all sorry to see Miss Willa Mae go. She's a bright light here. Even in her weakened state, she brings joy. We'll surely miss her."

Before Mimi can respond, the nurse turns quickly and leaves down the hall.

Mimi looks over to check on Willa Mae, surprised to find her eyes open and seeming alert. Before Mimi can ask how she was feeling, Willa speaks.

"You know what, baby?" she says, her voice stronger than expected.

"What, Willa?" Mimi asks, sitting down on the edge of the chair.

"God is good all the time. You know that?"

"He really is, Willa," Mimi says with a soft smile, dismissing any tears about to flow. She knows there is a task before her. Those emotions have to be put aside for the moment.

Over their sixty-five years of life together, Mimi has heard Willa say those words thousands of times. And yet, every time, she says them with the same deep joy and unwavering belief.

"Is Effie here yet?" Willa asks.

"Not yet, her plane was delayed because of the weather. Andrew's picking her up at the New Orleans airport later tonight. She says that she can't wait to see you."

Willa closes her eyes, satisfied with Mimi's answer.

"Ohhh, that is such a blessing," she murmurs as her voice drifts off.

Mimi leans back in the orange chair beside her, only to hear something suddenly pop beneath her. She jumps up and looks down at the cushion.

"I knew that was coming soon," she mutters.

The tear in the chair had finally given way.

I guess it's truly time to leave, she thinks. *Now, how do we explain to Willa that we're moving her to a new place?* As she ponders the question, Mimi dozes off, close beside her beloved second mother.

Soon, Mimi feels a gentle tap on her arm.

"Mimi," Anna Beth says softly.

"Oh, Anna Beth," Mimi whispers, disoriented. "I ... I guess I fell asleep." Quickly standing up and looking around, "What time is it?"

"It's seven fifteen. The ambulance will be here soon. I told the front desk to be on the lookout," Anna Beth says.

"Oh gosh, I'm so sorry. I didn't even start packing her up yet, and I was waiting for you to come so we could tell her about the move together," Mimi replies. "I'm really hoping that Effie and Andrew will be here soon before she makes the move. Willa is so anxious to see Effie, and I don't want ... "

Anna Beth gently touches Mimi's arm, "Mimi ... look at me. Take a deep breath.

Don't worry about all of that; this is not an easy time. We are all doing the best we can right now."

Mimi gives Anna Beth a hug as tears fall. "Thank you, sis, neither of us could be doing this alone, especially since Mary Grace is out of the country."

Anna Beth goes to the table and pulls out a Kleenex for Mimi. She looks over at Willa Mae, who is still asleep.

"How has she been?" she asks as she begins to pack up Willa's belongings.

Wiping her eyes and pulling herself together, Mimi opens the closet to pull out clothes and toiletries that she had brought for herself while there, placing them in the bag.

"Oh, her same joyful, chipper self," Mimi says. "Never complaining. Still saying, God is good all the time, and at times trying to boss me around."

Chuckling, Anna Beth says softly, "There will never be another Willa Mae."

They look at each other, eyes misting. "We gotta keep packing," Mimi says with a quick sniff.

A knock comes at the door. Expecting it to be Angel telling them that the ambulance has arrived, they turn as the door opens—but instead, a tall gentleman wearing a Yamaka peeks his head in. They have not seen him before.

"May I come in?" he asks quietly, offering a warm smile.

"Of course," Mimi says, motioning him in.

"Good evening," he says. "My name is Elimelech. I'm one of the nurses here. I came to talk with you ... if you have a minute?"

"We were just packing up Willa Mae," Mimi says. "The ambulance should be here any minute to transport her to another facility. But yes—we have a couple of minutes."

Gently closing the door behind him, "Thank you," Elimelech says. "Yes, I understand you're leaving soon. I spoke with the director and he let me know everything that has transpired. I am a fairly new nurse to this facility, and I was truly so sorry to hear what happened." Looking over at Willa Mae with a smile, he continues, "I have heard that she is a pretty special lady."

Looking back at the girls, he says, "I would be honored to be Miss Willa Mae's new nurse, if it might encourage you to stay?"

There is a stillness in the room. He has a quiet, gentle presence about him—and when he stepped through the doorway, it felt as though God's light had come in with him.

"Oh," Mimi says, flustered, her thoughts immediately going to the supervising nurse and what it would mean to stay in the same building with her.

She looks to Anna Beth for help.

Anna Beth only shrugs, her face showing the same uncertainty.

"I can assure you," Elimelech says calmly, "I will take good care of Miss Willa Mae. She will be in loving hands."

Willa stirs at the sound of voices.

Lowering his voice to a whisper, Elimelech looks at Mimi and Anna Beth with kind, compassionate eyes.

"Again, I am so sorry for what you have experienced here. It would truly be an honor to care for Miss Willa Mae. From me, she will receive nothing but love, kindness, and respect."

"Maybe we should consider it," Anna Beth says calmly.

Mimi slowly nods, looking from Willa Mae to Elimelech, then back again.

"We so appreciate your words—and how caring you are," she says quietly. "But if we stay, my concern is that we'll still run into the supervising nurse. She might even come into the room."

With a clear and affirming voice, Elimelech says, "She has been given strict orders to stay away from this room for the final two hours of her shift. By morning, you won't see her again."

The girls give each other a glance.

"Well," Anna Beth says, looking over to Willa Mae, "it would be much easier on her if she stayed here."

"She seems to be waking up," Elimelech says. "May I go and introduce myself?"

Both Mimi and Anna Beth nod.

There is something about his countenance, Mimi thinks— calm, warm, and full of light.

He walks over to Willa's bedside, kneels beside her, and gently places his hand on hers.

"Hi, Miss Willa. I'm one of the nurses here. My name is Elimelech, but my friends call me Elim. How are you feeling tonight?"

"Ohhhh, I feel happy to meet you," she says in a weak but cheerful voice.

Elimelech chuckles. "I feel happy to meet you, too, Miss Willa. I hear you're a pretty special lady. I'd really like to get to know you."

"Ohhhh," Willa murmurs, "that would be such a blessing, baby. You are a gift from the Lord. Now, how is your family?"

He chuckles again. "That's so sweet of you to ask. They're doing very well. They live in New York City."

"Well, that's good," she mumbles, her voice drifting as she closes her eyes again.

Elimelech gently lays her hand back down on the bed and returns to Mimi and Anna Beth.

"I can tell, she really is a special lady," he says. "One of a kind, it seems."

"That, she is," Mimi replies. "And she really took to you. Thank you for treating her so kindly.

Angel peeks his hand in.

"Sorry to interrupt, but the ambulance is here to pick up Miss Willa," he says quietly, a hint of sadness in his voice.

"Maybe you'd like a few minutes to talk about it?" Elimelech adds. "Angel and I will be just outside the door. Don't worry—we'll ask the ambulance to wait." He gives them a reassuring look as he gently closes the door behind him.

"He is so kind," Mimi whispers.

"I know," says Anna Beth. "Like an angel appeared from heaven and walked into this room to take care of Willa."

"Maybe that's exactly what happened," Mimi says, staring at her sister in quiet amazement. They stand there for a long moment, both still taking in what has just unfolded.

"Let's stay," Anna Beth says softly.

"I agree," Mimi replies. "And I know Effie would agree too."

"I'll let Elim know," says Anna Beth as she steps into the hallway and the door closes behind her.

Mimi looks over to Willa Mae, who seems to be sleeping peacefully. She then walks to the window. The sun is setting over the bayou. There is really nothing like it—the golden light filtering through the water oaks, casting soft rays that reach into the room.

"God," she whispers as the sun slips below the horizon, "thank You for Your light that dissipates the darkness—and for Your love that is still present in some of our most difficult moments on this earth."

The door opens again, and Anna Beth steps back in.

"The ambulance just left," she says. "Can you believe what just happened?"

"Yes," Mimi answers, her voice grateful as she sits down. "I can—because all we have to do is pray and trust in Jesus, and He will take care of the situation."

"Amen to that," says Anna Beth.

They heard another "Amen" and turned to see Willa smiling at them.

Without a knock, the door opens—and in comes Andrew, Anna Beth's husband, and Effie.

"Effie!" Mimi says with delight, jumping up to give her a big hug. "You made it!"

"We're so glad you're here, Effie," says Anna Beth, embracing her too.

Hugging the girls, she replies, "I'm so thankful to be here. It's been a long couple of days." Effie looks toward her mom. "How's she doing?" she asks.

"She's stable," Mimi says, "and she's been asking for you."

Effie walks quietly to her mother's bedside and takes her hand.

"Momma," she whispers.

Willa Mae's eyes flutter, then quickly open to the sound of her daughter's voice. "My baby," Willa Mae says, weakly reaching out for Effie's hand. "You made it. Sit with me. How long can you stay?"

"Don't worry, Momma. I'm not going anywhere. I'm staying right here."

Mimi, Anna Beth, and Andrew quietly leave the room to give them time together. They step into the lobby area, the hush of evening settling in.

"I'll stay here tonight and call if there's any change," Mimi says.

"You sure? Where will you sleep?" Andrew asks.

"In my orange chair, of course—even though it's now split open."

"I'm going to get you another chair," Andrew says, half-laughing.

"No need," Mimi replies with a smile. "We've got history. We've come this far—we'll see it through together. We've become close friends."

Shaking his head, Andrew says, "That's just a little weird, Mimi, but alright."

"Yep," laughs Anna Beth. "That's my sister, but I love her."

"Nonetheless, I'll ask them to bring another chair for Effie."

"Oh, that's a great idea," Mimi says. "Thanks."

"Okay then," says Anna Beth. "Call us if anything changes. The phone will be right by my ear. Otherwise, we'll be back first thing in the morning. I'll bring y'all some warm beignets."

They exchange hugs and say good night. Walking back into the room, Mimi finds that Willa has fallen asleep and Effie is sitting by her side with her hand over her momma's.

"Would you like a cup of coffee, Effie? They just put out a fresh pot," Mimi says with a smile.

"That sounds great," she says. "I don't want to fall asleep just yet. I want to be able to sit up with Momma for a while tonight."

"She seems like she is comfortable, and her breathing seems stable. Let's enjoy it in the lobby area for just a few minutes," says Mimi.

On their way, they pass by and are greeted by a black woman pushing an elderly White lady in a wheelchair down the hall.

"Hmmm," says Mimi. "I haven't seen them here before." Looking back over her shoulder, "she must have just arrived, but it's really late. Yet," she sighs, "I think here in hospice, time is a relative thing."

Walking into the lobby, Mimi and Effie sit down with coffee and an Aunt Sally's praline from the snack basket, grateful for a moment of quiet together. Taking a sip of coffee,

Effie says, "Ohhhh, this is balm for my weary body and soul. How I've missed this Community coffee. It brings back so many memories. Grandma Nellie always had it dripping on the stove before the sun came up. The aroma itself would wake me up. It sure takes me back to another time."

Settling into the couch, Effie then shares all about her exhausting day of travel, and Mimi fills her in on everything that has happened since they arrived at hospice.

"How are you holding up, Mimi?" Effie asks. "Including the hospital, you've been with Momma for almost two weeks straight. Thank you for staying by her side."

"There's absolutely no other place that I would want to be," Mimi says.

She then takes a bite of praline, letting the rich caramel sweetness melt on her tongue as the pecans add their buttery crunch. "Mmmm," Mimi says, savoring the moment. "Oh, how I have loved these since I was a child. Whenever we were in New Orleans, Daddy would drive down to the French Quarter and buy a box of Aunt Sally's pralines[85] to bring home."

"I know," says Effie, "because your daddy would always give Momma some to take home to me and Grandma Nellie."

"I didn't know that," says Mimi.

"Your daddy was a good man, Mimi. He watched out for Momma and our family."

"Thank you for sharing that with me. That means so much," says Mimi. "I sure miss him."

Mimi gets up to refill her and Effie's coffee.

"Has AJ been here yet?" Effie asks.

"Yes, it was nice to see your cousin. He left earlier to pick up a friend from the airport—someone coming to speak at Southern University. I need to tell you about that visit too," Mimi says, giving her a wide-eyed look and shaking her head.

Mimi sits back down, giving Effie a fresh cup of coffee, and goes on to share everything that has taken place with the supervising nurse and AJ—and how Elimelech had stepped in.

"Wow, that's a lot to process," says Effie, "but it does seem that God opened a door. I'm so thankful. I look forward to meeting Elimelech."

They both fall silent.

This is the moment, Mimi thinks, *feeling her heart begin to race. It's time to bring it up. You can do this, Mimi.*

"Effie," she says, looking into her eyes. "Can I ask you a question?"

"Of course, Mimi. Anything," Effie replies as she takes another sip of coffee, the aroma seeming to comfort her.

Mimi shifts in her chair, feeling her insides begin to shake.

"It's something I've needed to ask you for a long time. I've just been afraid."

Effie's forehead creases, sensing the weight behind the words.

Putting her coffee on the side table, she asks, "What is it, Mimi? You can ask me anything. It's okay. What's on your mind?"

Mimi takes a deep breath and shifts to face her.

"Was it ever hard for you, Effie, when your momma was with me and my sisters six days a week? I mean … I guess I never thought about it when I was a child. But … I should have. But," she adds hesitantly, "I feel like we had your momma more than you did. With our parents often out of town, as you know, your momma was always sleeping over."

Effie grows quiet. Mimi swallows hard, suddenly unsure she should have said anything at all.

"Yes," Effie says at last. "It was really hard sometimes. Especially when she spent the night at y'all's house. I mean … it was–" Effie pauses, her words catching. "To be honest, Mimi–and this is hard to admit–but I was often jealous of you girls. Sometimes, I even felt angry. You had my momma, like you said, with you all the time. She gave you girls a lot of love, that's for sure."

"I knew she loved me," Effie continues, "but I missed her. I was her baby, she always said. But I knew deep down that she had other babies, too–ones she loved dearly."

Effie looks out through the front doors of the lobby.

"She talked about you girls all the time. Sometimes she came home late in the day, so tired, and … well … there would be nothing left for me."

Effie becomes quiet again, looking down at her hands.

"Effie," Mimi says softly, placing her hand over hers, voice heavy with grief. "I am so sorry. I want to ask you– please–forgive me."

Looking up, Effie states, "Mimi, you didn't do anything wrong. You and your sisters were just little girls."

"I know, Effie," Mimi concedes, letting go of her hand. "But now that I'm older ... I see it all through such a different lens. And I needed to say this to you. And I'm truly sorry for any pain you went through. I was so unaware. And that makes me truly sad."

Effie looks at her with gentleness.

"Mimi, do you know how I think of you today?"

Mimi takes a slow, unsteady breath, bracing herself for what might come next.

"I see you as my sister. We are family."

Mimi has no words. Tears stream down her face as she reaches forward and hugs Effie.

"Thank you, Effie," is all she could say.

"Mimi," Effie says, looking at her. "Momma told me one time that she felt like God called her to your family. And I believe now that He gave her enough love for all her girls, including me." Hugging Mimi, Effie says, "Come on, sis, let's get back to Momma."

Walking back to Willa's room with their arms around each other, Mimi feels a quiet peace settle over her. *This is a redeeming moment,* she thinks, *finally feeling peace replacing the guilt that she had been carrying for so long.*

When Mimi and Effie enter the room, they are both surprised to see the elderly White woman in the wheelchair they had just greeted in the hall. She is now sitting beside

Willa's bed, holding her hand. Her attendant sits quietly in the orange chair.

Mimi leans toward Effie and whispers, "Do you know them?"

"No, I don't think so," she says quietly.

Walking over to the wheelchair, Effie offers a kind smile. "Hi, I'm Effie, and this is Mimi. We're Willa Mae's daughters."

Mimi is taken aback by Effie's words. They catch her off guard—yet cause her heart to soar.

Looking at the girls, the elderly woman replies warmly, "Oh, so many wonderful stories to hear, I see."

Willa stirs and speaks up. "This is my dear old friend," she says, patting the woman's hand.

Effie and Mimi exchange a confused glance.

"My name is Clara," the woman says gently. "And this is Edna, who cares for me." She smiles toward the woman in the chair. "Your momma and I were best friends when we were little girls."

Mimi suddenly can't believe what she is hearing. She walks over to stand beside Effie.

"You're the one in the photo," Mimi says.

Effie stands in silence, overwhelmed, trying to take it all in.

Mimi quickly walks to the table, picks up the frame with the embroidery, and opens the back. Pulling out the photo, she hands it to Clara.

Clara looks at it in silence. Her hand trembles as she lifts it closer to see better. Tears well in her eyes.

"We were so young," she whispers. "I had the same photo, but it's been lost for decades. We called ourselves sisters forever."

"Edna, can you please get–" Clara begins.

Before she can finish, Edna nods. "Of course," she says, already reaching into Clara's purse. She pulls out an identical embroidery and frame. Mimi and Effie both gasp.

"My mother made these for us," she says softly. "Do you see the white and brown hands?"

"Oh yes," Effie speaks up. "I noticed those hands when I was a teenager. Grandma Nellie never got the chance to finish telling me the story about them."

Clara looks at Willa. "My momma would read Bible stories to Willa Mae and me while Nellie cleaned and cooked. And after each story, we'd say a prayer that ..."

"Faith can break the sky in two," Willa whispers from her bed.

Clara joins in, "and let the face of God shine through."

Their eyes lock, and in that moment, there is a rejoining of a bond so deep that none of the others in the room could begin to understand it.

"You see," says Clara, shaking her head slowly, "my mother saw the prejudice all around us. She wanted to teach us not to carry hate–but instead to be ..."

"Image-bearers of God's love," Willa finished again, her voice full of memories. "The same words," Willa takes a breath, "my daddy used to tell me, too."

Clara reaches out for Willa, and as both their trembling hands meet, they form praying hands, as though they'd done it a thousand times before. Black and White. Together again, as one.

"Then," Clara says, as their hands separate, "that awful night happened—on the way to Christmas Eve service. It was cold, and sleet was falling. Our car began to slide. I remember the lights of an oncoming car. I don't remember anything else ... except that when I woke up in the hospital, I was told my mama and daddy had gone to heaven. It was a most horrible time for me. My aunt came to take care of me, and within a few days, I was packed up to leave Louisiana to go live with her."

She pauses and looks at the embroidery. "I was just fourteen. Before I left with my aunt, I asked if I could drop something off at Willa's house. I remember that night. It was very late, and my aunt wouldn't let me knock. I just left it sitting by the door."

She reaches for Willa's frame on the table.

"It was this," she says softly. "My mama had just finished one for each of us. She wanted us to remember that prayer—for God's justice to reign down. That we are all image-bearers, no matter what color. I slipped the photo behind the embroidery in Willa's frame, not knowing if she'd ever find it."

Clara lets out a quiet laugh, picking up the photo in her lap. "Willa and I always thought it was somethin' else that my mama and daddy had a camera. Not many people did back then. One day while we were playing by the bayou, Mama came and took our picture—because," pointing at the arc in the weathered photo, "she knew how much we loved rainbows."

"I knew that was a rainbow in the photo," Mimi says, smiling.

"Yes," Clara nods. "My mama always told us rainbows remind us of God's hope and promises."

Effie comes and sits on the edge of the bed close to her momma and Miss Clara.

"Where have you been living?" Effie asks.

"I've been in Missouri. When my parents died, I felt lost. I didn't want to think about home anymore. It made me too sad. Life went on, and sadly, Willa Mae and I lost track of each other. About a year ago, my son moved me back here from St. Louis to be close to him. I tried to find Willa. I found a number in an old phone book he had. I called the number, but no one ever answered. I even checked the obituaries—nothing."

"Yes," Effie says, "we had already moved Momma out of her house to assisted living."

Clara nods. "Well, after that, I kept the embroidery close. I knew—even if we weren't together—it kept our hearts and our hands together."

She looks back at Willa, now asleep. Her face softens. "I now feel at peace," she says, before growing quiet.

"I think maybe we should go now," Edna says gently. "You're lookin' tired, Miss Clara."

"Before you go," Mimi asks, "how did you know Willa was here?"

A knock comes at the door, and it slowly opens.

"Can I come in?"

Joseph walks into the room.

"This is my husband, Joseph," says Edna. "He made the connection."

Mimi's eyes widened.

"Joseph? Oh my goodness."

He smiles. "I went home and told Edna all about the embroidery. I asked if she remembered where I might've seen something like that before. Her face lit up. She then told Miss Clara the story, and, well—as they say—the rest is history," he says, laughing.

"That's such a God story," Mimi says, her eyes misty.

"It's just beautiful," Effie adds.

"Miss Edna," Mimi says, quickly wiping her eyes, "I hear you make the best red beans and rice.

"Joseph sure thinks so," she replies, smiling at her husband. "I just might have to bring y'all some tomorrow."

The room suddenly grows quiet.

Clara turns to Willa, lifting her hand softly and pressing a gentle kiss to it.

"I love you, Willa Mae," her voice cracking. "I know we'll see each other again—soon."

Willa squeezes Clara's hand, and Clara squeezes back. Clara gently lays Willa's weak hand on the bed and turns to Edna.

"I'm ready to go home now," she says.

Effie stands and hugs Clara. "Thank you for coming."

"Well," Edna chimes in with a chuckle, "once Miss Clara heard about the frame, no one was going to sleep tonight until we came here."

Everyone laughs.

Strong-willed like Willa, Mimi thinks.

As they leave the room, a quiet settles over everyone.

"What a gift God gave to Momma and Miss Clara tonight," Effie says.

Willa Mae now appears peaceful—her expression soft, her body at rest.

God's loving presence at the end of life, Mimi thinks, can be something far beyond our earthly understanding.

CHAPTER TWENTY-NINE

August 7, 2019

Mimi awakes from a restless night. Her whole body aches from the fatigue of the past couple of weeks. Gaining her bearings, she looks over and sees that Willa is sleeping peacefully, but Effie's chair is empty. Mimi rises slowly, lifting her arms in a long stretch. The grogginess of sleep lingers. But it is more than that, the kind of heaviness that settles in after days of keeping watch. Looking down at her chair, she smiles. Well, the blanket did its job, she thinks. The tear in the cushion hadn't been enough to make her give up her old friend. But maybe it's tired too, worn down by the weight of too many painful goodbyes.

A quiet yawn slips out as she walks to the window.

Dark clouds loom above the water oaks. The day feels heavy. Still, the sun makes an attempt to break through the dense fog, casting faint streaks of light across the dew-covered ground.

She turns away from the window, just as Elim steps quietly into the room.

"Good morning, Miss Mimi," he says with a gentle smile, his voice barely above a whisper.

"I came in a few times last night to check on Miss Willa. You and Miss Effie were sound asleep. I hope you got a little rest."

"Yes ... I woke up a few times to check on Willa as well, but always drifted back off. I was probably snoring when you came in."

He chuckles.

"I can't deny I might've heard a few snores from both of you."

"How did Willa do through the night?" Mimi asks.

"She seemed to be in a little pain, so I adjusted her meds. She may sleep more today. Her blood pressure has dropped a bit—we'll keep an eye on her," he says. "I let Miss Effie know just now when I saw her in the hall."

Elim walks over to Willa and kneels beside her bed. He gently strokes her hand.

"Good morning, Miss Willa," he whispers, though her eyes remain closed. "I hope you slept well. We're going to take good care of you today. I'm right here if you need anything."

He stands. "I'll be close by if you need me," he says to Mimi, and quietly steps out.

Mimi turns her gaze back to the window. Her pelican has returned, sitting quietly on its perch, as if once again, keeping vigil.

Mimi's phone buzzes from under the chair, likely fallen there during the night. She pulls it out and answers groggily.

"Hi, Anna Beth… yes, she's stable, I'll fill you in when you get here. See you soon. Oh, wait, Anna Beth, you're not going to forget the beignets, are you…? Oh yum. See you soon."

Effie walks into the room carrying two mugs.

"I brought you coffee, Mimi. The comforting smell of it woke me up this morning, just like the old days at home," she says with a grin.

"Nothing like it," Mimi replies. "And always Willa's favorite. Oh, and Anna Beth is on her way."

A gentle tap is heard at the door, and it creaks open.

"Angel," Mimi says gratefully. "I'm so happy you're here."

"Yep, I'm here until two this afternoon," he replies.

Glancing out the window, he adds, "And Andre's somewhere out there on the Zydeco Zoomer. I just wanted to check in to see if y'all needed anything, and to see how Miss Willa's doin'."

"She seems stable right now," Mimi says. "Have you met Effie?"

"I sure did," he answers, looking over at her with a smile, "I had the pleasure of meeting her in the lobby kitchen."

Angel steps over to Willa's bedside, bending down.

"Miss Willa, it's good to see you today," he says softly.

She remains quiet.

"Elim and I will take good care of you. And maybe Andre will roll past in the Zoomer and toot the horn to say hi."

"She would really love that," Mimi says with a smile.

Walking back over to Mimi and Effie, Angel says, "Now I'm guessing that Miss Willa won't be too hungry today, but Andre fried up some catfish this morning, and made biscuits too. He told me to bring some for all y'all. Says you'll likely need the nourishment. It's in the lobby kitchen."

Mimi puts her hand to her stomach. "Oh my goodness," she says. We are going to have a feast today. Fried Catfish, Biscuits, Beignets. Oh, and pralines for dessert. Only in Louisiana," Mimi says, laughing.

"I can't remember the last time I had fresh fried catfish or beignets," Effie says. "Not too much of that in Detroit. It all sounds so good.

Mimi takes a sip of her coffee.

"You go grab some breakfast," Mimi urges. "I don't think you've eaten since lunch yesterday."

"Well, Momma seems okay. I might just go have a quick bite," Effie says, setting down her coffee.

"Oh," says Angel, "and did I mention there's fig preserves from Andre's Mama?"

"Well, now you've totally sold me," Effie says with a laugh, and heads for the kitchen.

As Effie turns the corner into the lobby, she stops in her tracks. She sees him.

A wave of recognition hits her, people and places from different times suddenly colliding. She stares.

Could it be? she thinks.

"Wilton?" she calls out.

"Effie," he says, eyes wide. "I can't believe it. It's so good to see you. AJ said that you just arrived last night. You look … I mean, you look great!"

Everything seems out of context.

"What are you doing here?" Effie asks, stunned and a little confused. "How did you even know … I thought you still lived in Nashville?"

Wilton smiles. "Well, can I get a hug first, please?"

"Sorry, you just really caught me off guard … in a good way." They walk toward each other and embrace as though no time had passed at all.

"Do I get a hug too, cuz?" comes a familiar voice.

"Of course, AJ," Effie says, turning to hug him.

"You two go and catch up," AJ says, his smile full of warmth. "I'm going to go visit Tee."

"Let's sit in the lobby," says Effie.

They sit down on the couch, a quiet awkwardness between them, neither quite sure how close to sit.

"It's been a minute, hasn't it?" Wilton says.

"Where do we even start?" Effie asks. "So much time has passed and so quickly.

Wilton shakes his head. "How did we end up drifting so far apart?" he says, as his gaze drops to the heart around her neck. "I can't believe what I'm seeing–you're still wearing the locket I gave you that night at the graduation party."

Her hand clutches it.

"Of course I am. I think of you often, Wilton. You've never stopped being a part of me."

His eyes gaze into hers. "And you of me, Effie."

"I tried to keep up with you through your daddy for a while," Effie says. "But it seemed like you were so involved in your studies at Fisk, and then the Civil Rights Movement. Well..." She shrugs her shoulders.

He looks at her with genuine curiosity.

"And you, Effie? I bet your designs ended up on the covers of those fancy fashion magazines."

"Maybe not in magazines," Effie says with a smile, "but I had a nice little boutique before I retired, where I was the couture."

Wilton chuckles. "I know a lot of words, but that's a new one for me."

"Wait," Effie grins, "this has got to be a first for Wilton Ambrose."

They both laugh, just like old times.

"It means I design clothes made specifically to someone's measurements and tastes."

"I knew you could do it, Effie."

"I took some design classes while apprenticing with my aunt in Detroit," she says. "Eventually, I saved up enough to go to school."

Wilton leans back, thoughtful. "I guess we both had our own unique gifts to share with the world. Just like my pap said the day I left Bayou Grande."

"Yeah," Effie says. "I've thought about that often—how God called us in such different directions."

"I thought about that many times, too," Wilton says. "I think if we had stayed together back then, we might've held each other back."

Effie nods, then gently shifts the conversation. "I heard you got married."

"Well ... I'm a widower now," he says.

"I'm so sorry, Wilton."

"It's okay. It's been a while. We met when we were both with the Freedom Riders."

Shifting on the couch to face her, he starts, "You know, Effie, I came down here several times while I was at school to visit my dad. I would always go by and say hi to your momma and Grandma Nellie, until she passed away. Your momma gave me your number. I thought about calling you so many times, but when she told me you were seeing someone," he shrugs, "I figured I'd lost my chance and ended up getting married that next year."

Effie gazes out the window. "Yes ... I was seeing someone for several years, but it didn't work out. That was a long time ago, Wilton. I knew that you were deep into your studies and your passion for the movement kept you busy, then I heard from your daddy that you got married."

Effie tilts her head. "So what brings you back to Louisiana?"

"Well," he says, "I'm speaking at Southern University. It's a conference on Reparative Justice and Racial Restoration."

"Well, look at you, Mr. Valedictorian," she teases.

"I love it, Effie. It's my passion."

Looking right at him and shaking her head, she says with a chuckle "Really? I would never have guessed that."

"Now you're just teasing me like you used to do," Wilton says, laughing and giving her a little shove.

"Then, after graduation from Fisk," he says, "I went on to Howard Law School. A few years later, I got my theology degree."

"That's wonderful," Effie says warmly. "Your pap would be so proud, following in his footsteps."

"You know, Effie," he continues, "I think we both followed our dreams. It was all meant to be."

"I think so, too," Effie says quietly.

He looks at her again, a question lingering in his eyes. "Did you ever marry after your breakup?"

"No," Effie says. "I never found the right man."

They share a long look.

"Well, you were so brave to head North for a new start. Did you come home often?"

"Not really. I was happy in Detroit. I felt free to be who I was there. Mr. Benoit would fly Momma out every year for my birthday."

"I was sorry to hear about your daddy," Effie adds, "and your pap before that."

"I miss them both," Wilton says. "I've been thinking about moving back down here into Daddy's house. I'm mostly retired, but I still love to speak and preach. There might be an opportunity for me at Southern University."

They continue talking with the comfort and ease of high school days.

"Well," Effie says, standing, "I should get back to Momma."

"And I need to get over to Southern," Wilton says, "and get ready for my talk." Wilton pauses, "Can I see you again?"

"I would love that," Effie says. "Before you go, can you come and say a quick hi to Momma? She may not be fully alert, but she'll know you're there."

"I was hoping that I would be able to see her," he says.

Walking into the room, Effie smiles and says, "Wilton, I want to reintroduce you to my sisters, Mimi and Anna Beth, and her husband, Andrew.

"Oh my goodness," Mimi says, standing up. "I think the last time I saw you was during that whole library incident when I was just a little girl. That was a traumatic day for me, etched into my earliest memories. I still vividly recall how kind and comforting you were to me."

She reaches out and hugs him warmly.

"Well, I could also be a little grumpy back in those days, but I've softened," Wilton says with a grin.

"You always had a soft side to you," Effie adds.

Wilton looks into Effie's still-beautiful deep brown eyes and smiles.

He crosses the room to Willa Mae's bedside, bending down and taking her hand.

"Miss Willa, it's Wilton, Effie's friend. It's good to see you."

Willa partially opens her eyes.

"I want to thank you, Miss Willa, for always showing me so much love and ..." he chuckles, "for making a welcoming spot in your pew for me and my daddy back in the day.

Willa Mae's eyes open. "God is good all the ..." Her words drift off.

Wilton's throat tightens as he turns to Effie. Her eyes brim with tears, but she gives him a gentle nod, the kind that says, *It's okay.* He turns back to Willa Mae.

"You know, Miss Willa," he continues, gaining his composure, "my daddy always told me how much you prayed for me after I went off to Nashville. I want you to know your prayers sustained me. That was your powerful voice during those turbulent times. You are a prayer warrior, Miss Willa," he pauses, tapping her hand lightly. "You and your church community made a real impact on my life."

Willa squeezes his hand.

Tears now stream down Effie's face as she watches this tender moment between Wilton and her momma. She had always known that gentleness was inside him, and seeing it again, even after all these years, stirs something deep in her.

Just then, Angel steps through the door.

"I'm sorry to interrupt, but I wanted to let everyone know that there's lots of food for you out there," he says. "You need to eat and keep your strength up today. There's plenty of catfish and biscuits to go around. And Miss Edna says to tell you that she dropped off red beans and rice with cornbread for later. Still a few beignets left and pralines for your sweet tooth."

"Southern hospitality," says Mimi warmly.

Smiling through her tears, Effie says, "I'm gonna have to go back for seconds."

"I'll go with you," Wilton offers.

"Yeah," says AJ, standing up, "we can grab some food for the road."

"Well, I need to say goodbye," AJ adds. "I have to get Wilton over to pick up his rental car, but I'll be back. Please call if anything changes."

Wilton walks over to Effie and hugs her. "Don't worry I'll be back later on."

AJ bends over Willa's bed and kisses her gently on the forehead, not knowing if it will be the last time he sees her on this side of heaven. A cloud of sadness hangs over him as he walks out the door. A boat horn echoes from outside. Angel quickly moves to the window.

"Miss Willa," Angel says, "Andre and his crew are tootin' their horn at you to say good mornin'. The crew's wavin' too."

Willa raises her hand just slightly above the sheet and gives a tiny wave.

"She's getting weaker," Mimi says, her voice cracking.

"It's so hard to watch," Effie whispers.

"I wouldn't go too far today," Elimelech says gently, coming to stand with them. "We'll be right here by Miss Willa Mae's side, and yours too."

"That's right," says Angel. "If you need anything, you ring or call down the hall. We're as close as can be."

"You're all angels," Effie says, her voice trembling. "Thank you for loving on my momma so much. She feels it. Trust me."

"She's hard not to love," says Elimelech with a smile as he leaves the room along with Angel.

Pulling out her cherished handkerchief, Effie turns away toward the window.

"I have an idea," Mimi says. "Let's sing some of Willa's favorite songs. Willa Mae asked me to bring her songbook from church."

Mimi retrieves the songbook from Willa's bag and opens it. Everyone gathers around Mimi so as to see the words.

"What should we sing?" Anna Beth asks. "Any thoughts?"

"How about 'The Old Rugged Cross'?" Effie suggests. "Momma loves that one."

"And it's okay," Effie says, wiping her eyes while smiling. "I don't need to see the words. I know that one by heart."

As they begin to sing, Willa's hand moves ever so slightly above the sheet, like a quiet symphony conductor. It brings her joy and a smile to those gathered around her. When they finish the hymn, Mimi speaks gently. "I remember Willa always singing 'Precious Lord, Take My' ..."

Looking down at Willa, Mimi's expression tenses.

"Her breathing seems to be changing," Mimi whispers urgently.

"I'll get Elim," says Anna Beth, running quickly down the hall.

Within seconds, Elim is by Willa Mae's side, his hands gentle as he checks her breathing and pulse.

Without missing a beat, he says calmly, "Let's all gather around her, let her know you're here."

"I can't do this," Effie sobs. "I can't watch my momma die," she whispers through her tears."

Mimi wraps an arm around her shoulder, "You're strong, Effie. Your momma needs you to be by her side, as hard as it is. Let's keep singing."

"We're okay," Elimelech says, his voice steady. "We're all here together. And God is right here in the middle of us."

"Let's just keep singing," Mimi says. "It will comfort Willa—and she'll hear all our voices."

As hard as it is, they continue singing "Precious Lord, Take My Hand," their voices trembling and cracking.

Mimi's mind drifts back to when she was a little girl, and the first time she had ever heard Willa sing that hymn. Back then, she hadn't understood the weight of the words or the depth of Willa's journey. Now, standing here, the meaning was crystal clear, and achingly beautiful.

A loud clap of thunder startles everyone in the room, and the rain starts pounding against the roof. Still, they keep singing, even louder, glancing to one another for strength.

"*Precious Lord, take my hand, lead me home,*" their voices weave together.

"*Let me stand. I get so tired. I get so weak. I get worn. Through the storm, through the night, lead me home. Take my hand, precious Lord, lead...*"[87]

Looking down at Willa, they stop singing.

"Gather even closer," Elimelech says quietly. "Continue to let her know that you are right here with her."

He moves behind them, giving them space to lean.

"Momma, I love you so much," Effie says, her voice breaking, tears streaming freely. "You have been such a good momma to me."

Taking Willa's hand, Mimi whispers, "Willa Mae, I love you. Thank you for loving us so, so much," her voice catches, "and for the faith in God that you instilled in me."

Anna Beth can hardly speak, but she leans forward and says softly, "I love you, Willa. You gave us so much love ... and so much care."

As Willa's head rests against the pillow, her eyes slowly open. She looks up toward the ceiling, squinting slightly, as though a brightness has filled the room. Her gaze moves from one side to the other, but it is clear to everyone ... she isn't looking at the ceiling.

It is a sight none of them can see, a glory none of them can comprehend.

Willa's eyes linger a moment longer, as if she does not want to miss a thing.

Then, very peacefully, her eyelids close.

Elimelech kneels by the bed, feels for her pulse, and looks up at them all.

"She's gone home," he says tenderly.

They circle the bed. And weep.

"Precious Lord," Mimi says through her tears, "thank you for leading Willa home."

For a long moment, no one moves. They simply stand in silence, unwilling to leave her side, unwilling, just yet, to say goodbye.

Elim's gentle voice breaks the quiet.

"If it's okay," he says, "Angel and I would like to take care of a few things here. You can come back and be with Miss Willa Mae as long as you'd like."

They all nodded in gratitude. At the door, Angel stands watching, trying to hold himself together.

Mimi turns to gather her purse from the chair by the window. Just then, through the rain and mist, she catches sight of her pelican lifting into flight. Beyond him, there in the grey sky, as if painted by the hand of God Himself, arches a vibrant rainbow over the bayou.

Mimi presses a hand to the glass, her voice choked with emotion.

"Willa ... you're not here anymore, are you?" she whispers through tears. "Jesus came for you. He came to take you home."

She swallows hard, barely able to speak.

"And… He sent the most beautiful rainbow to light your way."

Mimi turns and quietly walks out of the room.

Sitting together in the lobby, they are silent, overwhelmed not by grief alone, but by gratitude—giving God the glory for His magnificent send-off for Willa from this earth and all the love she left behind. Minutes later, Elimelech and Angel come to find them.

"You can come back into the room now," Elim says, "and continue to say your goodbyes."

Mimi rises and turns to them, tears welling up again.

"Elim, Angel … I know it's way past your shift. You must be so tired."

Elim smiles softly with Angel at his side.

"Miss Mimi," he says, "we're not going anywhere until we've escorted Miss Willa Mae out those doors."

Hearing him, Anna Beth, Effie, and Mimi break down again, moved beyond words. They return to Willa's room, and when the door opens, there she lies—beautiful and peaceful. Elim and Angel had brushed her hair, smoothed the sheets, and placed yellow roses gently in her hands, taken from the front desk bouquet.

She looks like an angel.

Sitting together around her bed, they share memories—of Willa's laugh, her stubborn side, her singing, her fierce love, and unshakable faith.

The door opens quietly, and AJ and Wilton walk in, faces solemn. They had returned to retrieve Wilton's briefcase, but upon hearing the news, they stand there, reverent.

Effie rises, and Wilton immediately pulls her into a tight embrace.

"You are carrying on a beautiful legacy now, Miss Effie Rose," he says.

"I'm so glad you're here, Wilton," she whispers.

"God orchestrated it all," says Wilton.

"I'm not leaving town for at least another couple of weeks," Wilton says. "I want to check on Daddy's house. And I thought … maybe it's time I visit my momma's gravesite in Mississippi. First time."

Effie squeezes his hand gently.

"That means you could come to Momma's funeral," she says. "And then … I would be honored to go with you to visit your momma's grave, if you'd like."

Wilton smiles, his voice tender.

"I would like that very much. It would mean everything to have you by my side, Effie. And maybe on the way … we'll stop for a milkshake at River King, this time at the front window."

Effie laughs through her tears and nods, squeezing his hand once more. A light tap sounds at the door.

Elim steps quietly inside.

"The hearse is here for Miss Willa," he says.

In tears, they say their final goodbyes, laying soft kisses on her forehead, whispering their love.

Elimelech and Angel come to her side, ready to escort her.

Before they leave, Angel asks them to look out the window.

They gather around.

There, floating gently on the bayou outside their window, is the Zydeco Zoomer.

All of Andre's crew stand solemnly on the deck looking towards the window, hats in hand, honoring Miss Willa Mae.

Andre says, his voice thick with emotion. "They wanted to be part of the ceremony—as Miss Willa Mae is escorted home."

The captain blows the horn three long times, a sound that rings through the misty bayou like a final hymn. Mimi presses her hand against the glass again, then lifts it in a soft wave.

Leaving the room, following behind Elim and Angel, who wheeled Willa's bed gently forward, they find the hallway lined with nurses, aides, and patients' families. Doors open down the corridor as people stepped out to honor her journey.

There at the door stands Mr. Joseph, waiting

As the doors swing open and the breeze drifts in, Mr. Joseph takes off his hat and bows his head as he tenderly says, "She's gone on into glory."

The doors close.

Somewhere beyond the bayou and the rainbow, Willa Mae is finally home.

THE END

Lillie Mae, backporch of author's home (circa 1950s)

Lillie Mae with Linda (the author, center) and sisters (circa 1960s)

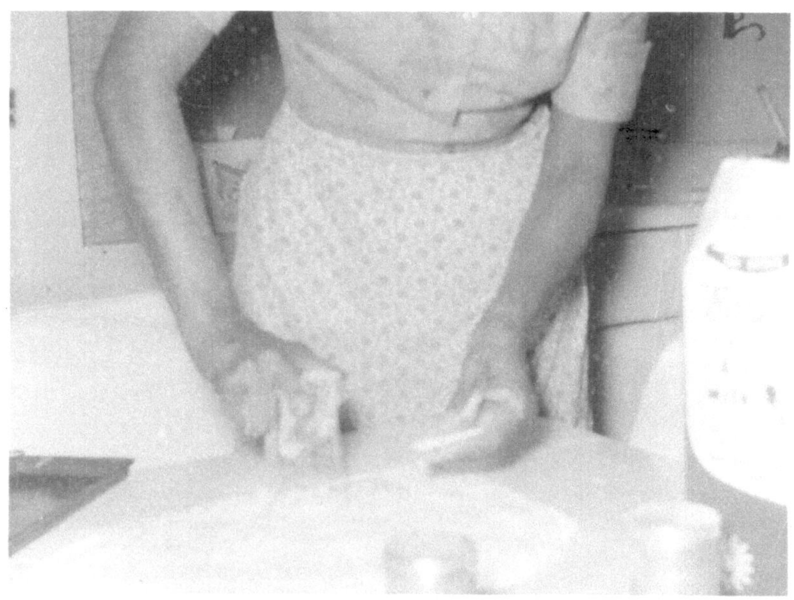

Lillie Mae's loving hands making her
famous homemade biscuits (circa 1960s)

Lillie Mae and Linda, the author (circa late 1980s)

WITH HEARTFELT THANKS

To Jesus Christ, my Lord and Savior:

I could not have written this book without You, Jesus, by my side. I am deeply grateful for Your ever-presence and the strength You gave me as I worked through those many years in my writing room. Thank You for being the pen in my hand. I humbly ask that this book be filled with Your Streams of Living Water, flowing out from the pages into the hearts and lives of all who read it. May these words give You all the glory, and may they bring hope, healing, and reconciliation to every life they touch. Amen

To Bruce, my husband and the love of my life for 42 years and beyond—you are my shining star. You were my cheerleader on this long journey, believing in me even more than I believed in myself. Thank you for the beautifully plated meals you brought to my writing room door and the bowls of Ben & Jerry's on those long, weary days. You went above and beyond—cleaning the house, doing the laundry, editing chapters, and keeping me laughing when I felt like giving up. Your patience was beyond amazing! You are my calm in the storm. I love you to the stars and back again. Most of all, thank you for your unwavering and unconditional love, and for the love you always showed Lillie Mae–she loved you dearly. Bae, this book is for you, too.

To my family–the ever-growing "Erley Squad." I know you don't believe me, but yes... I'm really, finally done with my book! Thank you for standing beside me and offering constant, unconditional love and encouragement through the years.

To my three sons, Christopher, Matthew, and Patrick–I've loved writing this book, but I've loved even more raising my three little tugboats, who have now grown into incredibly beautiful tall ships with families of their own. I know you loved Lillie Mae, and she prayed for you and loved you deeply–may you carry her legacy forward.

Thank you to my three beautiful daughters-in-law–Katie, Katherine, and Shannon–you are precious gifts to me from God. I am filled with gratitude for your love, your encouragement as I wrote, and the girl talk when I need it.

To my eight precious grandchildren–Ingrid Mae and Mae (both named in honor of Lillie Mae), Conrad, Winifred, Eleanor, Maxwell, Reese, and Sullivan–and always, Christmas: you are Nene's joy and the light of my life. You keep me smiling and laughing, and you remind me to see the world through the wonder of a child's eyes–especially when Nene needed a break from writing.

To Matilda, Tilly, our sweet Portuguese water dog (remembered)... my faithful and loving writing companion under my desk. You almost made it to the end, girly-girl, but age caught up with you. Thank you for all the love, kisses, and therapy during my writing journey. You were one special girl!

To Suz, my dear long-time friend, sister, and prayer warrior: your abundance of prayers has been a sweet, fragrant offering to God along this journey. Thank you for every cup of coffee and bag of goodies delivered to my door, every encouraging text and call, every laugh, your patience, love, and every moment you held me up–like Aaron and Hur holding up their dear friend and brother's hands–when I was discouraged and weary.

Thank you, Nance, my dear friend and powerful prayer warrior. You walked alongside me this entire journey!

To my prayer team–thank you. Please know how much your faithful prayers and encouraging words carried me through. I thank God for each of you.

To my Beta readers–thank you for cheering me on through a rough first draft. Your time, grace, and thoughtful feedback helped me to see my book through others' eyes and improve it.

To the Sarasota Seven–my fellow writers, encouragers, and dear loving friends. We began this journey together, and your prayers, support, and companionship have truly been a gift from God. We just "get" each other.

To hope*books, my wonderful publisher–wow, Brian... you, Hope, and your amazing team set me up for success. Thanks for sticking with me through every cohort, Teaching Tuesday, conference, counseling, and for always being there on the other end of an email, message, or phone call when help was needed. You believed in me! And to all the Hope authors and co-horts: those Wednesday Zooms spurred me on and were a lifeline.

To Dr. Zoe, my editor, who believed in me and my story: your ongoing encouraging words, kindness, beautiful spirit, and professional wisdom kept me writing. I am thankful to God for you and your friendship.

To Brenda, my new hometown friend, and one of the brave seven to be the first to integrate Port Allen High School in 1968: I admire you (and your classmates) for facing this challenge head-on and paving the way for many who came after you. Though we grew up in the same little town, we never knew each other until this book brought us together. Thank you for sharing your stories, your honesty, and for cheering me on. I thank God for our new friendship.

To Rosalie (remembered)–your beautiful smile would light up a room. Thank you for sharing your momma with me, and thank you, from deep within my heart, for calling me "sister."

Thank you to my sisters–Letti, Libbie (remembered), and Laurie–I feel blessed to have grown up with you in our little Louisiana town. I cherish the memories of Lillie Mae helping to raise us–the "Lowe girls," as we were called–together as sisters.

To my parents, Bessie and Herman (Monday) Lowe, and my MawMaw, Rema Hebert Guerin (all remembered). Thank you for your love, memories and the foundation of faith and courage you gave me to help write this book.

To all those who kindly and graciously allowed me to interview you–thank you. I was humbled by your stories from the Jim Crow era; they brought both heartache and beauty to these pages. And thank you, Sergeant Todd. I'm so grateful for all of you.

To my long-time *Up With People* friend—Cyndy—thank you for believing in me when I wasn't sure I could do it. Your faith and input into this book were God-sent. And to all my *Up With People* long-time friends, Myriam, Leigh Ann, Rajean, Deb, Julie, Retta, the Phab Phive, and so many more that would take up a full page. Thank you. We learned valuable lessons about "pressing on" from being on the road together, and this is what I did throughout this writing journey!

To my dear neighbors and friends who have surrounded me with love and support, including—Cindi, Pam S., Beth, Jillie, Shirley, Myriam, Tricia, Jodi, Pam R., Kathy A. and so many more that I wish I had space to write them all—you didn't abandon me during long stretches of silence and writing confinement, you are treasured gifts in my life.

To Char and Mary, I felt your spirit with me as I wrote. You live on in my heart.

To Mary at the Louisiana Old State Capitol—thank you for your wisdom, resources, and kindness.

To the angels of Hospice—God has given you a rare and beautiful gift. Thank you for the love, support, and care you've shown as I've walked beside so many dear ones, including Lillie Mae, in their final days.

To my endorsers—thank you for your time, your words, and your encouragement. I am both honored and humbled to have your names in my book.

To Angelique and the team at the West Baton Rouge Parish Museum, thank you for your kindness and help with research.

To Catherine Newsome, former State Archivist and Executive Director of the Louisiana State Archives (now First Assistant Secretary of State of Louisiana)–thank you, and thank you to your staff for your incredible support and help with archival research.

Thanks to my hometown of Port Allen, Louisiana, and the people in it–you will always hold a special place in my heart. My roots are there, and they run deep.

ADDITIONAL INFORMATION GLOSSARY

Acadians

Acadians are descendants of 17th- and 18th-century French settlers of Acadia (Nova Scotia). Many were exiled during the Great Expulsion and resettled in the bayous of southern Louisiana, where their traditions evolved into what is now known as the **Cajun** culture. They are known for preserving their unique dialect of the French language, Catholic heritage, and rich storytelling traditions. They have a distinct, vibrant culture of rural communities that are filled with lively folk music and rich culinary traditions, including dishes such as gumbo and jambalaya.

Black Codes

A set of discriminatory laws passed by Southern states immediately after the Civil War (1865–1866) during the early Reconstruction era. Their primary purpose was to restrict the freedom of African Americans and maintain White supremacy by controlling Black labor, movement, and civil rights. Though the **Thirteenth Amendment in 1865 abolished slavery,** Black Codes attempted to preserve a system of economic and racial control. They laid the foundation for later Jim Crow laws, which formalized segregation and inequality.

Brown v. Board of Education

A landmark 1954 Supreme Court decision that unanimously declared racial segregation in public schools unconstitutional, as it violated the Equal Protection Clause of the Fourteenth Amendment. The ruling overturned the previous "separate but equal" doctrine from the 1896 Plessy v. Ferguson case, stating that separate educational facilities are inherently unequal and create a sense of inferiority among Black children. Although it did not immediately desegregate schools, it provided the legal foundation for the Civil Rights Movement and for future court rulings and legislation aimed at ending racial segregation.

Chattel slavery

The enslaving and owning of human beings and their offspring as property, able to be bought, sold, and forced to work without wages.

Chicory

A bitter-rooted plant whose roasted root is often blended with coffee, especially in Southern Louisiana tradition. Popularized during the Civil War, chicory remains a cultural staple in New Orleans, where it's known for adding a distinctive, slightly nutty flavor to coffee.

Civil Rights Act of 1964

The Civil Rights Act of 1964 is a landmark piece of federal legislation in the United States that prohibited discrimination on the basis of race, color, religion, sex, or national origin. Signed into law by President Lyndon B. Johnson on July 2, 1964, after being proposed by President John F. Kennedy. It was one of the most significant legislative achievements of the Civil Rights Movement.

1. Outlawed segregation in public places, such as restaurants, hotels, theaters, and parks.

2. Banned discrimination by government agencies that receive federal funds.

3. Prohibited employment discrimination based on race, color, religion, sex, or national origin and established the Equal Employment Opportunity Commission (EEOC).

4. Authorized the federal government to enforce desegregation of schools and other public facilities.

5. Paved the way for future civil rights protections, including the Voting Rights Act of 1965.

Civil Rights Movement

A mass social and political movement in the United States, primarily during the 1950s and 1960s, aimed at ending racial segregation, discrimination, and securing equal rights for African Americans under the law. Rooted in nonviolent protest, inspired by Christian faith and leaders like Dr. Martin Luther King Jr., it challenged Jim Crow laws, voter suppression, and systemic racism in housing, education, and employment. Used boycotts, marches, sit-ins, freedom rides, and legal challenges to spotlight injustice.

Creole

A Creole refers to a person from a culturally distinctive community in Louisiana, whose identity stems from the colonial French and Spanish periods, blending European, African, and Native American ancestries. It evolved to encompass a diverse group, including people of mixed race. Today, this term denotes a connection to this specific culture, which influences food, music, language, and traditions.

Emancipation Proclamation

The Emancipation Proclamation was an executive order issued by President Abraham Lincoln on January 1, 1863, during the American Civil War. It declared all enslaved people in Confederate-held territories to be forever free. It did not immediately free all enslaved people, especially in Union-controlled slave states, but it transformed the war's purpose into a fight against slavery. While limited in scope at the time, the Emancipation Proclamation became a symbol of hope and liberation for millions of enslaved African Americans. It marked a turning point in American history, aligning the nation's moral direction with the cause of freedom.

Fourteenth Amendment

The Fourteenth Amendment to the United States Constitution, ratified on July 9, 1868, is one of the most important amendments in American history. It was passed during the Reconstruction Era to guarantee equal protection and citizenship rights to formerly enslaved people and all persons born or naturalized in the U.S.

Freedom Riders

Groups of civil rights activists, both Black and White, who rode interstate buses into the segregated Southern United States in 1961 to challenge non-enforcement of Supreme Court rulings that had declared segregation on public buses and terminals unconstitutional.

Great Migration

The Great Migration refers to the mass movement of over six million African Americans from the rural South to the urban North, Midwest, and West between 1916 and 1970. This migration occurred in two major waves:

First Great Migration (1916–1940): Spurred by World War I, labor shortages in Northern factories, and increasing racial violence in the South.

Second Great Migration (1940–1970): Accelerated by World War II and postwar industrial growth, particularly in cities like Chicago, Detroit, Los Angeles, and New York.

African Americans sought better economic opportunities, educational access, and freedom from Jim Crow laws and racial terror. The migration reshaped the cultural, political, and social landscape of America—fueling the rise of movements like the Harlem Renaissance, and later, the Civil Rights Movement. It transformed major cities, giving rise to vibrant Black communities, churches, newspapers, and activism.

The Great Migration is one of the most significant internal movements of people in U.S. history and marks a profound shift in African American life and influence.

Gumbo

Gumbo is a hearty stew from Louisiana that reflects the rich blend of African, French, Spanish, and Native American culinary traditions. It's often considered the unofficial state dish of Louisiana and is a symbol of Creole and Cajun culture. Ingredients include the trinity: onions, bell peppers, and celery. Thickened with a dark roux (flour and fat cooked until brown), and okra, a West African influence.

Imago Dei
(Latin: "Image of God")

Imago Dei refers to the teaching that human beings are created in the likeness and image of God, a foundational concept in Christian and Judaic theology.

Jim Crow

Refers to the system of racial segregation laws and customs that were enforced in the Southern United States from the 1870s to the mid-1960s. These laws institutionalized racial discrimination and upheld white supremacy by legally separating Black and white Americans in nearly every aspect of public life.

"Separate but equal" doctrine (established by *Plessy v. Ferguson*, 1896) legally justified segregation in schools, transportation, restrooms, restaurants, and more.

Voting restrictions: Literacy tests, poll taxes, and grandfather clauses were designed to disenfranchise Black voters.

Social norms (often enforced violently) required Black Americans to act subserviently in interactions with Whites—known as "racial etiquette."

Enforced by violence: Those who challenged the system faced threats, lynching, and attacks from groups like the Ku Klux Klan.

Laissez les bons temps rouler

A Cajun French expression that means "Let the good times roll." It's a joyful, celebratory phrase often associated with Louisiana culture.

Lagniappe

(pronounced *LAN-yap*) is a Louisiana French-Creole word meaning "a little something extra." A small, unexpected gift or extra favor, often given as a token of appreciation. Common in Louisiana culture, it reflects warmth, generosity, and the joy of going beyond what's required.

Mais'

Mais' (pronounced like "meh") is a common Cajun French exclamation used throughout southern Louisiana. Though it literally means "but" in French, in Cajun conversation it functions more like an interjection or verbal shrug—a way to express emotion, emphasis, or surprise.

Middle Passage

The horrific transatlantic journey that enslaved Africans endured as they were forcibly transported from West Africa to the Americas as part of the triangular trade between Europe, Africa, and the New World. Enslaved Africans were chained, packed tightly into ships, and endured inhumane conditions, including malnutrition, disease, abuse, and death. The Middle Passage was not only a physical journey but a devastating rupture from homeland, identity, and family–marking the beginning of centuries of racial slavery and oppression in the Americas.

Plessy v. Ferguson

Plessy v. Ferguson was an 1896 United States Supreme Court case that upheld the constitutionality of state laws requiring racial segregation under the doctrine of "separate but equal." The case arose when Homer Plessy, who was seven-eighths white and one-eighth Black, deliberately sat in a Whites-only train car in Louisiana, challenging the state's Separate Car Act. Plessy argued that the segregation law violated the 13th and 14th Amendments to the Constitution.

The Supreme Court ruled against Plessy in a 7-1 decision, stating that as long as the separate facilities for Black and White citizens were equal, segregation did not violate the Constitution. This ruling provided legal justification for Jim Crow laws and sanctioned institutionalized segregation across the American South for decades. The "separate but equal" standard established by Plessy v. Ferguson remained in place until it was overturned by Brown v. Board of Education in 1954

Reconstruction Period

The era in American history from 1865 to 1877 immediately following the Civil War. It was a time of profound transformation as the United States attempted to:

1. Define the legal status and civil rights of newly freed African Americans.

2. Reintegrate the Southern states that had seceded.

3. Rebuild the South's economy and infrastructure.

Sha'

Sha' (also spelled cher, or chère, pronounced *sha*) is a Cajun French term of affection meaning "dear," or "darling." It is commonly used in Southern Louisiana among family, friends, and even neighbors, regardless of age.

Sauce Piquant

(pronounced *soss pee-kahnt*) A spicy, tomato-based Cajun and Creole stew from Louisiana. The name comes from French, meaning "spicy sauce." It's known for its bold, peppery heat, rich flavor, and deep cultural roots in Cajun cooking traditions.

Zydeco

A rhythmic, accordion-driven music genre born from Louisiana's Creole culture, blending French folk roots with blues and R&B. Known for its infectious energy, washboard percussion, and danceable beat, zydeco remains a cultural treasure of the bayou region.

ENDNOTES

1. King, Martin Luther, Jr. *A Testament of Hope: The Essential Writings and Speeches*, edited by James M. Washington. HarperCollins, New York, 1986, p. 296.

2. King, Martin Luther, Jr. *Loving Your Enemies* (speech, January 12, 2021). https://kinginstitute.stanford.edu/king-papers/documents/loving-your-enemies-sermon-delivered-dexter-avenue-baptist-church.

3. Evans, Farrell. "Reconstruction: A Timeline of the Reconstruction Era." *History*, January 25, 2021, https://www.history.com/articles/reconstruction-timeline-steps.

4. Ibid.

5. Davis, Ronald L. F. "Jim Crow Etiquette." *Jim Crow Museum*, Ferris State University, https://jimcrowmuseum.ferris.edu/question/2006/september.htm. Accessed June 27, 2025.

6. Parks, Gordon. "A Man Who Tried to Love Somebody," *Life Magazine*, Volume 64, No. 16, April 19, 1968, p. 34.

7. King, Martin Luther, Jr. "Where Do We Go From Here?" *Plough*, January 18, 2021, (originally delivered at the 11th Annual Convention of the Southern Christian Leadership Conference, Atlanta, August 16, 1967), https://www.plough.com/en/topics/justice/social-justice/where-do-we-go-from-here.

8. Scofield, *Scofield Study System Bible*, pp. 1559–60, comment on Phil. 2:14–16.

9. Wilkerson, Isabel. *Caste: The Origins of Our Discontents*, Penguin Random House, chapter 2, paragraph 3, https://www.penguinrandomhouse.com/articles/caste-excerpt/. Accessed June 27, 2025.

10. Scofield, *Scofield Study Bible*, p. 721, on Psalm 23:1–3.

11. Sternberg, Hans J. *We Were Merchants: The Sternberg Family and the Story of Goudchaux's and Maison Blanche Department Stores*, Louisiana State University Press, Baton Rouge, LA, 2009.

12. "The Negro Health Problem." *The Red Book of Houston: A Compendium of Social, Professional, Religious, Educational, and Industrial Interests of Houston's Colored Population*, Sotex Publishers, Houston, 1915. Quoted in *To Bear Fruit: A History of Public Health in Houston*, University of Houston Center for Public History. Available upon request.

13. Yousafzai, Malala. "9 Inspiring Malala Quotes," United Nations Foundation, 2025, https://unfoundation.org/blog/post/9-inspiring-malala-quotes/

14. Ardoin, Chris. "Talk 2 Me Gud Whiskey." *Unleashed*, Maison de Soul Records, 2012, track X.

15. Scofield, on Ephesians 6:12, p. 1556.

16. "God Put a Rainbow in the Clouds." Traditional African American spiritual, 1800s, https://secondhandsongs.com/work/236365/. Accessed July 16, 2025.

17. "You Hear the Lambs A-Cryin.'" Traditional African American spiritual. *Songs of Zion* Abingdon Press Nashville, 1981, https://hymnary.org/text/my_savior_spoke_these_words_so_sweet.

18. "God Put a Rainbow in the Clouds."

19. Wilkerson, Isabel. *The Warmth of Other Suns: The Epic Story of America's Great Migration*. Random House, 2010.

20. "Dem Bones (Dry Bones)." Traditional African American spiritual, performed by Allen Prothero's Quartet at State Penitentiary, Library of Congress, American Folklife Center, AFC 1999/0005–559, https://www.loc.gov/item/afc9999005.559. Accessed July 16, 2025. Recording available upon request.

21. King, Martin Luther, Jr. Brown Chapel, March 8, Selma, AL, 1965.

22. "Cohn High School – Port Allen, Louisiana." *African American High Schools in Louisiana Before 1970*, https://africanamericanhighschoolsinlouisianabefore1970.com/cohn-high-school-port-allen-louisiana/. Accessed July 18, 2025. The book's fictional "colored" high school was inspired by Cohn High School.

23. Fisk University, "History," Fisk University, https://www.fisk.edu/about/history/. Accessed June 28, 2025.

24. King, Stride Toward Freedom, p. 190.

25. Southern University and A&M College, "Southern University History," Southern University, https://www.subr.edu/page/southern-university-history. Accessed June 28, 2025.

26. Jones, Howard J. "Southern University [Baton Rouge] (1880)," BlackPast.org, November 8, 2010, https://www.blackpast.org/african-american-history/southern-university-1880-0/. Accessed June 28, 2025.

27. King, Stride Toward Freedom, p. 63.

28. "Ain't Gonna Let Nobody Turn Me 'Round." Traditional African American spiritual (public domain), originally published as "Don't Let Nobody Turn You Around" in Clarence Cameron White, Forty Negro Spirituals (Philadelphia: Theodore Presser Co., 1927), Public Domain Mark 1.0.

29. CreoleGen, Charity Hospital in the Jim Crow Era (1878 – 1964), September 27, 2019, https://www.creolegen.org/2019/09/27/charity-hospital-jim-crow-era/.

30. "Rosa Parks, Tired of Giving In" Smithsonian National Portrait Gallery, facetoface: A Blog from the National Portrait Gallery, December 1, 2016, https://npg.si.edu/blog/tired-giving#:~:text=As%20Parks%20later%20explained%2C%20%E2%80%9CThe,its%20contingent%20humiliations%20and%20sorrows.

31. King, Martin Luther, Jr. Stride Toward Freedom: The Montgomery Story. Harper & Brothers New York, 1958.

32. Onion, Rebecca. "Take the Impossible 'Literacy' Test Louisiana Gave Black Voters in the 1960s," Slate: The Vault, June 28, 2013, https://slate.com/human-interest/2013/06/voting-rights-and-the-supreme-court-the-impossible-literacy-test-louisiana-used-to-give-black-voters.html.

33. King, Martin Luther, Jr. "MIA Mass Meeting at Holt Street Baptist Church." The Martin Luther King, Jr. Research and Education Institute, Stanford University, 5 Dec. 1955, kinginstitute.stanford.edu/king-papers/documents/mia-mass-meeting-holt-street-baptist-church.

34. Momodu, Samuel Dingkee. A Capstone Project Submitted to the College of Online and Continuing Education in Partial Fulfillment of the

Master of Arts in History (Nashville, TN: Southern New Hampshire University, May 2019), https://academicarchive.snhu.edu/server/api/core/bitstreams/7c824c16-66f2-4ca6-b8a2-648ead828fc7/content, pp. 42-44.

35. Halberstam, David. "Nashville Sit-Ins (1960)," BlackPast, https://www.blackpast.org/african-american-history/nashville-sit-ins-1960/. Accessed July 17, 2025.

36. King, Martin Luther, Jr. A Testament of Hope: The Essential Writings and Speeches of Martin Luther King Jr. ed. James M. Washington, HarperOne, San Franscisco, 1991, p. 447.

37. "Our Story," Community Coffee. https://www.communitycoffee.com/heritage/. Accessed July 18, 2025.

38. King, Martin Luther, Jr. Stride Toward Freedom: The Montgomery Story. Harper & Brothers, New York, 1958, p. 163.

39. Ibid, 164.

40. Martin Luther King and the Montgomery Story (comic book). Originally published in 1957 by the Fellowship of Reconciliation. Reprint: Fellowship of Reconciliation, 2006.

41. Brundage, W. Fitzhugh. Lynching In the New South: Georgia and Virginia 1880-1930. University of Illinois Press, 1993.

42. "Oh Freedom." African American Spiritual, https://hymnary.org/text/o_freedom_o_freedom_o_freedom_over#google_vignette, public domain.

43. Scofield, Jeremiah 23:5, p. 773.

44. The Holy Bible, English Standard Version (Wheaton, IL: Crossway, 2001), 2 Chron. 20:15.

45. Heinz, H. John, ed. 1959. Crises in Modern America: A Series of Lectures on Two Areas of Conflict in Our Society: Civil Rights and Economic Life. Yale: Dwight Hall, Yale University. Manuscripts & Archives, Yale University Library. https://onlineexhibits.library.yale.edu/s/mssa-kings-at-yale/item/12761#?c=&m=&s=&cv=&xywh=-396%2C-89%2C1833%2C1777.

46. Ibid.

47. Ibid.

48. The Scofield Reference Bible, King James Version, Oxford University Press, 1917, New York, 1 Cor. 13:1.

49. Scofield, *Scofield Study Bible*, Matthew 12:34.

50. Nolfi, Joey. "Stevie Wonder Addresses Rumor that He's Not Really Blind: 'You Know the Truth.'" *Entertainment Weekly*, July 15, 2025, https://ew.com/stevie-wonder-addresses-rumor-not-really-blind-11772236.

51. King, Martin Luther, Jr. *Where Do We Go from Here: Chaos or Community?* Beacon Press, 1967.

52. The Ku Klux Klan. "50 reasons to join" (leaflet, Student Digital Gallery, Bowling Green State University), https://digitalgallery.bgsu.edu/student/items/show/8860. Accessed July 18, 2025.

53. U.S. House of Representatives, Committee on Un-American Activities, *The Present-Day Ku Klux Klan Movement: Report by the Committee on Un-American Activities, House of Representatives, Ninetieth Congress, First Session*, December 11, 1967, p. 369.

54. *Scofield Study Bible*, Acts 17:26.

55. Stevenson, Bryan. "Lynching in America: Confronting the Legacy of Racial Terror," Equal Justice Initiative, https://eji.org/reports/lynching-in-america/. Accessed July 19, 2025.

56. Wilkes, Tom, and David Stevenson. "What Color Is God's Skin?" *Up with People*, 1964. Used with permission.

57. Mark 12:29–31, *The Scofield Study Bible* (New York: Oxford University Press, 1945)

58. Slack LaMotte, Brenda. (retired Drug Enforcement Administration agent), interview by author, Port Allen, Louisiana, March 7, 2024. Reflecting on her experience as one of seven Black students to integrate Port Allen High School in 1968.

59. Hebrews 12:1, *Scofield Study Bible*.

60. Kirkland, Tarabu Besarai. *Remembering is Resistance: Tarabu Besarai Kirkland Touches Hearts and Minds with 'One Hundred Years from Mississippi,'* East Bay Express, Sharon K. Sobatta, April 6, 2022.

61. Douglass, Frederick. *West India Emancipation Speech.* 3 Aug. 1857, Canandaigua, NY. *The Frederick Douglass Papers: Series One, Speeches, Debates, and Interviews*, vol. 3: 1855–1863, edited by John R. McKivigan, Yale University Press, 2001, p. 204.

62. *Days That Shook the World: The Dream of Martin Luther King.* Directed by Andy Webb, BBC Two, 2003.

63. "History." *Franciscan Missionaries of Our Lady University*, https://
franu.edu/about/history.

64. Alexander, Otis. "Martha White (1922-2021)," BlackPast.org, March 12,
2022, https://www.blackpast.org/african-american-history/martha-
white-1922-2021/.

65. Melton, Christina. "Baton Rouge Bus Boycott." *64 Parishes*,
Louisiana Historical Association. https://64parishes.org/entry/
baton-rouge-bus-boycott. Accessed July 18, 2025. Notes that
Horatio Thompson "sold gas to boycotters at cost" from his Esso station
during the 1953 protest.

66. Johnson, Kenneth L. Associate Judge, Baltimore City Circuit
Court (1982–2001), speech, "1960 Baton Rouge Sit-Ins," Folks,
Louisiana Public Broadcasting, 1985, https://www.youtube.com/
watch?v=oN8mRFp5mvs. 0:30–0:45

67. Lee, Harper. To Kill a Mockingbird. HarperCollins, 1960.

68. Chhaya, Priya. "The Power of Place and Racial Trauma Healing with
Dr. Justin S. Hopkins." National Trust for Historic Preservation, July
25, 2023, https://savingplaces.org/stories/the-power-of-place-
understanding-racial-trauma-healing-with-dr-justin-s-hopkins.

69. "Lynching in America: The John Hartfield Story." Equal Justice
Initiative, https://www.youtube.com/watch?v=x-7sVFQBBIY

70. "John Hartfield Will Be Lynched, 1919." Flyer, Records of Rights, National
Archives, https://recordsofrights.org/records/342/john-hartfield-
will-be-lynched?utm_source=chatgpt.com. Accessed July 18, 2025.

71. Rohr, Richard. "Transforming Pain," Center for Action and
Contemplation – Daily Meditations, October 17, 2018, https://cac.
org/daily-meditations/transforming-pain-2018-10-17/. Accessed
July 18, 2025.

72. Archbishop Rummel High School Newsletter, p. 2, Archbishop Rummel
High School, Metairie, LA. Accessed March 7, 2024.

73. Woodward, Mary. "New Orleans Archbishop Committed to Ending
Segregation, Remembered by Bishop Emeritus," Diocese of Jackson
Archives, Jackson, MS., posted May 30th, 2021.

74. Wicklein, John. "Catholic Archbishop Backs New Orleans Integration;
Rummel Will Act Despite Protests, Calls Segregation 'Morally Wrong
and Sinful'—Says Schools Must Conform." New York Times, July 8,

1959. https://www.nytimes.com/1959/07/08/archives/catholic-archbishop-backs-new-orleans-integration-rummel-will-act.html.

75. Scofield, C. I. *Oxford New International Study Bible*, rev. ed. (1967), 740, Isa. 61:1–3.

76. Waterhouse, Rosalyn. "I Am a Negro." *Freedom School Poetry*, Meridian, MS, poem lines 8–12, in *Freedom School Poetry*, 1964, https://www.crmvet.org/poetry/64_fskool_poems-r.pdf. Accessed July 19, 2025.

77. John 4:1–5, Scofield Study Bible.

78. Matthew. 27:51, Scofield Study Bible.

79. John 10:10, Scofield Study Bible

80. John 1:4–5, Scofield Study Bible

81. Revelation 12:11, Scofield Study Bible.

82. 2 Timothy. 1:6, Scofield Study Bible.

83. Rascoe, Ayesha, and Danielle Kaye. "He was with Emmett Till the night he was murdered. The horror haunts him still." *NPR News: The Civil Rights Generation.* March 5, 2023, https://www.npr.org/2023/03/12/1162677900/emmett-till-wheeler-parker.

84. Stevenson, Bryan. *Lynching in America: Confronting the Legacy of Racial Terror*, third edition, Equal Justice Initiative, 2017, Montgomery, AL.

85. Aunt Sally's Pralines, 810 Decatur Street, New Orleans, LA 70116, Official Website, http://www.auntsallys.com/. Accessed July 18, 2025.

86. "Going to Shout All Over God's Heaven." Hymnary.org, hymnary.org/text/ive_got_a_robe_youve_got_a_robe. Accessed 10 Oct. 2025.

87. Dorsey, Thomas A. "Precious Lord, Take My Hand," (1938; text and tune), public domain spiritual. The melody drawn from George N. Allen's tune "Maitland." See hymnary.org. Accessed July 18, 2025.

RESOURCES FOR FURTHER READING

1. **Stevenson, Bryan**. *Just Mercy: A Story of Justice and Redemption*. Spiegel & Grau, New York, 2014.

2. **Arsenault, Raymond.** *Freedom Riders: 1961 and the Struggle for Racial Justice*. New York: Oxford University Press, 2006.

3. **Wells, Ida B.** *Crusade for Justice: The Autobiography of Ida B. Wells*. Edited by Alfreda M. Duster. Chicago: University of Chicago Press, 2020.

4. **Cone, James H.** *The Cross and the Lynching Tree*. Maryknoll, NY: Orbis Books, 2011.

5. **Wright, Richard.** *Black Boy*. New York: Harper Perennial Modern Classics, 2007. Originally published 1945.

6. **van Wormer, Katherine, David W. Jackson III, and Charletta Sudduth.** *The Maid Narratives: Black Domestics and White Families in the Jim Crow South*. Baton Rouge: Louisiana State University Press, 2012. Paperback edition, 2015.

7. **Chafe, William H., Raymond Gavins, and Robert Korstad, eds.** *Remembering Jim Crow: African Americans Tell About Life in the Segregated South.* New York: The New Press, 2014. Paperback reissue, 2021.

8. **Brogdon, Lewis.** *The Gospel Beyond the Grave: Toward a Black Theology of Hope.* Foreword by Stephen G. Ray Jr. Eugene, OR: Cascade Books (Wipf & Stock), 2025.

9. **King, Martin Luther, Jr.** *Stride Toward Freedom: The Montgomery Story.* New York: Harper & Brothers, 1958.

10. **Tisby, Jemar.** *The Color of Compromise: The Truth about the American Church's Complicity in Racism.* Grand Rapids, MI: Zondervan Reflective, 2019. Paperback edition, 2020.

11. **Baldwin, James.** *The Fire Next Time.* New York: Dial Press, 1963.

12. **Humez, Jean M.** *Harriet Tubman: The Life and the Life Stories.* Madison: University of Wisconsin Press, 2003.

13. **Washington, Booker T., W. E. B. Du Bois, and Frederick Douglass.** *Three African-American Classics: Up from Slavery; The Souls of Black Folk; Narrative of the Life of Frederick Douglass.* Dover Publications, 2007.

14. **Walking with the Wind: A Memoir of the Movement** – John Lewis with Michael D'Orso A powerful first-person account from Civil Rights icon John Lewis, filled with moral clarity and historical insight.

15. **Kasher, Steven.** *The Civil Rights Movement: A Photographic History, 1954–68.* New York: Abbeville Press, 1996.

16. **King, Martin Luther, Jr.** *A Knock at Midnight: Inspiration from the Great Sermons of Reverend Martin Luther King, Jr.* New York: Warner Books, 1998.

17. **Hampton, Henry, and Steve Fayer.** *Voices of Freedom: An Oral History of the Civil Rights Movement from the 1950s Through the 1980s.* New York: Random House Publishing Group, 1991. Paperback reissue 2011.

18. **Marsh, Charles.** *The Beloved Community: How Faith Shapes Social Justice from the Civil Rights Movement to Today.* New York: Basic Books, 2005.

19. **Olson, Lynne.** *Freedom's Daughters: The Unsung Heroines of the Civil Rights Movement from 1830 to 1970.* New York: Scribner, 2002.

20. **King, Martin Luther, Jr.** *Where Do We Go from Here: Chaos or Community?* Boston: Beacon Press, 1967.

21. **Wilkerson, Isabel.** *The Warmth of Other Suns: The Epic Story of America's Great Migration.* New York: Vintage Books, 2010.

22. **Wilkerson, Isabel.** *Caste: The Origins of Our Discontents.* New York: Random House, 2020.

Online Resources

1. **National Park Service.** "The Middle Passage." *NPS.gov.* https://www.nps.gov/articles/the-middle-passage.htm. Accessed June 20, 2025.

2. **History.com Editors.** "Black Codes: Definition, Dates & Jim Crow Laws." *History.com*, A&E Television Networks, November 20, 2023. https://www.history.com/articles/black-codes. Accessed July 20, 2025.

3. **History.com Editors.** "Jim Crow Laws." *History.com*. A&E Television Networks. Last updated January 22, 2024. https://www.history.com/topics/early-20th-century-us/jim-crow-laws. Accessed July 20, 2025.

4. **Equal Justice Initiative.** *Lynching in America: Confronting the Legacy of Racial Terror.* Equal Justice Initiative, 2017. https://lynchinginamerica.eji.org/report/. Accessed July 20, 2025.

5. **Ukins, Graham.** "Showcasing Louisiana: Group Uncovers Forgotten Plantation Cemeteries." *WAFB.com.* Originally published May 30, 2019; updated August 5, 2020. https://www.wafb.com/2019/05/30/showcasing-louisiana-group-uncovers-forgotten-plantation-cemeteries/. Accessed July 20, 2025.

6. **African American High Schools in Louisiana Before 1970.** "Cohn High School – Port Allen, Louisiana." https://africanamericanhighschoolsinlouisianabefore1970.com/ https://africanamericanhighschoolsinlouisia-nabefore1970.com/cohn-high-school-port-allen-louisiana/. Accessed July 20, 2025. (Stories in this book were inspired by this historical school)

7. **Historical Marker Database.** "Old Cohn High School –Home of the Mighty Eagles –1949–

1969." *HMdb.org.* https://www.hmdb.org/m.
asp?m=249404. Accessed July 20, 2025.

8. **Hymel, Susan.** "The River Preacher." *Country
Roads Magazine.* October 1, 2004. https://
countryroadsmagazine.com/art-and-culture/
people-places/the-river-preacher/. Accessed
July 22, 2025.

9. **Rascoe, Ayesha, and Danielle Kaye.** "The Civil Rights
Generation: Emmett Till's Cousin Reflects on His
Life and Legacy." *NPR News,* March 5, 2023. https://
www.npr.org/2023/03/05/1161192431/reverend-
wheeler-parker-jr-emmett-tills-cousin-reflects-
on-his-life-and-legacy. Accessed July 22 2025.

10. **"Archbishop of New Orleans Excommunicates
Three."** *Catholic Under the Hood: Catholic History
from a Franciscan Perspective.* April 16, 2010. https://
catholicunderthehood.com/2010/04/16/today-
in-catholic-history-archbishop-of-new-orleans-
excommunicates-three/. Accessed July 22, 2025.

11. **Woodward, Mary.** "New Orleans Archbishop
Committed to Ending Segregation, Remembered
by Bishop Emeritus." *Mississippi Catholic,* May
30, 2021. https://www.mississippicatholic.
com/2021/05/30/new-orleans-archbishop-
committed-to-ending-segregation-remembered-
by-bishop-emeritus/. Accessed July 22, 2025.

12. **Monet, Mila.** "A Historical Ellisville Lynching
Remembered." *WDAM7 News,* June 17, 2022. https://
www.wdam.com/2022/06/17/historical-ellisville-
lynching-remembered/. Accessed July 22, 2025.

13. **Hinton, Rob.** "1960 Baton Rouge Sit-ins." *Folks*, Louisiana Public Broadcasting, 1985. YouTube video, posted by LPB Louisiana Public Broadcasting, February 26, 2016. https://www.youtube.com/watch?v=oN8mRFp5mvs. Accessed July 22, 2025.

14. **Washington Informer Staff**. "Rev. T. J. Jemison, Civil Rights Leader, Dies at 95." *Washington Informer*, December 3, 2013. https://www.washingtoninformer.com/rev-t-j-jemison-civil-rights-leader-dies-at-95/. Accessed July 22, 2025.

15. **Jemison, T. J.** *Oral History from the Archives*. Recorded April 11, 1993. Posted by Louisiana Secretary of State, February 29, 2012. Facebook video. https://www.facebook.com/watch/?v=10101135929440325. Accessed July 22, 2025.

16. **Alexander, Otis.** "Martha White (1922–2021)." *BlackPast*, March 12, 2022. https://www.blackpast.org/african-american-history/martha-white-1922-2021/. Accessed July 22, 2025.

17. **Signpost to Freedom**: The 1953 Baton Rouge Bus Boycott. Directed by Christiana Melton. Louisiana Public Broadcasting, 2004, https://www.youtube.com/watch?v=6AONat-lKE4.

18. **Momodu, Samuel.** "Baton Rouge Bus Boycott (1953)." *BlackPast*, February 4, 2018. https://www.blackpast.org/african-american-history/events-african-american-history/baton-rouge-bus-boycott-1953/. Accessed July 22, 2025.

19. **Wesleyan University.** "Celebrating Dr. Martin Luther King, Jr.: The Legacy of and Memorial to Dr. King, Coretta Scott King." *Wesleyan University.* https://www.wesleyan.edu/mlk/posters/legacy.html. Accessed July 22, 2025.

20. **Jones, Howard J.** "Southern University [Baton Rouge] (1880–)." *BlackPast.org*, November 8, 2010. https://www.blackpast.org/african-american-history/southern-university-1880-0/. Accessed June 28, 2025.

21. **Equal Justice Initiative.** "Nashville Students Launch Protest; Face Violence and Jail Time." A *History of Racial Injustice*, February 13, 1960. https://calendar.eji.org/racial-injustice/feb/13. Accessed July 22, 2025.

22. **CreoleGen.** "Charity Hospital in the Jim Crow Era (1878–1964)." *CreoleGen*, September 27, 2019. https://www.creolegen.org/2019/09/27/charity-hospital-jim-crow-era/. Accessed July 22, 2025.

23. **"Cohn High Interviews."** YouTube video, 12:34. Posted by *Port Allen Historical Archives*, March 15, 2018. https://www.youtube.com/watch?v=OmSDFjy5x-w. Accessed July 22, 2025.

24. **West Baton Rouge Parish Public Library.** "Open to All: Cohn High School History." *West Baton Rouge Parish.* https://www.wbrparish.org/976/Open-to-All. Accessed July 22, 2025.

BOOK DISCUSSION QUESTIONS – RAINBOW OVER THE BAYOU

Personal Connection

1. As you finished *Rainbow Over the Bayou*, what word or phrase comes to mind that best describes your experience reading it?
2. Which character felt most like "you" in some way, and why?
3. If you could step into any scene from the book, which one would it be—and what would you want to experience there?
4. If you could sit down and ask one character a question, who would it be and what would you ask?
5. Was there a chapter heading or quote that really spoke to your heart or stayed with you?

6. How did the characters grow in finding their voice, and what did that journey mean to you?

Historical Understanding

7. What new insights did you gain about Jim Crow Laws and the daily life of Black Americans after slavery?

8. Which part of the Civil Rights Movement in the book had the biggest impact on you, and why?

9. Did the story change how you think about any historical figures or events? If so, how?

10. How did the author help you understand the era's social structure, culture, and laws? Were there moments where you felt transported into that world?

Spiritual Reflection & Insight

11. Where did you notice God's presence at work in the lives of the characters—quietly, powerfully, or both?

12. How did courage and faith come together in the characters' choices?

13. What emotions or spiritual thoughts came up for you while reading the present-day chapters?

14. Were there moments in the story that challenged you to rethink forgiveness, mercy, or reconciliation in your own life?

15. After reading this book, has your understanding of God, His presence, or His Word changed in any way?

Action & Application

16. How might this story inspire you to speak out in your own unique, God-given voice for hope, justice, or reconciliation in your community?

17. What is one tangible thing you could do to build bridges across racial barriers in your world?

18. When you look around today, what echoes of injustice do you see, and how does this story help you respond?

19. How can we, as a group of readers, lift up the voices of people whose stories have been silenced or overlooked?

20. Try writing a 'six-word essay' on justice or building bridges across racial barriers—and share it at lindaerley.com to become part of a living tapestry of voices (for example: "Looking back...Healing begins...Moving forward").